PRAISE FOR EMILY HAYSE

Emily Hayse immerses you in her writing with both rich detail and exquisite prose. Her world and characters immediately swept me away into an exciting adventure as wild and untamed as the land in the Western Territory itself.

— LANI FORBES, AWARD-WINNING
AUTHOR OF *THE AGE OF THE SEVENTH
SUN* SERIES

*These War-Torn Hands* rings with authenticity and the echo of legends. You can hear the saddles creaking, taste the smoke from blazing handguns, and feel the uneasiness of a territory hovering on the edge of lawlessness where outlaw bands roam, dragonlike creatures soar through the skies, and peace is a distant dream. It's a masterful blend of the fantastic and the familiar! So ready for book two!

— GILLIAN BRONTE ADAMS, AUTHOR OF
*OF FIRE AND ASH* AND *THE SONGKEEPER
CHRONICLES*

I0587922

One of the best westerns I've read, with a hint of fantasy. Cowboys, outlaws, and showdowns. Hayse's descriptions make you feel like you're in her western world, including the heat, the dust, and the coffee. Especially the coffee! I loved the cast of characters and could hear their drawl in my mind as they spoke. From the moment I started reading, I could not put this book down. Absolutely loved it!

— MORGAN L. BUSSE, AWARD-WINNING
AUTHOR OF *THE RAVENWOOD SAGA* AND
*SKYWORLD* SERIES

# THESE
# WAR-TORN
# HANDS

EMILY HAYSE

# CONTENTS

*To the tall cowboys and valiant knights who from my
earliest days taught me to be brave.*

# THE PEOPLE

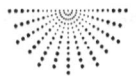

Doctor Sikes: Old as the hills with as many secrets. He set Archer Scott's life on its course and continues to watch him from afar.

Archer Scott: Governor of the Western Territory. A man used to cattle drives and open skies, he reluctantly takes the position to safeguard the land he loves from the hands of eager politicians. Yet, tired from war and toasts and fame, he dreams of a quiet life.

Alexander Mortimer: Outlaw King of the Western Territory, he's a man on fire. He sees the vast potential in an unclaimed land and considers it only fair that fate be on his side this time.

Rosamund Lacey: After hearing tales of the Western Territory from Archer Scott during his wartime visits, she accepts the young governor's proposal of marriage even though it arrives by post.

Raymond Lacey: A hero in the Croix-Savannah War, he came home and tried to throw his medals away. Not a man to sit idle, he goes west to start a new life where he can keep an eye on his younger sister, Rosamund.

Jesse Thatcher: Born in the Western Territory, he is a rancher at heart. He admires his cousin Archer's ability to charm the high circles of Eastern society but does not envy him.

Jack Selby: Rifleman, paid to guard sheep from the predators of the range. His shy demeanor and love of poetry belie his skill at tracking and killing.

Kate Carnegie: Showed up in Glory Mesa and took a kitchen job a couple years back. No one knows where she came from or where she's going, only that she's young and strong and just passing through.

The Swift Brothers: Laughing blond fellows, hard to tell apart and settled on a large spread. Jem is a veteran of the war back East, but the other two, Alan and Max, have never left the West and couldn't care less.

Maria Pike: Widow and businesswoman, she stands aloof from the rough dust of Glory Mesa.

Clay Carson: Owner of the only saloon in town. A hard man, but a good one to have at your side in a fight.

Peter: No-one's boy who cleans at the saloon and runs errands.

Holt: Hard-bitten outlaw, Mortimer's right-hand man.

# 1

## SIKES

THERE IS RAIN-SMELL IN THE AIR TONIGHT. THE WILD air—barely moving enough to stir the territory flag across the street—quivers with it.

I can remember when this land was wild nothingness. No town, no roads, meager and dusty as they are. I was there before there was anything.

I lower myself into the rocking chair on the porch, lean my back against the slats. Somewhere far off, I hear a bellow. Certainly it is someone's bull, but I am in a fanciful mood tonight, and I can almost imagine that it is a *darani*. Those that are left are mostly in the hills now, living in the deep caves, nursing their ancient reptilian grudges, no longer common dangers.

The territory is new. The governor even newer. But this, this town—settlement, more like—is a spark of civilization where once not so long ago was windswept plain teeming with bad ways to die.

Humans are fascinating. Clinging to places of earth where anyone in their right mind has no business being, insisting on seeing beauty in the most desolate and terrible places. It is like there is a compass in their hearts, and against all sense they follow the point of the needle.

Usually to their deaths, but sometimes to greater things.

And it is for the greater things that I have been waiting. Waiting like the barren hills for rain.

I fish my pipe from my pocket, raise my boot over my knee to strike a match against its sole.

But the pipe doesn't settle me tonight—rather, it makes me unsettled.

Governor Scott is young—too young for the men in tall hats back East. Against all their arguments for an older, heavier-handed man, he was chosen. Like they know anything. Really, it wasn't their decision to make.

Archer Scott is as much a piece of this land as the sagebrush is.

I was there then too, when he was born. It was I who laid him upon his dying mother's chest to ease her passing. It was I who gave him to a grim trapper with a quiet Auki wife.

There were no other women in the territory, see. None, to my knowing.

Thirty-six years ago, that was. Now there's sixteen women, and more coming.

Oftentimes it is not the doctors, nor the bankers, nor the politicians who flock to a place so remote and disconnected from the rest of the world. Not until there is something to hold them fast to the wild space of earth, where the wind would blow you off come a fortnight. It is the men who have nothing to lose, everything to gain.

But when this territory was newly bought—a pin's price to the Auki and Red Tree Clans, who lived nearest it and wouldn't set foot on it—I was there.

But who says that I ever came? Perhaps I have been here, old as the hills, from the beginning of time, waiting for something. Something I can feel in my bones.

The wind snaps the flag like a woman shaking out a tablecloth.

There is a storm coming.

## 2

## ROSAMUND

THE LAND IS EXACTLY HOW I IMAGINED IT. WILD, WIDE, and more alive than anything I've ever laid eyes on before.

The dusty land sprawls before me, brown and rocky, making the sky almost blindingly blue. I never believed there could be such variation in one place—the rocks are vast like mountains, but the driver hardly batted an eye when I pointed them out, and the flat ground shimmers and disappears to the horizon like the sea.

The stagecoach lurches beneath me and slams into a rut, jarring my spine. Even this, I welcome. There's something strong and real about it—something that whispers, *I am here*. I am, at last, in the Western Territory.

Most importantly, it means I will soon see my betrothed, my beloved, Archer Scott.

We haven't seen each other since the war six years ago, when my family took in sick soldiers in need of rest and care. He told me stories of the wild, spacious territory where he was born and raised, of the hills he loved, of the cattle he drove, of the storms that roared across the plains out of nowhere.

I knew then that he was the man I wanted to marry.

He's been appointed governor of this whole territory, and after our years of correspondence, he wrote me, sorry he could not come in person, asking if I would marry him.

Of course I said yes.

There is no one else in the lurching stagecoach. My parents are dead. My only brother, Raymond, sold our fine house and came west with me, but he rides his sorrel alongside. He was a cavalryman in the war—he doesn't look at home unless he's on his horse.

The stagecoach grinds to a jerky halt.

"All right." The driver climbs down from the seat and his boots scuff the ground as he lands. "Last stop before Glory Mesa. Horses need watering."

The horses shift and I hear the clink of their harnesses as they settle.

"Rose?" The lean figure of my older brother dismounts beside the door and he unlatches it, thrusting his head and shoulders through the opening. "How you holdin' up, Rose?"

"Just fine."

"'Course you are," he rumbles. His heavy mustache tilts in a hidden smile. "Want a hand?"

I gather up my skirt and take his heavy-gloved hand, stepping down.

The driver is watering the horses, stroking the neck of one; the shotgun rider is still up on the seat, his finger resting casually inches from the trigger as his eyes scan the horizon.

Raymond's gaze follows mine. "Precautions." He smiles, his gray eyes warming with pride. "You look mighty pretty in this bright sunshine, Rose."

I tug at the damp ribbons of my bonnet—it is very hot—and smile back. He's too kind, but he has always been like that.

In a couple hours I'll have this bonnet off, my hair down, the windows open in my new house, letting in the slight breeze. In the meantime, I'll make do with spring water.

I bend down and soak my handkerchief in it, bathing my neck and watching the spots of sun play on the sandy bottom.

"There now, my girl," Raymond murmurs low in his chest, leading his sorrel to the water and stroking her neck as she drinks.

He's soaked with sweat but hasn't had anything for himself yet—hasn't even wet his handkerchief. He loves that sorrel and she comes first.

I wet my lips with the water. It tastes of earth, so I let the rest run through my fingers. We aren't far from the town of Glory Mesa. I can afford to pass it up.

Raymond's sorrel jerks her head up, muzzle dripping, ears swiveling to the north. She lets out a low nicker.

Three young men are riding up to the waterhole,

dressed in gingham shirts and leather vests, sunshine blond and solemn-faced, on roans that look like they are from the same herd.

They stare at us as they ride up, their eyes narrowed against the sun. They have guns at their hips, knives strapped to their legs and stuck through their belts, and rifles hanging from sheaths on their saddles.

"That's just the Swift brothers." The driver raises a hand to them in greeting. "Didn't know they were riding this far south."

The newcomers rein in, their roans dropping their heads to drink.

"Hey, Jem!" The shotgun cups his hands to shout. "How come you fellows are so far south?"

"Business," answers one of the Swifts, flashing a white grin. He throws his leg over the saddle and drops down. "Can we ride into town with you?"

"Won't say no."

"Good," says Jem. "Max, head up onto those rocks there, will you? Keep an eye out."

The one called Max salutes and pulls his horse's head up, muzzle dripping, to head for a cluster of rocks a couple hundred yards off.

Jem finally looks us over, then takes a second look.

"Raymond! Raymond Lacey, what in blazes are you doing out here?"

"Settling." My brother smiles wryly.

"No. Not you? Thought you had a good place."

"Sold it. My sister's come out to marry the governor."

The other brother gives a long whistle. He grins, shy and a little crooked, and dismounts. "Archer Scott? Well, I'll be." He crouches down and dips his hand in the water, bathing his face and neck.

"Do you know him?" I ask. He has an intelligent face—something I noticed in Archer the first time I met him.

He looks up at me, raises his eyebrows. "Yes. I know him. Good man."

"This is Alan." Jem seizes his brother by the shoulders and gives him a shake. "Next one down from me."

Alan smiles, looks away shyly.

"The youngest, Max, is up there." He jerks a thumb over his shoulder. "And this must be your sister?"

"Yup." Raymond is a man of few words, but his eyes shine with pride. He draws me against him with a gentle squeeze. "She's much younger and prettier than me, that's for sure."

"I'll say. Ma'am." He pulls the brim of his hat.

I smile and nod in return.

"Rosamund, this is Jem Swift. We were in the same brigade in the war."

"Small world." Jem grins and dips his hand in the water, bathing his neck. "Do you know what we used to call him?" he asks me. "Old Steady. You couldn't faze him with a rainstorm of bullets."

I look to Raymond, tack the name onto his sun-browned face. It fits him.

The other brother is smiling, shaking water from his golden hair.

"It's good we met up." Jem's gaze wanders to the shotgun and driver. "Word is Mortimer's ranging near here."

"Alexander Mortimer? The Outlaw King?" I ask.

"So you've heard of him?"

"Archer's told me about him."

"He usually give much trouble?" My brother's hand naturally wanders to the butt of his pistol.

"Yeah. Enough."

"Noticed the extra watch." Raymond jerks his head to the shotgun and then to the third Swift up on the ridge.

"He warrants it. Max, get over here!"

The youngest turns his horse, picking his way back down to the spring.

"See anything?"

"A little dust." Max meets our gazes one by one, as if trying to decide whether or not to continue. He's got the sort of face girls fall for—both boy and man at once, somehow. "I don't like it."

The driver jerks the rein buckle tight over the back of one of the horses. "We should get moving. Horses are nervous too."

"There's something building to the south," offers Alan.

"A storm, most likely, but it's not that." The driver shakes his head. "The horses get nervous coming up on that Black Shaft Pass. Sometimes going through there, you almost believe this land is cursed."

"Did he tell you about the curse?" Max grins at me like a boy.

"What curse?"

The oldest smacks him in the head.

"No, I'm curious," I press.

"Well, this land was abandoned hundreds on hundreds of years. Only trappers and wanderers came here—not a single clan—because there's a legend it's cursed."

"You mean, this spot? Or the territory?"

"Both. Anything your government got on agreement from the clans out here would have been cursed land. Maybe a bit of desert, if it doesn't have a spring, but—"

"Miss Lacey isn't interested in that," says Jem pointedly. "He's referring to the Newcastle charter. Made this here a territory. Just stories, you know."

Max squints and scratches the back of his head.

"Let's get moving," cuts in the driver. "This ain't a goin'-to-meetin' social." He slaps one more rein tight and heaves himself up into the seat.

I climb back in on my own, without waiting for Raymond. I feel it too.

Something's not right in the air.

ENTERING the Black Shaft Pass an hour later, the driver has the horses going fast. The riders are at a fast lope to keep up.

The dark rocks of the pass tower over us, casting deep shadows between us and the blinding sun. The men are just blurred figures, whipping between beams of sunlight, leaning low over the necks of their horses.

I see the black glint of a gun in one of the Swifts' hands.

This isn't a precaution. They are expecting trouble.

A gunshot breaks the silence and the shotgun tumbles from his seat and falls to the ground. One of the Swifts drops the reins to his horse's neck and whips his rifle to his shoulder.

Raymond's pistol is out, smoking.

I duck low as more gunshots blaze out, and the stage gives a sudden lurch and comes to a tilting halt.

I drop to the floor, covering my head as more bullets whizz through the air.

It has to be Mortimer—it can't be anyone else, can it?

A chill runs through me. Perhaps he's here because he knows who we are. Who I am.

I pull my satchel down off the seat and onto the floor with me and pull out my packet of letters from Archer.

There are things in these letters that I suspect a man like Mortimer would love to read: Archer's worries, little details of the town, gentle words for me. They won't matter much longer anyway—just bits of paper. Archer is my own, and I scarcely need them to remind me of him.

I pull out one letter, the one with a blue territory stamp.

I fold it up and thrust it into the neck of my dress. That one stays with me, against the risks.

Striking a match, I set the others on fire. I wait a moment, keeping my fingers from the flame, then toss the mostly consumed packet out the window before it burns the floor.

The gunfire has stopped, but Raymond has not come to check on me.

"Get out!" The door is ripped open by a young man with his face covered. I step down quickly but steadily. Now is not the time to make a stand, but neither shall I lose my head.

The driver is slumped on the ground by my feet, shot but alive, his teeth clenched and his shaking hand trying to stem the blood trickling from his arm.

They are ignoring him.

He looks up at me and I cannot read his expression. He has a face both pleasant and plain. He is neither young nor old, and the wind moves a strand of his dusty hair. Perhaps I will be the last person to take notice of him in his life. The thought turns me a little sick.

The Swifts are lined up, the wind blowing their hair, their faces defiant and hands raised as outlaws strip them of their weapons. Raymond stands nearest me, his gun belt already on the ground. His eyes meet mine and they are tender, reassuring. But every line his lean body is tense.

The man in charge is dirty, with a scruffy, graying beard and piercing eyes like ice. The eyes light on me and there's a glint in them I don't like.

This must be Alexander Mortimer.

Raymond shifts so his body is between me and the outlaw. His hand slips behind his back and finds mine. I clasp it.

"Hands where I can see them!" barks one of the men. "You!" He points to Raymond.

Raymond gives my hand a slow squeeze and brings his out where they can see it.

"All right, both of you over there. With them."

Raymond waits until I move, until he can put himself between me and the leering outlaw with the dirty face, and someone shoves him impatiently between the shoulders.

We're lined up now—Raymond and the oldest Swift brother stand on either side of me as this Mortimer walks up and down, eyeing us as if we are horses at market.

He pauses in front of Jem Swift.

"Hm." He gives a short humorless laugh and hits him across the face.

"All right, on your knees!" he bawls, gesturing to us. He smiles as he approaches me. He's got a broad mouth and a jagged tooth that makes him look wolfish. "Ladies excused."

I stare back into his ugly, icy eyes, my face a mask. I can see it in his eyes. He's after me, and these men will die.

Everything is numb and silent. I can see my brother and the Swifts, surrounded, out of the corner of my eye. I should be feeling everything, and instead I feel nothing.

"That's enough, Holt!" A strong voice breaks in.

A red-haired figure rides in, draws rein so close that I feel the heat radiating off his powerful black horse. It's a huge beast, with a thick neck and a sweeping mane that nearly brushes me. The scent of leather and a sweet cologne overpower everything else.

I was wrong.

I need no one to tell me that this is Mortimer, the Outlaw King of the West.

He dismounts easily, thrusts the reins of his horse into the ugly outlaw's hands in a clear signal of dismissal.

"Miss Lacey." He tilts his head in a crisp bow.

He's younger than I expected. His eyes meet mine, sullen but intelligent, and gently blue. The lines of his face are sharp, like a river gorge cutting down his face.

"I suppose you must be Mortimer."

"You've heard of me?" A flicker of amusement enters his eyes. "Well, that makes things a little less awkward."

He goes to the stagecoach and looks it over slowly. He steps right over the dying driver and doesn't even look down.

"Who was burning papers?" He stoops and picks up the blackened ruin of my love letters. They crumble in his fingers and fly away on the wind.

Silence.

"I'm not asking twice." He takes a step toward us.

Raymond clears his throat to speak.

"It was me. They were mine," I cut in quickly before Raymond can take the blame.

"You? Burning papers?" There's a look in his eyes— almost of pleasure. "You'll do out here, Miss Lacey, you'll do."

He steps up to me, too close, his voice too gentle.

"And what were they?" The wind brings his cologne to my nose, sweet and strong.

I draw my head back away from his. "Love letters."

He nods and smiles as if he should have known this all along.

"All right." He lifts his voice just enough to be heard,

makes a sharp motion in the direction of the men. "Tie and blindfold them. They're coming along."

"We're not shooting them here?" It's the dirty outlaw.

"Devil's name, Holt, there's a lady present! Get to it."

He takes me gently by the arm and turns me around so that my back is to the men, my face to the southeast where the trail lies.

"I will make no bargains. The fates of the others are decided, only delayed awhile. But you—" His eyes soften in his iron face. "Have no fear. You will be safe."

I turn away from him. How can he mention protection and murder in the same breath? That's my brother he speaks of so lightly, as if I wouldn't care about him so long as my own life was secure.

He leans down, catches my gaze, and there is honesty in his eyes. "I swear it."

"I don't want the promise of a thief and a murderer."

Wry amusement enters his voice. "Nevertheless, I swear it."

"Sir." One of the men brings his horse up, points to a knot of dark, low-hanging clouds. "Looks like a storm's brewing over those hills."

Mortimer glances at the hills to the south. The warm wind pushes at his hair restlessly—something is brewing all right.

"Get her things, bring the men. I will require the life of any man who loses one of those prisoners, dead or alive, you understand me?"

He loops the reins over one arm and lifts me into the saddle as if I weigh nothing.

The saddle is of an Eastern style, light and without a high pommel, and he climbs up behind me, moving me forward and putting his arm around my waist.

As he wheels his horse around, I see the town of Glory Mesa, a pastel cluster of clean-cut shapes far down the valley.

We ride in the opposite direction, toward the gray-blue hills.

## 3

## THATCHER

IF YOU'D TOLD ME THIS TIME LAST YEAR THAT MY COUSIN would be named governor of the whole dang Western Territory, I'd have called you loco.

Archer isn't what I'd call on friendly terms with the powers that be. In fact, I'm pretty sure the last time he wrestled himself into that prison of a dandy's suit, he ripped both shoulder seams defending his honor. He's not one to look for trouble, but when it finds him, it regrets showing up.

It's for the good of the territory, him becoming its governor. He knows it, I know it. This is wild, unclaimed land, and if you're willing to ignore the sad price tag come with it saying it's cursed, it's a place where any man can make himself.

It makes it a place for wolves to gather, and not the kind with sharp teeth.

Still, I had reckoned we'd make a go of the ranch together. Instead, he's gone to Glory Mesa and left the ranch in my hands. Now I'll be able to tell the very few folks who pass by the ranch that it's my cousin governing this entire territory. Small consolation for running this outfit of ornery critters alone.

A low bellow breaks me from my ruminations. Speaking of ornery critters.

A calf's got himself caught in a tangle of brambles, twitching and bucking against the stubborn brush.

I dismount, leaving the horse to stand where he is.

"Well now, little thing."

I glance at his mother, lest she run me through while my head's turned. Those cows will let their young'uns get into every sort of scrape imaginable and then kill you for getting them out. That's how it goes.

I lean down, reaching in with my gloved hands—thorns come thick as nails out here—and pull the worst of the branches away from his woolly hide. I thread my arm below his belly and he kicks out at me, even though I'm nowhere near his hindquarters. One heave, helped along by an ornery buck that sends his spine straight into my chest, and he's free.

I drop him like a scalding pot and he dances off toward his mother, who gives me a sour look and shakes her horns like I've done her wrong.

Not always a gratifying business, this ranching.

My horse is waiting where I left him, ears back, hoof cocked. He looks about as happy about ranching today as I am.

He stirs as I remount and his ears swivel 'round. His whole body goes tense. Over the roving backs of the cattle I see a tall, good-looking sort of fellow leaning on his saddle horn.

Speak of the devil. It's my cousin himself.

He's wearing his hat low and at an angle, having no idea that it's things like that make the few unattached girls left in Glory Mesa go mad for him. Not to mention Maria Pike, a fine widow and the owner of the town's only restaurant.

From the outside, it looks like a good match, but it gives me the creeps somehow. Besides, he's got a girl back East.

"Jesse, how long are you going to stare and not say anything?" He spreads his hands in appeal and I feel a grin spreading across my face despite myself.

"Howdy."

He grins, a clean, white flash in his sun-tanned face.

I come over and he throws a long leg over his bay's neck and drops down.

"It is good to see you," he says almost fiercely, throwing an arm around my neck and giving me a shake.

"And you."

"How's ranching?"

"How's governin'?"

"Ah, well—" The smile fades a little from his face. The laughter, the easy manner was just a show. Something's wrong.

"Well?"

"The stage was due in at five o'clock yesterday."

"Didn't come?"

I can see it on his face now. He's not just worried, he's afraid.

"Not on time." My cousin peels off his sweaty gloves, pairs them and slaps them onto his horse's neck, tucked in front of his saddle. "A couple men rode out to the Black Shaft Pass last night. Found the driver partway down, half dead and riding for town on one the stage horses."

"Casualties?"

"Jeb, riding shotgun. But Jesse—there were woman's things aboard that stage."

"And no sign of the woman?" It wouldn't be the first time someone's been stolen from a stage.

He rubs his forehead like it pains him. "Carson and a couple of his hands scouted back a ways. Looks like there were four outriders, easy. Got stopped right around the pass. Mortimer's place."

"You think it was Mortimer?"

"Had to be, if he took down four outriders. Driver's in a bad way, Sikes won't let me see him."

"Whew!"

"Jesse." His voice is grim, held steady only by careful self-control. "I proposed—to Rosamund Lacey."

Realization slams into me like the point end of a stampede. "She was coming out here?"

He nods, hesitates. "I love that girl, Jesse. I'd do anything for her."

He means it. He doesn't talk like that unless he means it.

I let my breath out in a long whistle. It's bad enough

that Mortimer's got the girl, but I've got a bothersome feeling in my mind, like there's something else I ought to catch and can't put a finger on.

It's got the feeling of a trap.

"I want you to come back, Jesse. I need to move before we lose the trail. Before—it's too late."

I've seen my cousin stare a thirty caliber right down the barrel, and I've never seen him this close to losing his cool.

"I'll come." I whistle sharply to the hands on the far end of the herd, gesture with a couple fingers for them to move along. "Who've you called?"

"I sent riders out to the Gilchrist and Stanton ranches. They're the only ones close enough to spare men and the time. Some of the men in town'll ride."

"Well, I'll swing by the house and muster a couple more. I'll push back the roundup."

"Jesse, thanks."

I give him a brief nod. Kidnapping's been around since the beginning of days—or at least since there were enough people for one man to decide he wanted to steal something from his neighbor—but my cousin being afraid is smoking-brand new.

Archer reaches into his collar, scratching the back of his neck. He's still wearing linsey-woolsey. You'd think now that he's governor of a whole territory he'd start wearing linen or something.

I get on my horse, startling it.

"Let's ride."

. . .

THE TOWN'S quiet when we ride in, too still. A flag stirs listlessly on the end of a pole in front of a white-trimmed building, newly built. It's got a white mountain and a rising star set against a blue background.

I'd have expected red, the color of blood. But I'm glad they chose blue.

"That your place?"

Archer looks over at me and then at the building in surprise. "Yes, reckon it is. I have a house down the street and over, though."

"Where do you sleep?"

"Does it matter?"

He sleeps at the office.

I toss my extra hands a coin for the saloon and follow Archer to Doctor Sikes's trim establishment. My cousin dismounts and throws the reins of his bay over the post out front, not even bothering to wrap them around.

I tie my horse and give Archer's reins a couple turns, just in case.

The blue door is closed, but the windows are open, and from inside I hear the clink of solid glass on glass and the thin, sharp sounds of metal instruments.

Archer knocks on the door, a firm sound, and it breaks me out of the strange feeling I get when I hear medical instruments—all twisted up inside, like there's a snake in there.

The doctor answers the door, wiping his gnarled hands on a towel. His face is as gnarled as his hands, but the man who mistakes Sikes's age for weakness has had his last chance. Underneath, those old hands could be made of steel.

"Evening."

"Good evening." Archer clears his throat, removes his hat. "Hope you don't mind the intrusion. I was hoping to talk to Sam."

"He's not in any condition to be going anywhere." Sikes fills the gap in the doorway with his arm. He is every inch as tall as Archer and his face is twice as severe.

"I won't take him anywhere. I just want to talk."

"He can't take even an ounce of excitement. He should be dead for as much blood as he lost out there. I'll not be trading lives that might be lost already for one I can save right here and now."

"Sikes." My cousin's voice goes husky. "A couple questions is all, I swear it."

The doctor's fierce face relents. There's not a soul in the territory who doesn't know Archer's word is as good as gold.

Sikes steps aside, giving me a sharp look with one eye, like an eagle. I nod respectfully and whip my hat off. I know how to pick my battles, and if I can help it, none of them will be with Sikes.

Doctor Sikes has one sickroom, with a metal four-poster that looks older than I am, made up with white sheets. The shades are drawn, but they move gently back and forth like sea waves, so the window must be open behind them.

Sure enough, it's Sam lying there beneath the thin

white sheets with his buckwheat-colored hair and arms like whipcord. His whole right side, from neck to shoulder and down below the sheets where I can no longer see, is swathed in bandages. He's normally tanned from the sun, but everything under the tan's been drained clean away.

I'm mighty relieved to see him with the living.

He opens his mouth to speak and I barely recognize his normally dry, matter-of-fact voice. "Reckon I should call you 'governor' now."

Archer laughs under his breath. "I can see a bullet's no match for your sense of humor."

"No, sir. I figure it'd take another couple to knock it out of me."

Archer's eyes sober. "Doctor says you're lucky, Sam."

"Lucky I wasn't hit between the eyes like Jeb. That's about it."

"I just have a couple questions."

A hint of a smile. "I've got all day."

Archer takes in his breath and shifts, the floorboards creaking beneath his boots. "Was it Mortimer?"

"Yeah, it was Mortimer. He came for the passenger."

"That was my other question."

"Name's Miss Rosamund Lacey, said she was coming...."

"Yes?"

"Said she was coming out to marry you."

"I was afraid of that," says Archer softly.

"I didn't make free to comment on it myself," Sam says slowly, "but Mortimer brought out such a crew as I could believe it. Took Miss Lacey's brother and the three Swift boys."

"Took them alive?"

"All of 'em."

Archer rubs his face wearily. "Thank you, Sam."

"It's nothing." Sam gives a ghost of a smile. We've tired him out fast.

"You get better, hear?"

"Don't worry about me. Go get those dogs."

Archer smiles and puts his hand very gently on Sam's unharmed shoulder. "I'll do just that."

SIKES SEES us out of Sam's room, and it's not until I step into the fresher air that I realize how strong the smell of antiseptic and bloody dressing was. Usually a man notices it the other way around.

Sikes shuts the door from the inside and leaves us alone.

"You know Crook's Hollow?" Archer turns to me, his hands resting on his gun belt.

"'Course I do."

"There's a band of sheep herders on the grazing land there. Man called Selby'll be there with them. He's a rifleman, hunts the dragons drawn in by the sheep. I want him."

"Will he come?"

"Just tell him Archer Scott needs him. If he can come, he will."

"All the way out to Crooks Hollow for just another rifleman?"

"No, a tracker. Watched him follow week-old signs

from a *darani* in the rain three years back. Never seen anything like it. If any man alive can find Mortimer in his own territory, it's Jack Selby."

# 4

## ROSAMUND

THE HORSE JOLTS UNDER ME AND SCRAMBLES DOWN THE riverbank with a splash. Mortimer's arm tightens around my waist and he peers over my shoulder to see the ground.

I stiffen and I know he can feel it. I hate being so close to this man. The only decent thing about him is that he really couldn't care less that his arm is around my waist. Some men would.

We are drenched in sweat, he and I, and the black horse beneath us is streaked with foam.

He lets the horse have its head and we all pause a moment as the horses drink, their throats pulsing with each great gulp.

Mortimer's black raises its head, swivels its ears, then lowers its dripping muzzle back to the clean water.

"You're thirsty." The outlaw observes this without giving me a chance to affirm or deny it, but he's right. I am intolerably thirsty.

EMILY HAYSE

Mortimer removes his arm from my waist, turns around, and motions to one of his men, who wades out to us, knee-high in the river. The man takes the canteen and pours out the warm water, filling it fresh.

"No hard feelings." Mortimer takes the canteen back and offers it to me. I wish I could refuse it, but I'm not a fool.

I take it and drink deeply.

"How are you holding up, Miss Lacey?" His eyes are stony, but his question seems genuine.

I meet his eyes calmly. "Just fine." I pour a little water onto my handkerchief and sponge my neck.

I think my answer pleases him, which was certainly not my intent. He watches as I take another drink and wet my handkerchief again. "May I have the water now, or are you intent on seeing me go thirsty?"

I hand it to him, quietly.

While Mortimer drinks, I steal a look over my shoulder. I can't see my brother—only one of the Swifts, his shirt darkened and slick with sweat like the flanks of his mare. I hope they give them water. This heat is infernal.

Mortimer leans down, his arm so long that he can refill his canteen while seated on the horse's back. He ties it, still dripping, to the saddle.

"You shouldn't worry about them. Trust me, it's easier to let them go and try not to think about it."

I knot my hand into a fist to keep from saying anything. Under the circumstances, it would probably be something foolish.

"Ready?"

32

I don't answer.

He leans back a little, gives a single piercing whistle, and we're off again.

WE STOP for the night at the foot of one of the steep hills, under towering pines. Mortimer's men set up a rude camp and a watch—I see half a dozen of them fan out, some to high ground and some back the way we came.

The daylight is almost gone.

Mortimer lifts me out of the saddle and sets me on the ground before swinging down easily himself. He takes his horse's reins in one gloved hand, my arm in the other.

"Get that fire going," he orders his men. "I want food, and then I want it out. We have a moon tonight—the watch will cover for *darani* and wolves."

I have the privilege of being served food while the fire is still going. I sit on the ground in the travel dress I had picked out especially for meeting Archer—blue, with sleeves to the elbows.

For days before leaving, I'd had it laid out, dreaming of the day I would step off the coach in Glory Mesa. It's going to be a thing of rags before he sees me, if he sees me at all.

Mortimer crouches beside me, his rifle across his lap and a tin plate held firmly in his strong fingers. His hands don't look worn or browned, as my brother's do.

"Eat," he urges, noticing my neglected plate of steak and beans.

The smell of the fire-broiled beef is strong, so strong I feel the world swim like the slick hot air coming off the fire. I haven't eaten anything in hours and I am ready to faint with hunger.

"What about them?" I force the words out, trying not to look at the hot juices running down the slab of beef. During the war, a cut like this never made it to our table, save during a holiday. And I could be eating it all right now.

"Who?"

"The other prisoners."

"I thought I told you not to worry about them."

Something snaps inside me. "You must have missed the part where I didn't ask for your advice."

He looks at me, surprised for a moment, and then he bursts into laughter and turns to his men. "Go—feed them. They deserve one last decent meal, I think."

Even after his men leave with the food, I can hear him, still chuckling a little under his breath.


I SLEEP that night under guard, under the stars. They are so bright and distinct that I see why the astronomers wanted to give them all names. Just before I fall asleep for real, when I'm already dull with sleep, I hear a great bubbling groan that seems to come from the earth itself.

*They will protect me*, I think. But they're outlaws. Outlaws against wild creatures, in the middle of nowhere, the nowhere territory nobody wanted. Except, it seems, for Archer and Mortimer.

What a beautiful, terrible land I have come to.

. . .

IN THE FOLLOWING TWO DAYS, I am blindfolded before forks in the trail or around landmarks. Mortimer insists on this, though his man Holt laughs at it.

Unfortunately for my chances of escaping, Mortimer does not underestimate me. Perhaps his insight is what has made him great, over the rest of the killers and thieves.

But he apologizes, and he allows me to sit behind him with my arms around his waist instead of his around mine. I hate touching him, but I prefer it over him touching me.

From the noises and talk I hear, we must be arriving at his hideout.

He stops his horse and twists around in the saddle. He unties the bandana from around my eyes with surprising gentleness and stuffs it into his pocket as he dismounts.

"Welcome to your home, for the time being. Forever, if your fiancé is wise and chooses the alternative over you."

He says it with nonchalance, but this I know: I will never make a home with him, even if I cannot be rescued. As for Archer trading me away, the stars would fall first.

But it is beautiful, this spot where we are, and surprisingly civilized. I see a white house with blue trim and a white picket fence, a barn, extra stables and outbuildings, and flowers and fruit trees growing outside.

A woman must have lived here once.

"In the unforgiving shadows of the curse, there are always seeds of blessing," he says, noting my study of the homestead.

"You believe in the curse?" I raise my eyebrows.

The hot wind blows a strand of molten-iron hair off his

forehead as he studies my face. "You'll learn soon. It's cursed, but I'll free it. I'll make it a place worth living."

He holds out his hand to help me down.

The ground hits my boots, real and almost shocking, and the world tilts slightly.

"Ah—easy now." He takes me under my elbow and I stiffen.

"I'm all right." I try to brush him off, but he holds on.

"That other man we took, is he your brother?"

"Yes."

"And what's his name?"

"Raymond."

"Ah." He smiles as if this is friendly conversation over a dinner party. "And those other men, do you know them well?"

"I had only just met them."

"Well, that's good, I suppose. The Swifts will get what is coming to them. I've owed it to them for a long time now. But your brother—I can afford to wait and contemplate whether he may be of use."

He gives me a pointed look.

I remain silent. I am not stupid.

Nothing I do will change his mind in the end. He'll use us all how he wants, whether or not he allows me the illusion of power.

"A little water?" He leads me past a watering trough from which some of his men are unabashedly drinking and up onto the high porch of the house.

An older man sits there, hale and sturdy, with once-red hair that has turned a dull rusty gray and a thick beard of the same color. He's whittling, shavings decorating his lap and littering the boards of the porch.

He looks up at us slowly as we pass by him and through the open door.

I realize with sudden relief how lovely it is to be out of the sun.

"Water!" Mortimer calls sharply.

A short man comes limping from another room.

"Alexander, sir, you're back!" He hands Mortimer a glass of water and gives me a long, quiet look.

Mortimer hands the glass straight to me. "Yes, and how are you getting on? Leg bothering you?"

"Not more than the usual." He smiles, his eyes crinkling at the corners, and hobbles away.

The house is well-furnished, neat and trim, and our footsteps echo in it. The man from the porch has followed us in, a few shavings still stuck to the leg of his trousers.

"Who's this?" he asks.

The question seems to give Mortimer pause.

"It's—it's a guest, Pa."

"Not for you, is she? At last?"

"No," he mutters. "'Course not, Pa."

"Pity."

The man dusts off his hand, offering it to me. When I take it, he kisses it rather than shakes it. "I reckon I have an idea what you're here for, then. Have a seat, do," he urges, ignoring his son.

I sit, glad to do something that isn't Mortimer's idea. If I had given any thought to Mortimer the Outlaw King having a father—which I hadn't—I would have expected someone stern and cruel and distant. Not this mild fellow whittling and shuffling about.

Mortimer stands in the middle of the room, stiff and stern, as if out of place. The sun is in his hair, and he fingers his pistol as one might scratch a dog's head. "You'll mind her, Pa?"

"I'll get her a good room and have O'Meagher get her something hearty."

Mortimer looks at me, his face straight, almost emotionless. "If you promise to keep to the house and yard, I will not lock you up."

I nod.

"Good." He leaves quickly, as if the house is suffocating him.

My shoulders sag with relief, and yet the house feels strangely empty without his presence.

# 5
## SELBY

THE RAIN POURS DOWN THE DISMAL ROCKS, LASHING THE sagebrush and locoweed to the dusty ground. Won't be dusty for much longer. Soon it'll be mud, after that rivers, after that a torrent. I glance toward the huddled flock in the cave behind me, the couple shepherds huddled over a smoky, petulant fire.

On days like this the boredom sets in. I am useless. The *isarks* don't fly in weather like this, so my protection is hardly needed.

There's nothing to do but clean my rifle again, burnish my hunting knife, and read my one book—poetry—clean through again.

One of the sheep raises its head and bleats in protest, protesting what, only it knows. But a couple more join it just for the idea of the thing.

*Now falls the rain, to grateful ground in growing torrent....*

I saw a painting once that looked as the storm does

now—blurring gray over a desolate, green-dotted landscape.

Ah, but it's been years since I've seen anything one could call art.

"Coffee," grunts one of the shepherds, setting a tin cup on the ground near my boot as if I'm a wild animal to be fed at a distance.

I give him a nod of thanks and wait until he backs off before picking up the scalding tin in my insensitive fingers. The calluses are thick enough that heat and I get along tolerably well.

Better than the shepherds and I, in any case.

One of the dogs gets to his feet with a sharp bark and I rise to my feet, reaching for my rifle. "Easy."

The dog spares me a brief wag of its tail to assure me we are on the same side. The hair still stands in a ridge along its back.

The apprentice shepherd has gone stiff. "What do you reckon it is?"

I peer into the rain, searching for movement, any shape or color that was not part of the blurred landscape a minute ago.

The dog barks again, and now I see it—a blurred figure leading a horse, both of them blown back, half pinned to the ground by the nasty headwind.

I cup my hands to my mouth. "Halloo!" I shout over the rush of the rain. He'll be lucky to hear me at all.

The figure pauses as if considering the direction of my voice, and the dog barks again. The man swivels around and trudges toward the cave.

I step out to the very edge, where the rain spray flecks me with the edges of its swift current, and squint.

He's a young man, on the cusp of thirty or just past the edge, clean-cut with traces of a beard.

"Howdy." He glances up from under the brim of his hat, looking me up and down and then grinning.

"You have guts riding out here, in this storm."

"No choice." He dismounts and lets his horse follow him in out of the rain on its own.

I stand slowly, pushing down the uneasiness that trickles over me like the rain running off his bay's flanks. The old impulse to reach for my gun is strong, but I resist.

"Lonely out here, ain't it?" he asks genially, doffing his hat and shaking the rain off the brim.

"I haven't noticed." My fingers find the buttons on the open front of my shirt by habit, fastening them higher, hiding the cross that hangs cold on a chain against my chest.

"I'm Thatcher, Jesse Thatcher." He sets down each word like they're each heavy loads to be laid down.

The new governor's cousin.

"Welcome," I say, my mouth gone dry.

"Are you Jack Selby?" He holds out his hand.

"That's me." I hesitate for the barest moment before putting my hand in his. His handshake is warm and firm.

"I suppose the news has gotten to you somehow that Archer Scott is the governor of the territory now?"

"Reckon I've heard it."

"He sent me to find you."

"Indeed?" I steel myself.

"It's Mortimer. Trail's a day or two cold, but he figures if anyone can find it, it's you."

"I can. Near to here?"

"Black Shaft Pass. Mortimer's kidnapped my cousin's bride-to-be and the Swift brothers besides. The sooner we go the better chance we have of finding them alive. How soon can you be ready?"

I look out at the lightning. It's not all that safe to be out in right now. Get beyond these rocks, and a man's the only thing above the level of the ground in miles. Perfect way to die.

"I'm ready now. But we should wait a spell until this lets up. Have some coffee."

"Too kind." Jesse Thatcher's smile cuts deep dimples in his face. He saunters over to the fire, giving a firm nod of greeting to the shepherds.

The younger of the two hands him a tin mug of coffee without a word. They're cowed by his presence.

I linger nearby, waiting for him to speak what's on his mind. I've never come this close to the shepherds' fire.

"Say, how far back does this go?" Jesse Thatcher is admiring the dark recess of the cave beyond the dingy backs of the huddled sheep.

"Oh, 'bout twenty yards, I'd say. Don't worry, I checked it for *darani*."

Thatcher laughs in response. He tips his hat up on the back of his head so that he can watch the storm as he takes a drink of the coffee. "This rain ain't doing us any favors."

"No, reckon it'll wash nearly every sign away."

"Will there be any point then?" Concern flits across his

face for the first time.

"I said 'nearly.' Some things survive rain. No telling until we've given it a try."

"The governor'll pay you well for your trouble." He glances at the shepherds. "A gold piece and two pinches of dust."

I shake my head. "I'm coming. He asked. We will talk of payment when we know the end of this trail."

He nods, understanding. Pleased, too, I think.

"We're going back to the town first. Archer's rounding up a group to go after them. We'll leave as soon as we meet up."

I only nod and sip my scalding coffee. I haven't had this much conversation in a fortnight.

THE RAIN LETS up about an hour later, and Thatcher is eager to be off. Lucky for him, I'm always ready to leave at a moment's notice. I heave my saddle onto my horse's back, check the buckles on his bridle, and I am ready.

"When'll you be back?" One of the shepherds gets to his feet slowly, wrapped in his oilskin.

"Don't know. Guess after we find that girl."

"Don't get killed," he says, more worried for his sheep than for me.

"Sure." I tighten the cinch, take down the reins off the saddle, and lead my horse out into the drizzling rain.

"Two bit pieces he never returns," says the older shepherd sagely.

For a moment, I hope I never do.

# 6

# THATCHER

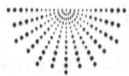

Most folks make camp for the night when it gets dark, but this Jack Selby is a born scout. He keeps on going like he knows every stone by heart, all the way back to Glory Mesa.

By the time we hit the town, the night's more than half spent, but the lights are on in Clay Carson's saloon and we find Carson at the counter going over the ledgers.

"Good morning, Jesse." He's a powerful-built man, tall with a bristling red mustache. He straightens and comes to meet us, grasping first my hand then Selby's in his strong grasp. "Can I get you boys a drink?"

"I'm fit to sleep," I say.

Behind me Selby sits down, pulling his shotgun out of his coat and setting it on the table in front of him.

"How 'bout you, sir?"

Selby shakes his head. Out on the range he moved with the ease of a cougar, but inside four walls, he's shrunk inward, like a man who's trying to take up as little space as he can.

"A room, then?" Carson presses. He's a man who sticks to an idea. "You could sleep a couple hours before we ride."

Again Selby shakes his head.

"Then I'm getting you grub. A man can go without sleep or grub, but he shouldn't go without both."

I stand numbly, watching them both a moment, too tired to move.

"You stick around here, Jesse Thatcher, and I'm forcing coffee on you. I'm up for the morning, and it's coming on us quick."

For once, Clay Carson's got a point. If I'm going to sleep, I'd best get a move on.

I stumble out the door, leave my horse at the hitching post, and head down the street until I reach the small room behind my cousin's office.

I let myself in and hear Archer's soft snore.

"We're back," I announce. "Selby's at the saloon."

My cousin sits up and rubs his eyes. "I should go talk to him."

I slump into a chair. "I'm beat as a racehorse." I wait with my eyes shut, dozing, until Archer is gone, and then I crash in his bed, boots and all.

He doesn't come back the rest of the night.


MORNING COMES with a heavy headache as a forceful hand shakes me awake. It's Peter, the errand boy from the saloon.

"Excuse me sir, Mr. Thatcher," he says eagerly. "Governor sent me to wake you. It's almost time to be off."

"Time?" It's still dark out.

"A quarter past five."

I moan and force myself up.

Peter falls into step behind me like a stray dog. "Are you really going to shoot outlaws?"

"Well, if we have to. Sure would be nice if we could settle it without lead, but—you know outlaws."

Even in the dusky light, I see his eyes gleam. "If I was older, I'd go with you."

"I'm sure you would."

"Anyway, you can have these."

He holds out a fistful of bullets, warm and a little sticky, like he's held them in his hand or maybe his pocket for a few days.

"They fit your gun. I checked."

I chuckle slowly, feed the bullets one by one into my belt. "Thanks. If I have to shoot an outlaw, I'll let you know which one you helped with."

He claps his hands sharply and I reach over, ruffling his stiff dark hair.


A DOZEN or so well-armed men stand in the street now, milling and talking: Archer, Selby, Carson, and the handful we've rounded up from nearby ranches. The air smells of horse and leather and coffee.

My horse nickers low in his throat. I reach for him and

rub his face. Someone's already rubbed him down and readied him for me.

Carson fingers a shotgun, his reddish mustache bristled like one of those scrub brushes he sets Peter to work with on the floorboards. "Are we ready?"

"Almost." Archer grunts as he tightens his cinch.

A horse stamps impatiently. My gelding swishes his tail at a cluster of flies, catches me with the edge of his tail. Most horses know it stings and do it so you can share their misery, but with this fellow, it's a mild show of friendship. I stick my fingers in his mane and scratch his neck so he knows the gesture is appreciated.

I'm itching to be off.

"All right." Archer mounts his horse, his voice filling the open air of the street around us.

A hint of light glows on the horizon, and against it, I see him gather his reins as I've watched him do on more cattle drives than I can count, turning his horse around as if they're one.

"We're riding out. Jack Selby here is one of the finest trackers I've ever met. We follow his lead. You hear?"

A murmur ripples through the men.

"Good. Let's ride."

He turns his horse's head and sets off at a gallop for the heights.

## 7

## ROSAMUND

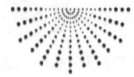

"Would you do me the honor of a walk after supper?" Mortimer looks over at me, setting down his fork.

I hesitate, glance to his pa. It's been awkward, the three of us having meals together for the last day and a half. But awkward meals are hardly new to me—after all, they were an almost weekly occurrence in high society back East.

"Well?" Mortimer asks impatiently, wiping his mouth on his napkin. "Is it yes or no?"

"Come now, Alexander," his father grunts, serving himself a generous second cup of coffee. "Give the lady the courtesy of a moment."

Mortimer wipes the look of distaste from his face. "Take your time."

He reaches for the serving fork and spears another slice of meat.

After supper, he takes me out near the edge of the

property where the grassy ground turns sandy, with towering pines and dry, reddish rock. We walk in silence—my arm in his, as he insists—and I am glad for the quiet. If I have to endure his presence, at least he isn't talking.

The trees thin to the rocks and we halt. Sunset is still a few hours away, but the light is changing, casting deep shadows and bringing color out of the trees and rocks.

"Beautiful, isn't it?" he asks pleasantly.

I nod without a word. It is beautiful, though austere.

"Come, now. I thought you wanted a walk." His eyes are disappointed, as if he expected me to find him charming. As if I would be here if I had any choice at all.

"Yes, I wanted the walk."

"Then what is it?"

I look away, laugh softly at his arrogance.

"Ah." He gives a slow nod, tilting his head down to catch my gaze. "You are the first woman I've kidnapped. I don't make a habit of that."

"Perhaps not." I meet his gaze directly. "But you clearly have no difficulty doing it when you want to. That makes you no better than someone who does make a habit of it."

"I hope it makes me a little better." He shoves his hands into his pockets. "This territory is bigger than all of us. One must make sacrifices."

"But they aren't your sacrifices to make."

He looks at me and shakes his head. "You have greatness in you, Miss Lacey. You see beyond what most men see. But you know nothing of what you speak. Many of the sacrifices have been my own. Everything I have, I fought for against wicked men. And when you fight such men, you cannot keep your hands pristine."

"In some cases, I think it stains a man entirely."

"What about your Archer Scott? What about his wartime deeds, those battles he fought, the orders he carried out? I'll wager his hands are stained with more blood than mine."

"A war is an awful thing. I have seen it. But it is not the same as choosing to steal and kill people in cold blood who would do you no harm otherwise."

"How much do you really know about him?" He stops and turns to me, releasing my arm. His gaze is curious, amused.

"Enough to know he's on the right side and you aren't."

"You don't fool me, Miss Lacey. I didn't know one thing about you, save your hand and manner of address—"

"My hand and manner of address?"

"I would be a rather poor outlaw if I couldn't get my hands on the mail." He gives me a long look before continuing. "But you don't fool me. You have ambition beyond that of common men. What you want, you get."

"I'm hardly getting what I want now."

He looks at me with narrowed eyes and a smile. He believes he can see through me, but he is wrong. He is seeing what he wants to see.

I try a different tack. "Well, then, shouldn't that scare you?"

"It thrills me. There's nothing common about any of us. We'll all be legends."

I start on without him, striding back toward the house.

"Miss Lacey—this territory is something new. It is unlike anything else. Unclaimed land, a place where a man can make himself."

"Forgive me for pointing it out, but you certainly aren't making much of yourself."

"Do you know what they call me?" He stalks straight up to me, leans into my face. "They call me the Outlaw *King*. Tell me how that is not making much of myself."

I've touched a nerve, but I stand my ground quietly. "Thievery is the lowest thing a man can do. I don't care how good you are at that."

"I won't have to thieve all my life. When Scott is gone, I'll have no more rivals. There won't be a need for it."

"You won't stop. Wrong eats you alive when you coddle it."

"Not if you don't coddle it long."

"You really believe the law will let you do this? Raise yourself to power by violent means and just switch sides?"

"Oh, darling—" He stretches the word out, more a condescension than an endearment. "I will be the law."

He holds out his hand to me like a peace offering. "You and I are lucky. Young and strong and alive in this time of history. They'll write books about us."

"Perhaps," I reply, ignoring his outstretched hand, "But I'll be at Archer's side in them."

IT IS EARLY AFTERNOON, and I am alone in the front parlor with the sunshine. Mortimer's pa has gone to speak to the cook about supper, and the solitude is a relief. I close my eyes and breathe in, picturing Archer's face as it was when I last saw him.

I wish I knew what he looks like now.

When I first met him, he was recovering from camp lung and he was too thin—in full parade dress, he looked as if he could hardly hold up his chestful of medals. But nobody thought him a weakling, even at half his proper weight. The men stood out of his way, the women checked their appearances when he approached.

He was handsome in his way, with a firm jaw and a mouth quick to smile, and eyes the most beautiful blue. He was a catch, but he wasn't looking to be caught—he wanted family, someplace to belong. His only family, he had told me, was a cousin named Jesse from his deceased mother's side, but they hadn't been raised together.

I rise a few inches from my chair and peer out the front window, listening for footsteps. Everything appears quiet and peaceful. I reach into the collar of my dress and pull out my only remaining letter.

*It's late. I shouldn't be writing to you when I'm this tired, Rosamund, but if I say something strange, I know you will forgive it.*

*I've had a vision. I can see clear as day in my mind's eye that there will be homes in this territory. Families. This will be a good place where tired folks can start afresh. Where they can build something. From the star-crowned mountain peaks to the forests of tall timbers, standing since the beginning of the world, to the flat lands shimmering with heat and the cactuses that bloom despite the drought. I wish I could show it all to you right now.*

*It's never been something I've had, you know that. To me, home has only ever been a dream. But we'll have it.*

*It's you and I, Rosamund, and together we'll live to see this not just a beautiful place, but a good place.*

I hold the letter close and let my heart beat against it.

A noise outside startles me and I shove the letter back into the neck of my dress. Mortimer's pa hurries in from the next room and peers through the window. I stand and crane my neck to look.

A cluster of horses is coming in, a swarm of men. Holt shouts, making wide sharp gestures with one arm—with the other, he leads Mortimer's black from the back of his own horse. The men are surrounding it, helping a figure out of the saddle.

"It's Alexander." The man beside me blanches and bolts for the door.

I remain at the window, torn. I cannot wish death on anyone, but neither can I help the small hope that roots itself in my heart.

If Mortimer were to die, his father might let me go.

Holt storms through the front door with another man I do not recognize, half-carrying Mortimer, who is white and clutching his arm. Blood trickles over his fingers.

"The doctor's coming," says Holt. "We had to ride a ways—it's just a bullet in his arm."

I let my breath out silently.

I don't know if I'm relieved or disappointed.

. . .

I STAY out of the way. I want to go up to my room, but that would take me past the room where the doctor treats him, and also past Holt.

It's better not to draw attention to myself.

I pick up a book of poetry from the side table—Mortimer's pa has been trying to tempt me, in a sweet, apologetic sort of way, with interesting books.

Holt stomps into the front room, looks around slowly. His gray-brown hair has fallen into his face, and his beard is so mixed with dirt I can't tell where one ends and the other starts. He smells of dirt and leather and man.

I continue to read with great outward preoccupation until I've read the poem three times over and not taken in a word of it.

"You're still here," Holt growls, as if somehow he expected to find me in the middle of an escape.

I turn the page on the unfortunate poem serenely.

"Does Mortimer know you got that book?" He strides over to me and stands too close. Apparently Mortimer is the only one who wears cologne in this place.

"His father gave it to me." I don't look up.

"I reckon you hope he's dead."

"I wouldn't wish that, not on my worst enemy." I look up and give him a thin smile, then notice the fresh bullet hole in his coat.

I wish Mortimer's pa would come back—I don't like being alone with Holt.

"Well, he's tough. He ain't going anywhere yet." Holt grunts and stomps out.

I wait until the sound of his boots dies away, then look

out the window over my shoulder. He's leading the horses away.

Mortimer's pa stumps back into the room, mopping his brow, a minute too late to be my hero.

"Will he be all right?" I ask. I know the answer, but he looks so distraught I feel I must say something.

"I reckon so." His heavy brow knits. "He's in a sight of pain. I wish I could take it all away."

"He's a lucky man then, having you. Not all fathers are so good."

"I'm lucky to have him," he counters with conviction.

"Is he going to be down long?"

"Oh, he'll have to rest, but nothing keeps my son down long." He pours himself some water from the pitcher on the table and sinks down in his chair.

By and by, the others trickle out of the house: Mortimer's companions, the doctor, even the cook who had been providing them with hot water.

The house is quiet in the heat of the day. Mortimer's pa is snoring with his handkerchief over his face.

Setting down my poetry, I go to the window. The yard is empty.

Escape isn't on my mind, for I know nothing of the surrounding land and the idea of being chased down and eaten by wild animals is not a pleasant one. But if no one is around, perhaps I can find Raymond. After a few days of watching the comings and goings as well as I may from the windows, I have a suspicion as to where he and the others may be kept.

Another glance at the old man proves he is truly asleep.

Crossing the room as softly as I can, I open the door and slip outside.

I head in the direction of the garden, where the purple clematis climbs its neat trellis beside the fence. With a quick glance around, I gather my skirt and climb over.

I pause. No sound, no disturbance stirs the hot, still afternoon air. I press on, quickening my pace toward the barn.

First, I peer in through one of the dusty windows, then duck in through the open door. It's musty and smells of hay and horse. I keep to the shadows, moving behind hay and stacks of grain, searching for anything that looks unusual.

In the floor at my feet is a hole, barred for drainage.

Heart pounding, I kneel in the dirt beside the grate and peer into the gloom.

I see four figures, someone's stiff blond hair, smell the stale stench of sweat. Their boots are gone, anything of use taken—just them in their shirts and trousers, but they are there, alive.

I glance up, listen carefully to make sure no one is coming, then lean close.

"Raymond," I hiss.

Someone stirs below.

"Rose?"

"Yes, it's me."

"Hold on." Another soft rustle, and then his face appears just below the grate. His hand reaches through the bars to take mine.

I grip his hand fiercely. It's gentle, enveloping mine.

"You all right, Rose?"

"Fine. I'm not supposed to be here, but I have run of the house and the yard. The—the food is good." My laugh cracks.

"Go back," he urges gently.

"I came to see you. I wanted to know you were still here."

"You've seen me. I'm all right. Now go."

He's not all right. His face is drawn, and below him, I see one of the Swifts with blood caked in his hair and down the side of his face.

I want so badly to tell my brother that we'll make it out the other side. I feel with a strange certainty that I will, but I have nothing for him—only Mortimer's promise to kill them all.

A lie would mean nothing. He knows his situation as well as I do.

"I just—" I'm not ready to let him go.

His eyes take me in as if I'm a dream that will disappear any moment, but he smiles, just a crooked line in one cheek.

"It's all right." His thumb caresses my hand comfortingly.

My eyes fill with tears but I refuse to let them spill.

"I love you, Raymond."

"Love you, Rose." He releases my hand. "Go on. I'll see you later."

But he stands there, his eyes tender and reassuring, gleaming with tears, watching me as if trying to memorize my face.

"Raymond—"

"Go, Rose. I'll see you later."

I stand slowly, afraid to look away, prolonging the moment as long as I dare.

He dashes me a wink, almost too fast to see, and steps down from the grate, making it easier for me.

I turn and make my way back, moving quietly over the straw-strewn floor, wiping tears out of my eyes. Around a wagonload of hay, I find myself face to face with O'Meagher, the cook.

My heart is hammering in my throat, but the surprise in his face slowly melts into something like sympathy. He shifts the basket of eggs he's collecting from one hand to the other uneasily and gives a quiet, awkward smile.

"Let's walk back together, shall we?" he offers.

We walk back in silence and he leaves me in the flower garden, safely inside the gate. I have no heart to go inside, and the faces of the flowers are cool and sweet. Whoever plants them has an eye for color.

I bend down and pluck a bachelor's button, soft blue like the territory stamp Archer sent me. It's so perfect in its design, symmetrical yet graceful, like poetry.

I pick another and another and keep on picking. I refuse to admit to fear or even think of being afraid.

I stare at the flowers, every shade of pink, white, blue, and yellow, as tears stream down my face.

It will pass. I will look again at flowers in a better day, in a better time, and I will know that I survived.

"What are you doing?"

I turn around to see Mortimer, his face white, swaying a

little. His arm is in a sling, and he really shouldn't be out here, up and about after losing blood.

My hands are full of flowers, my cheeks stained with tears. I have no words—I just stare at him. Let him form his own conclusions. I care nothing for his opinion at this moment.

"You didn't think I was running away, did you?" I give a short laugh with no joy in it.

"No," he says slowly. I cannot tell if it is the truth. He offers his arm.

"I don't need it," I say. "You're the one who does."

I brush past him, and a few flowers fall out of my bouquet and trail behind me on the grass.

I STAY in my room the rest of the day.

O'Meagher brings my dinner in right on time and doesn't even ask me to come eat with the others. "Thought you'd be more comfortable here." He smiles sadly.

"Thank you."

He sets the food down—it's chicken pie, my favorite.

"How did you know?" I ask suspiciously.

He winks. "Can't tell. But from that same source—" He pulls out a rose, yellow, soft, and sweet as summer.

Raymond. It is an old language between the two of us, as I am his Rose.

"Don't tell," he says softly and gravely.

"Not a word. Thank you."

He goes to the door and pauses. "Miss Lacey, I am a

simple man, and the struggles of men like Mortimer and Scott are beyond me. I do what I can. But please—" His eyes fall to the fresh-scrubbed floorboards. "If Mortimer loses, remember me?"

8

THATCHER

THE FIRE CRACKLES AND SPITS. IT'S ONLY TO WARD OFF
night animals. We ate pan bread and jerky for supper,
washed it down with coffee.

That's one thing Carson is good at—he makes better
coffee than the rest of us.

Jack Selby settles himself a little apart from the group,
his rifle across his folded legs, and sets to cleaning his
pistol.

Archer lowers himself onto the ground beside me and
rubs his hand over his lightly stubbled face. Right up next
to him like this, I spot a couple gray hairs in his dark head.

"Jesse."

"Mm?"

"I've been a fool," he murmurs under his breath.

"Why, because Alexander Mortimer is a dirty
scoundrel? It's not your fault he hates you."

"I should have been watching. I should have known he'd do something. It wasn't my own neck at stake."

"She had the Swift brothers and a brother of her own, by Sam's telling. That's a mighty good escort."

"But she came out here for me."

"It's done now, Archer. We'll get her back."

He leans back on his elbow, regarding the coffee he swirls in his tin mug. The firelight plays across his face, casting half of it into blackness. I hear a wry chuckle. "You sure aren't much comfort to a man."

"Don't mean to be."

I lie back, arms behind my head, my chin tipped to the stars.

After it's been so long that I figure he's fallen asleep, he says, "I envy you, Jesse."

"Me?"

I laugh. He's the governor. He's the handsome one, the one who didn't need to grub for a living on a ranch because he earned himself a brilliant pension in the war.

He's the man everyone aspires to be.

"If I could go back, I'd make sure somehow I'd never have joined the Croix-Savannah war."

"It's done you a sight of good. I mean, it even brought you Rosamund."

"I mean it, Jesse. Sure, you won't have the stories. Which battle you were in, where you were wounded, that place where your whole regiment was commended for their part. But I tell you it's not worth a carcass. It was the meanest, bloodiest thing I ever saw."

"Well." I cast about for something good to say. "It's sure made you better for this job."

"A little, Jesse. But I look at you, and you need nothing more. You're tough as the land itself. You know cattle, shoot straight. This land might never stop surprising you, but the tools you need aren't all that complicated."

He rubs his hands over his eyes and we just stare at the stars for a while.

"Y'know that legend," he says. "Straight out from the beginning of when they started keeping track of that sort of thing? About this here land."

"Mhm?" I'm tired, my listening lagging. I have to sleep now because my watch starts halfway through the night.

"They say it's bound, cursed since the beginning of the world. And it'll be freed one day by a man with war-torn hands."

"Yep. Could be you," I mumble.

"Don't be absurd." He shifts his long legs. "It's a beautiful legend. Long and twisting like the rivers. I spent an entire night in the house of the Far Hill Clan just listening to them tell it. It was like—like watching a woman spin wool into thread."

I grunt in appreciation.

"All the same, I intend to help make this land a place where people can come. Not just men like us, with guns at our sides. No, a place for families. For painters and singers, and people wanting rest...."

. . .

I'M STARTLED awake by a hand on my shoulder. The night's dark, the fire sunk to sullen embers.

"Your watch," mutters Gilchrist, one of the ranchers. He's hardly more'n a kid. Lost his father after Mortimer ransacked his ranch three years ago.

"That fire needs to be stirred," I mumble. A yawn takes my entire body powerful hard.

I drag myself to my feet and see that Jack Selby is still up, drawing in the sand.

"He's been at it—may not sleep at all." Gilchrist shakes his head. "Well, I'm turning in. Short night for both of us." He claps my shoulder and disappears into the muffled darkness beyond the campfire.

I pick up the stick with the charred end and poke the fire back to life. It's in these thin hours of the night that wolves and evil things creep around the shadows of camps. I've woken on other occasions to find large reptilian tracks circling the dust just outside the reach of the firelight. Just because you can't see it or hear it doesn't mean it's not there.

The very idea gives me the creeps.

Jack Selby glances up as I stir the fire, and the light flares against him. A huge scar from a set of claws is slightly visible through the open front of his shirt, beneath the chain around his neck.

"Not sleeping tonight?"

He doesn't reply. I settle back on my heels, my rifle on the ground beside me, within reach.

I watch as he works—draws in the dust and in a note-book he keeps tucked in his shirt. He's different from other trackers. Has something more. A sixth sense, almost. As if he could reach up with his fist and catch the very air of someone who had passed that way.

Somewhere out there a coyote yips, and I hear something groan—one of the dragon-kind, most likely, that hide under the ground. It's not a sound I like.

A horse comes out of the darkness; I catch the shape of its dark head, thrown back in protest.

"Who is it?" I peer into the dark.

"Just me. Terhune." A lean figure swings down, stalks over to the fire. "Heard there was a to-do. Thought I'd come lend an extra gun."

Harrison Terhune is rich as far as we ranchers go, and he's charming to boot. He's got a voice like smoke and whiskey, eyes the color of cornflowers, and lines in his face like he's seen too much.

Out here, he probably has.

I stretch my stiff arms slowly. "There's coffee if you're not inclined to sleep."

He smiles and his eyes crinkle at the corners. "That'll be just fine. I've been up most of the night, might as well go the rest of the way."

I reach out and pour him a cup. He crouches beside the fire and tastes it. "Now if only I could tempt Carson out to my ranch—he makes it like no one else."

I grin and reach out to pour myself a cup. The fire spits petulantly.

"I have it," says Jack Selby softly. "He must be up between the arroyo and the Ruby River." He gets to his feet, tucking his notebook away.

Terhune looks at him quizzically.

"Governor, sir." Selby bends over Archer, shaking him gently. His voice slips lower and he talks intently.

Archer stirs, listens, rubbing his face, and throws his blanket off. "I knew I could count on you, Jack." My cousin hauls himself to his feet and claps Selby's shoulder hard. "Come, we're not waiting. We can make it up there by the middle of the afternoon tomorrow, if we ride hard."

I guess I was one of the lucky ones. I actually got to sleep tonight.

# 9

## ROSAMUND

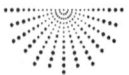

THE COLOR IS BACK IN MORTIMER'S FACE THE NEXT morning at breakfast. I am drained and weary, and he won't meet my eyes. His father is the only contented one, cutting his ham loudly with his knife and chewing industriously.

"It's good to see your appetite is back," he comments cheerily, seeing that Mortimer has emptied his plate.

Mortimer glances up and gives his father an indulgent smile.

His pa continues to talk. "I'm off rabbit hunting this morning. Wish me luck and we'll have coneys for supper." He winks at me.

I can't help smiling back.

"Yes, Pa, do." Mortimer wipes his mouth with a napkin.

"Do you have—" The old man glances at me before he continues. "Business today?"

"Something like."

"Well, mind yourself."

"I always mind myself." He butters a piece of bread with a pleased smile.

Boots stomp up outside and I know without seeing that it's Holt. "Mortimer?"

Mortimer sets down the knife and heads outside without a word.


BY LATE MORNING, Mortimer's pa is back, two fat rabbits hanging from a string gripped in his fist.

"Supper," he beams, showing them to me.

He stumps up onto the low porch and drags a chair out with his foot. It creaks under him as he settles himself and pulls out a skinning knife.

I watch with fascination as he makes the initial cuts around the feet and begins to skin them, leaving the hide intact.

"This is his favorite thing," volunteers Mortimer, stepping up onto the porch, into the shade. "I never see him happier than when he goes out to hunt."

"Animals, I assume. Not your poor victims."

Mortimer's jaw hardens.

"Pa doesn't hold with this." He gestures at the camp. "But he ain't got a choice." He almost snarls the last bit. "I remember the old land, before we came here. And I'd take *darani*, wolves, and lawmen any day over what we had back then."

"Where are you from?"

Mortimer, with his long coat and gloves, gun belts strapped across his hips and chest, his flame-red hair and that face with lines like a river gorge, seems as naturally a part of this land as the arroyo and the dry river bed beyond the pines. I can't see him anywhere else.

He motions for me to follow and we start down the path, out the gate and out of earshot of his father.

"Place called *Ioraich*." The word rolls off his tongue, and for a moment I hear in his voice that he's accustomed to a different language entirely. "Rich soil, too many rocks. We were farmers. Dirty land-workers."

"Was it just the two of you?" In my curiosity, I almost forget that I don't want to be around him.

"No. Had a—a mother, a sister."

That doesn't seem possible. My eyes go to his face, try to see if he's lying. But his eyes are hard as rock, every line in his body tensed.

No one I've met ever braces themselves so hard against a lie.

"My father and I worked hard on the land—I started in the field when I was six. No one worked harder than my father. But the landowner was a greedy pig. And then my mother got sick. We tried every doctor."

He cleared his throat and clasped his hands behind his back.

"After a while, my father couldn't pay—he couldn't stand to not buy my mother medicine, even though she was dying. He—he couldn't stop hoping she'd turn a corner and get better."

A cruel smile spreads across Mortimer's face, but his eyes—they are still hard as stone.

"So the landowner, can you guess what he did? When you don't pay your rent, do you know what they do?"

"Evict you?"

He nods and I don't like that smile.

"Oh, but that's not what he did. He was angry, had it in for my father, good soul who never hurt anyone in his life. Do you know what he did instead?"

I shake my head and take a step back involuntarily. Suddenly I don't want to know. I've learned too much too fast about the cruelty of men these last seven days, and I'm on the edge of learning more than I can take.

"He came in the night, with torches and the law. Didn't take my pa. He hauled my sister and I out of our beds, beat me in front of everyone as if I was a man who could resist." He reaches up with his thumb and caresses the silvery scars on his cheek and jaw. "My sister screamed the whole time. Then they hauled us away to prison. Prison, mind—she was eight and I was eleven. And I was deported for labor here. Never saw my sister again."

"And your pa?" I glance over at the man industriously skinning rabbits. He's an ugly, coarse-featured fellow, but there is genuine pleasure on his face and the tune he whistles is happy.

"Found me four years later, working corn. Said my mother was dead, sister had died in prison according to the records, and I was all he had left. I bashed my guard's head with a rock that night and ran away."

I recoil—I can't help it.

He looks steadily into my face. "There wasn't another way. I was sick of working for no other crime than my father's poverty, I was sick of being treated like dirt. And they wouldn't have let me go."

Silence lies between us.

"Despise me all you like, Miss Lacey. Yes, I chose crime, but crime chose me first."

The wind sighs through the pines, making them restless.

"You still had a choice," I whisper, but my heart's hardly in it.

"Yet from your perspective, our landlord is the better man, as he did not break any laws."

"I would not. There are moral laws that stand whether men write them or not. You have crossed that line yourself."

"That's the world, Miss Lacey. A man gets so that he goes after the weak to hurt the strong. We were my father's weakness, and that man knew it. By the time I came out here, I swore I wouldn't have weaknesses."

I look away. The sky is clear and cool beyond the pines, and I very nearly wish I had never come out here to the Western Territory at all.

He takes the gesture as disgust and speaks more insistently. "After that, after seeing what it had done to my father, I swore he would live in luxury the rest of his life. I have carved us a good life—more than that, a destiny—out of the rocks and the barren land. How is that a bad thing?"

"But by robbing and killing others?"

"Life's not fair. You have to snatch your share from it if you want anything."

I shake my head. "Where does it stop? Where does the

justification for one father erase the fact that you are perhaps depriving some other person of their father? It doesn't make sense. I am sorry that life was so cruel to you, but—"

"I do not want your pity," he snarls.

"I'm not giving it," I bite out.

A muscle twitches in his cheek. I can't understand him.

He takes a deep breath, offers his arm stiffly. "I apologize, Miss Lacey. On this, I suppose we must disagree." He gives a sad smile.

We walk toward the house, both quiet. His father still sits on the porch, happily at work on the rabbits.

It's a strange, powerful thought—I nearly stagger with the heady feeling, but I see it—there are men like Mortimer, and there are men like his father. Ones with their heads stuck in destinies and stars, and ones who find utmost satisfaction in something like preparing supper from food they have caught themselves.

And I am like Mortimer.

"Are you all right?" he asks. Perhaps I did stagger.

"Perfectly." I step ahead of him as he opens the gate for us, and I do not take his arm again.

I give his father a smile as I pass him on the porch.

Mortimer follows me into the sitting room. "Miss Lacey—"

"I'm no longer in the mood for talk." I reach for a book.

He sits down on the other end of the sofa. "Watch your back, Miss Lacey. No matter where you are, whether you think you're safe—"

I turn on him. "Is this a threat?"

"No." He fixes me with a direct look. "In fact, if this territory wasn't so important, I think I would do anything to keep you by my side."

I draw back from him, surprised, but his eyes are honest.

"In the best sense, of course." He rubs the side of his finger with his thumb. "A woman with your determination and pride wields more power than a regiment. Governor Scott is lucky."

Outside, I hear the rumble of hooves.

"You think he'll trade the territory for me, then? He doesn't have that kind of power."

Mortimer looks at me strangely. "Miss Lacey, how do you think men get power? Do you think I walked into the middle of that rabble out there, most of whom would gut another for his birthright—gut me, if they thought they could—and demand that they follow me?"

The door bursts open.

"Sir, they're coming!" Holt is dust-covered, jerks a thumb over one shoulder.

Mortimer raises himself halfway off the chair. "What? How far?"

"Five miles out. Stopping now and again to scout."

"Good. Send a party to meet them well out. I'll be along. Warn 'em if they start something, I'll—" His gaze wanders to me. "Tell them not to start anything. Nothing. Understood?"

"Sir."

But he lingers, wanting Mortimer to follow him.

"Holt, get. I'm coming."

The door slams behind Holt louder than it needs to.

My heart lifts. *Archer is coming for me.*

But Mortimer is still frowning, determined to make his point. "A man nowadays gets his power from bullets and paper. I have the bullets, Archer Scott's got the paper."

"But he has integrity—something you're missing entirely."

He laughs softly, condescending. "If only you knew, Miss Lacey."

"You could start now. You don't have to go through with your plans, you know." It's a hopeless cause, but I'll try.

"I'm too far along this path to look back now, at least in the way you suggest. But I'll do what your Archer is trying to do, and by any means necessary."

"But what if you did put a stop to this? What if you gave yourself up and tried to help him? I know him, Mortimer—he's reasonable."

"I know him too. I don't need his help, nor would I want it if he offered. I'll make this territory something, you'll see. And I'll do it without him. Despite him."

He gets up, stalks to the door, and opens it. He pauses, framed with sunlight, and glances back. "It's too late for him, Miss Lacey, but it's not too late for you."

The door shuts and I hear his boots tramp across the porch and up the stone walk to the gate.

. . .

THE AFTERNOON SUN is too bright. I shut the book I'm pretending to read and set it aside. Archer is close, within a few miles, and likely has been for the last few hours.

I cannot concentrate on anything.

I wonder if he has changed much—if he's put on the weight he sorely lacked when I bade him goodbye on my doorstep that pale spring morning when the lilacs were just beginning to bloom. He must have. It's been years. I wonder if the years and the responsibility have deepened the proud lines of his face.

It's hard to know that he is so close—face to face with Mortimer, more than likely—and I cannot see him. I wonder if we will be shy when we see each other again.

I want to hear his voice again—not have to imagine it in my head as I do with his letters, trying to remember the way it sounded. Feel the warmth of his hand in mine, work-worn and real.

But mostly, I just want to be with him.

A clatter of hooves comes over the rocks, turning into dull thuds as the horses reach the soft dust and grass of the yard. I stand up and lean against the sill to look out the window.

It's Holt.

He reins in his horse sharply and shouts something, pointing to the barn. I straighten, dread rising in my middle.

Something terrible is about to happen.

Two men drag out Alan Swift, the middle brother with the shy smile. Holt stands in the middle of the yard, and the others back the horses a safe distance from him. He's feeding a bullet into his pistol.

I'm out the door before I even realize I've moved. The world is clear and still and mad.

"Holt!" I shout from the porch.

He turns. "Get out of here," he snarls.

"You can't make me do anything." Fear makes me bold. "I'm more valuable to Mortimer at this moment than you are."

His face turns uglier, if possible, than it already is.

"Stay, then. But you won't want to see this." He turns his back on me deliberately and motions for them to bring Alan.

"Get some rope and tie him up. This has to be quick— better than he deserves." He closes his gun and spins the chamber.

In an instant, I've snatched up the rifle Mortimer's pa left on the porch. I'm through the gate before Holt looks my way again.

"Don't do it!" I train the gun on him.

He sees me and stops. He puts his hands up, slowly, mockingly, the pistol still in his hand.

"Drop the gun." I can only keep my hands from shaking a little longer, but I know how to shoot, and I'm close enough that I really can't miss.

He gives me a nasty smile and moves the pistol toward his holster.

"I said drop it!"

And I see it. A split second movement of his hand—I

squeeze the trigger and his pistol fires into the ground as he falls, clutching his shoulder.

One of the horses screams and breaks free, bucking and twisting through the men.

A rush of movement—Alan is free, the men are fighting, tangling, the horse whips past and I drop the rifle as its shoulder slams into me.

Someone grabs the horse and hoists onto its twisting, plunging back. It's running at me. The rider seizes my arm.

The ground slides out from under me as I'm hauled upward with a sudden wrench.

Gunshots are going off around us and he puts his arm around me as the horse bolts forward. It's Alan.

We're whipping through the trees, scrambling down a sandy bank and splashing across a stony river. The gunshots are nowhere near hitting us now, but I still hear shouts. The horse scrambles up the bank. Alan whistles sharply to him.

We shoot from the cover of trees onto a great flat that shimmers.

I hold onto Alan for dear life as the world blurs and jolts with strides as quick as my heartbeat. I can feel the horse's muscles beneath me as it eats up the ground in a frenzy, its mane whipping into our faces, its ears pinned.

The thought hits me as we streak across the flat: we're running free. We cannot undo this. There's no going back.

# MORTIMER

He's here.

The heat of the day rises from the very ground, making it quiver beneath us. Every step is rising dust and shivering air.

He's standing back from us but apart from his party, only two men flanking him with rifles. I wave off my main escort and bring two of my own as security, mirroring him.

For all the grief we have caused each other, I have only faced him a few times.

His face is like granite, his hat pulled low, his hand hanging beside his hip, fingers twitching with nervous energy.

Patient and afraid.

I wet my lips and smile to myself. In this moment, we stand in our rightful places. I am king. He wants to hear my demands. He wants to know how to satisfy me.

"Mortimer," he acknowledges.

"Archer. At last." I drag the words out.

The air is still and hot.

"You never sent a ransom note. I'm surprised at you."

There it is. That way he has of making sport in the worst situations. I do believe he'd laugh in the face of the devil himself.

"Perhaps I decided I don't want to be rid of her."

He stiffens slightly.

There. That struck a nerve.

"What is it you want?" His voice is like steel—hiding, I am sure, a pounding heart. I've seen faces like these a dozen times. They break eventually.

"I want the territory."

Archer's face relaxes into a white grin and he laughs a little under his breath. "Mortimer, you know you can't ask for that. It's not mine to give."

"Don't play with me." I keep my tone flat. "You are its governor. Changes and orders from back East are slow and scarce. The law stops with you. You alone are its master, and true, the time will come when it's not the case, but today—look me in the face if you dare, and tell me it isn't so—you have no one to turn to for help. If I created a war with you, you would be defeated like that." I snap my fingers.

"And you think those men back East won't send an army if they find you've taken over?"

I laugh. And here I had thought Archer Scott was intelligent, a man of the world who knew how these things worked.

"They certainly wouldn't send you an army to fight me with."

He knows that. I see the assent in his eyes.

"I am a reasonable man," I continue. "Even Miss Lacey would tell you that—"

He interrupts with a forbidding sound in his throat. "Bring her out then and let her tell me herself."

He's serious. I hesitate a moment and then choose the simplest path—ignoring him. "You get Rosamund Lacey when you write me a full pardon. A pass to do as I will, no questions asked. You remain governor in name."

"Never." He barely sounds interested.

"You would rather see me dead than your fiancée safe?"

"It's not a matter of revenge, Mortimer. It's a matter of principle."

A sudden burst of anger takes me. I want to hit something, shake him until his teeth rattle.

I laugh, instead, at the irony. I would take better care of that proud, clever girl than this man would, give her more power than he ever would, and yet she trusts him as she never will me. I feel it again, the brick wall of fate deciding for me that I should have a hard, unhappy life, rewarding instead men in authority who abuse it.

"Is ancient principle more important to you than a human life?"

"It's one because of the other, Mortimer. But you'd never understand that."

*Hypocrite.* I'd like to see how many lives he's willing to spend before he gives up the girl or the territory. We'll see soon. Holt's gone back to dispatch one of the Swifts, bring the body down to prove I mean business.

I wave one of the other men over, and he bends his head to me so I can whisper. "Any word from Holt? How long ago did he return?"

"He ought to be back any time."

"Good. Ride back a ways, tell me when he's coming."

"Yes, sir."

"Can you wait?" I ask lightly, when the man has gone.

"We're not going anywhere." Archer's jaw is hard as a rock. "And let me tell you this. You harm one hair of her head, and I will make you pay, do you understand me? I will not rest until you swing."

I wave him off with a laugh.

Let him worry. Let him think me a monster. So long as he does as I say. And he will, when he realizes his righteous stubbornness has cost the Swifts their lives.

A horse comes riding in, lathered.

It's Tora-Teth, my tracker, who comes, not Holt. He swings off the horse before it has stopped, like a bird landing from the sky.

You can never tell from his dark eyes what he's thinking, but he is hurrying, and for him, that is not good.

He jerks his head and I bend to hear.

"There's been an accident," he whispers.

# 11

# ROSAMUND

COOL NIGHT FALLS. THE HORSE IS SPENT, ITS RAGGED breathing the only sound in the night. The horizon is a darkish purple and orange, casting strange light across the rocks and illuminating Alan Swift's strong, lean face.

I let out a long sigh, feeling I haven't breathed or thought clearly until this moment.

He stops the horse with a word.

"Well." He gives a short, disbelieving laugh. "That was an adventure."


THE ROCKS we shelter behind are small and still warm with the sunlight.

"Sleep," Alan says. "We're only stopping for an hour or two."

I lie down on the warm rock. It's getting cold already.

Alan perches on the rock above me, holding the horse's reins.

"You aren't going to sleep?"

"I can't," he admits. "That's all right. My brothers and I have cattle, and sometimes on the drive you can't sleep for days."

I close my eyes, but the sounds of the night crowd around me. Far-off wild calls, a strange tapping like wood against a rock, the horse shifting and sighing, and after a while, Alan's breathing.

"What will happen to the others?" The thought comes to me and I have to ask before I can sleep.

There's just enough light to see him, but I cannot read the expression on his face. "It's best not to think on it."

"If you know, please tell me."

"I don't." He pulls at his jaw with his long fingers. "We got away. We have to make sure we don't waste it."

He's right. That's the only thing we can do now.

I close my eyes, try not to think.

It feels like a long time before the night sounds fade and I rest.


THE WORLD IS NEARLY PITCH black and only the stars are bright when Alan wakes me gently. There's only a sliver of moon.

"How long has it been?"

"Just over an hour. Hush. Don't make a sound."

I take his hand and stand up, feeling my way off the

rock and back to the horse. And then I hear it: a distant raised voice, a clatter of hooves.

"Is it them?" I whisper, leaning close so he can catch my soft words.

"No telling. But we can't take that risk." He hesitates. "I hate to ask, but do you have a petticoat I can use?"

I give him one and hold the horse as he quietly tears the cloth and pads its hooves.

With the excess, he wraps the rings next to the bit to keep it from jangling. Then he helps me up into the saddle.

"Aren't you riding?" I whisper.

"No." He takes the horse's head and leads it on.

The chill in the air makes the night more foreboding. I try not to think of Raymond. We hear the sounds of far-off men and riders for an hour or two, and then they fade away, swallowed, like the other noises, by the night.

Close to sunrise, Alan asks me how I am.

"Well," I answer softly. I am stiff and sore and my back hurts, but I am not about to say anything. Alan's been on his feet, and we are running for our lives without weapons or food or water. I can keep going for a good while longer, and that's all he needs to know.

"Have we lost them, do you think?"

I turn around, looking at the blank, rocky way we have come. It's hard to see anything in the light.

"I doubt it. But this particular set won't have had time for provisions or a change of horse. Or orders to follow. If we can elude them for the next day, we'll have some breathing room."

"We don't have provisions either."

He smiles, but his eyes don't follow suit. "Don't worry about that."

I hope he has a plan and isn't just trying to think of a way to tell me gently that we're going to die out here.

It's quiet between us, but he seems to have relaxed a little. We haven't heard any sounds of pursuit for some time, and the horse plods on unconcerned, no longer alert for danger.

Alan leads the horse carefully over the uneven ground, sometimes staring ahead with his face set like a marble statue I saw once in a museum.

A little over a week ago, I had never met this man, and now it's the two of us alone in the midst of a dangerous wilderness. If I am to live more than a few days, I must put my trust wholly in him.

"Why did you bring me?"

He seems surprised by the question. "Why wouldn't I?"

"You know you have a better chance without me. If they catch us, you'll die and I probably won't."

"I wasn't going to leave you with Mortimer as collateral. That was the whole point, I think." He laughs softly. "And you saved my life."

"That nearly didn't turn out."

"But it did. You'll soon find survival satisfaction enough out here. You no longer think about how close you came— just accept that it wasn't your time. And when it is—"

He shrugs.

"That's rather cavalier."

"The land out here changes you, Miss Lacey. You can't be the same person you are back East. It demands things of you. Some things that matter where you come from are pointless here, and likewise the other way around."

"For example?"

"Well, in the East, so I hear, every person of a particular age and class is expected to have a certain sort of job. Out here, it doesn't much matter what work you put your hand to, so long as you can find food and shoot straight, stick on a horse and pull your weight when asked. But that'll change as more folks settle."

"You make folks settling sound like a bad thing."

He shakes his head. "Humankind is always going to be flawed and run to its own nasty habits. Anytime enough of us get together, we end up with trouble. You and I may not live to see it, if that's a comfort."

He means, of course, that it may not happen in our lifetimes, but I still shudder inwardly. At this rate, we may not live to see much of anything.

The horse sighs, long and low.

"Do you know where we are?" I ask. From the lay of the land and the rising of the sun, it seems we are headed roughly southwest.

"I've only got a very rough idea," he admits. "But travel long enough and you find landmarks, if you know the country well enough."

"And where are we going?"

"Someplace where we'll find help. He'll have sent fresh men by now."

I shudder. "But do you know where?"

"Sure, I do. I'm taking you home. Our hands are good as gold, and the ranch is as easy a place as any to defend."

"I'd hate to have him tangle with your ranch."

"Don't worry one bit, Miss Lacey. Out here, it's always a risk. Might as well risk it for something worthwhile."

"Alan...."

He looks up at me expectantly.

"Please, just call me Rosamund, or Rose. I want to be ready, no matter what happens, and I couldn't possibly die with someone calling me Miss Lacey."

A smile starts across his face and spreads to his eyes. He understands.

"Very well. Rosamund. But it's Miss Lacey again as soon as we're out of danger."

DAY RISES in the form of an all-encompassing, majestic sun that casts little shadow for us as we travel. We have had no food or water.

Around noon, judging by the light, we stop for a brief rest. Alan leaves me the horse and heads back the way we came to scout from the tops of the rocks.

I stroke the animal's neck and it leans into me, appreciating the attention. And I wait, listening for sounds, for anything.

A hawk cries, wheeling in the blinding blue sky, and something skitters through the tall rocks near my ear. The horse looks too, but I see the flash of a brownish tail, quick as a blink. Just a lizard.

"Rosamund—"

Alan comes scrambling back with his face so carefully calm that I know it can't be good.

"What?" The word falls from my numb lips.

"The party is on our heels."

"How many?"

"Three. They have canteens and guns, no food that I can see."

"What are we going to do?"

He swallows and gives a little smile. "I'll take care of it." He takes my hand and leads me on, searching the rocks. He finds a sturdy desert sapling and ties the horse. A distance beyond the horse, he finds me a small cleft, just big enough for me and just out of sight of the main way.

He gives me a hand up the rocks. "Stay there, and whatever you do, don't come out until I come back for you."

"All right."

"If no one comes by tomorrow morning, see what you can salvage. If you continue the way we are going, you will find a little water in three miles."

With that, he leaves me to the thunderous pounding of my heart in my ears.

A gunshot breaks the silence, answered instantly by another. I start, slamming into the rock, my heart pounding so hard I'm almost shaking.

It's quiet after that. I strain my ears against the silence and count my heartbeats to track the minutes. The world feels too slow.

Footsteps. I press myself back against the wall and my hand closes on a rock. Only Alan knows exactly where I am—the other men would have to search to find me. If it isn't him, I'll put up a fight.

I go weak with relief when the figure comes around the

rock. It's Alan, with a trickle of blood running down his face, leading the horse.

"What happened?"

"I took care of them." He's wearing two belts across his hips—one facing the wrong direction—and another across his chest. A canteen dangles from his fist.

"Drink, and don't think about where it came from." He tosses it to me.

And I do. I am so thirsty I really don't care.

"Are they...?"

"They're not going to trouble us anymore," he says quietly. "Come—we have a little time." He holds out his hand and helps me down.

The horse carries the rest of the spoils: a saddle sheath with a rifle, another gun belt hung on the saddle horn, and two more canteens.

"Any food?" I ask, not daring to hope.

"A day's worth of jerky. Eat, if you like. I'll hunt soon, before there's a chance of them catching up and hearing us."

"What if they—"

"Already? No, they'd have lost the light quickly. Tracking in the dark takes longer, and we would've had at least an hour's lead setting out. I'd wager we have almost half a day on them now."

He glances up at the sky as a shadow falls between us and the sun.

The breath leaves my body as I look up and see a long-beaked creature silhouetted against the light, the sun shining through its leathery wings. It's far away, but monstrous—large enough to carry away a sheep or a small child.

"An *isark*," Alan says grimly. "Let's go."

The creature screams, and I shudder.

I wonder if it's a scavenger.

# 12

## THATCHER

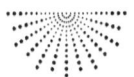

ALEXANDER MORTIMER MEETS US TWO DAYS LATER, which I think is right odd.

It would make sense for him to hold out on us, hoping to starve us out or at least make us uncomfortable enough to go home. But the way he took off, abrupt-like, and left a watch in the distant rocks—we could see the shine of their rifles—I can't make it add up in my mind. Even if I never was good at figures.

He's different today. Haughty and cold, not pleased with himself. The cool morning wind brings me a powerful sweet smell from his direction—in my opinion, not a smell that belongs out here in these barren places.

"I am afraid there is no longer a reason to parley," Mortimer says, pulling at his gloves, looking only at Archer.

"And why not?" My cousin is as still as cedars just before a storm.

"She's dead," he says, in a low voice.

"Dead?" He repeats it like an accusation.

Mortimer just nods, a little regretfully.

"How?"

Mortimer looks at him, sadly, blankly.

"This is your doing. The least you can do is tell me."

"You think I did it?" Mortimer laughs. "When I wanted to barter? I'm not a fool, Archer."

Archer's jaw tightens, ever so slightly.

"There was a—mistake. An underestimation on her part, too much zeal on the part of one of my men. He shot her as she was trying to escape." He tugs at his gloves again, glances up at us.

He's hiding something from us, not telling the whole truth. I see it in his face.

"If I find out you're lying—"

"Archer, I saw her body."

My cousin speaks low. "I'm holding you responsible for this, Mortimer."

Mortimer holds out his palms, spreads his arms. "Very well. I take responsibility. Though you might perhaps consider taking some yourself, as you were the one who asked her to come. And since you are no longer a law officer of Glory Mesa—"

"Mortimer, I am not here for my amusement." Archer's voice is unrelenting. "What about the others? Her brother, the Swifts. If they're still alive, I want to barter for them."

Mortimer gives a thin smile.

"The Swifts are my affair. There will be no trading for them." He seems annoyed that Archer has changed the subject. "But her brother—I will listen to what you offer."

Archer's fist knots. Those Swifts are good men, every one of them, and whatever Mortimer has planned for them, it won't be good.

But my cousin is smart and he's got a level head. His anger will wait for another day. He swallows it back and calms his voice as if lives were not in the balance.

"You give him to me, we'll turn around and leave."

Mortimer weighs this. If I had a right fine hideout, I'd do a little sweating until my enemy was out of its vicinity. But Mortimer has one advantage: he doesn't care if Raymond Lacey lives or dies.

And Archer cares.

"That horse." Mortimer points at Gilchrist's grullo. "It's a good one. I have another similar to it in color, and I fancy a match. Give me the horse and your promise to leave. And I'll be watching to make sure you uphold your end of the bargain. Anyone turns back, I'll shoot."

I'm glad Gilchrist is out of earshot. Mortimer doesn't seem to remember, but that grullo he has was the one he stole from Gilchrist's father same time he killed him. The two were sired by the same stallion.

Archer goes back to Gilchrist and they talk quietly.

"It's a deal," says Archer. "Bring him out."

Mortimer leans back in his saddle and whispers something to one of the men, who rides away.

"You will have to wait," he says, in mock regret.

"Did I say I had somewhere to be?" Archer raises his eyebrows and turns away.

. . .

AN HOUR LATER, Mortimer and two of his men bring out a figure in a stained white shirt and tall, dusty black boots.

I don't know what I was expecting—a kid brother, maybe—but Raymond Lacey's got a heavy mustache that's already graying, and you can spit in my eye if he hasn't spent half his life in the saddle. Cattlemen and cavalrymen get a look about them.

"He's yours," says Mortimer. "Now get me that horse."

Gilchrist is a better man than I'd be. He climbs off, undoes the cinch, takes the bridle off. He stands face to face with the horse a moment, holding its forelock, then leads it over to Mortimer's crew.

One of his men ropes it and they ride off, leaving Gilchrist standing in the dust. He trudges back our way, and Archer reaches out and claps him on the shoulder in sympathy.

We're up a man and down a horse, and I'm not looking forward to the dusty ride home. It'll be days, and we'll be slower for the loss.

Raymond speaks first.

"Reckon one of you must be Archer Scott," he says in a voice that's deeper than the ranch well and gravelly as the bottom of it.

"I am." My cousin holds out his hand.

Raymond takes it.

"I'm sorrier than I can say that we meet under these circumstances."

"Yep." Raymond looks grim.

"Well." Archer lets his breath out like it hurts and slaps his hand onto the man's shoulder. "Now that we've got you, we'll do our best to keep you alive."

Raymond Lacey grunts. He strikes me as a man of few words.

I glance toward Mortimer and his men. "Archer, let's be off." With the talks coming to an end, Mortimer could spin around and shoot one of us and maybe get away with it.

Harrison Terhune spurs his horse forward from the rest of our men and pulls up beside Archer. "The posse's restless, Governor. They figure we should take a couple with us."

"Hm?"

Archer's in shock. He's not catching the meaning.

"Open fire, take him out right now. They're within rifle shot."

"And leave how many of ours behind in a skirmish?" Raymond Lacey fixes Terhune with a steely gray eye.

Terhune slides his gaze uncomfortably from the newcomer to Archer.

"We are here under the rules of parley," my cousin says severely and pushes past us all to his horse.

As he mounts and settles in the saddle, I see his hand steal up and his thumb wipe at his eye.

The sun fades behind a passing cloud, casting a shadow over us all. It should be a welcome respite, but I only feel apprehension.

The sooner we leave this place, the better.

# 13

## ROSAMUND

Alan hands me the canteen. "Not too much," he warns.

I take a sip, just one, though my dry throat screams for more. The water is warm and a little bitter, but I don't care.

"One more."

I take another, grateful. Then I hold out the canteen and he accepts it, closing the lid and slinging it over his shoulder again.

It's been three days. The horse is no good for riding anymore, and we've had to give it water from our canteens, the same we have to drink. It's been two days since the last water source, and Alan thinks it may be a day or more before we reach another.

And the heat is infernal.

"I had an Auki grandmother. We did. Jem always says it

gives us a couple days longer before we die in the desert."
He gives me a quiet smile.

"Lucky," I murmur. The sun makes spots swim before
my eyes.

"Lucky for you," he says. "You will drink the water, and
I'll get you out of this desert."

I only smile. There's nothing to be said, and I don't
want to waste my breath saying it.

The ground shimmers before us as we plod forward,
and I wish I could see an end to the sand. A towering
collection of rocks on the horizon breaks the monotony
but gives little comfort.

"There could be water." Alan is panting but cheerful.
He must be thirstier than I am and twice as tired, but I
haven't heard one word of complaint from him. "Around
the clusters of rocks sometimes there are small springs."

I hope so. I grip the poor horse's saddle to steady myself
and close my eyes against the blinding sun for just a moment.

Already my throat feels parched again, and I am dying
to have another drink.

"How are you holding up?" he asks.

I don't know if it's been five minutes or an hour since
he last spoke.

I hate this desert. It's the first thing I've truly feared
out here.

"I'm all right," I answer him with a smile. "I just want
this desert to end."

"And it will." He looks me straight in the eye with a
knowing expression. "I promise you, it will end."

"I think I might even cry if I see pines and a cold river again." The words sound sadder than I intended.

"Then be prepared, for once we are out of the desert, we'll have just that. Our ranch is right up in the best timberland there is." He laughs, a little hoarsely.

I close my eyes to visualize it. *Courage, Rosamund.*

As we draw closer to the rocks, the horse begins to revive a little, pricking its ears and blowing.

"What is it?" I look to Alan.

"Maybe he's sensed water." He reaches up and scratches its forehead. "That or there's a predator around. But he doesn't seem afraid."

Alan shades his eyes and peers up at the rocks. "With the storm that passed through here a few days ago, there might be water up there. When it's wide like that at the top, it forms basins and catches the rain. If it's deep enough, the pools last a bit."

The horse continues to watch the rocks with perked ears, but he doesn't try to turn or bolt as we draw near. We walk with our own ears strained, the horse snorting now, uncertain.

Then we hear a slow grating shriek, like a crow but ten times louder and more horrible.

Alan freezes.

"Stay here—close to the horse." He hands me a pistol quietly.

"What?"

"Shh."

"What are you doing?"

"Going first." He gives me a smile that is meant, I think, to reassure me, but it doesn't.

He makes his way up the rocky, uneven ground, his boots grinding the stone softly as he moves. I hope, I pray the water is real.

He makes his way around the edge of the rock face ahead of us and pauses. Silently, he gestures for me to follow. And he inches forward.

A shriek tears the air and from nowhere a vast shadow hurls itself downward toward us. The horse shies hard and rips the reins out of my hand. I jar against the ground and feel the brush of a massive leathery wing just before the creature smashes into Alan.

It's an *isark*.

Alan's gun goes off and I grab mine, which I dropped when I fell. The air is full and thrumming with the shrieking of the creature, and through the cacophony comes a drawn-out cry from Alan.

I cannot see him under the creature, but the back of the thing's head is toward me and it's thrusting its beak downward like a pecking bird.

I take a breath, hold the pistol in both hands, and fire right into its head. It jerks, thrashing and thrashing, its broad wings beating first the air and then the dust. Its long, wicked tail slams into my knees, knocking me on my back.

And stillness reigns.

I struggle up, ignoring the grit and blood on the palms of my hands, and run to Alan, who is trapped under the wreck of the *isark*.

Its body lies partially on top of him, the hideous head

turned away at an unnatural angle, the wings spread and still.

"Alan!" I duck under a wing, trying to move it, but it only pushes back, stiff.

He's lying with his head tilted back, his eyes squeezed shut.

"Alan, you have to talk to me."

He forces his eyes open and looks at me with a strange, faraway expression. Dark blood pools beneath his leg.

He opens his mouth and closes it and then whispers, "I'm sorry, Rosamund."

"It wasn't your fault. I'm fine. Tell me—tell me where you're hurt."

"I don't know."

So I look myself. The blood pooling beneath his leg seems to be from a deep puncture just above the knee, and by the time I've figured that out, he says softly, "I think my wrist is broken."

It's discolored and limp and has an unnatural bulge.

"Anything else?" I try to sound cheerful.

"Ribs too."

No. Everything has gone wrong so fast. I don't think Alan can walk, and he's bleeding. And the *isark* is still on him.

"I need to move this. If I put my shoulder against it, can you roll out from underneath?"

"Try me." He gives me a brave smile.

The thing's underbelly is clammy and cool. I put my arms around its awful body and shove. True to his word, Alan rolls out, drawing his breath in with a hiss.

I let the carcass go as fast as I can and shed my second petticoat. It's dusty, but cleaner than my dress, and it'll have to do.

I rip it desperately, and the moment I have a strip, I tie it above the leg wound and draw it tight with all my might until the bleeding slows.

Leaving him on the ground, I run back around the rock, hoping to find the horse, but knowing better.

It is gone. With the rifle, the rest of the jerky, and one of our canteens.

The other two lie on the ground between Alan and the *isark*. I pick one up and kneel beside him.

"You can't use the water on my leg. We need it to drink. Check for a spring."

The bleeding has slowed since I tied off the wound, but it's not slow enough. I cannot delay. "Alan—"

"Just look." His voice is faint.

I get to my feet and step past the *isark*, moving up the rocks that Alan pointed out earlier. I climb high, sweat gathering against my neck and between my shoulders. There has to be water.

Near the top, sheltered by a taller formation, I see the sky reflected in a pool.

I run over and dip my hand in. It's cooler than I expect and doesn't taste bitter. There's enough to fill the canteens and then some.

"Find anything?" Alan sounds bad.

"Yes—I think it's rainwater." I scramble back down the rocks. I hand one canteen to Alan and keep the other, dampening another strip of petticoat.

"I'm sorry if I hurt you—" I begin.

"That's the least of my worries." He's sweating hard.

The wound is dirty and cut up inside, but there isn't much debris. I get it as clean as I can and bandage it tightly.

"Well done," he whispers. "Now go fill those canteens again."

I climb up, the canteens rattling over my shoulder. Standing beside the pool, I can see for miles around. I look back the way we came—it's clear and still and shimmering. I wonder if they're back there somewhere, Mortimer and his men.

With Alan hurt, we might not make it after all.

I turn around to look the way we're heading, and here, from the height of the rocks, I can see it—a darkish line of hills on the horizon.

There's no telling how far away that is, but it's enough for me. I bend down and fill the canteens, my resolve growing.

If I can see it, I can make it.

A sudden cry comes from below and I hurry to the edge. "Alan!"

"No—it's all right." He's gripping his bad wrist and he tries a shaky smile and fails. "It's all right now."

Since he's put the bone back in place, I help him splint his wrist, and the rest of the petticoat goes to make him a sling.

I build a fire, but we have nothing to eat. I want it to burn now and let it sink to coals by the time night hits—

that way I can revive it in an emergency, but it's not bright enough to attract attention from a distance.

"Can you eat an *isark?*" I've used a trickle of water to wash the blood from my hands and arms, but I somehow still feel dirty. It doesn't help that the body of the *isark* is there in front of me, sprawled out in twisted death.

"You shouldn't," Alan replies with a whisper of a smile.

I laugh because I don't know when I'll get another chance.

So we go hungry.


WE HAVE ONE RIFLE—ALAN was carrying it when he was attacked—so I settle myself against the rock with the gun across my lap and watch Alan and the embers. He didn't protest when I told him that I was keeping watch tonight, only made me promise to use caution. I promised, and he is asleep.

I wish I had whiskey—or anything stronger than water —for him to drink, but he seems to take pain as a matter of course. Mortimer, too, had been that way after his injury. I suppose accepting danger and suffering as a natural part of life is another way things are different out here.

Something cries in the dark. I check to make sure both chambers on the rifle are loaded, then settle back.

Back East, to stay up all night would be almost unthinkable. I never had call to unless I was caring for someone sick, and even then, I had doctors or the cook to help.

But tonight I am not tired. I am as awake as the stars

and the night animals. There is something real and desperate in facing down death like this, clinging to the edge of survival with your fingertips, willing the chance at life to stay with you. An entire dimension of your soul is asleep until desperation wakes it.

In the time since being captured, I haven't felt this determined about anything, not even when standing up to Mortimer. I will live, and I will marry Archer Scott.

Alan and I are not going to die.

I only nod off once—I do not know for how long, but I hear the howling of a wolf and I am fully awake again. Then a noise, loud and scrambling, comes near at hand, followed by a long, uncertain snort.

I set the rifle down and rise slowly. Just beyond the rocks, its ears flicking back and forth nervously, stands our horse, the reins wrapped around one leg.

The world goes still.

It wants to come, but the dead *isark* is spooking it. I step over the offending beast and inch toward the horse.

At last my hand is on the bridle. Holding it steady in one hand, I reach down and unwrap the reins from around its leg. It jerks its head but doesn't try to get away.

When it is freed, I lead it the long way around the body, reassuring it with soft words as it snorts and sidesteps.

I tie the horse securely to a tough scrub bush a comfortable distance from the carcass but safely within sight of the fire and give it a whole canteen of water. It laps the water greedily and then licks my hands with its dripping tongue.

Hopefully the water gives the poor animal more than enough reason to stay with us.


MORNING DAWNS PALE AND DRY. Alan wakes at first light, his face drawn.

"You caught it." He's looking at the horse.

"It came in the night. I gave it water."

He gives an approving nod. "Good, then. Give it some more and fill the canteens. If we wait any longer, we run the risk of being caught."

"Can you make it?" I suddenly wish I hadn't asked. We don't have a choice.

"Now that we have the horse, we can. It's had a rest and water. We'll be all right now."

His confidence pours life back into me, tired as I am.

*We'll be all right now.* I hold those words tight to my chest.


IT FEELS LIKE A MIRACLE. By nightfall, we reach the edge of the desert and climb up the sandy soil into pine woods again, and in the fading light of the day, I climb off the weary horse and walk knee-deep into the running water of a mountain stream.

## 14
## THATCHER

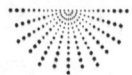

He's mourning her. I can tell by the set of his shoulders, by the tone of his voice, by the look in his eyes the whole way back.

No one else would know. Carson even made free to mutter to Gilchrist that Archer hardly seemed to be taking the loss of his bride-to-be to heart.

But I know him. I feel it in the very air around him.

This Raymond Lacey is a quiet customer. He and Gilchrist didn't say much more than a dozen words to each other in the last few days, but they were almost amicable when we stopped at the Gilchrist ranch and they parted ways.

I suppose it might help that it was the grullo that bought his life.

Carson mutters to himself as we rein in outside the saloon. I don't know what he's worrying about. He left the place with Kate Carnegie, his one and only worker, and though she's young, she is more than competent.

Every time I see her, her wind-curled hair is falling loose, no matter how many times she ties it back, and those bright eyes of her take you in like the wide blue sky. But not a man even thinks about crossing her. She ain't like the other womenfolk here, but she ain't lowlife neither.

She's just Kate—there's no other way to put it.

I step through the doors into the smoky, sharp-smelling room and Kate looks plumb straight in my direction with a sudden longing. I stop short, making sure that it really was me she was looking at. No one else is in the doorway, and the view behind is just the restaurant across the way.

Her eyes are fixed on me, but they see straight through and out the other side. I look away; there's something too open and real on her face.

When I come up to the counter, she sees me properly and smiles. The look is gone.

"What can I get you?" She tilts her head in a way that says *try me.*

"Whiskey and soda. Just a shot."

She turns with a brisk nod.

There's something powerful strange about this girl. For one, she has no family. No one really knows where she came from—she just showed up one day, and she's been here since.

The other's that when you talk to her, it's not like talking to other girls. The other womenfolk out here are sturdy enough, but there's a different kind of resilience to

Kate—as if there's something she wants powerful bad, and she's waiting for it and knows what's taking her there and what's just a distraction.

It makes her a good worker.

"Whiskey and soda." She puts it in front of me with a heavy thunk. "What? Is there something strange on the wall?" She whips her head around to look at the wall lined with Carson's spirits.

"Nah."

She glances up and down the counter and then leans her chin on her fists. "What was it like? What does Alexander Mortimer look like?"

"It was hot and dusty and we rode so hard even the best men were stiff."

She laughs. "And Mortimer? I've never seen an outlaw up close."

"Hopefully you won't have to." I grin. She's a bloody romantic. "He's got hair redder than rust and a lean face that looks like a coyote."

"Men don't look like coyotes," she counters shrewdly.

"He does."

"Carson said he was dandy. Tall and strong and fit to wrestle an ox."

"He can't wrestle an ox." I frown and shake my head. "No chance."

"Who is the new man?" She jerks her head toward Raymond Lacey, who has settled at a table in the corner alone.

"Name's Raymond. He was one of the hostages. The brother of a girl who was coming out."

"What happened to the rest?"

"The girl died," I admit. "The others he wouldn't trade."

"She died?"

She's whispering. Even so, one of the men at the counter seems to be listening close.

"It was an accident, supposedly."

She presses her lips together and the color mounts in her cheeks. "It's not fair. Why the girl?"

I shrug. I don't want to talk about it. It's going to be the most talked-of news in the town for a while, and it'll be rough on Archer.

"I wish I could march out and give that Mortimer a piece of my mind."

"And he'd love to give you a piece of lead in return." I push my hat back on my head and sip my whiskey and water.

"It's not funny." Her voice bites.

I almost choke on my drink. "Well—it wasn't meant—"

"People who treat others like their lives are disposable have no place here."

"Pretty sure that gets rid of half of the population out here, Kate."

Her face is like stone. "Doesn't make it right."

She moves down the counter to serve another customer.

I finish my shot and step outside. I'm hot and tired and so's my horse. It's a night for turning in early.

Across the way, Maria Pike stands in her doorway,

staring into the street, her arms folded against the world, her lips a little parted in a smile.

She notices me and goes inside, shutting the door.

# 15

# ROSAMUND

ALAN IS WEARY. HIS EYES ARE DULL WITH PAIN, AND I know riding must be hurting his leg and his arm, but he hasn't made a sound today.

"How much further?" I ask him. It seems like all we've done is wind upwards on piney deer trails and splash across shallow creeks. Traveling is much slower now that we have reached the mountains, taking twisting paths, navigating around fallen trees, but I wouldn't go back to the desert for all the world.

"Should be there before nightfall." Alan glances up at the trees. "We better, because there are lot more things in this forest to kill us than in the desert."

I'm sure he tells the truth. But I still can't imagine anything worse than that *isark* swooping down on us from above with its horrid screeching and sharp, pointed beak.

I shudder.

We pause at an overlook, the last glimpse back toward

the horrid desert before we go north over a ridge and leave it behind.

I shade my eyes, scan the horizon for signs of pursuit. I glance back at Alan for his opinion. He's staring northwest, the way we came, with a strange look on his face.

"What is it?"

He doesn't answer. It's as if he's heard a distant sound and he's listening for it to come again.

"Alan, what is it? Do you see them?"

He snaps out of it and I can see that whatever he was thinking about, it wasn't pursuit.

"It's nothing." He looks again at the horizon, scanning as I was.

Then I see it.

"Alan...." I can't get the words out.

A cloud of dust stands on the horizon behind us. Above it, the sky is clear and blue and hot.

"Yep, they're coming all right." Alan gives a sniff, pushes his hair back from his face. "They'll find that *isark* and know they're on the right trail. Pity we haven't lost them. I almost dared to hope."

"What can we do?"

"Run for it. If we make it to the ranch, the hands will protect us. I just wish they hadn't tracked us here. Means it isn't over yet. Means a lot more trouble."

He gathers the reins and shouts to the horse, and we're off.

. . .

ALAN IS white as a sheet and the horse is lathered and panting, but we don't stop. I keep praying that we turn a corner or come to a break in the woods and find the ranch. But we go on and on for what feels like hours, and still there is nothing.

"Alan—"

"I know."

And he does. If we don't make it by nightfall, if he loses consciousness, if the horse falls and breaks its leg on this steep climb, we're as good as dead.

The horse stumbles. One leg slams into the steep ground and Alan catches his breath as we almost go down.

"I'm walking." I throw my leg over the horse's hindquarters and drop to the ground. "We cannot keep this pace anyway."

"Rosamund—"

"This once, don't argue."

We don't have time for it, and he's not looking any better. I take hold of one of the reins and we forge on.

The climb is hard and I am covered in sweat. It's a warm day, the sort that would be too hot if it weren't for the shade of the pine trees. The ground under me is sandy but growing increasingly rockier, and my feet ache terribly.

It's Alan's white face that keeps me going. If he can risk a bullet to the head or the deaths of his brothers for me, I'll do anything keep him out of their hands.

We reach a plateau and I pause to catch my breath. Only desperation is giving me the strength to keep going.

The sun is rich in color, fading toward the horizon.

"Are you recognizing anything?" I ask.

"I'm sorry, Rosamund," Alan whispers. "I can hardly see straight." His cheeks have too much color in them, the rest of him none. I reach up and set my hand against his forehead.

He's feverish.

I glance behind us. There's no sign of our pursuers, which is even less comforting than knowing where they are.

"Hang on." My eyes still linger behind us. "We're going to make it."

I should be afraid now, but I'm not. I think of Raymond and how he might already be dead, and I tell myself I am a Lacey and will go as bravely as ever one did.

The horse is a game thing, plodding up the bad ground, and Alan has his wits about him enough to hold on. But as the sun drops, my fear rises. Alan cannot defend me against anything in this condition, and I cannot shoot and hold onto the horse at the same time.

I steel myself against these thoughts. In an hour or two, we'll know whether we live or die.

After a bit, the steep climb lessens and I find we are crossing a ridge. That's when I see them, behind and below: a cluster of horsemen. Just horsemen, no cattle.

And I know, with startling clarity, that I am more afraid of being hunted down than I am of the unknown dangers ahead.

I break into a run and the horse follows at a trot. It's hard on Alan, but we are out of time.

It has to be now or we lose our chance.

The horse stops short, jerking me back, whickering low in its throat, neck arching.

"Hullo?"

A tall fellow starts through the woods toward me—a ranch hand—and my legs go weak with relief.

The reins fall from my numb fingers as I crumple.

"It's a girl!" I hear, and the answering shouts barely register. Strong arms are around me.

# 16

## THATCHER

THE SLOW CREAK OF THE DOOR WAKES ME.

Archer lights a candle across the room, takes his hat off and tosses it on the table. Then his boots, which he lines up neatly next to the cot where he sleeps.

He sits down on his bed and stares at his hands. Just stares at them, turning them first palms toward him, then backs, then tilting them so the candlelight falls over them.

He keeps at it until I think there must be something the matter with him more than his thoughts.

"Is something wrong with your hands?" I raise myself up on my elbow and peer at him.

His hands snap closed as if to hide something invisible.

"How long were you going to sit there watching me?" he asks in a dry voice.

I heave myself up. A bedroll on his floor is surprisingly less comfortable than the ground outside. "Oh, I dunno. Until you did something interesting."

He smiles. "Reckon you saw it then."

"You're back real late."

"I talked a little with Raymond. Figured I owed it to him."

"You got him to talk?"

Archer throws one of his boots at me. I grin and throw it back.

"Business, mostly. About what he'd seen of Mortimer's hideout. A little about the war. He'd heard of me."

"Nothing good, I hope."

He ignores me.

"Is he staying?"

"He means to. He's pretty set on trying to get the Swifts back. Jem and Max are still alive, as far as he knows, but Alan disappeared two days before we last saw Mortimer. Raymond figures he shot him."

Disquiet stirs in my chest and I frown. Something doesn't sit right, and I can't put my finger on it.

"I just really hoped, Jesse. You know, I really hoped." His voice has changed. He's thinking about her again.

I let him talk.

"If I hadn't thought of her, or hadn't asked her—I know she said to look before the summer, but I could have sent someone out."

I sit up and push my blanket aside. "Archer, an escort wouldn't have made a difference. Mortimer took a stage with four outriders. We've been over this already."

"I would do anything to go back and try it again."

And then something clicks into place, like the cocking of a gun, in my head.

"Two days. That means Alan disappeared the day we first talked with Mortimer. The day there was an accident."

Archer thinks on this. "That Mortimer can be a liar when it suits him."

"What if Alan got away?"

"Wouldn't he have come to us?"

"Probably." I scratch my chin and rub the stubble that's grown over the last week or two. He's right, of course. It doesn't seem likely.

Archer lies back on his cot with a sigh, one arm tucked under his dark head. "Maybe I'll talk to Sam in the morning."

"What for?"

"See if he knew where the Swifts were headed last week. If they were going to the Auki Nation, we might get some help from them."

"Do you know how he is?"

"Well, Sikes says he ain't dead yet."

That's good enough for me. If Sam survives a week, I'll wager my stock he'll survive. He's that kind of man.

I lean back and pull the blanket over me. It smells of horse and oiled leather.

I still can't shake the feeling—something ain't right. I may not be as clever as Archer, but I know a liar when I see one.

That Mortimer had something to hide.

ARCHER IS STILL ASLEEP when I wake the next morning with the light. It isn't like him to sleep long, but I'm glad he is. Sleep hides the sadness I've seen in his eyes for the last three days, and erases the worry lines from his face for at least a few hours.

Stretching, I cross the room in my stocking feet, debating whether to commit to my gun belt and boots.

A glance out the window shows there's already a wagon in front of the mercantile, and Peter is out sweeping the low porch in front of the saloon. He stops his work to catch a lizard and I smile.

He's such a solemn, silent fellow I forget he's still a boy.

Kate comes out to scold him and gets caught staring out toward the Black Pass.

I open the door softly, glancing behind me to make sure that it hasn't disturbed my cousin. I step out into the fresh morning air and trip.

There, in a crockery bowl on the step, covered in a floury cloth, is a pan of Maria Pike's bread.

A neat note on top has Archer's name on it. I'm an ethical man—I don't go reading other people's letters—but this one I pick up and I scan over.

I know she's been eyeing Archer, and I don't like it one bit.

*I am sorry,* it reads in soft, flowing script, *for your loss. May she rest with the angels.*

# 17

## SELBY

I'M PACKING MY THINGS WHEN ARCHER SCOTT HIMSELF comes out of the governor's office and calls my name.

"Selby, you heading out?" He looks disappointed.

"Got to."

"Look, I have another job for you if you want it."

"What is it?" I shouldn't take it, but I am curious.

"Raymond's got ideas about getting the Swift boys back."

I raise my eyebrows. I'm not one to judge, but trying to get the Swifts out of Mortimer's hands is like trying to dig a rattler out of its den.

"But we would need you."

I give my horse a pat and unbuckle its halter.

"I'll pay you well."

"I don't need pay to do it."

"You're a good man," he says. "You deserve to be paid."

I slide my rifle into its sheath and fasten it in.

"Nah. Those *isarks* will be flying again. The shepherds need me. We have a contract."

"A written one or a spit-in-your-hand one?"

It's the latter, and he knows it. Still, a man like me's got to be careful about keeping my word.

Archer presses on. "I'll send another rifleman out to the herds. I'll pay him myself. I need your tracking skills."

I open my mouth to speak, then close it again. I've had the advantage of seeing what things look like from the losing side—from the wrong side. I don't like the looks of what's in front of me.

"Well, how about it?"

I shake my head. If he makes me talk, he's just going to hear things he won't want to hear.

"Selby, I know what's happened in the past, but you must know that your skills place you deep in my respect. Don't let that get in the way."

I lift one side of my mouth in a wry smile. "It's not that."

It would be simple if that was the only problem. Some men are ashamed of their pasts. I am ashamed of who I was, but not of what happened to me.

So many men I know have it backwards.

"Well, what is it, then?"

"I have no easy way to say this nor any way to make you believe me." I pull on my gloves slowly.

He's waiting. I wait too, biding my time until he bails out of the conversation, but he does not, and I must concede.

"Governor, I've seen my share of ruined men. I have

watched causes die. I've seen the world on fire. If you continue this, that is what you will have."

"Sometimes a just cause requires sacrifice."

I see it in his eyes—that hopeful, noble streak that sets him apart from all the other lawmen I've known and makes him a man good for upholding the law, not just shooting the opposition.

When you just shoot the opposition, morality is decided by who shoots faster. And I can't believe in that.

He's looking at me, imagining it may be his sacrifice that is required and rising like a young visionary to the call. He's not thinking what I'm thinking—that we've already had sacrifice, and it was a young lady.

"I can't be a part of it." I reach down and unbuckle the loose girth, pulling it tight.

"Jack, there's men's lives at stake. The least you can do is explain to me why this is the wrong way. I'll listen."

I finish the girth and come around to the horse's front, giving it a brief scratch under the chin while I think, working to put every thought and word into its place.

He lowers himself onto the porch in front of the hitching post and moves over so I can sit near him on the lower step. I thrust one leg out in the dust to give my gun belt room and scratch my head before pulling my hat brim low again.

Again, he's patient. A good thing in a leader. He gives me all the time I want or need.

"There's men like you," I begin. "And there's men like Mortimer. But it isn't a simple thing, one good side and one bad—it isn't as easy as all that."

He gestures for me to go on.

"Mortimer will not play clean. Twisted people twist life. I know your type—if he said, 'Let me shoot you down and I'll leave the territory,' and you knew it to be true, you'd do it in a heartbeat. And it would be the easier choice. The way things are now, if you win—if somehow you fight and overcome his dirty schemes—you will have to live with watching your hopes and dreams and those of others burn and die before their time."

He looks sober. "It's how this territory is. I've been fighting Mortimer for years as a lawman. I know what he's like."

I nod. It's true enough. "But—" I clench my hand, debating whether or not to say it. "But people will say this is your doing, and it will be true. Your violence will breed more violence. You'll have to do things you will regret. And you will have to live with the consequences."

He lets out a long sigh and I wonder if he's thinking of the girl.

"So be it. Someone has to stand up for this town, and that's the job I've been given. My question is, will you help me?"

The wind brushes my hair. I've always thought of the wind as freedom.

The words of a poem come to my mind.

*...and on the wind I shall go, yes, it shall carry me,*
*beyond the reach of men and bars, into the stars to be free....*

My hands are already stained with blood. What more can a man like me lose?

# 18

## ROSAMUND

I WAKE IN A DIM ROOM, COOL SHEETS LAID OVER ME. Curtains in the window rise and fall with the breeze. I try to sit up and lie back down with a moan. My head is pounding.

"Miss?"

I open my eyes again. I am in a comfortable, well-furnished room with walls of log.

A boy sits across from me, a bit dirty, wearing a stained vest.

I start up, and he startles too.

"Easy, easy now—" He holds out his hand as if I'm a spooked horse to be calmed. "No need to get up."

"Where am I?" I look around at the room, trying to take in more than the furnishings. Why can't I remember the last thing I did? Where I was? Surely not the desert....

"You're at the Swift ranch. Alan brought you in. Or—" He gives a little laugh. "You brought him in, more like."

"How is he?" I push myself up. I'm in someone else's clothes, a man's clothes.

"He's all right. We ain't letting a Swift die on our watch, anyhow. He'll be right enough with rest."

Silence falls. He's afraid to talk, I think—from the way he looks at me, I suppose he hasn't seen many women— and the world is still too fuzzy for proper thoughts.

"Are you hungry?"

I think about this, slowly. "I think so."

"I'll bring you some soup. Cook made some."

He gets up and goes out.

I push the sheets off. The clothes are too large for me, but they're clean. One of my hands is bandaged—a cut from a rock, perhaps, or having the reins ripped out of my hand. At some point, I had stopped noticing where and when I was hurt.

The light in the window is pale and pleasant. I hear the wind moving the branches of the pines and smell the clean air as it pushes past the lace curtains.

The Swifts must have had a mother or a grandmother living here once, with curtains like that.

The boy returns with the soup, true to his word. It's a rich soup with cream and vegetables and it takes all my willpower to eat it slowly. He disappears again and brings back a pitcher of water and a glass, which he sets on the table beside my bed.

"The hands are getting the guns all loaded," he says by way of conversation. "Just in case. They might not come here at all."

"Don't you think he'll track us?"

"Ain't easy in those woods. And a bunch of scrub cattle went down the way you came up, last night. Saw it myself."

A small flame of hope rises in me. Perhaps there won't be a fight. Maybe I can hide here, small and safe, and let Mortimer ride on by like a storm on the wind.

"May I see Alan?"

"Alan must rest as long as he can, and so, for that matter, should you," he says, as if quoting directions carefully. "If he wakes and feels better, I will tell you."

"Are you a doctor too?" I ask, smiling.

He jumps to explain. "Oh, I ain't been in a sickroom before. But the boss is out and it's just the cook and us hands here."

"I will rest then," I say, and lay back down, my head tilted toward the gentle light of the window.

We made it.

I smile, just to myself. We made it.


Noon comes, and the boy takes me to visit Alan.

He's still pale, but he smiles, wide and genuine, when I enter. He sits propped up in bed in a clean nightshirt, his arm in a clean sling. I can't see the leg under the bedclothes.

"How are you feeling?"

"Better," he says, and means it.

I sit down in a chair across from his bed and take a good look at his face. There are gaunt lines in it from the strain of the last few days, but this is important to me.

All my life I'm going to remember this. And I'm going

to remember that this man saved me, and that I shot an *isark* and rode for my life across a blurring plain.

I want his face burned into my memory so I will never forget why I am still alive.

"Miss Lacey."

I realize what he's called me, and the weight of the last few terrible days crashes in on me. We're safe now, and I'm crying.

"Is something the matter?"

I shake my head, but I can't stop. The boy, lingering by the door, offers a handkerchief and beats a hasty retreat. I wipe my eyes, but now I'm sobbing.

"Is—something the matter?" Alan tries again.

"It's nothing," I manage. "Just relief, I suppose. It's silly."

"It isn't silly." He finds my eyes and holds them with his. "You faced down death and you lived. That's not nothing."

"I suppose not. But without you—"

"And without you," he echoes.

It's a sudden feeling, strange and powerful—something I've never felt before. We, practically strangers, had cheated death together.

And here we are, safe, ready to live lives that nearly ended.

I remain composed long enough to return to my own room. I shut the door and I cry and cry until I feel calm and quiet in my soul again.

In the quietness, I feel almost invincible.

I will show Archer and Mortimer alike that I am a match for this territory.

A distant gunshot pierces the stillness. I start up and go to the window, pushing aside the curtains ever so slightly. There must be a dozen reasons to shoot during the day on a ranch, but deep down, I have no doubt—it is Mortimer's men.

A knock on the door. "Come in."

It's the boy. I still haven't caught his name.

"Are they here?"

He nods.

"Can we hold them off?"

He smiles, reassuring. "Sure, miss. There's a dozen of us hands and only five of them. But I'm taking you to the cellar, just to be safe."

"Alan?"

"He'll stay where he is. We just want to be careful, being that you're the governor's—" He trails off.

The governor's intended, I assume he was going to say.

I follow him downstairs. The house is vast and well-furnished. A proper table, set for supper later in the day, stands near a window. A huge hearth and fireplace tower in the middle of the main room, and above them hang antlers larger than I imagined could exist.

Hastening on through the kitchen, we come to a small door which leads down to the larder. I press in among the smoked meats, cheeses, preserves, and fresh butter while he strikes a match and lights a candle.

Another gunshot cracks above us.

He thrusts the lit candle into my hands and shuts the door. The larder goes dark.

I settle uneasily. Perhaps in another set of circumstances I would be content to remain out of harm's way, but today, straight off of the wilds, I am restless.

I almost wish I could be up there instead, defending this place and my person. And defending Alan—I am the object of their search, but he's the first one they would kill.

Another volley.

The candle flickers, dancing hard as if to some current of air I cannot feel myself. And I remember, suddenly, clearly, being four years old. It was storming, and my candle danced just so.

I was afraid. Of the storm, of the restless candle. And my mother came to me in her soft white nightgown, her long hair draped over her shoulder, and she held me and sang me a song. She used to sing it with her sister, she said —and from that moment, I wanted a sister.

I didn't understand then that I would be the last. My parents were no longer young.

The song is a gentle one, hopeful with its wistful tune. The words are old, but in the last five years, it has become an anthem for young hopefuls, fresh off the war, eager to forget its horrors in building a new life.

I sing, my voice soft in muffling darkness, gunshots still ringing above me.

*Now comes the time for gathering, for reaping, for bringing in,*
*the season of gold.*
*With my scythe and your twine we shall build a future*

*and know, come snow, we will be safe.*

*Let us go to the fields and be merry.*
*Do not cry, do not be afraid;*
*For we shall be glad in the abundance of the earth,*
*And we shall dance together in fields of plenty.*

*We shall work with our hands and rest by the water.*
*Do not hang back, come be at my side;*
*It's bluebells for me and hollyhocks for you,*
*And the song of the reapers at dawn.*

*Let us go to the fields and be merry.*
*Do not cry, do not be afraid;*
*For we shall be glad in the abundance of the earth,*
*And we shall dance together in fields of plenty.*

There are more words, but I stop. The firing has ceased.

# 19

## THATCHER

MARIA PIKE IS ONE OF THOSE WOMEN YOU CAN'T REALLY imagine being any other age than the one she is now. She's stunning—I'll say that for her. Nearly forty, with a strong face and an even stronger air about her. She dresses in black and dark colors and keeps them scrupulously clean, but local legend says even the dust is afraid to cross the Widow Pike.

She's a woman who's out to get her way, and that's what terrifies me this afternoon as I see her leave her restaurant in her best dress and hat and head down the street toward my cousin's office.

I set down my drink and stand up. Kate Carnegie, who's washing the bar in front of me, gazes over my shoulder at the street.

"So the hunt begins," she comments. "How long's his girl been in the grave, a week?"

"Excuse me, will you?" I finish my drink and head out into the street. Kate's dry laugh follows me.

If I know anything, the appearance of a loyal cousin five minutes or so after Maria will be just the thing Archer's praying for.

I unwrap my horse's reins from the rail outside and head down the street in the general direction of the governor's office, walking slow so as not to arouse suspicion.

Not that Maria will be doing much looking out the window when there's my cousin to be looking at.

I stop at the trough in front of the livery stable and let the horse drink. The sun's hot today and it's powerful dry. We'll have to mind our water and our stops when we ride north in the morning. Another couple days of this and half the watering holes will be dried up.

My horse finishes and looks back mildly, inviting me to partake. I scratch his withers and keep walking.

I'm a little early for the five-minute mark, but she's been in there long enough. I tie my horse out front and mount the steps to my cousin's office.

The door swings open, nearly felling me, and Maria breezes out with a brow like a stormcloud.

"Ma'am." I touch my hat.

She stops and regards me with a cold smile. "Think you're clever?" Gathering her skirts so they don't brush me, she steps down into the street.

"What was that?" I ask, stepping inside and glancing behind me to make sure Maria is out of earshot.

Raymond Lacey is sitting across from my cousin, in the chair nearest the cold wood stove, his boots on top of it.

"Afternoon," he drawls.

"Afternoon." I pull off my hat and hang it on the peg by the door.

Archer is industriously going through the mail that came in on the stage this afternoon. I can tell from his face that mention of Maria won't be welcome.

"Did you talk to Sam?" I ask instead.

"Yep."

"And?"

He drags his gaze up from the official-looking mail. "Don't think we'll gain anything by going to the Auki Nation. It's all right." He tosses one of the letters aside. "We've got no call to drag them into our mess."

"Is everything set for the morning?" I say instead, fingering the smooth top of his paperweight.

"Should be. Convinced Selby to stay on with us."

"Saw him up on the rented-room balcony above the saloon. I wondered why he was still in town. How many men are going?"

"About the same." My cousin shrugs. "It's not like there's more to be found."

Raymond Lacey drags his feet off the cold stove and unfolds his lanky form like a rattler uncurling. "Reckon I'll go down and see if Gilchrist needs a hand."

"What's that?"

"He's not riding tomorrow if he doesn't get his breeding stock penned." Raymond gets to his feet. He moves deceptively slow for a man with a quick eye.

"You'll be back?" Archer looks up, and I get the feeling

he doesn't much like the idea of letting this man out of his sight.

"I'll be ready to ride." Raymond's eyes are quiet, emotionless. There's an odd tightness in the air between them.

"Please tell Gilchrist anything he's short on, I'll make up out of the supply house here."

"I'll do that."

Lacey ambles out.

It's quiet as Archer starts on the mail again.

"I like Raymond," I say. I don't know why I feel defensive.

Archer doesn't answer.

"You know he was a war hero?"

"He doesn't trust me," says Archer, looking at me straight. He's not offended—it's just a fact.

"Give the man time. I'd be suspicious if I had a sister and she packed up to marry a man I'd never met."

He winces ever so slightly.

"Sorry."

"No, it's true. I can't hold it against him." He rips open a letter with a little more force than necessary. "But if you like him, I suppose you don't think he's leading us into a trap?"

"No." I'm usually the one who smells a trap first, and I don't smell it on Raymond. He sees too much—he wouldn't be duped into helping a fellow like Mortimer.

"Hmm." Archer crumples up a letter and throws it away.

"What did Maria want?"

He's in a businesslike mood, and I'm beginning to wonder if he actually sent her packing.

"Nothing," he says, but he's not meeting my gaze.

"Come on."

Finally he raises his eyes and laughs with perplexity. "Look, I don't know, Jesse. She was offering sympathy, wishing us luck for tomorrow. She didn't want anything."

"What's this world coming to?" I mutter.

"Jesse."

"She'd have offered you a sight more than sympathy if Raymond wasn't here. She's set her cap for you, Archer."

"Even if she has, why would she waltz in here and show it in front of the whole town?"

"There's no 'even if.' It's a definitely. She's not the kind to let grass grow under her feet. With Miss Lacey out of the way—"

Archer grunts. "Jesse, I'd appreciate it if you don't mention Mrs. Pike to me."

I nod. I don't have time for a fight. Neither does he, I guess. "Reckon I'll be on my way, then."

Archer doesn't even look up from the mail. He's scratching the side of his head behind one ear, lost in his own thoughts again.

It's a pity. He needs a woman to make sure he takes care of himself. But Maria Pike sure ain't the one, and there's no one else in Glory Mesa suited for the job.

I snatch my hat from the peg and step out into the street.

Peter stands next to my horse, patting its nose, examining the buckles and straps of the bridle.

"What are you doing?"

The boy turns and shrugs.

"Aren't you supposed to be—I don't know, working at Carson's?"

He returns his attention to the bridle. He must have finished his odd jobs early today.

"Well, if you don't mind, I'm going to take him." I unwrap the reins from the post and Peter steps back.

I shove my foot into the stirrup, swing up.

Peter breaks his silence. "Are you really going to go fight Mortimer?"

He's tall for a kid his age, like one of those scrubby range horses that are all leg and thin, shaggy mane.

"Ye-up."

"Do you know where his camp is?"

"We will when we get out there. That Mr. Selby's a good tracker."

"Yeah, he is." Peter's tone is like a man who knows what he's talking about. I suppose when you have only men around and no other children to play with, you pick up on things fast. "And one day, I'm going to go with you."

"Are you, now?"

"I'm already a good shot. Kate's taught me."

"That Kate's a sharp one."

"Yeah." Peter shrugs again. "And it won't be long either. Maybe just a few years."

He'd still be a mite young, but who knows, with the way things are. We might need him before he's ready.

I drop that thought to the dust where it belongs and back the horse up.

"Sure, Peter. You keep practicing and it won't be long. If you're working at the saloon tonight, I'll probably see you there."

"I'm always at the saloon," says Peter brightly.

He throws up his arm and waves enthusiastically as I urge the horse into a trot.

THE PLACE IS smoky and dim and smells of beer and whiskey. Carson's ain't my ideal spot—give me wide open space and a horizon a hundred miles away and a fire licking upwards to the broad blue sky—but it's the only public spot that serves food and drink besides Maria's, which is as respectable and dim as a funeral parlor.

Perhaps that's what Maria Pike has against the world. Her place is too respectable for this wild outpost of a capital, and Carson gets all the patrons, though he's done nothing to earn them.

I'm having a whiskey, my third in a week. It's not my favorite, but I don't trust the brandy or the beer here as far as I could throw it. When this business is over, I'll be happy to go to back to cattle dust and coffee.

Raymond ambles up from somewhere beyond my left shoulder and leans his elbows on the bar. His shoulders have a restless tilt. He doesn't belong in this dim, smoky place any more than I do.

"Evening," I greet. "Can I buy you something?"

"Nah."

"You sure? This is my last night in here for a long time.

We ride out tomorrow, and I'm going straight to the ranch after."

"Not cut out for the town life?" His mustache tilts in a hidden smile.

"Not by a long shot."

"Well, it may be some time before you see that ranch of yours. Mortimer's not exactly going to take this lying down." He toys with one of the empty glasses as he speaks. "He may not even be there when we arrive."

"You think he'll move?"

"He was dug in, but a man like him will give up just about anything for an advantage."

"Well, we got to get those Swift boys back. No better men in the whole territory, if you ask me."

"I knew Jem back East. He's a good man."

"What about Max?" Peter appears beside me, leaning his skinny elbows on the bar in a perfect imitation of his elders.

I grin down at him. "Yep, Max is a good man too."

"He taught me how to throw a switchblade last time he was in town."

"Did he?"

"Yeah. Until Kate caught him. Max says it ain't any more dangerous than a gun. But Kate was worried because I always have my knife. She says I don't get to carry a gun, so it's different."

"Well, Kate only means to protect you from trouble."

"But what if there's danger?"

"Here, out back of the saloon? Not with Carson

around. Besides, it ain't like Mortimer's going to walk in here."

Peter folds his arms decidedly. "I've seen Mortimer."

"Where did you see him?" I grin. The kid's seen Mortimer like I've seen the Blue Cattle of Rio Jefe.

"Here in town."

"No you haven't."

"Yeah I have."

"He came around a long time ago, maybe, but you wouldn't have been alive then."

"I'm ten."

"My point exactly. Look, kid, if Mortimer rode into town, someone would recognize him."

Peter looks at me as if I'm the one being difficult. "Who says they didn't?"

He moves on before Kate notices he's not working.

Raymond smiles slowly. "Some boy."

"No kidding." I shake my head. "He sure says the strangest things sometimes. But when he first showed up he didn't talk at all, so he's coming along. It was Kate who did it."

Raymond's roving eyes light on Kate as if he's only just noticed her. "She been here long?"

"Long enough. She came here after the war. Lost her folks back East. But she likes it here, I think. Acts like she was born here, and I should know, because I was."

I reach out and turn my glass in my fingers. I'm starting to regret shelling anything out for a drink. Wouldn't have done it if it weren't dry as gunpowder tonight.

"You headed back East? When this is over?"

I swear when I started the question, I didn't care what his answer would be, but as the words come out, my gut tells me different. I want him to stay.

He's a good man and a good gun, and I'm not above counting every single head in this territory.

Raymond leans against the bar, tilts his head to run his fingers slowly through his dusty hair. "Reckon I'll put down roots here. Nowhere else to be, now that—"

He shrugs.

I haven't seen him shed a tear over his sister, but he hasn't talked about her neither. Just quiet resignation.

But I'm powerful glad he's staying.

"If you need any help scouting out prime land, you just tell me." I give him a halfway smile. "I'm out on three thousand acres of good ranch land. But out here there's room to spare."

Raymond chuckles low and something gentles in his eyes. "Suppose you'd better just show me round when we get back."

I nod, take another sip of my whiskey. Yessir, he'll be a good man to have around.

## 20

## ROSAMUND

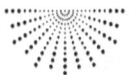

THE MORNING LIGHT STREAMS THROUGH THE PINES AND dapples the sandy ground around the ranch house. It's been three days since we arrived, and while broken wrists and *isark* wounds don't heal in three days, Alan looks so much improved that I chide myself for my former worries. He's sitting in a chair out in the sun, near the front door. Beside him stands a low, log-hewn table set with a pot of coffee and a few teacups.

"Miss Lacey." He glances up as I approach, squinting a little from the sun. "Have a seat. And help yourself." He leans forward slowly, with a bit of an effort, to pick up his teacup. I busy myself pouring out my own.

I take a small sip. It's thick and black and strong enough to wake the dead. Raymond used to describe soldiers' coffee just so.

I take another quick sip and try not to think of Raymond.

"Good?" Alan is watching me with a slight smile on his face.

"Good."

"Our cook used to go on our drives before his horse fell on him, and he never learned the difference between trail coffee and the coffee you serve to guests."

"It's all right." I laugh and take another sip.

The screened door along the far side of the house bangs, and a figure appears—a short, bewhiskered man.

"Alan, are you going to take your breakfast here or in the house?"

Alan takes a deep breath as if rousing himself and his breath catches. "I will take it inside. Out in the yard is no place for Miss Lacey to eat."

The cook looks at Alan with a grim twist to his mouth. "Are you walking back in there yourself? You're broker than a bronc."

"I'll get one of the hands to help me if I need it. I don't need your coddling."

He follows this with a grin that bears no ill will, but the cook doesn't move. "Sometimes you boys could use it." The man stumps back inside.

"Miss Lacey, do not wait for me," Alan urges. "I'm too slow to be your escort, I'm afraid."

I rise to my feet, knowing that he wants to be alone, but the sound of hoofbeats arrests us both.

The boy who brought me the soup and took me to the larder three days ago comes galloping in, dismounting before the horse has quite stopped.

"They're coming!" He snatches his horse's reins and

leads it close behind as he crosses the yard toward us, pulling his hat off to reveal tousled hair. "I saw them myself."

"How many?"

"Fifteen, twenty men."

"Mortimer?"

"Didn't see the men proper, but his black isn't among them. That I can swear to."

"How far out?"

"A couple hours at the most. They were at the southern creek bed."

Alan rubs his chin with his fingers and scowls slightly. "Get the rest of the men. Right away."

"Sir." The boy replaces his hat on his head and tugs the brim in acknowledgement.

Alan turns to me with a grim look. "I don't think I'll be eating breakfast with you this morning, Miss Lacey. I hope you will excuse me."


"MORE COFFEE?" The cook hovers at my elbow with a steaming pot.

"No, thank you. I have had my fill. It was very good." I smile up at him and see gratification replace the worry in his eyes for the barest moment.

He had prepared a table fit for a king, or at least a cattle baron. Eggs, flapjacks, bacon, coffee, fresh bread with wild berry jam, pie, ham, molasses and beans— certainly too much for my uneasy stomach. But I sampled everything, and the cook is happy.

The men have gathered across the room, standing around in their boots and vests and jackets, pistols at their hips and rifles in their hands. If you count Alan, there are six of them, and the smells of sweat and cow almost overpower the banquet on the table.

"The breeding stock are already being moved up to the far range," one of the hands is saying. "I only sent two men, figure that's all we could spare."

"The range is fresh," adds another. "They won't be hard to handle."

"And this is it?" Alan looks at the other five men—all tall, rangy fellows, like pines in human form.

The first man, a tall fellow with an air of authority and more years to his credit than the others, meets his gaze stolidly. "I dismissed the extra hands after the spring roundup, like always."

"Of course." Alan nods briefly. "Well, we'll have the advantage of the ranch house. At least we'll have that."

Five men, the cook, and Alan who can't walk and has a broken wrist. Against fifteen or twenty of Mortimer's men. I make a quick calculation of the odds and then wish I hadn't.

I wipe my mouth on my napkin and get up.

Alan speaks briskly and calmly, as if planning a siege defense is an everyday occurrence on a cattle ranch. "I want two of you boarding up windows and barricading doors. Do what you need to do—I'm not concerned about damages today. Frank, I want every firearm, every piece of ammunition this place has got right here, in this room."

"Yes, sir." The young one with the tousled hair gives a

nod and swings on his heel to leave. He pauses the barest moment to acknowledge me as he passes.

I approach the circle of men, addressing myself half to Alan and half to the tall fellow who I presume is the ranch boss. "I want to help."

The ranch boss glances at Alan. "It's appreciated, ma'am, but you're best out of the way and safe."

"But I'm the one they want. I can help, and I'd like to."

Alan nods slowly. He knows I'm made of sterner stuff than I appear to be. "I don't doubt you've got a good eye, Miss Lacey, but with these windows, you've got to expose yourself for a clean shot, and I can't let you run that risk. How are you at loading?"

"Competent."

"Good enough for me." He nods to one of the hands. "Set her up with the shells and ammunition."

When he turns back to me, I summon up a smile. "Thank you."


AN HOUR LATER, we are ready.

The young one comes back with a report that they're half a mile down from the ranch. The men set the saddle horses loose but keep three behind, holding them in the kitchen in case one of the men needs to ride for it.

But riding for it wouldn't help us much. The town is too far away and doesn't have enough men. One would have to ride for a week to pull more than twenty men together, Alan told me, and by then, either we'd have held them off or all died.

The windows are boarded up, gaps left for the men to shoot through. The hands help themselves to the cold breakfast, laughing and talking, making jokes about death.

Something cold and uncomfortable slides in my stomach. I feel responsible for these people. Someone's sure to be killed who wouldn't have been if I hadn't come here.

I ask their names as we wait, and they sound off swiftly: Frank, the young one; Joe, not much older; Ted, the cook; then Jim and Paxton and Lee. The names come at me, stick briefly as I repeat them back.

I may never have a chance to use their names, especially in the heat of a fight, but I still want to know them. If they are going to fight for me, I ought to know their names.

They swarm back from the cold food, a couple of them carrying cups of coffee, and gather at the low table next to the hearth where the ammunition and extra arms are piled.

Lee, the boss, walks me through loading the guns that are unfamiliar to me. I may not be perfect, but I should be able to keep the guns coming fast enough to keep them firing.

Only Alan is already in place. He sits in a chair, a rifle propped up in one of the front windows.

"Are you going to be able to shoot, sir?" one of the men asks with a laugh.

Alan grins. "You worry about yourself, kid."

I should have known, growing up during a war, that this was how a fight to the death would be—the joking, the bravado. But even in a war, men have superior officers and duty and country to stand behind. Here, it's only them and the outlaws, armed with guns and naked courage.

Hate for Mortimer wells up in me. In the face of such bravery, how else can I respond?

"Never saw a powder boy as pretty as you, ma'am." Frank gives me a wink, picking up a pair of pistols and shoving them into his belt. "No offense."

He picks up a rifle and heads upstairs to the bedroom windows, which face the back of the house.

Two more follow him, and the others come to the table to grab the extra firearms. I am left kneeling beside the low table, waiting for them to use their rounds.

"They're coming!" shouts the cook from the front window.

"How many? I don't have them in my line." This is Alan.

"I see four...five...nine."

A shot rings out from upstairs.

"And they're out back too," Alan mutters.

The guns crack upstairs. I count four shots. Then more, farther away, and the smash of a glass pane.

All of a sudden, without a word spoken, every gun across the room is blazing.

"Cover me!" shouts the one named Jim—he's got a bandy-legged walk and bristly mustache. He runs to the table, hands me his hot rifle, and grabs a ready one.

I reach down and pull out the shells, jamming them in and clicking it shut. No sooner have I finished than another warm rifle clatters down in front of me.

I'm loading as fast as I can, and they are bringing guns as fast as I get them loaded.

Alan is the only one who isn't coming to the table for fresh guns, but the cook keeps him supplied. A minute later, Frank comes tearing downstairs, carrying five or six guns. He drops them in a pile and loads himself up with as many as he brought.

"Hitting anything?" I make an attempt at a joke.

"I'm used to varmints," he grins over his shoulder.

I will my hands to move faster. A bullet whizzes past and buries itself in the wood above the fireplace with a *thunk*.

"Stay low, Miss Lacey," warns Jim as he comes back for another gun. "We have them coming through the window."

As if to corroborate this, a bullet shatters a decorative piece of pottery on the mantel, raining sharp shards down onto the hearth.

"Was that my mother's Auki pitcher?" Alan asks, dead serious, but it elicits a laugh.

"Stay low." Jim winks, making light of it, as he can hardly do anything else.

I crouch low, loading from my knees, shoving the guns up on the table above my head, raising myself up only long enough to reach new ones.

My fingers are smeared with black powder from reloading so many times, my clothes stained. If Raymond could see me now....

Another bullet whizzes past, safely above my head, and buries itself into the wall. I am almost glad for the distraction. I do not want to think of Raymond right now.

"Holding up?" A lull comes in the shooting—just a stray shot here and there—and Frank appears again above me with a grin, depositing an armful of empty guns.

"Well enough." I smile back, out of instinct more than anything else.

"We need our own loader upstairs. It's getting hard loading up both ways."

He means it, but he's saying it to lighten the mood. He turns, and just like that, crumples to the floor with a fresh bullet in him.

My voice is gone. Everything is clear, but I cannot seem to move fast enough. I close the few feet between us, see the dark blood starting through his shirt near his ribs. It's not a good place.

"Frank's shot!" I call, unbuttoning his shirt to assess the damage.

He's open-mouthed, a little shocked, breathless. "Is it —bad?"

I don't answer him. I'm not a doctor.

"Let me see him." Ted the cook pushes past, kneeling beside me, reaching in and pulling Frank's shirt open.

I can barely look.

"We've got to get to work on him now."

Frank has taken my hand, and he's holding it hard. I press his hand back, reassuring.

Jim comes from the window to take his shoulders. Ted whips out a kerchief and grabs my free hand, directing me to press the cloth against the wound. He takes up Frank's legs. "All right—on the count of three."

They lift him and his hand tightens on mine so hard I wince.

We make it to the nearest bedroom somehow and he's already looking worse, shaking.

Ted lights a candle and sticks a penknife into the flame. "Get the boy some sugar and water and a shot of whiskey. And one of you should give him something to bite on and a hand to hold."

"I'll hold it," I volunteer, as I am holding it already.

"No." Frank gives me a shaky smile broken by a hard grimace. "I'd squeeze your hand off, ma'am."

Jim kneels beside the bed. "I'll do it." He lifts his head to pour a generous amount of whiskey down the young man's throat.

I turn to the cook. "I'll get the sugar and water. Is there anything else?"

"Bring hot water and some cloths—there are clean ones in the hutch beside the larder door. And stand by to hand me the knife when I ask. If you have the stomach."

I nod. My hands are shaking, but I'd rather do something than nothing. Just then, the shooting begins afresh.

I gather my skirts in my hand, duck low, and run.


THE FIGHT WANES AGAIN before we are done. Frank is as stoic as can be, but he loses a lot of blood by the time the cook extracts the bullet.

He's as white as the sheets he's lying on, and I don't like Ted's expression as he lays the clean cloths over the wound and begins to wind the bandage around the young man's body.

For the last few minutes of the job, it's eerily silent, except for the slow, carefully measured breaths of the men around me and the pounding of the blood in my ears.

Finally Ted ties off the last of the bandage and straightens. "Kid's lost a lot of blood." He looks grim. "If he hasn't lost too much, he might pull through. But we'll have to keep it quiet in here."

"Can't say a rainstorm of bullets is going to be much help," says Jim.

"They still out there?"

"Yeah. Counted maybe a dozen bodies. Lee thinks they might have a few wounded too. But they've pulled back, probably to dig in. It's going to be dragged out, I think."

"Heaven help us," mutters Ted, limping across the room to rinse his bloodied hands.

I HELP watch and care for Frank for the rest of the day and on and off through the night. In the dark before dawn, Ted wakes me for a turn, his eyes gray-rimmed and bloodshot.

I'm sleeping in my clothes; my hair is a mess. "How is he?"

"He's sleeping. Best thing for him. Keep him asleep as long as you can."

"Of course." I get up, pushing an unseemly lock of loose hair back over my ear. I can tell from his voice that the boy isn't doing well.

I go softly into the room and settle into the hard, high-backed chair beside his bed. He's so changed from the day before. Even by candlelight, I see that he's worse—white, frail, and almost translucent, his face skeletal, his features drawn. I wouldn't have recognized him yesterday.

I press my fingers to my temples. Every bone in my body aches.

I have been trying not to think it, but I think it now— that if I had not come here, if I had not come west to marry Archer Scott, this boy would be living on, just as strong and hale as he was a day ago.

I can be strong at the idea of death for myself, but now, staring it in the face, someone else's life, not mine....

Simmering hate for Mortimer wells up in me again.

His hand stirs faintly on the coverlet. "Miss Lacey?"

"Yes?" I keep my voice soft, in case he is speaking from his sleep.

"Can I have some water?"

A pitcher and a glass stand on the table beside the bed. I pour a few swallows in the bottom, then put my arm under his neck and help him drink.

"Thanks." His voice is as thin as the worn sheets pulled up to his chest. "I've never had a lady help me like that before. Not an Eastern one."

"Are we so different?" I ask with a smile.

"A little. But it's right the governor should have a sophisticated wife, begging—begging your pardon."

I touch his hand to let him know there's no offense.

A silence.

"You're going to marry him, aren't you?"

"You should be resting."

"I want to talk," he presses, and I don't fight it.

"Yes, I'm going to marry him."

"Fancy that."

"Did you ever meet him?"

"Couple times. He knows Jem a little. He's a fine man, miss."

I take his hand gratefully, and he holds onto it like a drowning man.

A bird sings a little in the darkness, heralding dawn. The dark squares of the windowpanes are changing color.

I hear quiet footsteps downstairs and the hard, muffled clank of a rifle. The men must be up, getting ready. It will be light enough to shoot soon.

I smell coffee. Dawn is coming—another day—with the gentle blue and pink before sunshine.

"Miss Lacey?"

"Yes, Frank?"

"I'm better. Not in much pain now. You should see if they need help."

"All right." I release his hand and then look at his face. His eyes are afraid. He's trying to send me away because he knows what's coming.

I slip my hand back into his, and there's no strength in it. "Never mind," I whisper. "I can stay."

He gives me a ghost of a smile and it's such a nice smile —boyish and shy, with wing-lines like he's spent most of his life smiling.

"Thanks." His breath rattles in his chest and catches. He looks up at me for reassurance, like a boy looking for his mother.

I don't know what else to do, so I stroke his damp hair back from his forehead, moving my hand in gentle, soothing motions like my mother used to when I was ill, and hum low under my breath:

> *Let us go to the fields and be merry.*
> *Do not cry, do not be afraid;*
> *For we shall be glad in the abundance of the earth,*
> *And we shall dance together in fields of plenty.*

He relaxes, closes his eyes with a smile, and just like that, gentle as a whisper, he's gone. It's quiet, the morning still too pale and sacred for shooting. A bird calls quietly, a sweet, happy sound.

I'M STILL HOLDING his hand, some time later, when one of the men comes to check on us.

## 21

## THATCHER

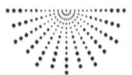

It's a long, dusty ride to the flats northwest of Mortimer's camp. Long enough and dusty enough for Carson to be cursing up a storm at Selby for leading us this way. Selby wouldn't care even if he knew, but I can hear the cursing plain as day, and I'm getting plumb sick of it.

The flats shimmer with heat. To the north lie distant rocks and the desert, a cruel trap for folks wanting to reach the good timberland. To our south lie the pine scrub and sagebrush arroyos where Selby thinks Mortimer's like to be holed up.

A stupid gamble, Carson has said more than once. I want to ask him why he came, then, but I know better. Growling helps him bear the dust and heat as it has many a man before him.

I uncap my canteen and take a warmish swallow. It's been two days since we filled up—we had to skirt the decent land to come out north of the camp.

Archer turns his horse out of line and circles back to us.

"All right, men. We'll be waiting here a spell. Selby's going ahead to scout out the scrub, catch the lay of the land. He wants one volunteer."

"I'll go." Carson jerks his horse back as it fidgets. "I'm sick of this dust."

"Wait." Raymond points west of us. "Look."

A white blur, maybe a mile or so off. I peer from under my brim, raise a hand to block the sun, and I still can't make it out.

But I see Selby's face give a sort of twist, and he's spurring his horse forward toward the shape, leaving a small burst of dust behind.

My heart sinks.

Everyone is urging their horses into a brisk trot, except Archer, who gallops breakneck after Selby, face set like stone. I start after him.

I wonder which one it is—Jem or Max. There's only one, from the looks of it.

It's Jem. I can tell from the outline of his strong shoulders and arms. Max is strong, but still thin as whipcord.

He's tied to a post that's been pounded into the ground, his wrists bound behind him. He's slumped like a dead man, his face blistered with heat, the wind blowing his half-buttoned white shirt like washing on the line.

Selby reaches him first, dismounting before his horse has halted. He whips his knife out and begins to saw through the rope at Jem's knees.

There's no blood to speak of—a mercy we got here before the *isarks* or other scavengers.

Archer whips out his knife, saws through the ropes at Jem's wrists. I help catch him as he falls forward.

Archer rolls him onto his back, presses an ear to the man's chest.

"Water," he orders.

Selby unties his canteen. He tosses it over and I catch it.

"Is he—?"

"He's with us," Archer says briefly, pouring a little water into his cupped hands and bathing Jem's face with it.

"Keep the canteen," says Selby, quiet-like. "I'm taking Carson to scout."

Archer glances up. "Go ahead. Be careful."

Selby touches the brim of his hat and swings into the saddle. The hoofbeats thunder away, disappearing into the noise as the rest of the riders pull up beside us.

Raymond walks up behind me and my cousin, taking it in silently.

"He's alive," I offer.

Raymond's hard expression doesn't change. He crouches down, silently picks up one of Jem's wrists, and presses a couple fingers to it.

"Sunstroke." Archer pours another handful of water into his palm. "We need to get him into the shade."

Raymond mutters under his breath and one lean hand makes a fist.

All I can say is Mortimer better have a fast horse, because Raymond Lacey sure has a lot to avenge right now.

A few of the men help sling Jem over Raymond's saddle and we walk the horses off the flats. It's a risk leaving the open ground without word from Selby, but it's Jem's life.

Once into the cooler air below the trees, Archer pulls Jem down from the saddle and gives him more water, which revives him.

"Well." Jem's voice is rough and cracked, but there's a smile, sure enough. "You weren't exactly what I expected to wake up to."

Archer smiles back dryly. "We were just in the nick, looks like."

"What day is it?"

"Day, um...." My cousin casts about for an answer.

"The fifteenth," I supply.

Jem looks up, dazed, at the others. His eye falls on the man towering beside me. "Raymond."

Raymond's face doesn't change, but there's a sparkle in his eye. "Save your breath."

Jem pushes himself up on one arm, addressing Raymond. "Have you seen Max?"

"No. Hoped you had."

Jem rubs his face gingerly. "A fool's hope anyway."

"If we ambush the camp—"Archer begins.

"No, no." Jem shakes his head, then closes his eyes as if even that takes too much effort. "They're gone. They rode out."

"When?"

"Yesterday, before dawn. They emptied the camp, left me."

"Where did they go?"

Jem shrugs and lies back, exhausted.

Something in my stomach goes tight. Knowing Mortimer, he's put a bullet in the boy's head long since.

"I'm sorry." Archer clears his throat. "You should be resting. Gilchrist!"

"Yes?"

"Take your horse, ride out after Selby, tell him the camp is abandoned. There's got to be water up there."

"Very good." Gilchrist mounted up and headed out into the brush.

Jem sits up slowly. "Do you have a spare horse?"

"You shouldn't be riding." Archer's voice is dry.

"I can make it. You'll need someone to show you the way in."

"And you can?"

Jem nods. "Only I can."

THE BUILDINGS LOOK TOO fine to be abandoned, but the grounds are already windblown, tumbleweeds rolling back and forth, a stall door creaking open and shut in the wind.

"So this is the camp of the notorious Mortimer?" Archer takes in the sight, one hand on his belt. His tone is almost amused, but I know him too well. He finds no humor here.

Selby meets us, leading his horse. "There's a trough over that way. Water's fresh enough. I recommend staying the night unless we want to give pursuit."

"What is he doing here?" Jem's voice drops low as he looks at Selby.

Selby moves his hands away from his belt, backing slowly. "I don't know you and I don't want trouble."

"If I'd known there was a man here who rode with Abernathy—"

Archer steps in. "He's my tracker, Jem. Take it easy. I know who he is."

Jem grunts and turns away.

Selby, a shade paler than before, leads his horse off to water.

We build a fire in the yard as the sun goes down, and the flames cast dancing shadows over the outbuildings. There's something haunting about Mortimer's house—it's like finding an empty cave with year-old *darani* signs. Even if the beast is long gone, you know you couldn't sleep a wink inside.

Being so close to the outlaw king's den gives me the creeps.

Jem and Selby don't speak a word to one another all evening. I'll admit to curiosity, but Jack Selby's past is none of my business. If my cousin trusts him, I reckon I can. And little as Jem likes it, he listens to Archer.

He is the governor, after all.

Governor. I try to tack that name on him as I watch him across the fire, his dark hair finger-combed off his forehead, staring into the flames, turning a stick in his hands.

Some days the title sticks. Tonight it don't.

We'd brought two extra horses, in case a miracle happened and we managed to find both of the missing Swifts. Jem picked one out and he's bedding her down. He stays with her longer than needed, and when he comes back to the fire he's stone-faced.

"Thanks for the mare," he says. "I'll pay you next time I'm in town."

Archer accepts this with a nod, but clears his throat. "Aren't you riding back with us?"

"No, I'll be heading out at first light."

"In your condition?"

Jem gives a short laugh. "That'll be my problem. I'm going home."

"Reckon I can't blame you. But I don't like the idea of you going alone. You'll have to cross the desert or take another two days to go around."

"I'll take my chances."

"And I think I'll come with you." Archer tosses his stick into the fire. "We have no idea which direction Mortimer's gone. You could run smack into him."

"And you with me. You're the governor now, Archer. You have responsibilities."

"And I'll see them through." Archer's voice takes on a firm edge.

"I'll come." This is Raymond, rubbing his stubbled chin slowly. "Three's better than two, and the governor won't ride back alone. It's only sense, Jem."

Raymond doesn't say it in so many words, but he understands. Losing someone can make a man reckless. I've seen it more than I've felt it, but out here, I reckon every man feels it at least once in his days.

Archer blinks as if to clear away dark thoughts. "Then

that settles it. We'll break camp at first light. Selby, I reckon you and Carson can handle the ride back?"

Selby gives a brief nod, and with that assurance, Carson clears his throat. "Naturally, Governor Scott. Nothing'd happen to a party of our size. I'll mind he gets us back as quick as possible."

"We should turn in, then."

"I'll take first watch," Jem says.

Archer opens his mouth as if contemplating argument, but he doesn't say anything.

We bed down, more comfortable under the stars than under any roof. The fire crackles comfortingly and one of the horses lets its breath out in a long rumble.

Jem alone sits at the fire, his rifle over his knees.

Snores mingle with the popping of the embers. We are a hardy bunch that sleep well and sleep quick from long habit.

A noise catches at my senses. I open my eyes and look over. Jem is bent over his rifle, wiping his eyes with the back of his hand. A tear falls from his chin.

He is crying for his brothers.

## 22

## CARNEGIE

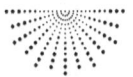

BEFORE LAST MONTH, I COULD COUNT ON ONE HAND how many times Carson left the saloon for me and Peter to mind, and now he's been gone twice in as many fortnights.

Not that there's much to mind. The stage has brought in handfuls of passing travelers, mostly people headed for other towns or starry-eyed, shiftless young men who spend more time boasting in their drinks than making good on their boasts.

But a few—more than before—are folks coming here to stay. People interested in the land office and the surveyor's place down by the livery stables.

I can feel the change in my bones, the same way I feel the wind change. It's as if someone's primed the pump and you can hear the water coming up before it gushes out.

There's people coming, heaps and heaps, ready to make this land settled.

But I don't want this wildness to be gone just yet—I must have my chance first.

"Peter!"

It's early yet and he's supposed to be sweeping, but I haven't seen him this morning. He's not given to sleeping late. "Peter!"

I step out onto the porch. The street is quiet and still. Peter isn't on the porch or down in the street. The sun is dawning golden, ducking in and out of the clouds. If I were a dreamer I'd hope for clouds, but I know the look of a day like this. It's going to be stark and hot.

I step back inside and check in the back, where sometimes he gets distracted memorizing the names on the bottles.

He's not there either.

I step out the back door, look up and down the alley. "Peter!"

What a boy he can be still. I just wish he hadn't chosen today.

Mr. Jensen, the livery stable owner, stamps up the boardwalk. "Kate?"

"Yes?" I smooth down my apron hastily and meet him at the swinging doors.

"I have your boy. He's rustling around in my loft. Not doing any harm, but I heard you calling."

"Thank you so much."

I gather up my skirts and hurry across the street.

"Peter?" I duck into the slightly cooler shade of the livery stable. "Peter, we have work to do. What are you doing up there?"

"Watching a dust devil."

"A dust devil? We have more important things to be doing. While Carson's away, you need to help me mind the saloon more, not less."

"But Carson would be mad if I ran off while he's here."

"And you think I'm not?" I put my hands on my hips and tilt my head up to the loft. I can't see him, only hear him; and I don't fancy climbing up after him.

"It's a strange dust devil. It's almost like the stage."

"You know the stage isn't due until this afternoon."

"Yeah." Peter appears at the edge of the loft, knocking down pieces of hay that drift slowly to the ground.

"Are you going to come down now, or must I come up after you?"

"I'm comin'."

Peter's shoulders sag in silent protest as he descends the ladder.

I start back across the street toward the saloon. The breeze catches at my hair; it's warm, with no relief to it.

Maria is standing on the front porch of her restaurant, gazing out beyond the town. I follow her gaze, but there's nothing there.

I don't think a lot of her, not since she set her cap for Archer Scott. He's governor now, but he's always been the best sort of man. The two of them just don't suit. Still, every time he avoids her, she follows.

As a widow, she must have her own griefs, but this cat-and-mouse game makes me shake my head. I know all about being a woman and wanting to get someplace in life, but I also know better than to think myself above the rules.

"When I'm finished sweeping and drying dishes, can I go back?" Peter's voice breaks into my thoughts.

"I guess so. If you don't bother Mr. Jensen. Promise?"

"Promise!" Peter claps his hands sharply. He dashes on ahead of me and nearly runs me over in the doorway coming back out with his broom.

"What do you say, Peter?"

"Excuse me, ma'am!" he calls.

It is good to see him acting like a child.

I walk to the bar where the washed glasses sit out on rags and begin to dry them thoroughly. Carson likes them done so that you can see straight through, clear as a mountain stream.

I listen absently to the methodical swish of the broom, a sign that Peter is doing his job. He's a dutiful fellow, but without Carson, he's a little wilder.

The doors swing again and Peter appears.

"Kate?"

"Mhm?"

"I was thinking about the dust devil."

"I see." My mind isn't on the conversation. We have ones like this every day.

"I don't think it's a dust devil."

"Really?"

"No, it looked like riders."

"Maybe there's a wagon train?"

"No...."

I turn on him. I cannot concentrate when he leads me on like this. "Well, what then?"

"I don't know, maybe Mortimer."

"Don't be silly." I pick up my rag and reach for the last batch of cleaned glasses.

But what he's said sticks in my mind.

"Peter, how about you go tell me if you can still see that dust devil. See if it is riders or not."

"Sure!" He drops his broom and runs.

I'm uneasy all of a sudden. It may very well be my imagination, but everything feels hot and still, like a held breath.

It seems like an eternity before Peter gets back.

"It's riders, not a dust devil!" he proclaims proudly.

It's too soon for Archer and the others to be back.

"How many?" My breath comes short, but my mind is clearing swiftly.

"Twenty? Thirty?" Peter shrugs. "Nobody I recognize, but one. Guess who I saw?"

"It's Mortimer." The words come to my lips even as the thought sticks in my mind with utter surety.

"How did you know?"

"Peter, go get Mr. Jensen. Tell him to sound the alarm. Quick."

He dashes off. I'm left looking around the saloon, lost. There's no way to block or bar the doors on such short notice. I grab an armful of the better drinks off the back counter and shove them all into the spare room, locking it.

The bells are ringing across town.

Now what? What will do the most good? I gaze out into the street, where folks are running up and down, carrying guns. Peter hasn't come back. The men are all off riding with Archer, save those who have businesses to keep up here in town. Jensen, Trasker who owns the general store, Garth Levine the surveyor—they're all congregating as if for a fight.

And then it hits me: Carson's saloon be hanged, there's no one to protect the governor's office.

I take the old rifle Carson keeps around in the back room, grab his spare gun belt, check to make sure the gun in it has something.

He didn't reload after he shot it last, but there are five bullets in the chamber. Good enough.

I'm small enough that the belt fits better across my chest than my hips, so I duck into it. I snatch the box of shells off the shelf and plug a couple into the double chambers.

I glance out at the street. I can hear the hoofbeats of Mortimer and his men descending on the town, but there's no better way to the office than straight across.

A shrill whoop breaks over the noise of horses and men.

It's now or never.

I dash across the street, my skirt held up in one hand, the rifle like an iron weight in the other.

I run up the steps, throw myself against the door. It's locked, of course. I set the rifle down, thrust my thin fingers into the crack of the window, and heave.

It was a lucky guess. Archer, for all his good points,

wasn't raised in towns and doesn't think to turn the latches on his windows.

I snatch up the rifle and give the street another glance. Puffs of smoke accompany the hard staccato of gunshots.

It's beginning.

From around the edge of the furthermost buildings, they stampede in. Peter was right: there are thirty or forty of them. Some of them carry firebrands.

They are going to burn us down.

I slam the window shut and fasten it. In another minute they'll make it up the street and see the sign, the territory flag.

There's a pair of saddlebags hanging on a peg by the door. I pull them down and go to the governor's desk. He keeps it neat as a pin.

That may just have saved this territory.

I pull every paper I can find and shove them into the saddlebags. I am rummaging the drawer when the first gunshot shatters the window. I duck behind the desk.

Another bullet, then another and another. A horse clatters onto the low porch to the sound of laughter. The door rattles as the man tries to ride his horse straight into it. The horse throws up its head and half rears, sending the man down onto its shoulder. Its hooves scrape the porch.

Is there a back door? I glance around. There's another room—that's better than nothing. I shove the rifle across the floor and crawl after it with the saddlebags.

The horse crashes against the door again.

I scramble through the doorway into a back room— looks like where he sleeps. Thank goodness, there's a door to the back street. Slinging the saddlebags over my shoulder, I pick up the rifle and run out into the hot air.

Another crash, louder than before. Maybe he convinced that poor horse to smash through the door. Horses aren't meant to do that.

I dash down the alley, hear blows and splintering in the governor's office. I made it out in the nick. It'll be a coin's toss whether I make it around the side of the next building before they come out the back door.

I duck low and run.

Gunshots fill the air—I can hardly hear anything else. Perhaps this is how my father went at Square's Run, in battle, where all your senses disappear in thunderous noise.

A shout behind me, a scrabble of hooves, and the crack of a pistol.

A bullet whizzes over my shoulder. I instinctively shy away, then another plows through the leather of the saddlebags and burns like fire into my arm.

Getting shot was not part of the plan.

I duck around the corner and throw myself under the raised boards of the nearest porch. I wrest the saddlebags off my bleeding shoulder, shove them as far away as I can. If they find me, they're not finding that too. I drag the rifle into position and watch the narrow gap between the buildings.

The stables and the stage office are aflame, the black smoke billowing upwards in a great thick column, red flame licking skyward, defying the still sky.

A tall, stone-faced figure on a striking black horse

stands in the street, riding out the black's every jerk and sidestep. He shouts orders.

So that is Mortimer, Outlaw King of the Western Territory.

And he's got us in his grasp. Archer is easily three or four days away, and there's no resistance to speak of here. Every man's got what he had in his belt. The town is burning. With the heat and the breeze, we would be lucky to save half the buildings, even if Mortimer rode away now.

And he sure doesn't seem to be contemplating that.

I dig a handkerchief out of my pocket, taking my eyes off the gap for only a split second to knot it over my arm with my one hand and my teeth.

It's not bleeding too much—I'll probably survive.

I return my hand to the trigger, check to make sure it's cocked. Screams and shouts and shots fill the air. The fire is roaring now.

And then I see him.

Doctor Sikes is standing on his porch, his black coat pulsing in the hot wind, one hand on the post at the porch's edge.

He's watching, just watching, and a chill runs through my whole body. Not a bad one, but strong.

Doctor Sikes strides out into the street, moving fast, but with every movement unhurried. The hot slick air ruffles his gray hair, pushes his long coat open. Dust rises with every footfall.

Mortimer swings his horse around and reins it in hard. Every line in his body is taut. He carries himself like a king.

Then he spurs the black forward into a slow walk, up the street toward Sikes.

Their eyes are locked.

Mortimer reins in again, his lean face amused. The horse stamps impatiently, but he doesn't relent. And then Sikes stops.

Mortimer's horse is foam-flecked now, worrying the bit, throwing its head side to side. It wants to break away, run back to the fire from the doctor.

Mortimer senses it, too. He fiddles with the reins, watching the doctor keenly, the amusement still on his face and in the relaxed lines of his shoulders.

"Got a complaint, old man?"

Sikes just stands there.

A rumble of thunder comes from the distant hills, like a growled warning.

The horse gives a drawn-out, throaty cry. Jerks, pulls sideways at the reins. Mortimer slaps it reassuringly and sets his hand on his gun.

The sky over the hills is darkening swiftly. I've never seen a storm come on this fast.

"You'd better beat it," says Mortimer, his humor suddenly showing thin.

Sikes doesn't speak, but he steadies his stance, bracing his boots and lifting his shoulders.

Mortimer's horse backs into a half-rear of protest. The outlaw brings him back to the earth.

"I said beat it, old man. You got a complaint, you say it!" There's a crack in his voice, ever so slight.

The darkness is spreading from the distant hills,

spreading toward us, and suddenly, from nowhere, a flash of light falls and a roll of thunder splits the sky apart.

The world is going to ruination right on top of us.

"What is it you want?" screams Mortimer over the noise.

The horse is desperately trying to end their standoff—it's backing, sidestepping, throwing its head, trying to twist out from under him.

Sikes stands like stone, mere feet from the frantic beast.

I can hear nothing for the crackle of the fire and the tearing roar of the thunder. But I see his lips. He speaks.

*Get out of my town.*

The wind rushes like an answer through the street, shrieking, flinging rain like bullets against the hot, dry dust. Thunder shakes the ground and lightning splits the air, crackling.

It overtakes them both, and the last thing I see is Doctor Sikes standing like a statue, unmoved, in the middle of the street.

I reach for the saddlebags and shove them into the dirt under me, sheltering them as the rain slams, hail-like, into the porch overhang, against the slats above my head, smothering the dry dust by my face.

I curl in on myself to protect my head and the papers and wait it out.


WHEN THE RAIN stops twenty minutes later, the street is deserted and the burning buildings only smolder. The townsfolk are appearing again, assessing damage, talking in a swift murmur of incredulous voices.

My arm is stiff and blazes like fire when I move, and I go lightheaded.

Sikes is nowhere in sight.

I crawl out from under the porch—I see that I'm under the surveyor's office—and stumble down the muddy street toward the doctor's place.

Maybe he'll be full up. Jensen is used to patching up horses, so if Sikes can't see me, maybe he'd look me over.

But the office is still and quiet, untouched by fire or storm. I go to the door and knock. The world is swaying and I shake my head to clear it.

Doctor Sikes answers the door. He's dry as a bone.

I must look worse than I am, gripping my arm with its bloody handkerchief, wet and muddy and bedraggled. I can't read his face.

"It isn't bad," I protest.

Something in his face relents. He looks at me quietly, assessing me as much as the bullet crease in my shoulder.

"Step inside."

I've never been in his office before. It's neat, with a small examination table, instruments laid out, bandages. It looks like he's been preparing.

Sam is there, sitting in an armchair next to the window. A rifle leans against the wall within reach. I haven't seen him in weeks, as he's kept indoors—he's pale, but looks to be on the mend.

He gives me a nod.

"Come on back," invites Sikes, and I follow him into the back room.

He brings in water and bandages and a brown medicine bottle, saying nothing. He gives a pensive sort of grunt as he sits down beside me on the four-poster and peels my right sleeve off. It's stuck to my arm with dried blood and it hurts bad.

He cleans the wound to his satisfaction and bandages it, and I breathe slow and careful, knotting the fist that's hidden under my skirt.

"Keep it clean," he says.

"Thank you." I get up to leave.

"And stay off your feet. Go home. Leave the saloon alone. Carson's lucky it's still standing."

"But Peter—"

"Peter's better off than you. Go home."

I have no more energy to protest. The courage and presence of mind that came to my aid during the attack are wearing off into utter weariness.

I had better leave before he sees that too.

"Better?" Sam asks wryly as I step out of the back room.

I nod and go straight to the front door.

It's a strange sensation, stepping out onto the porch. I have never seen the town from this perspective before, and it all looks new, somehow. The air is cool, and there is a freshness in it that not even the smoldering buildings down the street can hide.

## 23

## ROSAMUND

THE SUN STREAMS IN WHEREVER IT CAN THROUGH THE closed curtains, as if defying danger to bring its cheer. Coffee and bacon provide a homey scent to help cover up the inhospitable smells of gunpowder and shot that fill the house.

It's now the fifth day that we've held out.

We buried Frank at night, with lookouts posted. Alan was against it at first, since at least two men would have to risk exposure to do it, but we buried him close to the house, in the family plot, and the lookouts saw nothing.

The bandy-legged hand, Jim, was shot two days ago. He can't do anything with a gun, but he's not getting worse.

"They're late this morning," the foreman jokes over his shoulder. "Must be sleeping in."

"Getting complacent, maybe," replies Alan, shifting his gaze from the window to me. "Miss Lacey, have you eaten?"

I nod.

"I promise you, when we win this, I'll get you back to civilization. We've been terrible hosts."

I give a little laugh and the men join in good-naturedly.

We're all tired to the bone and about to start another long day. It's not only the weariness of long days and longer nights, but the weariness of trying to take lives, of wondering which of us will be next, of trying not to imagine what will happen if they overcome us at last.

The report of a rifle from outside heralds the beginning of the day. I duck low and head for the loading table. We're running low on ammunition. There's been less shooting the last three days, but still our supplies are stretched thin.

Since our meager guard is down two men, I carry the loaded guns to the men in the front room and bring the empty ones back, and the men upstairs load their own.

I set down a brace of pistols beside Lee, the foreman. "Leave the rifle," he says, picking up one of the pistols. "I've got the bullets here."

His rifle is a single-shot, old, and he's only using it because we found a box full of old bullets downstairs. It isn't very accurate, by his own admission, but we're desperate.

I go to Alan, his lean face too weary, every line in it taut. He shouldn't even be up and about, but he's been standing guard—well, sitting guard—for the better part of a week.

"I'll take those." I give him a smile.

"Thank you." Alan trades his empty guns and meets my eyes for a brief moment. "We'll make it." He smiles back.

We get braver the closer to death we get.

EMILY HAYSE

Gunfire from upstairs comes now and again, but it is not heavy. The muted sunlight plays in the men's hair, turning it gold, casting obscure patterns on the floor around them.

I hear a gunshot to my right, out near the kitchen.

"They have to be spread thin," shouts the foreman to everyone. "Keep at it! Keep 'em hopping."

The gunshots from outside are growing thicker and faster.

Maybe today we lose.

"Alan! Alan, sir!" It's one of the men upstairs.

Alan turns around, keeping his head against the wall, away from the window. "What is it?"

"Sir, they're throwing down their guns."

"What?" Alan starts up, reaching for the windowsill to steady himself. "All of them?"

"Yes, sir," answers the foreman from the window. "Look."

Alan pulls aside the curtain and I see one man fleeing back into the trees, another raising his hands in surrender.

"It's Jem!" One of the hands from upstairs lets out a whoop. "It's him, it's Jem!"

The house erupts in cheers as the men from upstairs rush down. They shout, slap each other's backs, whoop and lift each other into the air. One of them throws open the door, shouts to us that there are prisoners taken. Everything is laughter and shouting and hollering. These hands and cattlemen, they know how to use their lungs.

In the middle of the cacophony, I lower myself into the nearest armchair, stare at the worn carpet under my feet.

It's over. As fast as it had begun, it's over.

In this moment, all I can think of is Frank and how he doesn't get to celebrate. Strange, how calm I felt when death was on all our minds, and how terrible it seems now that someone has been left behind.

The front door opens and the cheers double.

"Rose!"

I start to my feet. It's Raymond, dust-covered, a rifle gripped in his hand. He's alive.

I run to him and throw my arms around him. He wraps me close, pressing his face to my hair.

"I didn't know if you were dead—Raymond, I've been so worried." I reach up and kiss my brother's cheek, not caring if it's ladylike. We're alive.

"Not more than I was." His arms still grip me tight as if he's afraid I'll melt away. "Mortimer said you were killed."

"That liar! And you believed him?"

"Not anymore." His growly voice is gentle, almost playful. Relief is in every line of his body, deep in his twinkling eyes. "Are you all right?"

Yes, no. I haven't any idea. The words come tumbling out.

"There was a boy—no, you have to listen to me—he wasn't very old, barely a man—he was killed, and if I hadn't been here—"

"No, Rose." Raymond's hands are on my arms, his fingers gentle but firm.

"You don't understand—"

"I understand." He leans forward and kisses me slowly on the forehead. "It's all right. It's over."

I know he understands. He still remembers every man lost under his command. That is more comfort in this moment than anything else could be.

"Rosamund?"

The new voice is familiar, gentle, and for a moment the world goes still.

There stands Archer Scott, frozen in the front room, looking like he's seen the dead.

He's older than I remember him. The lines in his face that made him handsome are harder, more noticeable. But his eyes are the same color I remember—that stormy blue —and my heart begins to race.

"Rosamund?"

It takes me a moment to find my voice. "Archer."

His hat's off, but he reaches up again to smooth his hair down. He smiles, bringing out dimples, and his eyes twinkle almost sheepishly. "Morning."

"Good morning," I echo. We are a little shy, but I don't want to be. I want to throw my arms around him and know he is actually here, with me. My heart is beating loud in my ears.

"At last." I hold out my hand. "I feel as if I met half of the Western Territory before I met you."

He laughs, sudden and brief. "I'm mighty relieved to see you," he manages. "Mortimer—"

"Said I was killed?" I supply, as he seems to be finding it difficult to get the words out. "That man has trouble telling the truth."

He laughs, reaching out to take my hand, but I throw my arms around him instead.

He is here. It takes him only a second before his arms are around me too, holding me close.

He smells of sweat, but I never want to let go.

After a minute or so, we part and Archer looks down at me, earnest. "There's about to be some proper order again in this territory. We've got his man Holt out there."

Holt. I barely suppress a shudder. I'm glad I didn't know it was him shooting at us.

"And Mortimer?"

"He's not here. Only wish I knew where he got to."

"Alan and I, we came from his camp. Alan might be able to map it."

"He's already moved on." Archer shakes his head. "Always one step ahead."

"Alan, you rascal!" Jem Swift bursts in the door and seizes his brother, lifting him off his feet and shaking him. "I knew you were too tough to die out there!"

"Max?" asks Alan.

Jem shakes his head.

Alan's face goes still and sober.

"He was a good boy, was Max," says Raymond.

"Well." Jem banishes the sorrow from his face with an effort. "There'll be time for all that. I thought I was the only Swift left an hour ago. At this rate, maybe the kid's found a pocket of luck."

Alan makes a brave attempt at agreement, and Jem claps him on the shoulder again. "But I can't believe it. No water, no supplies, no map. Just clean across the northern spur of the desert on an outlaw's horse. But if anyone's too tough to die, it's you."

"And Miss Lacey," puts in Alan. "She shot an *isark* in the head."

"You what?" My brother's voice is equal parts horror and amusement, and Archer looks down at me, astonished.

"I don't plan to make a habit of it," I say, and Raymond begins to chuckle, eyes twinkling like mad.

It is at this moment that I know beyond a doubt—I will survive this territory. I will be well.

"Are there any steers still living around here?" asks Jem.

His face is businesslike, but his eyes haven't stopped glowing since he saw Alan. "I say, let's have fresh beef tonight. Where's Ted? We'll have a mess of bread and pies and green beans to go with it, if I have to lend a hand myself!"

# 24

## MORTIMER

"SIR, THEY'RE HERE."

In the stark light of the lantern I can see only half of Tora-Teth's face and that ghastly *isark* claw hanging on the tight strip of rawhide around his neck.

The *isark*, to the Red Tree Clan, is a symbol of power. That's why Tora-Teth wears it, renegade though he is.

He doesn't wait for me, and I follow the light of his lantern to the cluster of waiting men. In the poor, flickering light, the red horses of the Abernathy Clan look made of flame.

A dozen of them are gathered in the sullen light.

The Abernathys are a mean lot. After fighting for the losing side of the Savannah-Croix war, they defied peace and raided their way west, giving me grief for a couple years before I kicked them out of my territory.

Uncouth as they may be, they're the largest, most dangerous oath clan there is. And they have connections with others—others who bend to them when they cross paths.

"Evening, Mortimer," greets Marion, the head of the clan. He's a powerful-built man, and four years hasn't changed that, nor the heavy beard. "Been a while."

"It has." I extend my hand, shake his. Withdraw my grasp as soon as I can. He smells of cheap chewing tobacco.

"The boys said you wanted to talk." He folds his arms, slow. "I hope you know we ain't crossin' your borders."

"No, it isn't that. You've respected the terms, I know."

"Then what?"

"I have a proposition for you."

He stuffs the tobacco into his cheek slowly and grins. "Shoot, preacher."

## 2 5

## ROSAMUND

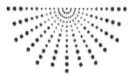

SOMETHING IS WRONG. I SEE THE BLACKENED PATCH outside of town, see Archer's face darken slightly as he sees it too.

He shades his eyes and stands a little in the stirrups.

"Looks like fire," I comment.

"An accident? It's been hot," my brother suggests.

"Maybe." Archer reaches down to scratch his horse's shoulder absently. "I still don't like it. Doesn't set right with me."

"Nor me." Raymond glances back at the second horse he's ponying—we're bringing Holt back to Glory Mesa for a trial.

The outlaw is blindfolded, trussed up too tight to move. But I see a smile tug at the corner of his mouth.

A chill runs through me. Whatever happened here, he knew it was coming.

Archer's blue eyes flicker upward in concern. "We better hurry. Looks like rain."

Raymond squints up at the sky, taking stock. "Yep. And someone's comin'."

A lick of dust stands in the air between us and town, in its center a flicker of movement.

"Hup!" Archer urges his horse forward.

My stomach sinks.

The rider meets us halfway and reins in smartly. He's wearing a checkered cotton shirt under a worn leather vest, and under his hat is a boyish face with a man's expression.

"Archer, Raymond." He tips his hat to me, revealing sandy hair, and looks inquisitively to Archer.

"Jesse, this is Rosamund Lacey. Rosamund, meet my cousin, Jesse Thatcher. I've told you about him."

So this is the beloved and notorious cousin. I smile. "Good afternoon."

"Ma'am." He tips his hat again. If he's surprised to see me alive, he says nothing.

"Archer," he says breathlessly, as if there's a weight on his chest. "Mortimer attacked the town."

"When?"

"A little over a week ago. Right about when we were up at his place."

A guffaw sounds behind us. Archer looks back at Holt slowly but doesn't say anything.

Thatcher squints. "Who's that?"

"One of Mortimer's. Name's Holt, a right-hand of sorts. He won't talk."

"Looks it." Thatcher looks ruefully at the prisoner.

"Damages?"

"A few buildings burned, some property damaged, a dozen wounded, a few killed. But folks are shook up bad."

Archer's jaw tightens. "Did he leave on his own?"

"That's the strangest part. They say an absolute screamer came down from the hills out of nowhere. Mortimer's men had to retreat, and it put out the fires."

"Where'd they retreat to?"

"Dunno, but Selby's on it. He rode out alone a couple days ago, didn't want company. Said he was going to see if there were any signs to read."

"And your journey back? No problems?"

"No problems. Selby got us back in record time."

"How about the office?"

Thatcher's face falls. "Pretty much ruined. It's standing, but they sure singled it out."

Archer's shoulders stiffen even as his face goes very still. "The papers?"

"Not to worry." A dimple flashes in Jesse Thatcher's cheek. "Kate got 'em all, sure as shooting."

"Kate?" Archer gives an incredulous laugh.

"Yessir, that's what they say. Those papers'll be the least of your worries now. The town council wants to talk to you. I think they're starting to regret they didn't appoint a new sheriff after Nelson bit the dust."

"I told them no one man alive could do all the sheriff's work on top of the governing." Archer slaps his horse with the long end of his reins. "Now maybe they'll listen."

We urge our horses into a trot. As the town looms closer, the damage is visible. The twisted, blackened beams, the smashed signs, the lumber stacked in the street outside torn-up buildings.

"Welcome to Glory Mesa." Archer gives me a loving look over his shoulder, reining in his horse so I can come up abreast of him. "I wish it wasn't such a poor welcome."

He has a dozen worries, and yet he's thinking about how it's not the homecoming either of us expected. And worse—after all this time, I think of it—I have none of my luggage. The bulk of it is still on the way, and the things I had with me, Mortimer stole or left trashed on the stage. I'm wearing cut-down cowhand's clothes from the Swifts' ranch. What a sight I must be.

"It ain't much now, but it's going to be something," Thatcher adds loyally. "Just wait."

"Do you live here?" I ask.

"Naw, not me. Archer didn't neither, before they made him governor. I still live on the ranch, out thataway." He waves his hand vaguely beyond town.

"Is it a large spread?"

He grins. "Large enough. Not the largest, but I guarantee you, ma'am, it's the prettiest patch of land for a hundred miles 'round."

As we ride down main street, the stares begin. I see mostly men, but there are a few women—mostly the matronly sort—watching us, whispering.

A small crowd gathers before we're a third of the way down the street. Raymond rides up beside me, quietly shielding me from half the onlookers. We finally stop in front of a saloon.

"Carson!" Archer shouts.

A big, burly fellow with ruddy hair and a stiff mustache to match stomps out.

"Carson, we got company," says Archer wryly. "Wondering if I can leave this piece of riff-raff with you?"

Carson peers at Holt. "Is he one of Mortimer's?"

"Sure is."

"Yeah, I'll take him. Kate!" He strides into the street and Raymond hands him the horse's reins without a word.

A slim young woman appears in the doorway. Her eyes go not to Carson, nor to Holt, but to me. We gaze at each other for a long moment, and though I am sure we have never met, a glimmer of recognition appears in her eyes. She nods and gives me a slight smile.

"Kate, go and unlock the back storage room. Be quick about it."

Her gaze breaks from mine, and she sends a glance of disgust in the direction of the men—whether it is aimed at Carson or Holt, I cannot tell. Smoothing her apron, she disappears inside.

Carson ties the horse up at the hitching post and wrestles Holt out of the saddle, hauling him inside none too gently. It's quiet and still now, though there must be more than a score of people watching us.

Archer backs his horse and turns it away from the saloon. He speaks softly, for me alone, and his tone is apologetic. "Not the finest introduction to our little town, is it? How do you like the sound of a wash and a rest?"

I let my smile of relief speak for me. A wash and a rest sound marvelous.

· · ·

ARCHER'S HOME—OUR home—is small. It has a second story, but the outside is dusty, and the paint is a dull, muted blue of the sort one might see on a boat shed. It's nothing to Mortimer's place, but what can one expect from a homestead gifted by the government?

At least there is a plot out front for flowers.

I dismount slowly.

Behind me, Raymond clears his throat. He's headed back to his rented room.

He is horribly dusty, but he leans down from the saddle to kiss my cheek. "I'll come later and see how you're getting on."

He turns his horse out of line and I watch him ride back up the street. The wind kicks up a swirl of dust, and the sun disappears behind the clouds. A couple drops of rain fall onto my trail-stained clothes.

By the time I turn back, Archer has unlocked the front door. He throws it open. "Welcome." He hesitates as if wanting to say more, but decides against it.

The place is nearly empty. What few furnishings he has are covered in dust cloths. It's small and simple compared to my home back East, but many good things must begin small.

"Well?" His voice is hopeful.

"It's lovely." I turn from the closed curtains of the kitchen window to his face. His eyes are hopeful too. "Really."

In the middle of the room stands a covered table. I pull up the edge of the cloth and run my hand over the smooth grain. The tables in my old home were all too large to ship halfway across a continent; this one will do well.

I pull back the kitchen curtains and look out at the darkening sky.

"Rosamund, I'm going to be straightforward about this. If you have any second thoughts—"

I turn around. He's toying with the edge of the cloth over the table.

I close the space between us, take his hand in mine, and lean gently into his face. "About the marriage? I have no second thoughts. Not one. I'd marry you tonight, but—"

He's searching my face, pleased and puzzled, as if he's still afraid I'll disappear before his eyes.

"But I'm waiting for my things to come. When they do, I'll be ready."

He pulls my hand to his lips and kisses it softly, his eyes warm and soft and fixed on mine. "If you're sure."

"I am." I squeeze his hand before heading into the parlor.

The parlor is barer still. I check under the two draped cloths to find an upholstered chair and a lamp. Dust is gathered on the floorboards. "This place could do with a good cleaning," I sigh. "But I'll start right away. It will be beautiful by the time we marry."

He looks down at me—the governor of this whole wild territory—and smiles gently. At this moment, I remember exactly why I fell in love with him.

"Well," he says reluctantly, turning toward the door, "I should get to work. I've been away from my office long enough and you can see what's come of it."

"What are you going to do about it?"

My voice stops him in the doorway. He rubs his chin wearily. "Rebuild."

"I meant about Mortimer."

"Well, figure out a way to defend the town. I suppose—"

"But aren't you going to go after him? This was a cowardly attack. He knew you were gone. He's nothing but an overgrown child."

"I don't have the men right now, nor likely anytime soon."

"But he's proved himself a coward, Archer. Cowards run—they don't fight."

He steps back into the room, his face earnest. "We mustn't underestimate him."

"I just spent a week with the man; I think I'm in a position to know."

"Rosamund, nothing is too low for him. I'd bet my bottom dollar Max Swift died bad, and Jem, he nearly did. Mortimer would have done the same to you—to anyone else—if it suited him."

My voice is low. "I know that."

"Yes, but you haven't seen it." Again he wants to say more, but stops. A strange dullness floods his blue eyes. He repeats halfheartedly, "You haven't had to see it."

I reach up tenderly, push back the dust-caked hair from his forehead. "We can't run forever. One day, he must have his reckoning."

"He will. I promise. What I'm doing isn't running." His body is tense.

"I didn't mean to suggest that. He's the coward, not you. I know that, or I wouldn't have come back to you."

He takes my hands and holds them tightly.

I'm suddenly tired, so tired I can hardly hold myself up. It's raining. I hear the drumming on the roof. I wrap my arms around myself, unsure whether I'm chilled or too warm.

"Can I build you a fire before I go? Pump you some water?"

"That would be nice."

He nods briefly and leaves.

I mean to go after him, but I don't. I stand unmoving, staring at the dark curtains.

From a distance, over the spattering of the rain, I hear the hard staccato of wood being split. He's the governor, and still no one thought to split his wood.

I suppose this is Glory Mesa, not New Hartford.

I hear the cast iron stove creak open in the kitchen, the hard *thunk* as he stacks the wood. The door opens and closes, I hear the gentle clank of buckets.

It is several minutes later when he finally comes back to the parlor doorway, damp from the rain. "It's done. There are some supplies in the kitchen cupboard from a few weeks ago, and anything else you need, Trasker at the mercantile will put it on my tab. The bedrooms upstairs have clean linens. They may need airing, but...."

"It's perfect." I'm tired, numb. I should feel glad, but instead I just feel empty.

"Is there anything else I can do, Rosamund?" He hesitates just before saying my name.

"No." Only that I don't want him to leave.

"All right. I'll be back tomorrow." He gives a slight nod and backs out of the doorway.

"Archer, thank you."

He reappears. "It's my pleasure. Are you sure you don't need anything else?"

"I'm sure."

"Tomorrow, then." He ducks out, and I hear his boots cross the floor. The front door shuts. The only sound now is the rain.

I go to the door, open it, and lean against the frame. He mounts up with a creak of leather and sees me as he gathers his reins.

He tips his hat and I close the door before he's up the street five paces.

It's quiet in the house. Thunder grumbles softly outside.

I go upstairs, open my window. The wind is warm and finally smells fresh.

I stare at the blurred hills beyond the town, up where I know Black Shaft Pass to be.

The rain would drown out any sound, but it doesn't matter. I cry silently. Sobs that wrack my body, breaths that keen for the dead. For the boys who won't come back.

Every tear down my cheek, off my chin, is like the rain on the glass panes, washing the desert's dust away.

# THATCHER

Let the record state that the first prison of the capital city of the Western Territory was an unused back room behind the saloon with the walls knocked out into the storage room so as to extend another twelve feet. Write about that to your tall hats back in civilization.

It smells bad, too. The stench of blood and sweat are bearable in the open air, but in a hot, closed room, it's torture.

Holt is chained to an anvil set in one corner, the blood and dust and sweat of three days ago mingled into an unpleasant crust that stains the side of his neck and his shirt. Carson took away his coat and his vest and his boots, but the real reason he looks half-dressed is there's no rifle cradled in his arms.

"Did the doctor see you?" My cousin's voice is direct, all business.

Holt doesn't answer.

If he'd seen Sikes, I imagine Holt's neck would be sight cleaner than it is.

"Tomorrow you will stand trial. If found guilty of outlawry and murder, as it seems likely you will be, you will hang. But I am prepared to offer you your life in exchange for full cooperation."

Holt gives a weak guffaw.

Archer keeps his cool. "Is your loyalty to a thief and a murderer so strong that you would die to protect information we will eventually have, with or without you? Is your life worth so little to you?"

Holt's eyes glitter with hostility. "You'll get what you want out of me and hang me anyway."

"I uphold the law here. When I make an offer, it's good."

"Hardly fair to hold a man's life over his head like that."

Archer shakes his head. "Holt, you've taken more lives in cold blood and hot than I'd care to name. You deserve hanging, whether you help us or not. What I am giving you is a chance. Even your boss won't get that."

Holt chews on this for a long moment. Then his face and eyes go stony and he stares straight ahead.

He's not taking it.

"Jesse, go get Doctor Sikes. I want this man cleaned up for the trial—and the rest of it."

I head out and I don't look back.

SIKES IS CHANGING Sam's bandage when I arrive.

"One moment," says Sikes, his back to me.

Sam nods in greeting. It was one of those soft slugs that did his arm, so it's going to be a long time healing, but he's looking much stronger.

"See me in another couple days." Sikes sets down the bandages, and Sam puts his hat on and heads out.

"What is it?" Sikes glances at me as he packs his medical case.

"The outlaw we have needs seeing."

"Hmm."

"It's been three days, and he's got some sort of wound in his neck. Tomorrow's the trial and—"

Sikes breaks in quietly. "That man needs my help like I need a lizard's help."

"Archer wants him cleaned up."

"Archer, hm?" Sikes regards me as if he's trying to determine whether I'm telling the truth. I find him a strange character at the best of times, but the stare makes the feeling stronger than ever.

At last he nods. "If it's Archer asking it of me, I will go clean him up."


THIS TRIAL IS big doings for Glory Mesa.

People are in the streets already, crowding the survey office, which is doubling as a courthouse since the beginnings of our courthouse were burned up in the fire. I stand in the dim back room of the saloon, holding the lantern as Carson unchains Holt from the anvil.

"Last chance." Archer stands in the doorway, his hands shoved in his pockets.

Holt maintains a sullen silence. A fly buzzes in one corner of the room and flies out the open door.

"Very well. Let's get this started, then."

There was a time when Archer was the law here, and then there was Sheriff Nelson, who died a couple months back when his horse stepped in a hole. Nelson spent his nights telling rowdy ranch hands when they'd celebrated enough and his days keeping half an eye on suspicious-looking drifters. Archer traded bullets with Mortimer a time or two in his day, and they tracked each other plenty, but no one needs to be told that's not settled yet.

The folks of Glory Mesa are a sturdy sort and used to rough characters, but today they're touchier than a herd of wild horses. The muttering that starts when we step out onto the porch of the saloon with Holt turns into shouts real quick.

By the time we're in the street, it's a clamor, and they're fighting to get in a jab at him, jostling me and Carson. The only one they won't touch is Archer.

These folks are out for blood.

Carson takes Holt by the elbow and guides him into the survey office, to a chair up front. Holt slumps into it, one boot shoved out in front of him, careless-like.

Mr. Trasker of the general store stands at the front of the room, his hands folded neatly. "All rise for the honorable Judge Patterson."

A tall fellow with graying hair but a surprisingly young face enters as we rise and takes his seat behind the desk. He's come clear from Thrasher Creek—a small town, but more civilized than ours since it's near the Auki settlements.

"Court is now in session," Trasker announces, and steps down from the raised platform brought in for the occasion.

Holt shoves out his foot and Mr. Trasker tumbles over it.

The smattering of laughter dies down as Trasker brushes himself off, flushed. "I will never hit a bound man," he says coolly, soft enough that it is really only meant for Holt. "But if ever I find occasion before your demise to stand on equal footing with you, watch yourself."

Holt just sneers. The man has guts, I have to admit.

"Order," requests Patterson mildly, thumping on the table. "Will the charges be read against the defendant?"

Carson does the honors. He has a fine voice for it that carries clear to the back of the packed room.

And Holt sure has a pile. Murder, thievery, horse-thievery, kidnapping, looting, manslaughter. There's got to be a sight more, but this is what we had witnesses for.

"How does the defendant plead to these charges?" Patterson asks, enragingly polite.

Holt leans forward and spits on poor Mr. Levine's immaculate floor.

"The court asks for an oral answer from the defendant, Mr. Holt. How do you plead?"

Holt grins, his tongue between his teeth. "Guilty as sin, hombre."

"You will please address the judge as 'your honor.'"

Holt hacks and spits on the floor again, loudly. Dead silence.

"Mr. Holt, address the judge as 'your honor' or not at all."

He only licks his cracked lips and grins. He has a wicked-looking jagged tooth, and he puts me in mind of a *darani* I saw shot once, long and hulking with powerful legs, its bluish forked tongue out, its teeth bared in death.

I shudder.

Judge Patterson's voice is grave, still polite. "Does the defendant wish to speak to his defense?"

Holt shakes his head.

"As the defendant has pleaded guilty to the charges, the court arrives at the verdict guilty. Sentence, death by hanging. To be carried out tomorrow at dawn."

For a moment it is silent. Holt breaks it with a low guffaw.

"THAT WAS A FAST TRIAL, and thank goodness." I hike my boots up onto the cold stove in my cousin's office. The room's been swept clean of broken glass, the smashed windows boarded up, the wrecked furniture removed.

Archer is cleaning his gun at his desk, which is now decorated with bullet holes.

"Well, he was guilty as a man can be." Archer holds up the chamber to peer through it. "We didn't even need the witnesses."

"He didn't seem to care."

"Oh, he cared. Just knew he was licked."

"I dunno." I scratch my nose. It's all been so easy since we got back. Too easy.

The sound of hammering out where they're building the gallows reaches us through the one open window.

"You sticking around?" asks Archer.

"Nah, not me. You won't catch me in town when there's a hanging on."

He only chuckles wryly.

Feet pound up onto the porch, the door flies open and slams against the wall. "Governor Scott!"

It's one of the young hostlers from the livery stable. He's flushed and panting. "Governor Scott, they sent me to tell you. It's Mortimer. He's here."

"Mortimer is here?" Archer starts to his feet.

"White flag on the edge of town. Wants to parley."

Archer scratches his jaw, skeptical. "How many men with him?"

"Five."

"Five." Archer echoes slowly. "Well, round up a few of our own. Jesse, you'll come with me if you don't mind. And find Raymond Lacey."

I drag my boots off of the stove.


MORTIMER STANDS out on the hot ground, waiting. He looks oddly bare without his gun belt.

Under his hat, his red hair is plastered darkly to his forehead. His face is that same ironlike mask, arrogant.

He's holding a piece of the livery stable's sign. It's the only place I know of that had yellow lettering. The whole front of the building caved in when it burned.

"Archer!" he calls out, tossing the wood aside and taking

a step forward. "Back in town, I see. I wouldn't have thought it of you—hiding behind old men's tricks."

"You ran from that old man, so I'm told."

"But I didn't see you at all. Funny, I thought you were the governor of this place."

"The territory," he corrects, mildly.

"The territory? Just a name for a spot on a map. Really, Archer, I'd think—"

"What is it you want?" Archer demands, unbuckling his gun belt.

"To talk. Isn't that what parley usually means?" Mortimer pulls out half a cigar and lights it slowly. He shakes out the match and drops it in the dust.

"Mockery doesn't befit a parley." Archer drops his gun belt and steps forward.

Mortimer is taking his time. He pulls the cigar out and blows smoke. "I hear you have my man Holt."

"We do. But the trial's over."

"You don't waste any time, do you?"

"Can't afford to."

Mortimer gives a thin smile. "I want him back."

Archer shakes his head, slow. "Glory Mesa won't release a convicted criminal."

"Glory Mesa." Mortimer laughs through his nose and looks slowly over the blackened buildings.

"Is there anything else?" Archer's more patient than I'd be, that's for sure.

"One thing." Mortimer smiles.

He turns, snapping his fingers to one of the men. From the cluster of horses that stand with their backs turned to the snappish wind, they drag out a tall, limping figure in worn-out, dirty clothes, a hood over his head.

"If you're set on having blood, I'll give you another spectacle to go alongside it."

"You're the one who wants to talk to me, Mortimer. I'm not playing games. You decide you want to talk like a man, come back tomorrow."

"I'll swap this fellow for Holt. Refuse me a deal, and I'll kill him slowly, right here in front of you." He nods to his men and they jerk the hood off.

It's Max Swift. His face is bloodied, but there's a set to his shoulders and a fierce light in his eyes.

Archer's beat. I hate saying it, but Mortimer knows how to play on a principled man. He knows my cousin can't turn down the chance to save a life.

Archer turns to Raymond and says a few quiet words. Raymond mounts up and rides back.

Somewhere in the unburned grass out beyond the town, a meadowlark sings.

"I don't expect I'll see you for a little while, *Governor* Scott." Mortimer pulls the cigar from his mouth and regards it slowly. "At least two weeks."

My cousin just stands there with his arms folded.

"You may want to consider your position while I'm gone."

"My position's been considered for some time."

Mortimer breathes out a lazy stream of smoke. "I'll tell you this much—when I come back, I'm coming back for the territory. And nothing's sacred to me."

"And if we're not ready to give it to you?" Archer's jaw is like iron.

Mortimer gives a bitter laugh. He's burned the cigar to a cinder. He unfolds his arms, flicks the dead stub into the sand, and looks up. "Then I'm going to set your world on fire."

Raymond rides up, bringing Holt along on a paint pony, his hands still tied. Raymond's looking back, not forward, and he's got his gun drawn.

I can see from here a line of men watching from main street. They're about to be mad, fighting mad.

Holt was supposed to hang, not go free, Max or no Max.

"I'm glad you have some sense." Mortimer meets Raymond with a mocking smile and takes Holt from him, cutting his bonds.

They give Max a brief shove in our direction and mount up. Holt is laughing. He turns in the saddle and spits in our direction.

They ride off.

Max stands there swaying a little, and Raymond goes up and cuts his wrists free.

"You all right, boy?" he asks.

"Sure, I'm all right." Max manages a half smile.

"I think a drink's in order," says Carson brusquely, rubbing his forehead. He'd never admit it, but Mortimer makes him nervous. "They're on the house."

. . .

WE TIE the horses outside the saloon. Kate, waiting on the porch to watch us ride in, turns to go in ahead of us. I still see the bulge of that bandage under her sleeve.

We get halfway up the steps when Max crashes to the ground, no warning.

Archer's on his knees, lifting Max to lay him on his back, unbuttoning the front of his shirt. "Get Doctor Sikes," he says. "And I reckon someone should send word with the next stage to the Swifts."

# CARNEGIE

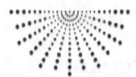

THE SUN RISES OVER THE HILLS EAST OF TOWN. I STAND on the steps and watch it spread its warm fingers of light over the hills like rivers of gold.

I've got beans cooking on the stove in back, and the coffee is fresh. On mornings like this, with the fresh bright air, the smell of smoked beans and coffee, I couldn't ask for a thing more in the world.

A lone horse and rider come up the street. It's Sikes, oddly. It's a little late for him—one rarely sees him out of his house unless it's dawn or dusk. Looks like he's coming in from the hills. Perhaps he was out picking herbs or the like. I wouldn't know.

He's been taking care of Max Swift for three days now. After falling down flat on the saloon's front steps, Max fell into a raging fever. I haven't seen him since—it's none of my business—but word is he didn't have any injuries bad enough to put a man in a fever like that.

Mortimer must have done something bad to him, but I'm beat if I know what it was. This land has secrets, and Mortimer knows more of them than most.

I wish I knew more of them.

The wind stirs, whistles a little as it runs past the buildings, whisks my hair back. It smells of clean air and sagebrush and a little of horse. I close my eyes and inhale.

There are so many mysteries left in this wild land, and I want to go look for them and learn them. It's a strong feeling, strong as love. I'm going to do it—I will do it. I feel it in my bones.

I was born for this place.

I don't know how long it is before I brush the wisps of hair back behind my ears and head inside. Carson's does good business, but hardly anyone comes here in the morning. Occasionally we have boarders in the rooms upstairs, but it's rare to get more than one or two at a time. They wake, usually too early or too late, and I serve them up the same coffee and eggs or beans and bacon that Peter and I eat in the morning. But we haven't had anyone regular since Jack Selby rode out of here two or three weeks ago.

After breakfast, Peter finishes his chores and runs off somewhere. He really should be having schooling, but I'm busy this morning. Carson will be back before noon and he wants all the laundry washed and aired.

It happens while I'm out back, pumping water into the cast-iron pot I made the beans in this morning. I roll up my sleeves and grab a fistful of sand to scour out the bottom with, and then I hear my name.

"Kate."

Archer Scott is standing in the back door of the saloon, above me.

I've never been scared of anyone. Shy, maybe, but never either with Archer Scott. But he's the governor now, and at this moment, the center of his keen attention, I'm suddenly flustered.

"Yes?"

"I hear from the men—they're telling me it was you who saved all those things from the office."

My mouth's dry and my fingers itch to continue with my work, but I can't. "Yeah, that was me."

"They tore the place apart."

"Yeah." I laugh, happy to break the tension a little. "I almost didn't get out of there."

He comes down from the doorway, crosses the empty space until he stands across the pump from me. "The papers were invaluable. I know 'governor' sounds strange, since I've been around here my whole life—"

"A little," I smile.

"But that doesn't change the fact that I have the responsibilities of a governor. Same as back East. You saved me from a world of trouble."

"It's what anyone would do if they thought about it for a minute."

"But it was you who thought of it. No one else did."

I shrug. I can't speak for anyone else.

"Anyway, you're a mighty resourceful woman, Kate. We're all beholden to you, and if there's anything you want, I'll do whatever's in my power to see you get it."

The clouds peel back from the sun, casting spotty, warm light over the yard.

I squint up at him, against the brightness. "Soon?"

"You've got it." He holds out his hand to shake.

I knock the sand off my hands and take it, firm and strong.

"See you." He pulls at the broad brim of his hat and heads back up through the saloon.

I stare after him dumbly, watch his silhouette move slowly past the bar and out the swinging doors.

Slowly, I get back to work, a sunny warmth creeping over me that has nothing to do with the weather. My sore arm barely hurts as I scrub vigorously, and a smile spreads across my face unbidden.

I can feel it. My luck's about to turn.


THE STAGE COMES IN, a tad early, at three forty-nine in the afternoon, bringing with it a powerful lot of new blood.

The first to amble in are Chet and Barnes, the two stage drivers who do most of the runs now—Chet was sent over from the El Terune line after Sam was shot. They'll be wanting coffee.

The stage office has some that the stage master keeps hot, but Chet is partial to mine and I let him have it on the house sometimes.

"Afternoon, Kate!" he greets, peeling off his dusty gloves. "How are the pickins today?"

"It's been quiet in town compared to the past week, but I don't think it's over," I say, laying out the mugs. "But with

EMILY HAYSE

what you hauled in, we might be headed for some more excitement."

"Aww, they're just tenderfoots and linemen." Barnes reached for the towel-wrapped handle of the coffee pot. "I'd be surprised if any of them stuck."

"How's Sam?" Chet glances up at me.

"Aw, he's good. Still too much under Doctors Sikes's thumb is his opinion, but he's getting ready to break his traces," I grin.

"Anyone would be." Chet gives an appreciative shudder. "Still crazy he made it all the way down from the pass with that hole in him. Yeah, he's one lucky son of a gun."

"That pass is real treacherous," agrees Barnes. "Saw some Tavachi scouts out there yesterday."

"Here? Thought Mortimer had his mark on that land." I pull the end of the towel down my shoulder to dry the glass.

"Well, he did. But I'd swear on my mother's grave they was Tavachi. They run with Abernathy. Either he's busted loose or Mortimer's up to something."

"Mortimer?"

"Well...." Chet takes a sip of his coffee. "See, it's pretty commonly known that the government back East turns a blind eye on Mortimer because he keeps out the smaller oath clans, the ones what came west after the war. But Abernathy, he was the hardest customer by a long sight."

"That's the government for you." Barnes fixes me with a direct look. "I ain't what you'd call a learned man, but I can see government fiddle-faddle a mile off. They used him, probably paid him, to clean out this place, and now

210

they've gone and sicced Governor Scott on him. Not that he didn't have it coming, but—" Barnes raises his eyebrows and takes a drink.

"We're going to need a marshal." I put the glass up with the others. "Probably a few."

"You can tell me if this is true," says Barnes, scratching the end of his nose. "I heard a rumor they're trying to set up another sheriff in this town straight off."

"I heard they're passing on sheriff and going straight to marshal," adds Chet.

"Seems to be true," I agree.

"Any talk on the candidates?"

I shrug. There's been talk, but nothing from anyone in a position to know. If Jesse Thatcher was still in town, he'd know, but he lit out three days ago like a cat with its tail afire before another catastrophe could happen.

Poor devil misses his ranch—I see it in his eyes every time he walks in here. Some folks just aren't meant to be cooped up.

"You know they'd ask Chris, but he'll turn them down flat," says Chet. "He's turned them down once before."

"Chris?" I'm trying to place the name.

"Cristobal Newton. Runs the Tree Hill brand."

"Oh, yes." He's a black-haired fellow I've only seen in town once or twice. Owns one of the richest spreads in the territory, and he was educated back East.

I wouldn't want to come down and be a sheriff or a marshal if I were him, either, but we sure could use a man like that.

"What about that old lanky fence-post?"

"Some days I don't know what yer talkin about, Barnes." Chet gives the man a halfway scowl.

"The governor's brother-in-law. To be."

"Oh, I dunno." Chet shrugs and takes a sip of his coffee. "You know anything about that, Kate?"

"I don't know if he'd take it," I reply. "But he looks to have a cool head."

"Is he proven, is what I want to know," says Chet. "What does anyone know about him?"

Barnes scratches his ear. "Governor Scott seems to think a sight of him already."

"He survived Mortimer's camp," I say quietly. "Not many men have done that. Survived the war, too. Heard he was a commander. And he knew Jem Swift."

"Well, then he can handle a gun, at least," approves Chet. "Men too, maybe."

"It takes more than that to marshal a town," says Barnes. "'Specially a boomin' one."

"The real question is whether he can—"

There's a quiet, slow step outside and Raymond Lacey strides in, his head nearly brushing the doorframe.

"Speak of the devil," mutters Barnes, raising his mug to his lips.

Raymond closes the distance in a couple slow strides.

"Afternoon," he greets the men, removing his hat and reaching up to loosen his collar. "Got any more of that coffee, ma'am?"

He smiles, just the faintest bit, but it warms me inside.

Funny, he's one of the few people who doesn't call me

plain Kate. It may change as he gets used to things around here, but for the moment, I find it strangely flattering.

He digs in his pocket for a coin.

I throw the bartowel over my shoulder. "It's on the house."

## 28

# MORTIMER

THE FIRES BLOOM RED-GOLD AGAINST THE DRY BROWN and green of the rocky, sagebrush-dotted ground. There are dozens of them. Enough men to fight a small war, which is what all this has come to at last.

If only it would rain.

I hear Abernathy's heavy-booted steps approach from behind. He still insists on uniform—none of his men have one, but he still wears the gold and brown of his old cause, thick gloves halfway to his elbows.

It's a wonder he doesn't die of the heat.

"Why haven't we gone yet?" His arms are folded across his strong chest.

"You will. Soon."

"Well, what's the holdup?" Abernathy never talks fast, but the man is impatient.

"Do you need me to spend all the day spelling out every

detail in order for you to hold up your end of the bargain? Be glad I have let you in on my conquest."

Abernathy grunts and lumbers off.

I'm waiting. Waiting like this dry ground waits for rain. Yearning as it yearns. It's a savage land—it takes and ravages and what does it give?

But it has been good to me.

Tora-Teth rides in, swinging off his still-moving pony. It's a quick thing, twitchy, faster than a rattler on a rock.

I stride across the hard ground, feeling the crunch of every stone under my worn boots. I need a new pair, but it hasn't been important, not on the very cusp of this glorious breakthrough.

The land is slick and hot. Ripe for burning. If only it would rain.

Tora-Teth shakes his hair out of his face.

"Tell Abernathy to move out. He knows the boundaries, he'll stick to them. Tell him the promised gold comes after. He can live off his raids in the meantime."

"Sir."

He turns and leaves without a sound. The man moves as easily as a snake over this rocky ground.

I heave in a hard, hot breath.

I was a fool to listen to anyone. This is my territory, this is my time. Soon there will be no reason whatsoever to bow to anyone's whims. They will bow to mine.

A bugle breaks the hot stillness, the clear clarion call of a now-dead cause.

Sometimes men hold onto their dreams so tight the

dream begins to smother them. But they cannot let go—it would kill them to let go—so they kill it. Their own dream.

A shrill whoop breaks through the air, echoed by a hundred throats. The earth shakes with the pounding of hooves as the horses get their heads, the sharp staccato of guns firing in the air.

It's deafening and then it fades to a rumble like distant thunder.

"Sir—are you still resolved?" Tora-Teth is back.

"I'm resolved."

"Can you trust them to follow orders?"

"Holt is with them. He'll tell me if they stray."

"Then what are we waiting for?"

Nothing. I'm waiting for nothing.

There's a beautiful lift in my chest, how a bird must feel when it soars.

But when I turn to Tora-Teth, I'm grim, detached.

"Have them saddle my black. I'm ready."

## 29

## ROSAMUND

Mornings come sun-drenched and early here, and every morning I am up with the sun, cleaning and scrubbing until my hands are raw, not going out, not wanting to see the rest of Glory Mesa yet.

Archer told me yesterday that I don't need to work so hard, but I do.

If I stop working, I start to think, and then I am too tired, too worn to do anything.

I think of Mortimer, of Holt, and of the boy Frank.

I look at my fingers slowly as the smell of coffee fills the kitchen. I wish my things would come. I want to marry Archer and not be alone here anymore.

A knock sounds at the door, interrupting the birdsong.

A tall, well-dressed woman stands on the doorstep. Her fair hair is piled below a black bonnet, and the dress she wears is black silk. She looks like a woman I'd see back home, not here.

"I am Maria Pike," she greets, holding out a black-laced hand. "As one of the few civilized women in Glory Mesa, I thought I would be neighborly and see how you were getting on."

"I am remarkably well." The rote words I've said all my life come to my lips before I can even think to ask her to call some other time. "Won't you come in?"

"Miss Lacey, I understand that you came out with the express intention of marrying Governor Scott." Maria lifts an eyebrow.

We are in the parlor, drinking out of mismatched china, eating the cake I had made for Archer today. I am thankful I had anything at all on hand. I explained that my things hadn't come, and she waved it away like a queen. Not to be helped, she had said.

Now she looks at me sagely. "That's rather bold. Even for out here."

"He asked me," I reply, and leave it at that.

"Did he? Now I am surprised at that, genuinely surprised. You are so young, my dear."

Raymond tells me this often, when he's lying in front of the fire of an evening, running his hand through the gray in his dark hair. He says it like it's a fine thing that makes him proud.

Maria says it in such a way that I feel I must explain myself.

"There are some things you should know about the

governor," Maria goes on, her rich voice dipping even lower. "You know, if you are to marry him."

I do not like her tone, but I nod for her to go on. Nothing she says will change my mind now.

"He's wild," she says confidentially, as if it's a most wonderful and scandalous secret. "A strong hand for a strong horse, as they say, and he's one of the best. He and Mortimer have had a rivalry—and I mean the word most deliberately —for years. The two of them are not so very unlike."

"Really?" I lift my cup and sip slowly. I think it's safe to say I know Archer better than this woman does, however long she's been here.

"And yet one has ten thousand dollars on his head and the other has the keys to the territory."

"One of them is a murderer." I try to keep the annoyance out of my voice.

"Rosamund, my dear, you must understand. In order to survive here, one cannot hold fast to the ideals of the East. Those who do, die." She looks meaningfully at me.

"I may be fresh to this territory, Mrs. Pike, but no one can say I don't understand what I am facing. I have already survived Mortimer, miles of desert, multiple gunfights, days of riding, and an *isark*."

She presses her lips gently together and regards me with a strange look. I cannot tell if it is sad, yearning, or both. "You poor girl. However did you survive a desert?"

"I was with Alan Swift."

A spark of recognition crosses her face, but not approval. "I see. Alan Swift."

She takes a sip of her coffee.

"Well, you seem a determined young lady," she says, when the silence grows long.

"Thank you."

She studies me quietly and I study her back. There is a strength in her pose—a subtle power, disguised until the moment of need. And she's a widow. No one need look further than her dress to know that.

"I find the determination required to raise oneself in station here quite amazing. You know, of course, that Archer Scott came from very humble means."

"No one knows who his father was."

"Exactly," replies Maria, lending more scandal than is needed to the tone of her reply. "And then he was taken on by the string-thin charity of a man named Hector Muley. And what a man."

She fans herself as if the stench of his sweaty, grease-stained clothing is filling the close air of the parlor now.

"One could scarcely call him a man," I say quietly. Brute would be a better description, from what Archer has told me. He has always been honest with me on the subject of his upbringing, but I hardly want to discuss it over tea with Maria Pike.

"It is true that he favored his own son well above Archer—a fault, but one common among men."

"And used Archer little better than a pack animal. Is that a fault common among men?" My voice is polite, but my patience is wearing thin.

"Well." Maria sets her cup carefully in her saucer. "For all his shortcomings, Hector Muley was among only a score of men with the audacity to set foot in this territory. He feared no legends. Such a man was Ian Swift; and Sikes, the doctor, was another. Archer and the Swift lads were some of the first to be born on this land. So much has changed since then, and so quickly."

I detect a note of wistfulness in Maria's voice. "And you? When did you come to this territory?"

"Oh, that's not an interesting story," she waves my question away with a laugh.

"I'd like to hear it all the same."

"Some other time, perhaps." Maria gives me a smile, and I can't tell if she means it to be friendly or patronizing. "I came to talk about you, and about Archer."

How kind.

"It seems," she says, setting aside her cup and smoothing her skirt softly with one hand, "that you have a great deal of faith in this fiancé of yours."

"Yes." I have the distinct impression that she came to set me right about him and found me less naïve than she expected.

"But—if you will permit me—there is one story I think he is not likely to have told you. Of how he came to leave Hector Muley."

I know there are things Archer doesn't tell me about his childhood, much of it for a reason. But there's a look in her eyes, and I sense that whatever's coming, it isn't plain gossip.

I look up at her serenely, bracing myself. "Go on."

"Archer Scott was twelve, or perhaps thirteen, and word moved from place to place slowly in those days. They had been trapping up in the mountains, or so Muley gave it out. I wonder if he hadn't been gold-searching. There are tales of gold in the hills, near the territory of the Far Hill Clan, but no real strike has been made. In any case, as it happens in the high mountains, winter came on early and without warning. They—Hector Muley, Hector's son, and Archer— found themselves faced with a brewing storm, and Hector sent his son ahead to scout the way."

Maria's eyes are quiet and bright.

"The son didn't come back, so Hector sent Archer ahead as well, to find him and hopefully a trail. Finally, he came upon both lads sitting at the side of the trail. Hector's son was bloodied and had a hurt leg. Archer helped him onto a pack horse and pointed the way out, but he unwittingly chose the Awaten-pana, or the Pass-Unbroken, a trail that had remained blocked by a great, impassable stone for many hundreds of years. The Far Hill Clan claimed it was a test of greatness, set by ancient forefathers of mankind. The one destined to free this land from its curse would crumble the stone at his touch."

I set my cup down quietly in its saucer.

"If they didn't find a way out, Muley knew they would be caught by the norther and likely die in the snow. He berated the boy for choosing that path, but of course, Archer hadn't known. He insisted it was clear—that he had cleared it. Muley threatened him with every oath he could think of, but time was running out, and Archer insisted the trail was clear. So they went on until they reached the place where the trail had been blocked. Only, as Archer had said, it was blocked no longer. The stone was shivered into a thousand pieces. In trying to pass over it, Archer said, Hector's son had fallen and become wedged, and to save him, Archer struck the rock, hoping to chip enough off to free him. But the whole thing crumbled at his blow."

"But—that's not possible."

"So said Hector Muley. He was fit to beat him for lying, but his son stopped him. Said he had seen it with his own eyes. Hector's boy, half Auki as he was, knew the legend well, and their kind take those stories as seriously as life and death. So they made their way to safety, and when they had passed beyond the mountains, Archer left Hector Muley. The man didn't raise a hand to stop him. It would be fighting fate, he said."

She's staring out the window at the heights beyond town, dotted with purple sagebrush, and there's a light in her eyes like she's seen glory.

A wagon clatters by below. Slowly, Maria turns her eyes to her hands in her lap and the look fades.

"Thank you for your hospitality." She stands up. "I should be going now. I will certainly see you again. In Glory Mesa, we can hardly avoid it."

I see her to the door and bid her good day.

The sun is up, casting cool shadows across the dust; someone is moving a dozen cattle up the street. I watch her leave, a dark figure in the middle of gentle sunlight.


It's impossible to miss the governor's office. Half the windows boarded up, walls pocked with bullet holes, and the territory flag flying bravely outside.

I step up onto the rough board porch and knock on the door.

"Come," the familiar voice calls, and I open the door.

Archer glances up briefly then starts to his feet, nearly upsetting his chair. "Rosamund, good morning! I apologize for the state this place is in, I wasn't expecting—"

He breaks off in a laugh.

The place is swept and uncluttered, but there is still evidence of the attack. A cold stove stands against the wall opposite his desk and bullet holes mar the plaster of the walls and ceiling.

"Good morning, Governor Scott." I smile and adjust the basket on my arm. "I thought you might like something fresh-baked."

"I would indeed." He grins and reaches out to take the basket. "Still no second thoughts, Miss Lacey?"

"Not one."

His blue eyes warm. "You know, most women who went through what you did would want to leave the territory." He pulls out a chair for me, then disappears into the next room and returns carrying a small table.

"Is it strange that I want to stay even more now?"

He looks at me with pride in his eyes. "No. Not for you."

He unpacks the basket—hot coffee and a pie. "I see you found Trasker's mercantile." He glances up at me, smiles. "He's a good fellow."

"He said the cherries were fresh from a farm near Thrasher's Creek. I didn't know there were any cherries out here at all."

"Thrasher's Creek is a nice place. Right across the border from the Aukis, so it's more settled than here. Got some good farms and orchards down there." His eyes flicker to a map tacked on the wall.

"Have the farms been there long?"

"Well, not long in the scheme of things, but some of them longer than you might expect. Take my cousin Jesse —his parents settled out here thirty-five years ago."

I walk over to the wall and study the map, which proclaims in gilt letters the span of the territory. Glory Mesa is easy to find. It's situated in the middle and slightly south, nestled near a speckling of mountains.

"So this is the Western Territory."

"Yes." Archer sets the cloth back over the pie and comes over. "There's Glory Mesa, of course. Looks much more impressive on the map."

I laugh.

"There's Thrasher's Creek, where the cherries are from." The dot on the map is near the border, as he said. "And there's the Auki settlement there. Their ancestral lands are further south, but these are northern Auki. Stopped just short of the border, as you see."

"Why is that? Was the border there when they settled?"

He shakes his head. "This land's always been set apart. We paid the Auki and the Red Tree Clan for it, as their territory abutted it, but they wouldn't set foot on it anyway. They say it's cursed."

"So I hear tell."

"Well, it's an old story. It would take a lifetime to learn all the stories about this territory."

"Do you believe it?"

"What?"

"That it's cursed."

Archer looks over at me. "I don't know. You see, legends are tricky things. Is it a real curse, like in a story, where there's one way and only one to break it? Is it like a mountain range that's called impassable because it's never been done? Is it like an unlucky spot where a tragedy took place and now it's tainted in people's minds?" He shrugs. "I won't deny there's talk, but I'm not going to let it stop me, either."

I reach out and take his hand. The wind stirs the bullet-torn curtains, fresh and sweet.

"What are these marks?" I touch a penciled *x*. Ones like it are scattered all over the map.

"Those are ranches and mines. That string of dots there, that's the progress the railroad is making. They'll get down our way eventually, but they're cutting through the good prairie land first. Settlers want that, and the towns are springing up as fast as the railroad can work."

He points to another *x* situated near two rivers. "There's the Swift ranch. Fine land they're on."

"What are the other ranches?"

"Well, this one is Jesse's." He touches a mark close to Glory Mesa. "I own some of that land out there. I'll show it to you sometime." Something like regret enters his eyes. "Before I became governor, I had hopes to build a ranch house."

"There's time." I lean my head against his shoulder.

"There's Gilchrist's ranch, just west of town. You

should meet him. He's a fine young man, and his grullo saved your brother's life."

"What?"

One side of his mouth lifts in a smile. "Long story. And that one, further east, that's Harrison Terhune's spread. He and Chris Newton—" he taps the opposite side of the map — "are the two richest cattle barons in the territory."

"Which ones are mines?"

His finger traces mark after mark as he rattles off names: Silver Heart, Wild Coney, Richard and Trace, Black Moon, Last Riddle Bet.

"Do they pay much?"

"A couple of them do. Decent ore, a lot of them. There's been some gold and silver, but we haven't had any rushes."

"What about all that?" I point in the direction of the northwest. The markings thin as the land spreads in that direction.

"Not many surveyors have made it up there. It's rough country."

"What's up there?"

"Mountains. A lot of trees. Caves and ridgebacks, wild animals. Some strange stories too."

"Strange stories?"

"You'll get used to it. Lore is thicker than dust here."

He squeezes my hand affectionately.

A knock startles us both.

I move toward the door. "I'll get it."

A trim, narrow-faced man stands on the porch, clearly travel-worn, but his thick brown hair looks like he's taken pains to smooth it with water from the trough outside before knocking.

"Good afternoon. Can I help you?"

"Is Governor Scott in?" he asks quietly. He's looking at me not quite like he's afraid of me, but something isn't right.

"Of course."

"I'm not—interrupting him?"

His clothes are dusty and he looks exhausted. Whatever business he has must be far more urgent than our chat over coffee and pie.

"No, of course not." I hold open the door. "Come on in."

He steps in, ducking a little, though he's nowhere near tall enough to hit the top of the door.

"Jack Selby." Archer strides across the room, takes the man's dusty hand in his. "You're just in time. This is Rosamund Lacey. Rosamund, Jack is the one who tracked Mortimer down."

"I owe you a debt of gratitude, Mr. Selby," I smile. "And I am pleased to meet you. Archer speaks very highly of your abilities."

He pulls his gloves off, takes my hand very gently. "My pleasure."

"Will you have a seat?" Archer offers. "There's food— you look like you've been living off jerky."

"Governor, I have news," he says, almost in protest.

Archer holds up a hand. "It can wait long enough for you to eat something."

Selby sits down quietly on the edge of the third chair.

Archer produces plates and a silver service from some other room, and I cut the pie, giving Selby a generous slice.

"Coffee?"

"Please." He dares something like a smile and I pour it out black into a tin cup. I serve Archer, then myself. By the time I sit down to take a bite, I see Selby's pie is half gone —and he's been holding back.

Archer was right. This man's been living on jerky...or less.

Selby wipes his mouth delicately, glances at me, and then proceeds. "Mortimer has let the Abernathys in."

I don't know who these Abernathys are, but Archer goes suddenly still. "I don't want to doubt you, but are you sure?"

"I'm sure."

"When?"

"I cut their sign three days ago. It was a lot of shod horse. So I followed it up and sure enough they had a camp up the Rio Jefe."

"How many of them?"

"Dunno. Maybe five, six hundred. That's not half of what could come if Mortimer allowed it."

"That many?"

"Well, if you think Mortimer's got a hand on well over a hundred men, when they're mustered, and the Abernathys have pull on just about every oath clan—"

"Oath clan?" I ask.

"They're bands of men, mostly renegades. Nothing like blood clans, just—outlaws, ma'am," supplies Selby.

"Ah."

"Did you happen to get any intelligence?" Archer pours himself more coffee.

"They're moving soon. Don't dare guess how soon, but —they're situated only a day and a half north of us."

He gets up and goes over to the map.

"With your permission—"

Archer motions for him to go on.

Selby picks up a pencil and begins to trace. He moves between hills and valleys, rivers and the scattered $x$ marks.

He's made a trail, from water hole to ranch to settlement, spreading like a hand's grasp across a third of the map.

He sets down the pencil.

"It's just a guess. It's been five years since I rode with Abernathy, but I think it's a good one."

Archer whistles slowly, comes over and studies the new marks.

"It's as good a line to ride as any," he says, after a minute. "I'll have to call a town meeting. Drag in as many cattlemen as I can, too. Thanks, Jack."

Selby just nods.

"Now go put yourself up someplace comfortable, you hear? I'm paying you for this information and I won't take no."

The two of them walk out, talking. I see Archer dig a few coins out and Selby take them.

They stand outside by the hitching rail for some time longer, talking quietly.

At last Selby mounts up and rides away, and Archer

comes back in. He looks tired, but when he glances over and sees me, his weary face lightens.

"I cannot tell you how much good it does me to see you here."

I take his hand, pull him into the chair beside mine. "Is it as bad as he says it is?"

He nods, his eyes troubled. "He's not a man prone to exaggeration."

"Who is Abernathy?"

"Leader of an oath clan—a bad fellow. Never thought I'd see the day that Mortimer would let him in."

"Let him in?"

"They're worse enemies of one other than either has ever been with us."

"And yet they're banding together?"

"Selby wouldn't lie about it. And Mortimer did threaten us with ruin last time we had the pleasure of speaking." His mouth gives a wry twist.

"Can we do something about it? Call for army support?"

"Too far away. Out here, we might as well be a different continent for as much help as we get. But we'll find a way."

He's worried. I reach up, smooth back his hair. I can see the beginnings of gray in it.

"You will. And you will take care of yourself in the meantime. I just got you back."

He smiles, and for a moment, sets aside the care in his face.

"Yes, ma'am."

# 30

## SELBY

Clouds cover the sun this morning. The wind is fretful. It's early yet, pale and sickly-horizoned. Reddish. Today is the sort of day when unpredictable storms sweep in, or the sheep stray far, or you stumble across *darani* tracks miles from where they ought to be.

The air itself is unsettled.

I lean my hand on the railing of Carson's balcony and take in the sight around me. There's comfort in being able to see the lay of the land around you. It is an old habit for me; I can think better up high.

There's a knock, and I go back in, unlatching the door of my room. It's Kate, the girl who minds the place.

"Coffee?" She's balancing a tray with a pot of coffee and a tin mug on it.

"Thank you. Let me get that." I reach out and take it.

"Anything else?"

"No, thank you. This is perfect."

She gives me a nod.

I bolt the door again and set the tray on the table. The noises of the waking town outside are sparse. I pour out a mugful, take my time. This Kate, she makes a fine, strong brew without the bitter dust of trail coffee. She makes it like a man.

I take the mug outside, cradle the scalding hot mug in my hands. They are so calloused now that heat doesn't bother them. The first sip of coffee is burning hot, strong. It soothes my weary head, helps me forget that I hardly slept, again.

A lick of dust rises on the flats northeast of town. I know, even from here, that it's a rider.

Peter runs in from the street, the coltish boy with the thick dark hair and no folks. Carson's place seems to collect strays. Kate's voice floats up from below, outlining the chores for the day, and I close my eyes, listening to it as if it were music.

Some men never learn, never come to appreciate the importance of normalcy. I savor it. I crave it.

I, who never will have it.

A minute later, I hear the scratch of Peter's broom on the porch below me. He thrusts his head sideways out from under the porch roof and waves, grinning.

"Morning, Mr. Selby!"

I give him a nod and he goes back to work.

"Peter," I say softly, and he needs nothing more. His head snaps up, he looks up at me expectantly.

His eager face, so hopeful and cheerful, strikes a strange, hard pain in my chest.

"Come on up here when your chores are done. I have a question for you."

"I will!"

He returns to his work—the scratch of the broom is faster than it was before.

Maria Pike stands in her upstairs window as she does every morning I've been here, her hair perfect, her neck shrouded in the high collar of her black dress. Her arms are folded as she gazes up and down the street.

Her eyes come to rest on me. She looks long, then retreats from the window.

I can feel her judgment from across the street, her distaste at the sight of me.

A shout or two rises from the street. The rider is coming in. He gallops up to the saloon, throws his long leg over the horse's back, and drops easily to the ground.

It's a well-bred horse, Eastern stock. The man is dusty, but his clothing is of good make.

"Harrison Terhune, what brings you here?" I can't see who the speaker is.

"Fortune!" he laughs. "No, it's business as usual. I was met by a rider halfway, he says there's trouble anyway. I'll want a room, Kate!"

I hear him stride in downstairs.

Peter is standing next to the hitching post, his broom loose in one hand. He goes over to the sweaty horse and unwraps the reins, letting it drink, then ties it back up with a pat to its nose.

That boy, he notices things.

IT'S LESS than an hour later when Peter comes up to my room. He stands, trying not to fidget, his hands folded, eyeing my coffee.

"Do you want some coffee?"

He nods.

I pour him out a cup, hold it out. It isn't as warm as it was an hour ago, but it's not cold yet.

He sips it hesitantly.

"Do you want to earn a little money? Do a job for me?"

He nods again, emphatically.

"Here." I hold out a silver coin. "Take this. You let me know if you see any men in town with a gun like this."

I hold out my rifle, let him study it carefully.

"Exactly like it?" he asks.

"Nearly. It'll have this gold mark on the stock, might be a little dirty. Might have some knife cuts in the wood, like this."

I cut a couple notches in the side of the already-worn table to show him.

He's nodding.

"I'll pay you the same if you see any men of Mortimer's."

"All right."

"One more thing. Have you ever seen an oath clan?"

"Maybe one or two." He shrugs.

"If you recognize any bad men, you tell me straight away, hm?"

"Deal." He thrusts out his brown hand.

I take it. If there's one thing I've learned in my years of living, good and bad, it's that sometimes the best ally in the world to have is a child.

I'M BENT OVER ONE OF THE SEVENTY-THREE LATE dropped calves of the season when I see a man riding in, and I know deep down that it's more trouble.

As to whether it's Archer or Mortimer who's neck-deep in it this time, I could flip a coin.

I grunt and turn back to my work. Hang trouble. Let it get here when it does.

"Hurry up with that iron!" I call to the saddle bum who is staring at the rider, his branding iron hovering over the ground forgotten.

He comes on over, and I hold my breath as the searing smoke comes my way and the calf under me kicks.

"Easy now." I thump his fuzzy, sweat-curled hide and let him up. He scrambles off toward the far side of the pen and the men rope another.

Again, they stop to glance out at the rider.

"Bring the next one!" I call, waving them in. "Let's keep it rolling!"

The next one is roped and I throw it, holding it down.

"Easy, easy," I soothe, and a few seconds later, the branding is over.

Hooves scrape against hard ground as the rider pulls up right beside the corral.

"Is there a Jesse Thatcher here?" asks the man, loud and clear.

"Go on without me," I tell the boys and hobble over to the fence. My back isn't as keen on bending over as it was when I was a stripling.

"Mr. Thatcher." The fellow is youngish, probably someone's clerk or stablehand. "I have a message for you."

"From whom?"

"The governor himself."

The governor himself. I try not to chuckle. "Let's have it."

"He says they're calling a town meeting and they want as many cattlemen as they can get in for it."

I think this over, shove my hat back to scratch my head.

Archer knows how long I've been away from this ranch. He'd only call me if he needed my help powerful bad.

I still can't help but be a little annoyed.

"Tell him I'll be there."

He nods, but he doesn't go away.

"Something else you need?" I just want to get back to riding fence and hauling hay and branding calves. The ranch is the life I was meant for, not these struggles of life and death and the twisted ambition of mankind. But they dog my poor cousin at every step, and somehow I always manage to get caught in the crossfire.

"He said to warn you the town's going to have a question to ask you."

"Can it wait?" I squint up at him.

The fellow shakes his head. "He said to get down to Glory Mesa soon as you can."

Of course. I take my hat off, beat it against my leg, wipe the sweat from my brow.

"I'll ride in as soon as the calves are done." I turn around and stride away. "Tell them not to get their hopes up."

"What's that?"

"Tell them not to get their hopes up!"


I KNOW what they're going to ask. I could have given that green stablehand my answer on the spot, but of course, we're a real town now and they couldn't be bothered to send a committee to me, so I have to leave my cattle and go meet the committee only to tell them what would have been said easy enough out in the open air: No.

I push the brim of my hat up and wipe my forehead with my neckerchief. The town is making a fine recovery. The burned buildings are mostly repaired, the streets are just as busy as—if not more than—when I was in last, and I swear there are womenfolk who weren't here before. It's positively civilized.

I shudder.

Get me out of here.

I stop in front of the governor's office and contemplate the territory flag hanging sadly from its pole. Most of the windows are still boarded up. You'd think the governor's office would take some sort of priority, but what do I know? I'm just a cattle rancher.

I tie my horse at the post outside and step onto the porch, peering in the one window that's intact. He's in.

I open the door without knocking, and he looks up from a letter, unsurprised. "I heard you coming."

"Figured."

"How was the ride in?"

"Fine. Why?"

He sets the letter aside and slices another envelope with his letter opener. "Well, you're not going to believe this, but Mortimer's buried the hatchet with Abernathy. And guess what over?"

Blast and bullets.

"Us?" I watch my dreams of having ornery cows as my sole concern tumble to the ground.

"Us." He throws the envelope down on the desk.

"So that's what the town's calling the meeting for? And they're going to ask me to put on a tin star and face Mortimer and Abernathy? I sort of fancied staying alive."

Archer chuckles deep in his throat. "I called the meeting. I'm calling in the cattlemen. Sent a message to the railroad and the mining syndicates. They won't have time to get here before we make our move, but at least this way they won't be hit blind."

I whistle long. "But the town's still going to ask me to put on the tin."

"Yep. I tried to tell them, but they wouldn't listen."

"Is there anyone else?"

"Harrison Terhune's been mentioned. I told them he was too far out, has too many interests of his own, but he carries a lot of clout, and when you're facing the likes of Mortimer and Abernathy, that's what folks want."

"They need to ask Raymond Lacey."

"I don't dare." Archer runs his hand over his face. "He's a lone wolf and he's new. The townspeople—the territory —want someone they know and trust."

"I dunno." I turn my hat slowly in my hands. "We might not have much choice soon."

For a long while there's no sound but his letter opener ripping open envelopes, his hands unfolding letters and then refolding them and putting them back.

He's a good man, Archer is. I don't know many men of his experience who'd risk their necks for a desk job.

His eyes look tired.

"You should have an assistant. Get a kid who wants experience as a clerk. You shouldn't have to handle every-thing on your own."

"I suppose that day will come."

I groan and get up. "Think about hurrying that day along."

"Meeting's at six. I'll see you there." He spares me a glance before returning to his letter.

"See ya."

I step outside, glance up the street as I untie my horse.

There's a pair of red roans riding in, ponying one with an empty saddle—that'd be Jem and Alan Swift, coming to collect their brother, maybe weigh in on the meeting.

Those Swifts are sharp ones.

Food and coffee sound mighty nice right now, but you'd have to drag me dead into Maria's restaurant.

I sigh and head for Carson's.

THE COMMITTEE MEETS inside Levine's accommodating survey office (since the courthouse apparently still lacks windows and a couple doors), and it is mostly made up of the businessmen of the town: Garth Levine, the broad-shouldered surveyor; Mr. Trasker of the general store; a half-dozen other faces you could tack a trade to. Then there's Jem Swift, his foot up over one knee, and Alan sitting quietly beside with his hat hanging from his long fingers.

Max hasn't got a vote yet. He stands in the back next to Raymond Lacey and—surprisingly—Jack Selby. I'd give a silver dollar to know what Archer said to keep him here in town.

Next to me is Harrison Terhune, smelling of soap and whiskey. On his other side sits Maria Pike, serene and dignified in black.

I sit on the edge of my seat in the front row and turn my hat round and round in my hands, fidgeting through the opening talk. I never have been good at sitting and listening.

My mother learned me to read and write and add, but

there was one winter a traveling schoolteacher came near the settlement where we lived, and I got sent to school. I couldn't concentrate a lick when I was stuck inside at a bench.

"Jack Selby has brought news that Abernathy is back in the territory, under Mortimer's direction." Garth Levine's voice cuts through to me. He's a tall, broad-shouldered fellow with dark eyes, and his face puts me in mind of craggy rock. "Anyone who's been in the territory long enough remembers the bloody days when Abernathy was—"

"Jack Selby?" One of the townsmen stands up. "Jack Selby was one of them! Why are we trusting his word?"

Across the room, Archer stirs slightly.

"Who else has seen Abernathy, or is this just another trick?" shouts another man.

"What is Jack Selby doing in this meeting?"

A quick mutter runs through the room. Carson opens his mouth to speak, but even he seems to have lost his words.

"Jack Selby is here because I asked him!" Archer raises his voice to a shout, not even unfolding his arms. "You have a problem with that, you bring it to me."

The place falls silent again.

Maria is fanning herself briskly, aloof from the hubbub.

"The fact of the matter is," Levine continues, "that Abernathy's clan is back in the territory. It'll be a matter of days, maybe less, before they move on our ranches, home-steads, and towns. That's the plain truth."

"Jesse Thatcher." Levine calls out.

I stand up at the call of my name, turn a little to give the men behind me a nod.

"This committee officially requests and calls you to the duty of marshal for this territory."

Poor fools, I've turned them down twice already and they're counting on me changing my mind the third time. I clear my throat, toy with my hat in my hands.

"Gentlemen, I'm mighty honored that you'd ask me. Abernathy turning up again makes my answer all the harder, but I can't accept this post. My ranch needs me, and a marshal has to be able to stand ready at any hour. I can't in good conscience swear an oath to that."

I sit back down and Terhune claps me on the shoulder. A murmur rises from the committee, but no one stands up to argue back, and I'm powerful relieved.

Levine calls again. "Harrison Terhune?"

Terhune stands, taller than usual in his boots. He's younger than he looks, but he has the weather-worn face of a man who has lived.

"This committee officially requests and calls you to the duty of marshal for this territory."

Terhune clears his throat and proceeds. "Gentlemen— lady." He spares a warm glance in Maria's direction. "It is with hesitance that I consider this appointment, for much the same reason as my good friend, Jesse Thatcher. I have a ranch to run, and while some upstanding man of trade must take up the badge for this territory, it's a heavy responsibility to do both. However, I remember the days when Abernathy came west."

Terhune pauses, shakes his head. "He was a bloody

terror. His raiding opened the territory to other oath clans such as the Flat Rock and the Tavachi, and I know I am not alone when I say I was relieved to see those bandits and raiders driven out for good. In the interest of seeing those days return, I do accept this territory's appointment, should the votes carry in my favor."

He gives a short nod of acknowledgment and sits back down.

He's sweating. We ranchers don't much like being the center of attention. At least, we real ranchers. Back East, I hear, some of them smoke all day and couldn't stick a bronc for a second.

"We'll take a vote," announces Levine. "All in favor?"

Ayes move across the room. Half the voters, maybe— it's hard to tell.

Maria leans forward gently to look around.

"Those against."

A handful of voices—more than I expected from a town and a territory in hot water and desperate for a marshal. Jem and Alan both have their hands up, against. Maybe they think, as I do, that Terhune's ranch is too far out for him to do the job well.

Again Maria leans forward, taking note. I reckon she's had to keep her wits about her in this town, being a businesswoman and alone.

Not that she hasn't tried to mend the alone part.

"For, twelve. Against, fourteen. Appointment has failed." Levine's voice is disappointed.

Archer pushes himself off the wall and walks out.

People start to leave. Terhune stands up quietly and

heads straight for the door, shaking hands and saying good-byes all the way out.

Garth Levine catches me as I get up. "Jesse, would you reconsider?"

I shake my head. "There's better men for this job. Raymond Lacey, for one. You should ask him."

"He's new in town."

"Doesn't matter. You wouldn't regret it."

"Well, we did ask Jem Swift before you, and—"

"He turned you down, didn't he? His ranch is too far from town."

"You are the governor's cousin. That looks good, and you're a good manager. Your ranch is in fine shape."

"And I want to keep it that way. Trust me, I'm not the man you want."

"Well, thank you for coming in." Levine offers his hand. "Safe travels."

I take his hand, then head for the door, shoving my hat back on my head.

Call me a fool, but I think they're making a mistake, overlooking Raymond Lacey.

# 32

## ROSAMUND

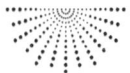

"I<small>F YOU ASK ME, WE NEED ABOUT A DOZEN MARSHALS.</small> One won't do, no matter who it is." Kate lifts her head and turns it, whipping her loose hair over her shoulder.

I stand on the other side of the counter, studying the dim bar and the girl behind it.

She's small, with fair hair tending toward red, and she moves quickly. Work is her aim, not conversation, and every so often she reaches up to tuck her hair back out of the way.

I tuck my shawl more tightly around my folded arms. "It seems strange to me that the town would call two men, have one decline and the other fail to be voted in. Doesn't that seem—odd?"

Kate glances up with a smile. "I'm still trying to figure this town out. I've only known two lawmen here: Archer Scott and old Nelson, who died early last year." She throws a towel over her shoulder, takes down a couple tin cups and sets them on the counter. "It is a pity, though. We need more men around here, not fewer."

"What about their choices? What do you think of those men?"

"Jesse and Terhune?"

I nod.

"Jesse's a good man. Hates town, I think."

"Why?"

"Some folk were just never meant to be penned in. Archer prefers the ranch, as Jesse does, but Jesse'd die in a town." She laughs humorlessly. "And Terhune, I don't know. He's rich and not around much."

"It was good of him to agree to it, then," I say. "Most rich people I know aren't quick to run into danger."

Kate shrugs.

A wagon passes slowly outside and a horseman rides by. I look out; Raymond rode out a couple days ago to scout some promising land despite the risks and I have been on edge since.

Kate's voice cuts in, matter-of-fact.

"Begging your pardon, you can see whoever you want, but I'll just have you know—I'm not really the sort of person people seek out for acquaintance. And you the governor's wife-to-be and all."

"Archer thinks well of you."

"Archer thinks well of most folk. He doesn't look at appearances, but most folks can't figure out where I belong and it bothers them. The ladyfolk don't want my acquaintance, and the men—most of them don't put me in the category of lady."

"Well, that's ridiculous."

"I didn't come up with it." She gives a wry smile. "Comes with the dust of this town."

"Maria seems to have avoided the dust," I say.

"I have other problems with Maria." Kate lifts her chin as if daring me to contradict her.

"She came to see me the other day."

"With a wash-bucket load of gossip about Archer?" Kate gives a dismissive wave. "Don't mind her. She's jealous. I know for a fact she locked him in her parlor once. Said she couldn't find the key. Carson had to go over there and break open the door, since hers is on the second level. Caused a bit of a scandal, not that the poor man could have helped it."

So that's it. Jealous.

"Why does she want him? Was it before his appointment to governor?"

"Oh sure, she's had her eye on him—she's a widow out here, life's not easy. But it got worse after his name was thrown into the ring for the governorship." She looks at me like she wants to say more, but decides against it.

"Well, it won't be a problem once I marry him."

Kate smiles as if she hopes I'm right.

"Do you have someone?" I ask.

"Oh, no." Kate throws down her towel and leans her hands on the bar. "I am a war orphan. My father was a captain for the Fifth Mounted Dragoons. Killed at Square's Run. My mother was good and healthy until the hour she died. Said she had a headache, laid down and never woke up."

EMILY HAYSE

"I am sorry."

Kate gives a small huff of laughter, pushes her messy, curling hair out of her face. "It's not as if you had anything to do with it. No—I belong out here, however unhappy I am working with Carson."

"You're unhappy?"

"Carson is bull-headed. Don't misunderstand me, if I couldn't stand it, I would go to the livery stable in a heartbeat. It is just that he is so close-minded about everything. There's only one way to wash a dish, one way to talk to the customers, one job for a girl like me. He's a good shot, I'll give him that. Masterful with a horse, though heavy-handed on the bit."

"Why do you belong out here?" I find Kate herself a far more interesting subject than Carson.

"Have you seen the land?" Kate laughs, and I see at once both a girl in love and a woman who cherishes something so deeply she doesn't have words for it. "The way the sun sets past those rocks, the way the *isarks* are first winged things of gold in its light and then black as cast iron when it slips past the horizon; the way those pines tower over rivers running clear as glass. It's in the air, it's in the black desert storms, it's in the Auki song that old Trevain sings every sunrise. Offer me one more day here or a thousand anywhere else, and I'd choose here in a heartbeat."

"But you have no family?" I press.

She smiles. "I don't need any."

And she believes it. Down to the bottom of her soul, she means it.

"If you don't intend to stay with Carson, what do you hope to do out here?"

She shrugs and picks her towel back up. That love-gleam is still in her eyes. "See the territory a bit, I guess."

She shines the glass in her hand with fresh vigor.

As I step outside Carson's, the heat is stifling. I stand on the edge of the street, looking up and down it, but there's nothing but the normal bustle of a town. A few wagons, riders walking their horses. A conversation outside the survey office.

"Hello, Miss Lacey!" The boy, Peter runs past me, up the steps and into the saloon. It hardly seems like the place for a child and a woman, but after all, this isn't the East.

I like Kate. She suits this place, and I think she and I will do well here.

I glance around to make sure I won't be run down when I step into the street, and I see a familiar figure riding in.

I've always loved how Raymond rides. His years in the cavalry show—he has a commanding seat and dignified carriage. Whenever he rode into town back East, I was proud to be his sister.

With such a presence, I wonder why he never married.

He draws rein beside me, bringing his horse up down-wind of me to spare me his dust.

"Afternoon, young lady," he greets, touching the brim of his hat. "Do you need assistance crossing this busy road?"

"Stop it, you cavalier."

He chuckles and swings down.

I reach for him and he shies back. "I'm dusty," he warns.

"I don't care."

He puts his arms around my shoulders and squeezes me gently. "How's my Rose today?"

"Very well, now that I see you back safe. What do you mean by riding off to look at claims when there are so many outlaws nearby?"

"Well, this might be my only chance in a while. I can't bunk with cowpunchers for the rest of my life."

I suppose not. Here I am starting my own life, with a home waiting for me, and he has to find his own way to put down roots.

"What did you think of the land?"

"I liked it."

"Enough to buy?" I look up at him, shading my eyes to see his face.

"Maybe."

"I have to see it, you know, if you are going to get it."

"If I file a claim, I'll take you out there myself." He clucks to his horse and we head up the street at a leisurely pace.

"Where are you headed?" I reach out and scratch the horse's neck. I don't know where he got this one; as far as I know, Mortimer still has his good ex-army mount.

"Take care of this old mustang and bathe, then I'm going to rustle up some grub, as they say."

"Come to my house for dinner, please." I take his arm and tilt my head up toward his. "Archer will be there, and I'm going to make a good spread."

He shoves his hat back and combs his hair flat with his fingers. "Well, I've never been able to turn down your cooking." He looks down at me and his eyes twinkle.

"I'm going in here." I let go of his arm in front of the mercantile.

"Reckon I'll see you in a couple hours then." He pulls the brim of his hat gently and walks on.

"GOOD MORNING, MISS LACEY!" Trasker looks up from his counter with a pleasant smile, a pencil behind his ear and an account book spread out in front of him. "Can I help you with anything?"

I look around the mercantile slowly.

"I'd like some baking powder, some flour, some sugar. And lemons, if you have them?"

"I have a few." He shuts his book and moves down the counter. "Maria Pike usually requires most of the lemons that make it out to Glory Mesa, but I keep a couple crates aside when I get them in from Santos Flores. These may be the last of them for a while."

I follow him to the back of the store. It's full of sacks and crates and smells of spices and fresh goods—fresh milled wheat flour, sweet butter, coffee.

"How many?"

"Four."

He reaches into the crate, pulls out a few, holds them out for inspection.

"They're quite decent," he says, with a quick smile.

"Look them over, choose them yourself. How much flour and sugar?"

"Five pounds each."

"Very good."

He hums to himself as he goes to the flour barrel and I examine the lemons carefully, selecting four of the best.

I set them on the counter beside the measured out goods.

"Anything else I can get you, ma'am?"

"A pound of butter...I nearly forgot."

"Right here." He heads down the counter and brings back a paper-wrapped package. "Freshly churned this morning."

"Are you baking?" Maria materializes at my shoulder as if from nowhere. "Silly of me, of course you are."

She answered her own question. I merely smile by way of greeting.

"Mrs. Pike," greets Trasker. "I have your order in the back. Have Danny fetch it around for you."

"Very good." She passes me with a serene rustle of silk.

"Will that be all?" Trasker tries me again over his spectacles.

"Yes, I think so."

"On the governor's tab, I assume." He gives a small laugh. "I'm still getting used to calling him the governor. Couldn't have picked a better man."

The bell rings as Max Swift walks in the doorway.

"The usual," he says, quietly, coming up to the counter. "Miss Lacey." He tips the brim of his hat.

Up close, he looks worn. He's vastly improved from the last time I saw him, but the illness took an undoubted toll.

Mr. Trasker produces a paper bag of horehound and peppermints and hands it over.

"I didn't know you were still in town," I say, as Max pockets them.

He scratches the side of his nose, shifts his scuffed boots. "There's business to do here. We'll probably leave today." He gestures to my things. "Do you want a hand?"

"Only if it's no trouble. It's not far to my house. I was going to carry them myself."

"Well, there's no need for that. I've got all the time in the world." He reaches for the basket.

"Max!" Maria appears from the back, holds out her hand in greeting. "You are looking well, if I may say so."

"Ma'am." He touches the brim of his hat. Seeing she does not withdraw her hand, he takes it.

"I am glad to see you safe and well. Is it something in the Swift breeding, or is Mortimer losing his touch?" she laughs.

"I don't rightly know, ma'am."

"Either way, you are a lucky young man."

"Thanks." He smiles, briefly, and she's looking him over as if seeing him with fresh eyes.

"When did you grow up?" she asks sweetly, and her tone strikes me oddly.

He's looking at her warily. "Ma'am?"

"You're quite a handsome man. I am surprised you have no sweethearts."

He laughs, uncertain. "Well, there ain't really—aren't—

any girls up Rio Jefe way. And I haven't been to see the Auki in a while. So I guess it's all business right now."

His ears are red.

"If you'll excuse me, ma'am." He beats a hasty retreat.

I watch Maria's eyes follow him out the door. I know what it looks like when a woman wants a man interested in her, and this was not quite the same. But whatever it was, it made me uncomfortable. "You shouldn't torment him so."

"He's old enough to take it," Maria says smoothly as she steps up to the counter.

I hurry after Max.

He's waiting in the street with my basket. As I fall in step beside him, he starts in the direction of my house.

"You know where I live?"

"Sure." He switches the basket around to offer me his arm. "I helped Archer build it."

"Really?"

"I was coming up from the Auki Nation and my horse needed shoes, so I stuck around for a day to help. Turned into three more days. The food was too good." He gives a slight smile.

"Whose food?"

"Mrs. Pike's." The name comes out in a laugh. "I think she had a hope then that the house would be for her."

Twice in one morning.

"Sorry, maybe that wasn't right of me to say." He ducks a little as he mounts the porch steps. I dig out the key, glad to not have to answer that.

I do not like how clear it is to everyone that this

woman wanted Archer. And now to have her around so very often.

We go inside and Max sets the groceries on the table, looking briefly around the house.

"It's shaped up quite nicely," he declares.

"It will be better when my things come. It's sadly underfurnished."

He shrugs.

"Well, thank you," I say as he starts to shift toward the door.

"Not at all."

He tips his hat, all gallant for a fellow barely out of boyhood. He strides out, stops, ducking a little in the doorway. "Is it true you shot an *isark*?"

I nod.

His grin is instant. "I'll be. It was going to be the first time I ever called Alan a liar."

He closes the door after him.


RAYMOND WIPES his mouth with a sigh and pushes his chair back. "That was good food, Rose."

I smile. He'd probably say it if I had made something terrible, but there's a satisfaction in the lines of his shoulders that spells contentment.

Besides, it's been years since I've ruined a meal.

Archer is quiet. He usually is, of course, but this is a different sort of quietness. The cares of the office came back with him today, of all days. Or perhaps I haven't been around enough to notice.

I wish I could take care of him better.

As soon as my things come, we can be married, and he will wake up here, to coffee and a hot breakfast and a home that is his own.

He breaks the silence to address my brother. "Raymond, you ever run across Abernathy?"

"Fought him twice in the war. Man's a bulldog."

Archer smiles. It's wry, but bright. "Yep. That's him. Mortimer hated him."

"Did you?" Raymond's eyes are narrowed, casually studying Archer.

"Hate's a strong word. But he sure did nothing to endear himself."

Raymond chuckles low, under his breath.

I get up to fetch the pound cake from the sideboard. "What are you going to do about a marshal?"

"Find a new one as fast as I can. I'm disappointed we had no takers at the meeting, but honestly, neither of them are in the best position to accept."

I cut a piece for each of us, serve them onto plates. "Are there any other marshals in the territory?"

"One, a fellow named Baker. But he's more of a sheriff. I haven't seen him in over a year. Hope he's still with us."

Raymond takes one bite of his cake and the slice is half gone. "Don't seem to be many men that fit the bill."

Archer leans back in his chair. "I wish you'd consider it."

"It should be a man who knows the territory," Raymond says slowly.

Archer accepts the statement in silence.

I stand up, check the coffee pot. There's a little left. "More coffee?"

The hard report of a gun silences any answer as the front window shatters. One of the cups flies up off the table with a twang. Archer's arm pulls me to the ground. Raymond kicks the table over, shoves it up between us and the broken window.

Two more shots crash in, making the table shudder. Something glass shatters. Another shot, but I don't hear it hit.

Silence.

"Anyone hurt?" Raymond's gun is out and he's raising himself cautiously.

Archer's arm slides off my shoulders. "Rosamund?"

I shake my head.

Archer checks himself. There's a cut on his arm from the glass.

A speck of blood stains the side of Raymond's long face. "Stay down," he says, his eyes on the window. "Both of you."

He walks toward the door slowly, crouched low, his cocked pistol in his hand.

My heart hammers in my ears. Archer starts to rise too, but I pull him down. Brave fool, he's the one they're trying to shoot.

I'm braced, waiting for another gunshot. The glass crunches under Raymond's boots.

I hear a rush of footsteps, running, the door being shoved open.

Jesse is the first one through, panting, his gun out. He stops short at the sight of Raymond.

"Any of you hurt?" he demands.

"No." Archer stands, helps me to my feet. Coffee and glass and crumbs from the remainder of my beautiful, light pound cake are all over the skirt of my dress.

"What happened?" Garth Levine shoulders his way in.

My porch and doorway are filling with people; I step back as the world goes muted and a little soft. There's a cut on my hand—I feel it keenly.

Everything is a mess. It will take time to clean this all, and on top of it, almost every dish that was on the table is broken.

I pick up the coffee pot, return it to the range, collect the two surviving plates.

"All right," Raymond raises his voice. "Out of here! Nobody's killed." The flow of people begins to reverse. Jesse stays.

"See anything?" Raymond lowers his voice to talk to him.

"Nothing. I figure whoever did it was careful enough to do it through an upstairs window."

"Reckon so." Raymond pulls out his knife and begins to dig a bullet out of one of the floorboards.

Archer comes to me and puts an arm around my shoulders.

"You all right?" Thatcher tips his hat toward us and then whips it off, remembering he's in my house.

"Yes. It was close, is all." Archer gives a short laugh. His grip tightens slightly. "I reckon Mortimer has his feet under him. Or maybe Abernathy."

"Abernathy," says Raymond, standing up. "Look."

He holds out the bullet. I cannot tell it from another, but Thatcher snatches it up and turns it this way and that.

"How do you know?" I ask.

"It's from a rifle that was standard issue in the war—for the other side. Long range, very accurate. Selby still carries one, and Abernathy and his boys would too."

An uncomfortable silence falls.

A movement catches my eye. Peter stands in the doorway, fidgeting.

Archer notices him too. "Yes, Peter, what is it?"

"They're trying to hang Mr. Selby up at the saloon. Kate told me to run and tell you."

Archer blanches.

"But he didn't do it," continues Peter. "He paid me to watch out for suspicious characters."

"Thank you, Peter." Archer is already snatching his hat from the rack beside the door. I gather my skirts and run after him.

The crowd outside the saloon is growing. There are shouts, words I don't understand and others I wish I didn't.

A sick feeling begins in the pit of my stomach.

Kate stands outside by the porch, her eyes hard and burning, her arms folded.

"I got them, Kate!" Peter calls, running up to her. Then he squeezes up the steps and disappears past the men who fill the doorway, through a gap only a cat or a boy would be able to find.

"They just marched right in, shoved us all out as if—as if they were the law." Kate's voice shakes just a little, but I don't think it's from fear.

Raymond and Jesse catch up; Raymond has a rifle.

"Can I have that?" Archer holds out a hand and Raymond hands over the gun.

"Enough! Let me through!" Archer raises his voice and steps up onto the porch.

The shouts abate a little and the men back up, parting as Archer strides through them, carrying the rifle.

I look around, then gather my skirt and start in after him. This town is my home now too, and anywhere Archer goes, I'll go.

The men press close around us, smelling of sweat. "What is this about?" asks Archer, a little more quietly, as the shouts are dying down.

Alan Swift stands on the steps to the rooms upstairs, his face set like iron, a rifle cradled in his arms.

One of the men closest to the stairs starts forward again, a face I do not recognize. "Glory Mesa's got no place for the likes of Jack Selby. I say it was him fired those shots!"

"And I say there'll be no hangings today," answers Alan, shifting the rifle.

I am learning quickly—men may take chances when facing down a pistol, but even a fool respects a rifle.

Archer shoulders past the men in front and mounts the steps to stand beside Alan. "Anyone who touches Jack Selby, they answer to me."

I see Selby himself at the top of the stairs in his shirt-sleeves and suspenders, arms folded. One sleeve is up, the other rolled down. Blood trickles from under his ear, drying partway down his neck.

He hasn't got a weapon.

"I paid Selby to stay here and watch for trouble," says Archer. He's bleeding too, from the cut on his arm. "Go home, men. Save your bullets. The time to use them'll come round soon enough."

There's muttering, and one man shakes a rope aloft in sullen defiance, but the crowd begins to dissipate. No one has the backbone to stand up to him.

Archer turns to Alan and holds out his hand. "Sure glad to see you. Hate to think what might've happened if you weren't in town today."

Alan sets his rifle against the railing and takes the hand. "Wasn't meant to be." He gives Selby a nod.

Selby dusts himself off, every inch of his tensed body slow, as if in the presence of a rattler. "Thanks," he says quietly.

"You have a lot yet to do, my friend," says Alan, thrusting out a hand. "My pleasure."

Selby hesitates a moment and then grips it.

Peter winds through the departing crowd like a fish swimming upstream. "Mr. Selby would never shoot at Miss Lacey."

"Peter, be quiet. You don't know what you're talking about," Kate snaps, shooing him off.

Peter jams the knuckles of one hand into the palm of the other and disappears around the corner into the back room.

"Alan!" Jem Swift troops in, Max at his heels. "I should have known you'd be in the middle of this. Out to put yourself in front of a lynching mob?"

Alan picks up his rifle with a small laugh. "And you'd have been with me, if you weren't so slow on the draw."

Max is looking around the room slowly. Thatcher and Raymond stand at the far end, just watching.

"Heading out?" asks Archer.

"Yep. We'll be off now." Jem's hand rests over the top of his holster. "A ranch doesn't take care of itself, and we've been away too much. If there's any mustering to be done, you know where to find us."

"I appreciate it." Archer thrusts his hand out and Jem's hand comes off the gun to shake.

"Miss Lacey." Alan pulls the brim of his hat and Max has the nerve to wink.

The Swifts troop out and the room goes quiet, save for the scrape of glass as Kate sweeps up something broken in the melee.

Selby lets his breath out, fixes his sleeves.

"Talk to me," says Archer, his voice lowered.

Selby glances up. "Someone rode out the back way while the town was gathering. Couldn't catch a shot or a good look."

"Did you see the horse?"

"A chestnut. But I didn't catch much more than a flank."

"Anyone else up here to see?"

Selby shakes his head. "I was alone. Harrison Terhune rode out this morning."

"Well, you watch yourself, hear?" Archer slaps Selby on the shoulder. "I can't afford to lose you."

"Understood." Selby's eyes go to me, of all people.

His eyes are a gentle blue; I never noticed it before. He doesn't look like the kind of man to ride with Abernathy.

His gaze moves on, back to Archer, but I have a strange feeling now.

It was like he was measuring me, trying to understand something he wasn't sure of yet.

## 33

## MORTIMER

"Why did they say this land is cursed?"

Up here, on the ridge of Old Grande, you can see for miles in every direction. The wind is slight, the air thin, the world spread at your feet.

Tora-Teth, standing beside me, folds his arms. "There was a great transgression made by a great man against his brother. It was said the land should lie barren; if it was disturbed, it would destroy the people in fire and ash."

"And yet people have been settling and trapping in these hills for years now."

"Perhaps the reckoning is yet to come."

"Do you believe the curse, Tora-Teth?" I have never asked him, after all these years.

He gives a sharp grin. "I ride in the face of curses. Let them catch up to me if they can."

"Well, curse or no, I aim to break this land. It'll heed the bit and spur, one way or another."

Tora-Teth doesn't answer. He's looking out at the dry land below us. The *isark* claw against his throat moves as he swallows.

The air is tight, holding its breath. It is hot and dry up here.

"Shall we proceed?" I ask.

Tora-Teth nods. "This is an old custom—a way to determine whether a man will meet with success. We rarely seek this testing, save in tasks of great importance." He looks at me with eyes that are closed, unreadable. "But this task, it is worthy."

"How will I know?"

"If your hand protects the hollow from the water, your strength is enough. If the hollow has even a drop of water, you will fail in your quest. It is an old test, and you must spend all your water, save none for the return journey."

I look out at the dry land. A man could make it to water from this mountain if he met with no accident. But lose a horse, injure oneself—it would be death.

"Rain too is a sign of blessing," says Tora-Teth. "Water for the man's journey down the dry hills."

I shove my hat back on my head, smile.

*Rain.* I search the blinding sky above, the horizon, for any sign of inclement weather. A small knot of clouds hovers over the shoulder of one of the far peaks. Mountain storms gather fast—it could be rain.

Tora-Teth kneels down on the rock, brushes the dust away until the rock is bare and clean. There's a small hollow there, a crack in the rock carved back to make a tiny basin.

I kneel beside him, press my hand over it.

He runs his hand over mine once, touching each finger, and then he opens his canteen, empties it. Then he empties mine.

The sound of the canteens falling empty against the rock is enough to strike fear into the stoutest heart, yet I feel nothing but courage right now.

I feel it in my heart, in the air, in the rightness of this moment, inside this year, inside my life.

This is my fate.

I leave my hand in place. The sun beats down, painfully hot despite the water on my hand, drying the darkened rock around me.

At last, Tora-Teth draws my hand away. He studies the rock closely, solemnly.

His voice is quiet. "You will succeed."

A cloud slides over the sun. I stand, drying my hand on my dusty pant leg. I smile up at that cloud. There are more, growing, coming.

The wind brushes past my cheek, sweet and cool.

Down the rocks a distance, I hear the horses snort. They can sense it too.

The clouds churn and darken. A smile spreads unbidden across my face. The wind whips through my hair, stings my face with sand. Thunder rolls over the peaks, and lightning streaks the dark with sharp bursts of light.

Then I hear it, the swift sweep of rain, watch as it races over the rocks toward me.

This storm—it is not hostile, driving me from this

place; rather it reaches to engulf me, stamp me as a part of this land.

To make me belong.

I tilt my head back and throw my arms wide. Every drop reaches to the very bottom of my soul.

I will succeed. I am the one.

"We must go," Tora-Teth shouts in my ear. "We don't want to be trapped up here."

I open my ears, smile to the rain as it streams down my face, plasters my coat to my back.

We won't be trapped up here. It is not my fate.

My black throws up his head, dancing, twisting his head away from the stinging wind. I shove my foot into the stirrup, drop into the saddle. He rears, a lift of nervous protest.

I turn his face to the east.

There is no stopping me now.

## 34

## ROSAMUND

ARCHER BOARDS UP THE BROKEN WINDOW FOR ME. IT'S an ugly sign of the risk he's taking, in front of me at every hour. But with the reminder comes a strange feeling of resolve.

Mortimer and those like him will see that they cannot drive us from here. They will learn what we are made of. In five years, they will be long gone and we will still be here.

Selby rode out after the shooting two days ago. Peter watches for his return—the sweet boy seems always to be around, appearing around corners, bringing me flowers he's found growing in the cracks of porch boards or behind the ruins of the old livery stable.

Once he brought me a snake, proud to declare that it was "not one of the poisonous ones."

I wonder at the sudden liking he's taken to me.

I'm out watering the peonies I have started in the

flower boxes out front when a horse comes trotting into town. Even from here, I recognize it as Selby's dun.

It stops in front of Archer's office.

My heart aches slightly as I watch Archer answer the door. I am tired of being separated from him, tired of this in-between time. I came out here with a purpose.

But my things were not so very far behind me. Any day they will arrive, and the waiting will be over.

Archer comes tearing out of his office, walks swiftly to the stage office across the street.

A whisper of disquiet starts in me as I go inside.

Three minutes later, the church bells begin to ring.


THE STREET IS loud and busy. Some men are preparing to ride, others riding out now. Archer comes to the house to tell me that Abernathy is on the move—some homesteads to the northeast are at risk, as well as the stage line. If a front is made at some of the stations, he thinks, the line might be maintained.

He is going.

"We don't have a marshal yet," he explains. "Until we do, I'm responsible."

I tell him he doesn't need to explain—I understand.

But I wish we had someone else.

Carson is talking to Kate outside the saloon, giving orders, pointing out loose boards, leaving instructions.

I expect Kate to be tired of shouldering more work once again, but when Carson turns away, the look on her face is light and free.

I head up the street and spy Raymond outside his lodgings, saddling his horse. On the ground beside him are saddlebags and his rifle.

"Raymond," I say, coming up behind him as he threads the cinch through.

"Yes?" He grunts as he pulls it tight.

I don't have the words yet. My heart is sinking, watching him. He sticks his fingers between the cinch and the horse's belly and gives it another tug before beginning the knot.

"Yes?" He turns to look over his shoulder and see if I'm still there.

We are in the street, but I reach up and pull his head down, planting a kiss on his dirty, scruffy cheek.

"Raymond, stay," I say, though I know it won't do any good. "Stay here, don't ride out."

He gives me a soft look, but he reaches for his rifle. "I'm able-bodied, darlin'."

"I can't lose you."

"If I can take care of myself for a week in an outlaw's den, don't you think I can do it against some rustlers?"

I press my fingers into his, but I know I am not going to convince him. "Just come back to me."

His mustache raises in a bit of a smile. "Sure. I've got to, you see—to keep an eye on that fellow there."

He gives a nod toward Archer, who is striding down the street, his dust-stained sleeves rolled up, his brows knit, issuing orders.

He sees us and his face lightens as he comes over. "Rosamund," he greets, raising his hat. "Raymond."

My brother grunts.

"You with us?" Archer asks, noting the gun in my brother's hand.

"Figured I'd come along."

"We could use you." Archer gives him a grateful look.

"Then you can count on me."

Jack Selby passes right by us, and Archer turns to catch him.

"Jack." Archer holds out his hand.

Selby hesitates a moment and then takes it. He's trail-worn, unshaven, and looks tired. But he's leading his horse out with the others.

"You're a good man, Selby."

Selby says nothing to this, and moves his horse on.

"I'm sorry to have to do this to you." Archer takes my hands in his. "I can't say how sorry I am."

The sorrow in his blue eyes is genuine. When Archer gives you his attention, you're the only thing that matters to him.

"Everything will be ready when you get back." I squeeze his hand. "I expected things like this when I came out here."

"Well—" He gives a small laugh. "Maybe I didn't. I'm sorry anyway. I'll be thinking about you the whole time."

"You had better not," I warn him with a smile. "You keep your mind on your work."

"If you say so." He gives me the barest wink.

We both speak lightly, but I know he hears the truth beneath my words.

I'm afraid I've just made it harder for him.

He starts to let my hands go, but I hold onto his. "You come back, promise?"

"I promise." He smiles sheepishly.

I have been in love with this man for years, but I am only just remembering the little things, like that smile, that I love about him.

"I'll be back as soon as I can." He mounts up easily, settles into the saddle as if it's his natural state. He moves his horse out, and I don't expect him to look back. But he does, and there's a raw longing in his face that I don't think he meant me to see.

He minds leaving just as much as I do, but he can't do less, and I love him for that.

Another minute and he's lost in the crowd, one back among a dozen others. I blow a quiet kiss to the milling space he occupied a moment before.

He will come back. I know he must.

"Sorry about your wedding," says Raymond slowly.

I take a deep breath, my resolve returning. "Everything considered, I'm lucky to be having one at all."

"Still." Raymond unwraps his reins from the hitching post. "I know you're disappointed."

It is sweet of him to notice. But he's had years of practice. He's the one person I can't really fool.

He backs his horse out, then puts his arm around my shoulders. We fall into comfortable step beside each other.

"Do you remember what Mama used to tell us?"

"Laceys keep their chins up, and they stick together. I don't want you talking like this, Raymond." My voice gets stern.

"Easy now. I'm not trying to say goodbye for good."

"But?"

"But you'll be marrying up soon. And—we're riding out there. I just felt like sayin' it."

I feel bad for flaring up at him. Of course he's feeling sentimental. When I marry, he'll be on his own. He's fine of course, but there's no denying it is different.

The riders are gathered on the edge of town, the horses eating up the men's nervous excitement like children with cake.

I should get out of the street.

"They said they could round up some of Gilchrist's hands if we waited another hour," Carson is saying, sawing the bit like fury.

"Don't bother." Archer gathers his reins and eases his own nervous horse down. "Thatcher's on the way. I figure he can spare an afternoon, two or three hands."

"Goodbye, Rose." Raymond gives me a squeeze and shoves his boot into the stirrup, swinging up into the saddle.

"Goodbye. Come back soon, you hear?"

His horse fidgets. He smiles, a slow, big one, and tips his hat.

I step back, out of the way, and the men let loose in a torrent of hooves.

I shade my eyes and watch them out of sight.

Kate is watching them too. Once they're out of sight, she reties her apron with something like resolve and heads back into the saloon.

"Miss Lacey."

Doctor Sikes is standing behind me. The wind pulls at the edges of his black doctor's coat.

He's a sharp-eyed man with a stony face—he's old, but it's impossible to tell what sort of old. He just is.

"Good afternoon, doctor."

"I was just about to have some tea. Would you join me?"

I HAD EXPECTED something simple when I arrived—everything is set out on the porch—but what he calls tea is equal to a luncheon back East. Sandwiches, tea cookies, sugar and milk for the tea, a small cake, fruit.

He pulls out a chair for me, and when I am seated, he pulls up another.

"You may pour out, my dear," he encourages.

He folds his hands and waits until we are served. I've barely even seen the man, but Archer tells me he is a person of influence and had a hand in his appointment as governor, so I pour out boldly.

He'll see what kind of woman I am, what I aim to be in this territory.

He tempers his tea with milk and sugar, stirs it quietly and sips it.

"I have known Archer Scott longer than any other living person," he says simply.

"Indeed?"

"Yes." He clears his throat as if getting ready to begin business. "In the time I have known him, two things have become clear: he is a most selfless man, and he, if any man I have ever seen, is the one to set this territory free."

"I can agree with the first." I smile with as much grace as I can muster. "As for the second, I've heard stories about the curse, but I know very little."

"The story is too old and long to be told over tea," answers Sikes with a faint twinkle in his eye. "It is better heard in the traditional way of storytelling. But it has existed for as long as these folk have told their legends, and for as long, they did not set foot on this land."

"It is a good land."

"Yes. But not worth the danger, for them."

"You live here, yet speak as if you believe the tales."

"Must one be without the other? Does not the soldier go to the front of battle where death waits, though he wishes to live? Victory is not found but at the battle line."

"I can understand that." I pick up one of the small cookies, take a delicate bite.

The intensity of his gaze is unnerving.

"I have known Archer all his life, and I know that should he be required to make great sacrifices for this territory, he will. But I want to know, Miss Lacey—what is it that made you want to come out to this place?"

I take a deep breath. "I believe he is the man who is going to make this territory a place worth living in. He wants that. He wants a place where people can live and thrive—it's a good thing."

"I know that is what he wants. But what do you want?"

I pause. I want what Archer wants, don't I?

Is there a part of me that wants to be history—that has the twisted glory-hunger that possesses Mortimer?

I think, at Archer's side, I could have both.

"I want what Archer wants," I say.

"Archer will be tested. If he succeeds, there will be no going back for him. But for you—you have a choice."

"I came out here. Isn't that choice enough?"

He wipes his mouth slowly, refolds the napkin and sets it beside his plate.

"Miss Lacey, you have great spirit. It isn't your courage, your determination, or your ability that I doubt. I do not doubt anything about you."

He picks up his teacup, takes a quiet sip, and looks out at the hills south of the town. The silence goes on so long that I wonder if that was all he meant to say.

"For you, there is a choice. There is a way out of this before you're tied to it forever. His fate need not be yours."

"Perhaps not." I set down my tea. "But I wouldn't have any other."

He accepts this with a solemn nod.

"Then I wish you joy, Miss Lacey. May you do this territory proud."

I step off the porch into the dusty street. There's a wind coming from the west, strong and warm, oddly sweet.

Perhaps I should be worried. After all, Sikes meant to warn me. But I feel nothing but certainty.

35

# THATCHER

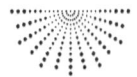

THE STATION AT HALF TREE SPRINGS IS A TWISTED MASS of smoldering beams and ash. We are too late.

"Drove off the horses," says Raymond, with a glance at the churned ground. "That'll slow 'em down if we want to catch them."

"Dare we?" I ask. Fresh horses can be got with little trouble. Once a man has tangled with Abernathy, he never forgets.

"It's Tavachi. They left their sign," Selby says. He's back from riding a slow circle around the ruined station and open corral. "If we send two riders on to the next station by the path up over the ridge, they could make it in enough time to at least warn them. It's unlikely a group of much size would take that way."

Archer gives a nod. "Do it."

Two men volunteer—a hand from Gilchrist's ranch and

a fellow I've never seen who rides like an Auki. They water their horses and ride north in a cloud of dust.

"Looks like they've had a late start," observes Selby, leaning over his rifle and saddle horn to look at the torn up ground. "We may stand a chance if we want to recover the stock."

"Water the horses," says Archer, dismounting. "We won't stay any longer than needed."

"Someone should bury the stationmaster," says Selby softly. "Poor devil."

"Where is he?" asks Archer, under his breath.

"'Round back."

"I'll have Carson see to him."

It's hot and bright out here, a tough day for riding. Or for driving a herd of a dozen or two horses. I get down off my horse and lead it to the stagnant troughs on the far side of the yard.

Selby's down on the ground nearby, examining the tracks. The man can't help himself. I let my horse drink, sips at first. I lead it away so that it won't overdo it, and stop over Selby.

"What do you think?"

He looks up at me, squinting to see my face against the bright sunlight in his face. "I think if we ride now, we'll catch them before dark."

"But where?"

He shrugs. "You can't hide fresh tracks that easily. Not on this ground, not from someone who reads signs."

Raymond rides up, switching his reins in his hands.

"They'll have to be headed somewhere with water. These are horses, not cattle. They'll start dropping."

Selby nods. "There's only two water sources in the direction they're headed. Clarke's watering hole and Arrow Creek."

"If they're smart, they'll go to Arrow Creek. This time of year, Mr. Clarke rides these holes watching for coyotes and *isarks*," I add. "At a hole, he'd be able to pick them off for quite a while, probably stampede the horses."

"Arrow Creek, then," says Raymond. "I'll go talk to the governor."

THERE'S A CRY OVERHEAD, and I squint at the blinding blue sky. No matter how hard I strain my eyes, I can't spot the *isark,* though I heard it, clear enough.

I inch forward on my stomach, lifting my head long enough to get a good look down below the rocks. There's a trim little canyon, only about a hundred feet square, and sure enough, it's crammed with the stock, tails swishing. A couple are lying down, and the rest stand there with heads hanging and hooves cocked, sweat-stained.

One, three, five. Five guards. Easy.

I inch back the way I came until I reach my waiting horse. I swing up and head back to the others who wait half a mile away.

"They're in the canyon, sure enough," I announce, drawing rein beside Archer. "There's a guard of five. Don't know if they have someone on the far side of the rocks."

Archer turns halfway in the saddle so his voice will

reach the others. "We'll move in carefully. Don't shoot unless you must. Is that clear?"

There's agreement.

"I'll lead us down in."

"Governor." Raymond clears his throat, his voice lowered. "Seeing how I promised a girl I'd see you back safe, it'd be my pleasure to lead the way."

Archer stares for a second, his eyebrows raised. Then a smile starts onto his face and he gives a nod.

Raymond straightens his hat and slaps his horse forward.

WHEN WE GET CLOSE, we dismount and walk in, surrounding the upper rocks and sending a couple men to watch the mouth of the canyon.

I'm covering Raymond, who is watching the canyon below like a hawk, his rifle in his hand. He glances over at me.

"You ready?"

I pull the brim of my hat and grin.

He shoves his rifle to his shoulder, takes aim, and fires. The horses jump, some rearing, and start to mill about, and the men scramble for their guns.

"Don't try it!" shouts down Raymond. "You're surrounded."

A bullet pings off a rock two feet from our heads, and Selby's rifle barks in answer. The offender's falls as he clutches his bleeding hand.

The canyon erupts with gunfire from below, sending

the horses frantic. Poor fools, all they had to do was throw down their guns.

I don't even need to fire. They manage a shot or two each and then they're dead.

There's one man left; he springs from his hiding place behind a rock.

"Don't shoot!" He throws up his hands. "Don't shoot, I'm not armed!"

Raymond lowers his rifle. "Take off that belt, then, and come on up here." Slowly, the fellow unbuckles his gun belt and throws it into the dust. One of the horses jumps.

"All right. Come on up," orders Raymond.

His hands held above his head, he moves up toward us. Raymond looks to me. "Do you have any rope?"

"Yeah, on my saddle."

"Go and get it. Tie him up."

I get up, slow and cautious, then turn and run back to my horse. By the time I've got my lariat, the fellow's seated on the ground with Raymond's rifle aimed at his stomach, five feet away.

"Tie him up good. He wants to talk."

I bind the man's wrists, tight but not cruel.

"Now how about you tell me what you folks were thinking, raiding a station."

Archer and the others are heading down the rocks, gathering up the horses, moving the bodies out of the way. All the better. Raymond will get more out of this man without an audience.

"Who are you?" He fixes Raymond with a suspicious glare.

"Just answer my question. I'm certainly not on your side, and that's all you need to know."

The rustler pales a little under his tan. He's almost a fair-haired mirror of Raymond, heavy-mustached, with a strong jaw. But there's a conviction Raymond wears on his sleeve that this man lacks.

"We were promised gold," he said. "By Mortimer. Said he'd make us rich, and until we had the gold, we could live off the spoils. We were hauling these south of the territory border to sell. Wasn't much to live on where we were camped."

"Where south of the border?"

The man hesitates.

"Come on, now. Chances are you'll get strung up for your part of this. Any hope you've got is in cooperation, and I can tell when a man's holding out."

"Coopersville."

"Interesting," Raymond rubs his chin. "And where were you going after that?"

The man doesn't answer.

"Remember, cooperation." Raymond moves his rifle meaningfully.

"Cold Bill Reed was our leader. He knew all them things, not me."

"Is Bill one of those down there?" Raymond jerks a thumb toward the holes a couple of our men are digging.

"Reckon so."

Raymond turns to me, lowers his voice. "Search him. Then go down and check those others before they bury them. If you find anything, you let me know."

He starts down into the canyon.

My unpleasant search yields one thing of use: a map in Bill Reed's belt. It's stained in one corner, and it sure ain't territory commissioned, but being born here, you get to recognize your land, even scratched out in bad hand.

Raymond and Archer are down on the rocks. The horses have been contained with a temporary rope corral and they pick at the scrub grass and whisk at the flies, mostly ignoring me as I pass.

Good stock, those horses.

"Found this." I hold the map out. "It's someone's sketch of the land hereabouts."

"Good," says Archer approvingly.

Raymond unfolds it slowly and holds it out. "Well," is all he says.

Archer glances up from the map, looks around. "Selby, come here a moment, will you?"

Jack Selby is seated on a pile of rocks cleaning his rifle. He puts away his things and gets up. "Governor."

"You worked the Lanoka tableland, didn't you?"

"I was up that way, now and again."

"What's the country like up there?"

"Pretty flat."

"Come look at this."

Selby leans over, runs a finger over his chin as he studies the crude map. "I think that's the railroad. Look— it makes perfect sense. They'd come down from the plains and across the tableland. Skirt that way, they'd be able to avoid the mountains and still come through Glory Mesa and on to Roan Hills and Thrasher's Creek."

"How would they know?" I ask.

"Mortimer could get railroad plans if he wanted them," says Archer grimly. "He hasn't taken much interest before. But the railroad's moving further in."

Raymond grunts. "How big are these oath clans?"

Selby looks up. "There are a few large ones, but most run in bands of only a dozen or so."

"I say we go up and disarm the lot of them."

Archer nods, but he looks at the map again and I see his shoulders sag. "They'd have my head back East if I got myself killed in a war with the clans. Resurrect me to hang me themselves. Officially, I'm only sanctioned for peaceful relations."

"What about a marshal of the territory?" Raymond takes off his hat and beats it against his leg.

"A marshal would have that authority, but we don't really—" Archer breaks off.

"Would you do it, Raymond?"

Raymond's got this look in his eye, a sort of gleam.


THE SUN'S made the black leather of the worn book burning hot to the touch, but I hand it over as Archer reaches for it.

Raymond sets one long, browned hand over it and raises his other.

We're all so drenched in sweat that our shirts are sticking to our backs, and the sun is in our eyes, but I reckon there's something more solemn to this, more right, standing under the cloudless sky next to the rushing creek, than any swearing-in done in a courthouse.

"Do you, Raymond Lacey, swear to uphold the laws of this territory, to administer justice, and to defend this land from wrongdoers and outlaws?"

"I do."

"Do you swear to conduct yourself only with honor, staying subject to the laws you uphold, and to act with courage and conduct befitting an officer of the law?"

"I do swear it."

"Congratulations, marshal." Archer holds out his hand and Raymond takes it firmly. "You're the first one I've ever sworn in."

"Hopefully not the last," says Raymond, a grim smile in his eyes.

IT'S DARK NOW, and we're eating jerky around the fire, which is doing little against the night chill.

Raymond sits just inside the circle of light, bent over a piece of paper. He's been making plans since the moment he swore that oath, asking questions about the land, hand-picking men to drive the horses up to the next station, others to erect a lean-to for the replacement stationmaster, and others to ride north with him.

He looks up from his writing and stares into the fire. Then he looks, slowly, differently, at Archer and goes back to writing.

A minute later, he folds up the paper and goes to my cousin, drawing him aside.

"Look, I want to talk to you for a minute."

Archer's face goes serious and he follows him out of the light. Just a flicker of orange reaches the edges of their faces.

"This ain't going to be over anytime soon. I think we both know that," Raymond says.

Archer nods, scratches his shoulder as he does when he's uncomfortable.

It takes Raymond a long space before he continues. Then again, he never rushes to say anything, much less anything important.

"My sister—she's got her heart set on you. And I wouldn't have given my blessing if I wasn't pretty sure of you. But it's got to be said. You take care of her, treat her right. Because if you don't, I'm only one step behind her."

Archer is man enough to smile at this. "Understood."

"Good. Now I figure I have the authority now to take this group of men and scour those places up north. And I reckon there's no reason you can't go on back to Glory Mesa now and get that wedding movin' on."

"Are you sure?"

Even at this distance and in the dim firelight, I see the twinkle in Raymond's eye. "I'm sure. Don't you keep my sister waitin'."

A dimple appears in Archer's cheek. "I won't."

"Give her this." Raymond smiles and holds the folded paper out to him.

Archer tucks it into his shirt carefully. "Thank you. I will."

Raymond slaps him on the shoulder and comes over to me at the fire. "Cold night," he comments, crouching down and holding his hands out toward the heat.

"Yeah."

"Look, I won't insist. I'm only asking once. But I sure could use you when I head up north."

I snap the twig I've been toying with, toss it into the fire. I've wanted to get back to my ranch. But this is big— big as the territory. And this land is mine just as much as anyone else's.

"I reckon I'm with you."

A gleam like a smile shows in Raymond's eyes. "Sure glad to hear it."


IT's STILL dark on my early morning watch when Archer gets up and saddles his horse.

"You take care of yourself, Jesse, you hear?" His voice is dim, almost nothing in the infinite expanse of sky above us.

"You too."

He shoves his foot into the stirrup and settles in the saddle. It's a short ride back from here. By the time dawn hits proper, he'll be almost there.

I reckon I would have been his best man, if I could have gone with him.

## 36

## ROSAMUND

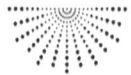

I'M CHANGING THE BEDDING FOR AIRING—ANYTHING TO keep my mind off the departure yesterday—when there's a knock at the door.

I come downstairs to find the clerk from the stage office standing at the door.

He whips off his hat, holds out a note. "This came in yesterday, Miss Lacey, and it was overlooked. I apologize."

"Oh, it's nothing." I give him a smile and take it from his hands. "No harm done."

"Have a good morning." He touches his cap and goes on his way.

I tear open the envelope and open the small leaf of folded paper.

. . .

*I REGRET to inform Raymond and Rosamund Lacey of the loss of freighted goods in a railway accident. Compensation may be sought with the railway co.*

AND THAT WAS IT. So simple, so quick. The words can't be compared to the loss they inflict. My mother's things, my chest with my household goods that I worked on all my life, Raymond's medals that I saved from the dustbin and refused to throw away, my mother's wedding dress. Were they burned? Scattered across the prairie?

*My mother's wedding dress.*

I press my fingers against my mouth as my throat closes with tears. I had held so many hopes coming out here—I was so full of excitement for the kind of life I would build, the life I would help Archer build.

My mother's wedding dress is gone.

I shove the note into my pocket and start walking before the tears can catch me. I will not cry in the street, and I refuse to go back inside and cry where I will have no constraint, where my misery will breed a languid manner for the rest of the day. I will walk, and not think.

The cool morning would be sweet normally, but it feels like a mockery as all my dreams crumble in my fingers.

I quicken my steps. There's a tree near the edge of town, one of the few around here that aren't young. If I make it there, I will let myself cry, if I must, under its gentle shade.

I round the corner and see a rider approaching. I turn away, starting in another direction.

"Rosamund!"

It's Archer's voice, cheerful. I press my fist to my mouth and take a deep breath. If I speak now, I'll cry.

"Rosamund," he says again, more quietly. "Are you all right?"

I shake my head.

I hear the creak of his saddle and the crunch of stones as he dismounts. "Can I do anything?"

I shake my head.

Gently, his hand comes up over my shoulder and I turn into him, burying my face in his shoulder and bursting into tears.

"Easy now, what is it?" He's rubbing my shoulder. His other arm comes around me and he's holding me as if to protect me from my sorrow.

"My things...they were coming out, remember?"

"Oh." It's like he knows already.

"They met some accident, and I don't know...I suppose they're gone. All my household things, our family heirlooms, my mother's wedding dress."

I feel him go still.

"Well," his voice is quiet. "Mortimer is trying to cut off the stage line. It's possible—"

"I needed those, Archer."

"I'm sorry." His hand rubs my shoulder gently. "I'm so sorry."

*Don't offer to buy me new ones, don't you do it.*

He pulls back to look at my face. "Do you want to wait, then?"

I nod. I will have to pick myself up at some point, but I

need to mourn this loss. These things were the last ties to my family, my old life. Now I have nothing.

"Here." He reaches into his pocket and holds out a folded letter. "This is from Raymond."

"Raymond?" My sorrow melts into fear. "Where is he?"

"He's all right," Archer tells me quickly. "He's not hurt, he's just not coming back yet. He wrote you this."

I take the letter in numb fingers and unfold it. Archer gives me a nod and walks on with his horse, leaving me to read it alone.

I see the handwriting, bold and familiar. I continue my course to the tree, reading as I walk.

*My dearest Rosamund,*

*I remember the first day I saw you, I almost cried. I was back on leave, and I only had two days. You had been in this world a few months already, and you were perfect. The moment I clapped eyes on you, I loved you. And I'm pretty sure you felt the same.*

*I'm writing to tell you that I won't be able to return for your wedding. I want you to go ahead and have it without me.*

*I am awfully sorry that I won't be able to keep my promise of walking you down the aisle in my parade uniform. I know we talked about it. We've talked about a lot of things, and I reckon you know me about as well as anyone in this world does. I'm sworn in as marshal, and there's work to be done up north, work that can't wait. This is a good territory, and I want it to be a good place for you to live in—for you to raise children, if it so happens.*

*I'm sending you your man back with my blessing. Go to my things—Levine or Trasker can show you where I've been staying—and inside is a little carved box. Take that out. It's for your use now. I don't figure on marrying, so you may as well have it.*

*I don't know when I'll see you again. I'll send word again as soon as I can.*

*Your loving brother,*

*Raymond*

I look up from my letter, wipe the fresh tears out of my eyes.

Sworn in as marshal. I should have guessed something like this would happen to Raymond. He's good at what he does.

I fold the letter gently and put it back in my pocket.


Mr. Trasker is setting goods out on the porch of the general store. I come up to the steps and he turns, wiping his hands on his apron.

"Good morning, Miss Lacey! What can I do for you?"

"Raymond says you can show me where he's been staying."

"Of course!" He unties his apron and lays it over the top of a barrel. "I'll take you right now."

We head up main street a ways, and then over onto a side street I've never walked. There we find a bunkhouse, new and without a porch.

"The hands who work the corral and the livery stable stay here. And your brother."

He turns the handle and goes in. It's empty and quiet, and it's a bit messy, but the corner he leads me to is sparse and neat.

Raymond's army trunk is set against the wall. It must

have been recovered from the wrecked stage after we were captured. It was the only luggage he brought west.

I kneel down next to it.

"Do you need anything else?"

"No. Thank you. Do I need to do anything when I leave?"

"The boys keep this unlatched, just let yourself out."

I give him a smile of thanks and open up the trunk. The small, carved box isn't hard to find. It's under Raymond's single spare pair of trousers, which I notice are wearing through and need patching.

I undo the clasp on the box and open it up. It's Father's wedding band.

I tip it into my hand, feel the cool hardness in my palm.

I remember playing with it on his finger. I never saw it off him a day in his life. I thought he had taken it to his grave, but I guess he must have given it to Raymond sometime after he knew he was dying.

I close my hand over it. Tears are springing to my eyes despite myself. I miss Father and I miss Raymond, and my things are important, but I feel like such a child now.

Things just aren't that important compared to people.

I put the ring back, close up his trunk, rub his worn army initials *R. H. Lacey* lovingly. Then I hurry out into the street.

I'm almost too late. Archer is riding past at a lope, heading for the low hills southwest of town.

"Archer!" I gather up my skirts and run after him. "Archer!"

He pulls his horse around, trots up to me. I can see the

storm in his face fading. He's disappointed, maybe about the wedding, maybe about the territory, but it's fading because he's looking at me.

"I've changed my mind," I say, panting. "I've changed my mind—let's just get married. Forget about the things. We'll buy new ones. I'll borrow a white dress if I have to."

His eyes melt.

"Thank you," he says, very quietly.

# 37

## THATCHER

"I FIGURE THERE'S ABOUT TWENTY OF THEM. WHAT DO you think?" Raymond Lacey hands the field glasses to me.

I hold them up, look carefully at the camp in the distance. Men are gathered around cookfires, cleaning guns, carving meat. From the looks of the meat on the spit and the hides, it was probably lifted off settlers.

"Yeah, I figure," I confirm.

"Looks like they started already."

So he noticed it too. I rack my mind, trying to think what settlements and homesteads are out here. The Thompsons, the Richter Mining Outfit, some trappers near the hills.

"Any idea who they are?" asks Carson impatiently. The man is no coward, but I do wonder why he came along. Raymond runs a no-nonsense sort of outfit, and Carson, well...Carson's got ideas that are his very own.

"It's Pete Slim's oath clan," I say. I recognized some of the men.

"What do you know of them?" asks Raymond in a low voice.

"They're dangerous." Carson spits. "Bloody dangerous. You don't go near them."

"Well, we're going near them now." Raymond fixes him with a slow look. The look comes around to me. "What do you say?"

"They're one of the rougher clans. There's a joke that Pete's vows are mighty simple—you just ride on up and they say, 'Hey, you want to go rustlin'?'"

Raymond doesn't laugh.

"That about sums them up. For a clan, they're meaner'n a cornered catamount."

At this, Raymond nods and gathers up his reins. "Good. I'm going down there. I'll give them a chance to put down weapons and move off. They don't, we'll fight." He turns in his saddle, fixes the dozen of us with a quiet stare.

"Is that understood?"

"Marshal Lacey," says Carson loudly, "I don't recommend the talking bit. Pete don't take kindly to talk." He laughs. "If old Pete's still alive."

"Well, I'm not opening fire without giving a man a chance to take the peaceable way out. We're starting new ways in this territory right now. I'm trusting you to cover me."

Selby cocks his rifle loudly.

"You'll have it," I say.

Raymond's eyes go to mine.

"All right, let's go." He urges his horse forward and we head down into the camp. Selby has his rifle cradled in his arms, his face like stone.

I'm mighty glad we've got him along.

"Afternoon, gentlemen," greets Raymond, pulling his horse up. Pete's men are starting up, disturbed. They weren't expecting company all the way out here and we've surprised them.

What comes of getting cocky, I reckon.

"Ah, ah—" Raymond moves his hand to his gun as one of Pete's men reaches for his. "I've only come down to ask you to move on."

"Why would we do that?"

"I'm a marshal of the Western Territory, and you are in possession of stolen goods. I'm willing to leave you with a warning this time only. But you have to clear out, leave your weapons."

Old Pete Slim is still alive. He stands up from the circle, one hand on his gun. He's got a face of graying stubble and a couple missing teeth as he leers up at Raymond.

"And who made you marshal? Only marshal I know of is Baker in Tres Hondo, two hundred miles south."

"I've been appointed a marshal by the governor himself," says Raymond calmly. "And I gave you your chance. Now are you going to take it?"

Three men stand slowly, unbuckle their belts.

"Irving, Kips—what are you doing?" Slim shouts.

"Gettin' out. I ain't picking a fight today," one says. "Can we ride out, marshal?"

"Ride out," says Raymond. He stands calm and stony as the three men mount up.

"You cowards!" bawls Slim, but it doesn't do any good. They ride out and we don't touch them.

"All right, boys, any more cowards?" demands Slim.

One of his men whips out a pistol and fires. Selby's rifle barks and the man falls. Raymond didn't even twitch.

"Last warning. He got his—you don't need to die today."

A half dozen men scramble for their guns and the place erupts in gunfire and blood.

SELBY IS SEATED ON A LOG, cleaning his rifle. He takes care of that thing as if it's his child. The fight went badly for Pete Slim's clan. Most of the band was killed, and we didn't even suffer a casualty.

They were all half-drunk.

The night is young yet, the food they left in our hands smells good, and Carson is turning a skilled hand to it, but I can't get the scent of blood and gunpowder out of my nose. My stomach is queasy from it and I'm not sure I'll be able to eat.

Those men were low-down thieves without enough sense to take mercy when a man like Raymond offered it. But I hate to see anyone die. They just had to pull their guns, had to put up a fight like fools.

And now they're six feet under. A waste.

Raymond is standing at the edge of camp, near where

we've picketed the horses, his arms folded, staring out at the first stars.

A click arrests my attention, but it's just Selby, putting his rifle back together. I reckon I'm just jumpy.

Out beyond our camp somewhere, probably a few miles off, a lone wolf howls. It's a wild, mournful sound.

Jack Selby glances up, his hand still burnishing the barrel of his rifle.

"They smell blood," Carson says morosely. I don't rightly know what's into him, unless it's the same thing that's into me—finding out that killing makes you sick, makes you die a little inside yourself. Even the worst sorts of men still have a life, and taking it does something to you.

Maybe that's why Archer is haunted sometimes at night.

Selby finally sheaths his rifle and sets it aside, next to his saddlebags. He gets up and comes over to the fire, pouring himself coffee.

"You are one dead shot," I say.

He thins his mouth in an effort at a smile and raises his tin cup to me. "I reckon those sheep herders don't miss me."

I laugh.

"This is better. Much better," I answer. "For one, those herders couldn't make a cup of coffee worth a lizard's hide."

Selby takes a quiet sip.

Raymond comes over, crouches beside the fire, gives Selby a brief nod. He's been quiet ever since the fight. Not to say he isn't quiet a lot of the time, but there's a different sort of quiet a man gets when he's doing a heap of thinking.

Raymond picks up one of the tin cups and fills it full. "This Carson's?"

"Yup," one of the men across the fire answers. "Carson makes the best coffee around."

Raymond takes a sip and makes an appreciative sound. Then he leans back on his heels and gives a long sigh, shoving his hat back out of his eyes.

"You must have nerves of steel," I say. "You didn't move an inch from the center when those guns set to blazing."

Raymond chuckles under his breath. "They needed to know I meant business."

"Well, you sure made yourself known as marshal clear enough, taking out Pete Slim's clan."

He scratches the side of his head slowly. "I hope so."

"I've lived here all my life." I stare into the fire instead of looking at him. "And apart from my cousin Archer, I've never known anyone who could've done that—what you did today."

Raymond sighs and smooths his mustache with his thumb and finger. "Jesse," he says slowly, "in the morning, I want you to ride out to the surrounding homesteads, warn 'em to hunker down for trouble or get to a town. Gather any volunteers who are willing. This fight's comin' fast and if we don't do it now, we might not get to."

"What do I tell them?"

There's the barest glimmer of a smile in his eyes. "Tell them what you want. Tell them there's a new marshal and he's going to set Mortimer's tail on fire."

"Whatever you say."

He chuckles under his breath and reaches for the coffee pot.

"Hey, Old Steady!" Raymond straightens. A half dozen or more men are riding in, at their head the three Swift brothers. They're a matched set all right, with their blond heads and red roans and bright smiles as they squint into the setting sun.

"Got room for a few more?" Jem grins and dismounts.

"Sure won't say no."

"Brought a few hands, some strays I picked up."

"Welcome." Raymond gives them a nod.

Max has his gun out and he's spinning it. The only reason he gets away with it is he's actually a crack shot.

"Your sentry tells me you're marshal now," says Jem. "Figure Mortimer and Abernathy are going to put up a scrap?"

"I reckon."

"Well, I wouldn't miss it."

"Well, set yourselves down. Food'll be ready soon. Talk's better on a full stomach."

Jem pulls off his gloves, shoves them in his belt. "Amen to that."

MORNING IS JUST a pale suggestion on the horizon when I saddle my horse and lead him out. Jack Selby is up, drinking coffee by the smoldering fire, and Raymond Lacey is up too. Two other fellows besides me are getting ready to ride.

Raymond comes up as I'm fastening on my saddlebags.

"Got any provisions?"

"I could use some."

He goes to one of the pack animals and brings back a small, heavy sack. I give my saddlebag strap one more hard jerk and tie the sack over it.

"Just mind you're back to Gray's Canyon before next week is out. Don't want to lose you."

"Got it."

I swing up and gather my reins. My pony is fresh and there's a wind today, stirring him up, making him eager and antsy.

"You take care of yourself, Thatcher."

"You too." I shove my hat down tight on my head and I hardly have to give the pony my heels.

He's off like a shot.

# 38

## ROSAMUND

I SMOOTH MY HANDS OVER THE WHITE DRESS. IT'S NOT ornate, but there is a little lace on the sleeves and high collar. It is a good dress.

I step out, and Mr. Trasker is there, biting his lip, his hands clasped in anticipation.

"It looks lovely, Miss Lacey. Quite lovely."

"It's beautiful." I'm touched by his genuine pleasure. "Thank you."

He beams. "And the bonnet? Did you try the bonnet?"

"Yes, it fits perfectly. I cannot believe you found something suitable on such short notice."

"Well, I always have something in the back. In a town like this, a ready-made dress can fetch quite a price. It just needed a few alterations."

I pick up the bonnet from its wrapping and pull out my purse.

"How much do I owe you?"

"Oh, it's—" He twists his hands. "It's a wedding gift. It was my pleasure, it really was."

I lean up and plant a kiss on his rough cheek.

"Thank you."

He wrings his hands further and turns a little pink. "I only wish I could do more. Archer Scott is a fine man, just a fine man, and I—I wish I could do something to help him in his cause."

"I think you're already doing it." I close up the strings on my purse. "Do come to the celebration. There will be lemonade and cake."

I step outside and into the street. I had hoped for a different sort of wedding. The sort where I would be driven to the church, not walk down the dusty street on my own. The sort where Raymond would meet me at the church doors and walk me in, wearing that fine dark uniform, his saber hanging at his side.

Many of my friends back East had such weddings after the war. But here I am, walking alone to the church like an eloper.

"Hey, Rosamund! Miss Lacey!" Peter runs up to me, carrying a handful of wildflowers. "These are for you."

They're fresh and strong. It's so dry and dusty around here—they must have been cultivated or picked a few miles away.

"Why, Peter, thank you! Where'd you get these?"

He just shrugs and runs on. He's either too modest or the messenger for some anonymous giver.

I pass the doctor's office, and Sikes is standing there on

his porch, his long black coat on, his arms folded and his eyes gazing out beyond the town.

"Good morning," he greets.

"Good morning," I reply. We haven't spoken since that tea we had on his porch.

"I assume you are on your way to get married?"

"Yes, I am."

"Then it's Miss Lacey, for the very last time." He descends his steps and holds out his arm. "Would you permit me to accompany you?"

I hesitate and then take it.

The town seems to be watching, riders pulling horses aside, stopping in the street to let us pass, as we walk down to the church.

"Your bonnet." Sikes gives it a nod. It's dangling from my other hand.

We stand before the door now, and I glance up at his face as I put the bonnet on my head. "Thank you for doing this."

"It is my pleasure." Sikes gives a slight smile, and I realize that his stern face is quite pleasant.

I tie the bow beneath my chin and pull the veil over my face.

Sikes opens the door and we step in.

Archer is standing at the front of the church. He's wearing his old uniform, the one with the gold braid and the medals.

I've always thought him handsome, but today—I don't think I've ever seen a finer-looking man.

"Go ahead," whispers Sikes, and he releases my arm.

I proceed down the aisle, my heart pounding with every footstep. The veil hangs over my bonnet in a gentle slant, like the sunbeams coming through the window. The waiting is over.

Archer smiles and holds out his hand to me.

Maria stands like a statue of marble at the front of the room, her proud face calm and still. I hand her my bouquet so I can take Archer's hands. Her fingers are cold.

In a haze that takes an eternity and yet no time at all, we say our simple vows.

He promises to be mine, until death, and I promise to be his.

He lifts my veil gently, and here I am, restraining my smile to a demure one, not the great beaming smile I feel in my heart. He sees that one in my eyes, and I'm glad of it —it's for him alone.

Today, in the dust, in the middle of unrest, this town feels so barren and wild, clinging to the earth against the odds. But I wouldn't leave it now for the whole world. This is where I belong.

He leans down and I tilt my head up, and we kiss.

My heart is going to burst.


THE PARTY PASSES IN A WHIRL. We dance. In Archer's arms, I weigh nothing. On this night, with every threat of destruction over their heads, Glory Mesa celebrates. The lanterns cast a golden glow over everything, the fiddle music races like my heart, the people clap and sing.

This is where I want to be for the rest of my life. In Archer's arms, surrounded by these brave, good people.

Most of the town comes, the tradesmen and businessmen, even some of the nearby ranchers. There are wedding gifts—a milk cow, a rocking chair, a bed, a quilt. Everyone is very generous.

I miss Raymond, and I know Archer is thinking of others too—Jesse, perhaps. People who should be here.

We hold each other's hands and don't let go all night.

IT'S dark when the festivities finish, and instead of going home, I climb onto his horse behind him and we ride out of town to the low hills that lie southwest.

The sky above us is a deep, deep blue, with stars so thick it's like someone poured out salt over a dark tablecloth.

"You won't ever see stars brighter than out here." His tone is low and reverent. "I used to camp in these hills all the time."

I'm leaning against him, one hand playing in his hair. The hills are pale under the starlight, and the moon is young. I'm tired, but I don't mind it since I'm with him.

"Rosamund—I'm glad you're here."

"So am I." I lean my chin on his shoulder, and he turns his head to kiss me.

"You know, I didn't think you'd come. It was too much to ask of life—to have you here, to know you'd be here with me for good."

"I was only waiting for you to ask." I laugh softly. "And

to sell the house back East, and to escape the clutches of an outlaw."

"Well, there's nothing in the way now." He kisses my cheek softly, and I turn my face to him and we kiss again.

"I still wish Raymond could have been here."

"I know." He turns in the saddle to wrap his arm around me, runs his hand up and down my arm.

"I just want to know he'll come back. He didn't have to tell me—the way he writes, he knows it's dangerous."

"Everything's dangerous here. But if anyone knows how to take good care of himself, Raymond does. I wouldn't worry."

"I wish that I could know that everything will be all right," I whisper.

"That's tomorrow." Archer's voice is gentle. "We have tonight." He gestures at the sky above us with a wide sweep of his arm. "Us and the stars."

I tuck the worry away into tomorrow where it belongs and feel the peacefulness of the open land spread over me. No one can take this night from me.

# 39

## SELBY

I'T's RAINING. NOT A HARD, HEAT-CLEARING SORT OF rain, but one of those drizzles that befriends the miserable heat and makes you wetter but no less sticky.

My horse plods on, impervious.

The original party of eight or nine riders has grown to over a score, men we've found along the way or who met Lacey's messengers and found us.

Two dozen is nowhere near what we'll need against Mortimer and Abernathy, but it's a start, and I don't care a whit about the odds. I can't tell if it's because I am tired today or if I sincerely do not care and will not, ever.

I'm tired of killing, even when it's what must be done.

A cockeyed sign with peeling paint announces that we're entering Hope Town. It's a sad cluster of dusty buildings, with the doors—what few are left—hanging off their hinges. Dust has drifted onto the porches and into the open doorways. Weeds stand in the street, surround a dilapidated corral, grow through the cracks in the boardwalk.

It was a mining town once, probably set up on a vein that dried up after a year. That's how it goes.

Raymond dismounts, eyeing the corral. "We'll set up here for a spell."

The rain patters on the old wood. Puddles of mud lie everywhere, splashing the legs of each horse as we walk up the street.

Raymond lifts a pole or two, kicks one of the posts that holds the corral up.

"We're better off staking them," he decides aloud.

We secure the horses around the back of an old hotel in a sagging barn with a little bit of dry hay left. We haul it out by the armful, feed the horses, rub them down.

I untie my rifle sheath from my saddle and haul the saddle off. Throwing it over my shoulder, I walk up the back alley until I find a low-roofed house that looks less rotten than the others. I shove the door open, step into the dusty, dark room. It was once a boarding house, I think. Rusted-out laundry tubs and washboards are propped against the wall. A pile of abandoned sheets and blankets sits molding in one corner.

In the next room, I find a table that would have been considered cheap even when new and a couch with half the stuffing ripped out.

It's not the prettiest place, but I've seen worse. I find the corner with the fewest cobwebs and settle down with the saddle beside me.

I pull my knees up, rest my rifle across my hips. Close my eyes. Lean my head against the wall.

I didn't sleep at all last night and my head hurts. For a long time I just sit, hearing the light patter of rain grow stronger until torrents rush in sheets off the roof.

I hope the men found a good spot, because this is about to be a real storm.

I can't sleep. I dig in my saddlebags and pull out a piece of jerky and my poetry book. It's an old friend, this volume, and I have read it through so many times I could quote the whole thing through without opening it. But there's a comfort in the sight of the words.

I flip it to the first page, one stained with dirt and a smear of blood.

*As a falcon with clipp'd wings, in the bottom of a cage I lie,*
*A broken thing, once used to sky.*

The back door bangs and I start out of habit. Raymond is standing in the doorway between the washroom and the parlor, taking off his hat as it streams water.

"Figured I might find you here." He shakes out his wet hair and wipes his face.

"Why's that?"

He comes in slowly, still sloughing water from his coat and hat.

"There's some men just good at surviving. You picked the house with the worst lookin' outside but the best roof." His mustache raises in a smile. "Am I disturbing you?"

I shake my head and return my book of poetry to my saddlebags.

He settles on the ground beside me, folds his long legs. "Rain's something else out there."

It's still running out of his hair and down his face.

He sighs. "Good thing is, if Mortimer's around, he's probably hunkered down too."

"Think he's around here?" I shift the rifle off my lap.

"Yeah, I figure he is."

I sit quiet for a spell.

"Do you mean to shear off and avoid him?" I ask finally.

"Naw, I reckon on surprising him. He's headed for the railhead and I mean to meet him there. I figured maybe you could—"

A cold sweat breaks out on my neck. I can't hear and I can barely see. It's like somewhere in the past, something's reached a hand out and grabbed me by the throat. I can't catch Raymond's words.

He stops talking and all I hear is the rain.

It's quiet between us. I catch my breath, let my slow breaths talk sense to my pulse.

"A number is all. Could you do that?" he asks, slow and quiet, after time has passed.

"Yes. When?"

"As soon as you can. When the rain lets up some."

I nod, catch my breath again.

"And Selby—keep this to yourself."

"Yeah."

He gets up slowly, heads for the door.

"Look—" The word comes out before I know it's coming.

He stops and looks back.

"If I don't come back—mind you, this is hypothetical— you get out and you skirt south round those hills, long way round, you hear?"

"You'll come back." He puts his hat on, raises his coat collar, and heads back out into the lashing rain.

40

ROSAMUND

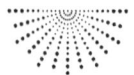

"Now that you're a married woman, you've got even less business in a saloon," Kate greets as I walk through the door.

It's late afternoon and the place is empty. For once, she's just standing there behind the counter.

"Even so, Carson is who-knows-where and took most of our business with him. So you are very welcome here." She gives a half smile and folds her towel.

"I was just coming to see how you are getting on. It's quite an establishment to be running alone."

"Ha. I run it mostly anyway, even when he's here. It's easier when he's gone." She turns over her shoulder. "Peter!"

I toy with the nicked up edge of the bar. I have no idea how long Carson has been in business, but it's been long enough for his place to get worn around the edges.

"Peter! Where are you?"

Peter comes dashing around the corner.

"Where were you?"

He shrugs.

"I need the aired laundry brought in. Mr. Terhune is back in town."

"Oh, yes!" He raises his eyebrows as if he knew this already and tramps out back.

"I swear, that boy manages to be everywhere."

"Is he your family?"

"No. He doesn't have any that I'm aware of. Carson's been good enough to give him a place in exchange for work, so I mind him. Or try to."

The stage comes down the street outside with a loud clatter, drawing a cloud of dust.

"This is only the third time it's been in this week," Kate takes down a tin of coffee. "Slim pickings on the stage line. The investors will be disappointed."

I laugh softly. That was my world, and it may well be my world again someday when this territory is grown, but it seems odd coming out of Kate's matter-of-fact mouth. "I daresay that's the least of our worries."

"I'd say," Kate replies with conviction. "The territory is running on a knife's edge, despite everything Archer Scott's done. And he's done a great deal. You should have seen this place two years ago when I came in."

"I hear he was sheriff for a time."

"Kept peace, in a way. Glory Mesa was enough trouble on its own then."

"Afternoon, Kate." Sam comes in, pulling his gloves off,

shoving them into the pockets of his long duster. "Does the coffee still stay hot for me?"

"Of course." Kate goes to the range, and in her absence, Sam gives me a nod, brushes the brim of his hat with his thumb and forefinger.

"How's the stage line?" asks Kate, bringing the coffee pot and a couple tin mugs hooked on the ends of her fingers.

"This might be our last run in a while. About half of the stations are standing, bristling with guns. No one wants to trust their mail or their persons on the stage. Been mighty lonesome on the runs."

"And what are you going to do?" I ask.

"Hunker down I guess." He gives a wry smile. "Maybe make a desperate run if anyone's got the money to will the stage out into danger."

"I think you live for that sometimes," says Kate under her breath.

Sam just chuckles.

"Hey Sam, you going to quit socializing and get the stage unloaded?" Barnes is standing in the doorway, his arms hanging on the swinging doors.

"You bet I ain't." Sam doesn't even look up.

"Now then, you've gotten mighty ornery since you got yourself almost killed. Come on out here."

"Don't see you doing it." Sam's face is as straight as a man's in church, but his eyes are twinkling.

"Impossible." Barnes stalks in, pours himself coffee, and leans his dusty elbows on the bar.

Sam takes a long sip of coffee.

"I should probably be going," I say, to Kate.

"I've got official mail on this run, probably for your husband." Sam looks over at me. "Is he in?"

"He ought to be. He was off early this morning. There's cattlemen and most of a mining syndicate taking shelter here."

"That'll do it, alright," drawls Barnes with a savage grin.

"Take care," says Kate, with extra meaning in her voice.

"Thank you." I nod to the men at the bar, and Sam salutes lazily.

IT'S EARLY MORNING, while we're still in bed, when the knock comes at the door.

Archer gets up quickly, thrusting his arms into the nearest shirt—his good white one—tucking it in without buttoning it.

I hear his voice as he answers the door, unnaturally low, talking to someone who is out of breath. I turn and look at the curtains—no light yet.

It must be an emergency.

I push the blanket off and pull my calico dress over my head, reaching backwards to button up the back.

Archer meets me as I'm coming out.

"What is it?"

His face and voice are taut. "Gilchrist's place is burning. They were hit in the night." He goes to the closet, pulls down a shirt that isn't his good white one.

I know he's thinking of the letter he got yesterday—the one with the official seal of the nation, turning down his request for aid from Fort Green. They've given him a nearly impossible task, defending the settlers here without any help from the outside.

"Mortimer?"

"Or one of his clans."

"Are you going over there?"

"Yes. The attackers moved on, but they need help putting out the fire and moving the stock." He's buttoning up his shirt quickly. It's a bit cockeyed.

"Do you have to go yourself?"

"I've always gone, when I can."

"Please be careful."

"Don't worry." He leans down and kisses me. "You can go back to bed if you want."

I shake my head. "Will you be gone long?"

"I don't know. If anyone comes around this morning looking for me, just tell them I'm not here. You don't have to deal with them, all right?"

"Yes, Archer."

"Good. Goodbye, my love." He caresses the side of my head briefly and then is gone.

I CAN'T SLEEP, of course. I've never been out to Gilchrist's place, but I have an idea of its whereabouts, so I take my chances and cook up a good breakfast. If the fire's not out of control, my husband could be back by late morning, probably hungry and exhausted.

Peter comes by mid-morning with a written message from the stage office for Archer, saying he checked the office first. I set it on the sidetable in the kitchen and feed Peter a good breakfast.

He says he's eaten already, but he eats like he hasn't.

The sun is bright and the yard is burning hot an hour before noon when Archer rides in at last. Black soot covers his clothes—they are ruined, I think—and smears his arms and face.

"Did they get the fire out?"

He dismounts slowly. He's stiff.

"Did they get it out?" I persist.

"Yes. He lost most of his buildings. Doctor Sikes is out there, Gilchrist got burned pretty badly."

"Is he going to be all right?"

"He's young. I don't think the burns were too deep, but they covered a lot of area. He refuses to come into town." He starts to walk around back.

"There's food on the table. I kept it hot."

"Good, I'm starving. I'll put the horse away and wash up at the pump and then I'll be in."

"I'll get you fresh clothes."

I reach up and kiss him. A twinkle of amusement appears in his eyes. He wipes his hand off, then tries at my chin where I brushed him.

"I think I just made it worse," he says, and moves on past.

I head in and take down a shirt from the closet in our bedroom, laying out new pants and socks. I pause at the mirror. Sure enough, there's a black smear across my face. I wipe at it with my handkerchief until it disappears.

The kettle I left on the range is whistling shrilly.

I'm pouring out coffee when he comes back in, dripping water. He smiles at me—he's tired—and goes upstairs to change.

At last I hear his footsteps descending the stairs. I am sitting across from his place, staring into my own cup of coffee. The china is still mismatched.

"Eat, and then sleep," I say, before he can propose otherwise. "Anything else can wait a couple hours."

"I will." There's no argument from him today.

He takes a sip of his coffee and closes his eyes.

"It's close, Rosamund. It's getting close," is all he says.

# 41

# MORTIMER

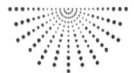

THE RAIL CAMP IS A SMALL SEA OF FLIMSY WOOD structures and muddy-hemmed tents. A black iron steam engine towers in the middle like a bull in a herd of cows. It doesn't look like much, but this is where I have found and taken my advantage.

My black blows and sidesteps, uncertain at the smell of soot and too many men too close together, uncertain at the tinny blows of the workmen's hammers.

I glance at Abernathy. He's seated on his stocky chestnut, eyes squinted against the sun, which pales the blue sky and brings it gently to meet the sea of grass. The railroad has found the easy way, straight across prairieland—nothing like the rocky ground just south of here.

"Move quickly," I say, sparing Abernathy only a glance. "Don't touch the headquarters."

He grunts. With the scent of conquest in his nostrils,

he's becoming unruly. But I must keep him in hand for the time being.

He waves one of his sons over and takes his cheap cigar out of his mouth to speak in a low, growling voice.

Ordering these men over here, more over there, a pincer move—it's laughable how easy this will be.

Abernathy gives a sharp whistle and waves his men forward.

The riders surge up and around me, sweeping past. I hold my black in, keeping him from following.

When they have all gone, I see Holt is still here.

"Go on." I wave him forward.

He just grins and urges his horse into a trot.

I rein the black in and sit in the hot sun, watching the path made straight before me.

Abernathy is not as quick and clean as I would be, but I'm not wasting my men when I can use his.

The workers' tents are on fire; I hear shouts and screams. The acrid smell of fresh smoke reaches me on the fitful breeze.

I glance over my shoulder, crook a finger to Tora-Teth.

"Sir." I have to look down to talk to him on his rangy pony.

"Scout out the situation, tell me how it is. I can't waste time."

His face lights and he gives a half-salute he picked up from my ex-army boys. Like a swallow he swoops in, shrouded in the smoke and chaos.

It's beautiful, all of it.

He reappears five minutes later and reins in sharply.

"They're almost through." He's soot-covered and his pony has blood on its legs.

"Good." I give the uneasy black a kiss of my spurs and we move in.

Smoke billows from burning buildings and tents. The resistance is almost gone. A couple railroad men, unarmed, streaked with blood and soot, see me and blanch.

It feels good to be feared.

"Sir, we have them bested." Holt jerks his horse to a halt beside mine. He's grinning like the devil.

"Good. Come."

The gunshots, which had been few and on the other end of the camp, die away.

Holt swears genially.

I ride straight up to the railroad office, purposely spared among the twisted ruin of the camp. I thrust the reins into the hands of one of my men and motion for Holt and another to follow me.

I kick in the door and step into the shade of the office to see a thin, older man with wispy white hair sitting in a chair and stuffing account books into the small pot-bellied stove.

He freezes and turns white.

I walk straight up to him. He doesn't move a muscle. My eyes still on his face, I open the stove and pull the half-burned books out, smother their smoldering edges with the heel of my boot.

"What's your name?"

"Homer Crenshaw?" He says it like a question.

"Get out, Homer Crenshaw."

I draw my gun easily, gesture him out of the seat. He moves quickly.

"What is it you do for the railroad?"

"Clerk, notary public."

"Perfect, you'll do."

I sit down in the padded chair, shove my feet up onto the desk. A man doesn't realize how sore his feet get in boots until he gets a chance to rest them.

"Who's in charge here?"

The clerk hesitates.

"Go on," I urge him with a brief wave of my pistol. "You've got a chance at life, you'd better take it."

"Matthew Preston. He's...not here."

"Hm." I laugh. "Holt, go find me Matthew Preston. Drag him here if you have to use his hair."

"Sir." Holt grins and stomps out.

"Now." I fold my hands and smile with just my teeth. "How about you fetch a pen and some paper?"


MATTHEW PRESTON IS a bolder man than the unfortunate, quivering Homer Crenshaw. He has black hair that's been oiled down and a suit that is wonderfully, enormously expensive. As Holt shoves him harder than necessary against the desk, I catch a whiff of good cigar.

Preston straightens his appearance and meets my gaze with some degree of defiance.

"Alexander Mortimer." He clucks and shakes his head. "Fancy seeing you."

"It'll be the last thing you see, if negotiations go badly. Have a seat."

I kick the chair opposite the desk and he has to dodge it or be slammed in the knees. He fixes me with a long look and sits down.

"Clerk!" I snap my fingers and he comes running from the other room.

I love that. The man is learning.

"Where's that document I dictated?"

"Here." He fumbles in his haste to give it to me, and Preston fixes him with a stern, betrayed look.

I look it over, slide it across the desk to Preston.

"I'm in charge of the railroad now."

He looks at me. "No, you're not."

"I am, and you can take it walking out of here or you can take it hanging from a tree."

He studies my face—I can see he wasn't appointed vice-president or whatnot for no reason. He's not a soft man with soft ideas.

I can respect that in principle, but he's in my way.

"Relief will come eventually, and they will oust you."

"Let them try." I shrug. Normally, he would be right. But this—this is only the beginning of my plans. Plans already set into action that cannot be stopped.

"Sign that," I order.

He's reading it now.

"But that's—a—an extortionate amount, that—that would sign away half of all the railway shares to you." His face is white with anger.

I grin, slowly. "Say it again."

# 42

## SELBY

THE OUTLAW CAMP IS QUIET, WITH FIRES SCATTERED around, low voices, horses fidgeting on the picket line. They are troubled, familiar sounds. The sounds of dead causes and exile.

They were home, my old life.

Dusk is creeping over the land, over the camp, muting and gentling everything in its dying light.

I had never thought to be back here, hearing those sounds and smelling the scents that haunted my old life.

But causes die all the time, taking their best sons with them. It's how the world runs. And what I thought was mine is now dead and had left me like a shipwrecked man, clinging to rock against the pull of the sea.

Ten, eleven, twelve tents on this side—two, three men to a tent.

I retrace my steps, head around to the other side of the camp. This side is more spread out. More tents. Fires.

"Mortimer's got everything all neat and tied up." I hear a voice, and I stop to listen.

"Says he's ready to draw them in, make an end." There's a low hum of laughter around the fire, accompanied by the clang of a cooking pot.

"The gold will come all the faster, I reckon. I aim to go straight under Governor Mortimer and make meself a marshal."

"He ain't gonna be governor."

"Who says he ain't? He'll do what he wants."

"And kick us out again?"

"I'd like to see him try. If we can take down the likes of Governor Scott, we can take down the likes of Governor Mortimer."

So Mortimer has a trap, and one that's in motion already. But these men won't know enough to give me the information I need.

If I don't return, Raymond Lacey will skirt south. I know that, and they do not. I have that advantage.

I wipe the sweat off my palms, drag them against my leg.

I must do it. I am expendable in the long scheme, and if it's the end of me, at least I know this: I will not talk.

That's more than most men learn about themselves in their lifetime.

I go back for the dun. He's waiting quietly, and I unsheathe my rifle and check my appearance. I'm dirty enough from all this riding; I look like I could have been alone in this country for weeks.

I take a deep breath. This sort of thing comes back

more easily than one expects—thinking swiftly in a passing of a moment, changing your plans to stay one step ahead.

I tug the reins gently so the horse knows we're going, and I step as naturally as possible out of the bluing dark and into the warm glow of the firelight.

"Howdy, boys. Can anyone tell me where I can find Marion Abernathy?"

"And what do you think you're doing walking into this camp, toting that rifle?"

"I told you. I'm looking for Abernathy." I hold out the rifle, stock first.

They hesitate at this.

"Here, but be gentle with it." I hand it over.

They turn it over, note the issue, the year.

"Who are you?"

I jerk my sleeve up, baring the raised, healed brand. OA, for outlaw, Abernathy. That's how they cataloged us, like so many cattle.

"Someone who has waited a long time for revenge."

"You're one of the old guard." There's respect in his tone.

I just nod.

"Well, Old Abernathy's up with Mortimer at the railhead, but Wade Abernathy is in this outfit."

Even better.

"Can I see him?"

"Reckon it won't hurt. This way."

The picket leads the way, the second fellow trailing, carrying my rifle. We stop outside a tent, lit from within by a lantern, and I hand my horse off.

Wade Abernathy's looking taller and more filled out than he was when I saw him last.

"Jack! You old devil, where have you been?" He throws down his gloves onto a map, spread across his field table. These fellows, they're full-blooded outlaws now, but they act like they're still fighting a war.

"That varies, depending on the last five years."

He laughs. "How long did you serve?"

"Long enough."

"Reckon only long enough to learn the guard rotation inside and out. Now what's the story? Want in on a slice of glory?"

I nod. "I was surprised to hear you boys were in the territory."

"Well," he says with a modest smile, "we came to something of an agreement. Catch 'em with honey, so my pa always says."

"And never followed his own advice a day in his life."

Wade throws back his head and laughs. "Right you are! Pa hasn't changed a whit."

"I rather counted on it."

"So—how do I know that you haven't pocketed some of our gold already? Or perhaps there's a bounty out for us?"

"I'd be a fool if I tried to collect bounty on you, out here. That would put me on the losing side, wouldn't it?"

He accepts this.

"Well, we're about to go meet Pa up at the railhead. Moving out tomorrow." His finger goes over the map briefly. "You acquainted with this land?"

"More or less."

"Well, the route is simple—north over these hills is shorter. Doesn't make any sense to go south."

"No," I agree, softly.

"Should make it there in a day and a half, don't you think?"

"Likely," I agree.

I let my fingers rove over the map—make it look accidental, the noticing. "Look at that." I point out the thin line denoting the tracks. "Do you know what you call that?"

Wade only scowls. Admitting ignorance is hard for the Abernathy kind.

I meet his eyes. "A back you can't cover."

"Well, it's always there. It's the railroad, of course."

"And Governor Archer Scott sent a wire to Fort Green, other side of Smith's Run, asked for troop support."

"He did?" Wade is thinking this over, slowly.

"Don't you remember how we solved that in the war?"

"We blew every bridge to high heaven."

"That's right." I smile. The action feels foreign. "We did."

## 43

## CARNEGIE

I DON'T KNOW HOW I KNOW, BUT AS PETER'S FEET POUND
up the back steps of the saloon, I sense trouble.

His face is flushed, his eyes bright and nervous.

"Kate, Kate! There's a telegram—it came from the railroad and then the wires up the line got cut!"

I dry my hands slowly on my apron.

"What did it say?"

"Said it was being attacked, needed help. Then it cut
out."

And we don't have the men to spare. Not really.

I glance out at the street. Word is spreading quickly; I
see Jensen heading up the street, trailed by two boys fourteen or fifteen years old, the only hired hands he has left
since the rest rode off with Raymond Lacey.

But what else can we do?

I untie my apron, hang it up.

"What are you doing, Kate?"

"Going down to the surveyor's office. You can come too if you like. This concerns us all."

"QUIET, MEN, LISTEN UP!" shouts Jensen, banging Garth Levine's tin cup loudly on the table. "I said listen up!"

Near the front I see Archer, Harrison Terhune, Maria Pike, Levine. A number of others stand around, ranchers and miners I do not know by name.

Silence comes in a slow trickle, and in the middle of the hum, Archer Scott stands up.

"As some of you know already, this morning we received a telegram from the railhead outside Shiloh's Crossing, requesting assistance. Mortimer attacked them. In person."

A low murmur spreads through the room.

"So that's where he is," mutters Levine.

"How many men with him?" asks Terhune quietly.

Archer shakes his head. "They didn't say."

He looks to the town again. They're restless, some ready to ride out and take Mortimer now, others unsure.

"It's my duty to consider all the consequences before risking more lives," says Archer. "Some of you men fought in the war, most of you can handle a gun. I don't doubt your courage or your will, but that doesn't mean we're a match for their numbers the way we are right now. Or that we should rush to empty the town for a cause that might already be lost."

His wife looks to him. Her mouth is slightly opened, and she's urging him—to what, I don't know.

"What about our new marshal?"

"He's out there, but he's running in wild territory. Last we heard from him was four days ago. With the wires cut, if he's around there, he'd have no way of letting us know."

"What do you suggest, Governor?"

Again, the urging look from Rosamund.

Archer looks sober, leans his strong hands against the edge of the table. "I say we bide our time. If we went now, we'd meet him outnumbered. We'd ride hard and maybe get there too late. If the council decides to muster a force, I am willing to lead it, but I won't advocate for leaving the town unmanned again, and I want you all to understand what would be asked of you. Riding in there blind is a risk."

"But we know where he is," speaks up a voice from the middle of the throng of townspeople. "We may never get another chance like this!"

"That's right," calls another.

Harrison Terhune clears his throat, looks to Archer for permission to speak, then stands up.

"People of Glory Mesa. This—fight with Alexander Mortimer is not simply the rounding up of another outlaw. This is a fight for everything we have. A fight for our homes, our ranches, and our families. Most of you know that yesterday, Gilchrist's place was burned by raiders."

A strong ripple of agreement.

"With all respect to the governor, I can't stand here and allow Mortimer to raze our homes and steal our livelihoods under our noses. Today, we know where he is and we know what he intends to do. I say this is the time. We go now, or resign ourselves to surrender in the future—on his terms."

"I say we go!" shouts a voice, a young one.

Cheers and stomps take over the room.

Terhune raises a fist, determination on his charming, sun-weathered face. "Then I say, I will go! And I hope you men will consider joining me."

He sits back down amid deafening cheers and clapping.

The thought comes to me, quiet and strong: *I want to go.* And Carson isn't here to stop me. Peter wouldn't say anything, I know that.

Archer stands slowly, turns to address the men with an odd sorrow in his eyes. "Very well. We will ride out of here in four hours. Volunteers meet at the oak outside town and be ready to ride."

I turn and hurry out before I get caught in the crowd.

ABOUT AN HOUR LATER, Archer Scott comes into the saloon.

"Kate," he greets, gives me a nod. He walks up slowly and leans his arm on the bar.

"Can I get you something? On the house." My heart is pounding.

I'm torn. I want to go, I want to ask him, but I'm afraid of pulling the trigger, leaving Peter alone here.

"No, I—" He looks down with a faint, sad laugh and starts to dig in his pocket. "I actually came to give you something."

"Oh?" I frown and set down the towel, coming around to his side of the bar. I can't imagine anything he'd owe me or this establishment.

He smooths a paper against the polished wood. It's his genuine governor's letterhead, made for official business.

*I, Archer Scott, grant as promised to Kate Carnegie....*

"What's this?"

"This is my promise to you. What I owe you. If another officer, governor, marshal, comes in, you can require it of them." He taps the paper with his finger.

This is the moment. I see it, clear as glass.

"I want to come with you," I say in a rush, looking up. For the first time since I've come here, I'm letting someone see what I want, what I truly want, and it hurts.

"Ride with me?" It's like he isn't sure what I'm asking.

"Yes, ride with you. I'm good. I promise I'm a good shot."

He's leaning his hands on the counter. He's going to say no, I know it. I'm shy now that I've spoken, but I had to try.

"Kate." His voice is gentle. "I'd let you ride with me. I mean that—I don't doubt your skills, I've seen them. And I owe you a debt."

He looks over at me.

"But please, don't ask it of me this time. I'm giving you this because I may not come back."

"But the other men—"

"Please, don't think it's a reflection on you," he cuts in quickly. "But this once, I ask you. You don't want to come this time. And—I feel safer leaving Glory Mesa with you in it."

It's a wonderful compliment, though I don't want it right now.

But he's right. Most of the men are leaving the town, and I think he's uneasy about it, as much as he needs every man.

I nod. I twist the towel in my hands. "I'll stay, then."

"Thank you, Kate." He means it, deeply.

I look up at him and nod. He pushes the paper toward me with a friendly wink and heads out.

Sikes's voice drifts through the open doorway. Was he waiting outside, listening to us?

"Archer Scott, this is the time of your testing."

"Is it?"

"Conduct yourself with honor. That's the difference between you and that rogue, Mortimer."

"And if I don't?" His voice is gentle and honest, humoring the old man.

"You will." What a strange man. I remember with a chill the storm that came down from the hills during the attack.

There's a laugh, from Archer Scott. "I'm planning on it. Take care of yourself, Doctor."

There's no sound after this. I keep expecting someone to walk in, but no one does.


ALL AFTERNOON, men ride by, getting ready. It's one of those hot afternoons, with a mild breeze. Dusty.

The noise grows outside steadily as the afternoon grows late. Across the empty room, full of tables and chairs no one is using and some of these men will surely never use again, the clock strikes four-thirty.

They will leave now.

I step out into the golden light, see from the porch the milling of horses and men. There must be sixty or seventy of them, almost all homesteaders and ranch hands driven into town to shelter from the raiders.

I pray with all my heart that they will succeed.

Archer is saying something, but I can't catch the words, just the tone of his voice. The men cheer, the horses take off in a rumble of hooves and dust.

I shade my eyes with my hand, watching until I can no longer see them.

The wind presses against me gently, sweeping my hair and my skirt in the direction of their dust.

I still wish I could have gone.

# 44

## ROSAMUND

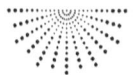

I AM USED TO BEING ALONE. ALONE WITHOUT ARCHER, alone without Raymond, without my parents.

But this feeling tonight is new. It's a heavy dread in my stomach.

I have never been afraid of the shadows, never—but tonight I am.

I am nervous even to carry a lamp from room to room, lest it show in the windows. It's not as if people don't know I'm home anyway, but this dread is so strong it starts to feel like the truth.

It's dark now. I certainly cannot sleep, but I should. I draw all the curtains upstairs and in the parlor and light a lamp.

I'll make tea to calm my nerves. There will be work enough in the morning. The railhead might be in danger now, but it could be Glory Mesa tomorrow.

I come down the stairs softly, with the lamp still in my hand. I take the tin of tea down from the shelf above the range, then open the stove door to stoke the fire.

Somewhere in the hills, a coyote yelps, going on and on.

It sounds too clear and loud. I whirl, and my heart jumps to my throat. The back door stands open, and there's a shadowy figure standing inside.

"Take it easy," a voice says in the darkness. "Don't move, don't make a sound."

I freeze. A chill runs up my arm. I don't dare set down the lamp.

"What do you want?"

I raise the lamp, slow and easy. The light slants onto the scrubbed boards near his boots; I let my eyes grow accustomed to the darkness. I see a man's figure, his mouth and nose covered in a bandana.

But I recognize his eyes. Only Harrison Terhune has those striking eyes, dusty-blue, lined at the corners.

It can't be. He rode out with the men—didn't he?

"Terhune?" I take a step back. Archer left me a gun, but it's hanging by the door. Even if I ran, I couldn't put my hand on it before I'd be shot.

"I'm sorry," he says. "You're a fine woman. If you weren't, I wouldn't have to be here."

"What do you mean?"

He doesn't answer, and that is answer enough.

"But why?"

He raises his gun a little higher, seems to be bracing himself.

"Why?" I raise my voice, try not to let it crack. "If you're going to kill me, at least you can tell me why."

I'm thinking quickly, trying to think of any way to cause a distraction. I could throw the lamp, but his gun would be faster.

"Because your husband is as good as dead now. Mortimer's trapped them. In two days, word would reach you. And when Archer Scott is dead, you will advocate for his causes—you and your brother. You're not the kind of woman to head back East."

"You are such a coward." My voice shakes, I'm so angry. "Are you sure you can live with this?"

He swallows. "Mortimer let you slip away. So it was up to me."

"Mortimer must be desperate to use you."

"I'm not with Mortimer. He's got orders, same as me, only he bucks them."

"Then who put you up to this?"

"Stop talking." His voice shakes slightly. He adjusts his grip on his gun. His finger twitches on the trigger, but he's waiting, or trying to gear up the courage.

I take in a quiet breath. "And the rest of Glory Mesa? Have you set a trap for it too?"

"I said stop!" He's sweating. He's losing his nerve.

"Don't do it," I say gently. "I'll tell Archer you walked away. He'll listen."

"It's too late for him. It's too late for all of us." He fights to steady his hand, puts his other hand on the butt of the pistol, takes aim.

I see it all, slow and clear. I'm calmer than he is.

"Hold it right there." Kate's voice breaks the darkness. I would know it anywhere.

Harrison hesitates.

"Don't think about it!" Kate's voice is sharp. "I'll have it in your back before you can turn around."

He goes white.

"You'd shoot me in the back?" His voice is slow, haughty. But I know it's his last card. Kate doesn't fall for that kind of talk.

"Under the circumstances, without hesitation. Drop it. Now."

His gun hits the floor.

"Step away from it."

"If you think—"

"I don't have to think," says Kate impatiently. "It's mighty clear what you were going to do, and you'd better be doing some thinking of your own. Mr. Trasker will be here any moment."

Slowly, Terhune backs out the doorway.

I hear footsteps, panting breath, and I see Trasker come around the side of the house, a rifle in one hand and a rope in another.

"Where is he?" he demands.

"Right here." Kate keeps her eyes trained on Terhune. "Tie him up, quick."

I step outside with the light and see Peter in the shadows, his dark eyes gleaming in the dark. He's watching everything solemnly.

Trasker hands the rifle to Peter, who adjusts it in his arms with an effort. "I wouldn't have believed it of you, Terhune," he says severely.

Harrison Terhune laughs bitterly.

"He says the men are riding into a trap," I say.

"And they are." Terhune fixes me with his eyes. "They are."

"Stop talking," says Kate. "You've said enough."

"It's too late for all of you." He gives her a grim smile. "For them, for Glory Mesa. You'll see."

Trasker doesn't say anything, just wraps the rope around Terhune's wrists again.

"Who put you up to this?" I look him straight in the eye.

His face is open, but his eyes are hard and I know I've lost him already.

"Does Mortimer know who it is?"

Fear flashes across his eyes before they're ice again.

I need to talk to Mortimer.

"Kate, where is Sam staying?"

"The place behind the stage office. Blue shutters." Kate is talking quickly, not even looking at me. Her hand on the gun is steady.

Trasker works quickly. "That'll hold. I had navy men in my family. If we know anything, it's how to tie something to hold."

He looks at me.

"Do you want me to come with you?"

"I'll be all right. Just—get him out of here." I suppress a shudder and remind myself that it's over—he can't hurt me now.

I shut the door behind me, lock it, and head down the street briskly before I can start imagining guns lurking in dark corners.

He says he was alone. I cannot trust his word, but it seems to be the case. Peter trots after me, doesn't say anything, but I do feel better with him behind me.

We reach the stage office. "It's on the right side," says Peter, pointing.

"Peter, how did Kate know?"

He shrugs. "I told her. Mr. Selby gave me five dollars to watch your house while he was gone. Said he'd pay me more when I got back and a gold piece if I caught someone. He said he thought somebody would try again."

He leaves me, running up the street.

Try again? They tried it before? This detail sticks in my mind strangely, but I cannot give thought to it right now.

I go around to the side and find a small outbuilding with blue shutters, just as Kate said.

A lamp is lit inside.

I knock, hard. Wait. Count the spaces by my pounding heart. Knock again.

A shadow crosses the lamplight and the door opens.

"Mrs. Scott?" Sam's plain, honest face peers out into the dark at me.

Thank goodness.

"Sam—"

"Are you all right?" He takes one look at my face and steps aside, ushering me in quickly. "What happened?"

"Nothing—I mean, well, Harrison Terhune tried to kill me, but—"

He reaches for his gun, heads for the door.

"No, it's over. He's taken care of."

"Dead?"

"No. But Kate's taking him down to the saloon. Mr. Trasker helped."

"I see." He sets the rifle down on the rough table. There's a book next to the lamp, some steak and beans, cold coffee.

"Have a seat," he offers.

I sit, out of habit. I'm so wound up I don't feel like it at all.

"It was a trap," I say, taking a breath to steady myself. "The men are heading into a trap."

"Did Terhune tell you this?"

I nod. "But he thought he was going to kill me. He seemed—desperate. Like he didn't want to do it."

"Well, as rich as he is, he ain't the biggest steer in the herd."

"Sam, I—" I stop, then look him straight in the eye. "I need to see Mortimer. I want you to take me to talk to him at the railhead."

He lets his breath out in a long whistle.

"If I can talk to Mortimer, I might be able to save the men. I think he's hesitant to kill me, and if I can just talk—"

"And what if he doesn't want to do that?"

"Sam, please believe me. I spent days with this man. I know his mind. And my husband's life may depend on it."

He turns his coffee cup by the handle, this way, then that way.

I try once more. "You're the best driver out here, Sam. Everyone says it. If we leave now, we may catch him in time."

He sighs. "I'll wake up Barnes."

"I wouldn't ask it of you if I knew the way." I stand up as he rises.

"It's not that at all, Mrs. Scott. I live for this." He gives me a wry grin. "And if I live past it, your husband will kill me. Pack something warm and a firearm, if you have it."


KATE SEES me to the stagecoach. I don't wait to tell anyone else. There isn't time for a discussion, and I don't trust anyone to know what I'm doing. If Harrison Terhune was compromised, who else might be?

"You know that I'd go if I could." Kate presses my hand.

"Of course you would. You'd go in a heartbeat." I look her right in her honest, open face. "But I have the best chance of not being killed on sight. And if Glory Mesa is attacked, you're a better help here than I would be."

"Yes."

"We have to hurry, Mrs. Scott." Sam comes back from checking the traces, he's knotting the reins over the brake.

"Goodbye." Kate lets go of my hand and steps back.

Sam opens the door and I gather my skirt and climb in.

"It's going to be rough," he says.

"Just get me through."

In the shadowy light, he smiles and pulls the brim of his hat. "If I can't, I'll die trying."

He shuts the door hard, and I hear him climb up into his seat.

"Ready?" he asks Barnes.

"Just drive."

## 45

## THATCHER

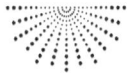

Selby hasn't come back.

I don't think many of the men even noticed he went. Alan did, I think. But I watched Raymond stay alert all evening, into the night.

I fell asleep watching him wait. And when a hand shook me awake in the thin night before dawn and I went to get my horse off the picket line, the dun was not there.

"Morning," Raymond greets. His face is like steel today.

"Morning." I'm not about to broach the subject—I'm too smart for that—but my eyes check again for the dun in case I missed it.

We're about eighty strong now, since I and the others mustered who we could find. It's not much compared to Mortimer's force, but it's something.

"We're moving on the railhead today," Raymond says in his slow way.

"North then?"

"South. Around the hills."

"South? That'll take far longer."

"Well," he says, still slow. "We better get moving, then."
He slaps his horse with the end of his reins and moves on.

I urge my pony after him.

"Raymond," I say, keeping my voice low. "Is it Selby?"

"He was going to scout. There's a camp big enough to
be a hundred or so, out northeast of us a few miles."

"Ah." My horse shifts under me. I feel her chewing the
bit uneasily through the reins, loose in my fingers. I finger
the reins reassuringly, so she knows I'm paying her
attention.

Raymond doesn't seem inclined to continue without
prompting.

"Do you think he's dead?"

"He could be." He looks over at me for the first time.
"Or he could be with them. Either way, he expects us to go
south, and I intend to give him that advantage."

"What if he defected?"

"It won't give him enough of an advantage to be
dangerous while I'm on my guard. I'm willing to give him
the benefit of the doubt. And he's clever. If he's joined up,
I'll warrant it's for some good reason."

"I sure hope so."

He smiles, grim, but still a surprise under the circumstances. "So do I, Jesse."

. . .

WE BREAK camp and ride south. We're setting a brilliant pace, and I'm glad our horses are bred to this land. When we stop, it's only to water them and let them breathe a little. Then we're off again.

Close to noon we reach the edge of the hills. They're plentiful, with high crests and deep valleys. In the distance, the Rio Jefe winds like a shining band of quicksilver.

"Who knows these hills?" Raymond's got his field glasses out and he's scanning the rising and falling ground before us as he speaks.

The Swifts speak up, and a few others.

"I want three of you to ride a little ahead. Stick on the south side and see what you can find. I want to know where the good ground is, any hollows that make for a good trap, tactically speaking. Any movement, I want to know about it."

Jem rides off, a couple other men with him.

"Are you expecting a trap?" asks Alan. His roan is champing at its bit. The horses are on edge, and I don't think it's all from the speed of our ride. They sense something in the wind.

"Can't rule it out," Raymond says, sparing Alan a glance and then returning his gaze to the land spread out before us.

"If they wanted to trap us, it would be past these hills." Alan gestures with a quick hand. "There's a mesa and canyons down beyond these, dry as a bone. If you want to end men easily, that's where you do it."

Raymond takes this and considers it with a soft grunt.

"Got an idea of the fastest way around these hills?"

"Just head on south of them. There's no faster way."

"Good." He pockets his field glasses and gathers his reins back up. "Let's move."

## 46

## ROSAMUND

WE STOP AS SELDOM AS WE CAN. THE STAGE HAS A ROUTE that runs roughly in the direction of the railhead, and for as long as we can, we stick to it. Of the four stations we pass, only one has any horses or inhabitants left.

We switch horses and get news from the stationmaster, a broad-shouldered man with scars on his face. He stares at me while he gives us water and a quick lunch of beans and bread, and none of us give him an explanation.

Five miles beyond the station, we leave the trail and the journey becomes rough. We pass through a couple dry-looking meadows and some high desert. The cactus blooms, brought on by recent rain, blur into the brown and green of the landscape.

Everything that has happened in the last week feels like a dream.

The men riding out, Terhune, even my wedding. It feels wrong to be out here, crossing wild country with only two men to my defense, leaving the town to possible destruction.

How eager I was such a short time ago, journeying out here for the first time, with such dreams—dreams I hope for but cannot count on now.

The stagecoach grinds to a halt. I'm sore all over, but they won't find a complaint in me.

"Last water stop. We're going into some dry country." Sam jumps down with a splash.

The horses are fetlock-deep in muddy water.

"Not broken yet?" jokes Sam, opening the door. "You may not want to get out, but I'd hate for you to suffocate from the heat."

The door being open manages to make a small difference.

Sam shoves his hat back on his head and looks around. "Mean country," he says conversationally.

"How much further?"

Somehow I had thought—hoped—that we would be nearing the railhead by now. But there's no sign of anything, just more wild country.

"I know which way the railroad was headed. Once we get up onto that ridge, we'll have an idea of how far it is. The horses were blown, these are fresher. But mind you stay inside and hold on. We're going to be taking that ridge at a good pace."

He means to be comforting, but there's a knot in my stomach now.

An unearthly screech sounds from above and Sam glances up.

"*Isarks*," he says briefly. "Too small to be trouble, though they might bode it. Legend has it there are some big enough to carry off a horse."

I shudder imagining those teeth, those beady reptile eyes, the wrinkles in the cold skin.

"All right, Sam. It's been five minutes."

"Hang on." He shuts the door. He sloshes back to the front and climbs up.

We're moving again.

The stagecoach climbs; there's no mistaking it. The trail is steep and narrower than I'd like. We move at a fast clip and I feel the tilt as we continue to wind upwards.

"Easy," I hear Sam from above. He whistles to the horses, clucks. Then he calls them up, cracking the lash. They start forward and we pick up speed.

He's urging them faster still, the lash coming fast and urgent. I don't know what he's seen, but I dare not try to look now.

The stage jolts and sways wildly, but we seem to be holding a steady course. Everyone in Glory Mesa says Sam is the best, and I pray they're right.

A rifle shot breaks the silence and I realize what is happening. Once again, I find myself being shot at in a stage.

I see again in my mind Sam lying bleeding on the rocks, the shotgun falling dead from the seat.

I cannot go through this again.

There are riders streaking from the trees around us. A rifle goes off again.

We are going to be killed, all three of us.

Guns blaze around us. One splinters the wood above me.

"Hey!" I hear Barnes bawl above me. "Easy, don't shoot!"

Sam eases the horses down with a long *whoa* and the stage comes to a halt.

Holt comes out of the trees, surveying us with a sharp eye.

"Throw down your guns!" shouts Holt. "Do it!"

Barnes lets the rifle slip out of his hands, clatter on the ground. One of the wheel horses shies off.

"All of them!"

The other rifle hits the ground, and a moment later, the pistol belts.

"All right, get down." Holt orders. He comes to the door and opens it, peering in eagerly as if expecting to find gold.

I smile at him, and he draws back in surprise.

"Good afternoon," I greet. "And before you say anything, I'm coming to see Mortimer. You will not touch these men, nor me."

"Get out." He's annoyed. I think he would have preferred the gold.

"If you will kindly remove yourself from the doorway." I gather my skirts.

He stiffens, but moves.

The others are getting down. Sam puts the brake on and knots the reins, looping them over it.

"Cut the horses loose," Holt orders.

"Look, we're on our way to talk to your boss. We're not

looking for trouble, and we'd rather like to keep our stock."
Sam's eyes are like ice, the wind in his hair the only thing
moving.

"Do it or I shoot him." He gestures to Barnes with the
muzzle of his rifle.

Sam obeys, slapping each horse kindly before turning it
loose. One bolts, but the others wander in among the
outlaws' horses, making them jumpy.

"What are you really doing here?" Holt demands. "If
you're thinking to warn those men, you're too late." He
grins. "It was smart, sending that telegram—the railhead
had been in our hands more than a day already when we
sent it."

He laughs, but he's alone in his joke.

"I know that already," I bluff. "Why else would I be
coming to talk to Mortimer?"

He gazes at me, a challenge in his eyes. "Shoot the
men," he orders his companions, as if I hadn't already told
him he wasn't going to touch them.

"Fool!" I step forward and pour every ounce of
authority I have into that step. "I said I have business with
Mortimer, and I meant it. It's none of my business if he
decides not to tell you his plans." It's a slight stretch, but
Holt's pushing me.

"What do you mean?" Holt freezes, defensive.

It was the barest thing, but he remembers. He remembers that Mortimer liked me better, once.

"You shoot them, and I'll have your head from
Mortimer," I threaten.

He looks at me, uncertain, and I stare right back.

He remembers that I shot him once, too.

I hold his gaze. I refuse to relent.

"Holt." A quiet voice breaks in, I look up with surprise to see Jack Selby standing among the outlaws, his rifle cradled in his arms. "Listen to her."

I stare. It is Jack, wearing two gun belts slung crosswise over each shoulder, another over his hips. I couldn't see him as an outlaw before, but now I can see nothing else.

"Bring them!" Holt waves to his men and they swarm around Sam and Barnes to tie their hands.

"Come along." Selby steps up beside me. His eyes are hard and closed off, but his voice is gentle. He offers me his arm.

"Selby." I curve my lips into a smile. "I don't need your help."

He looks away.

As I pass, Sam looks at me slowly. He knows what a knife's edge we're walking.

I only hope I've done the right thing.

# 47

## CARNEGIE

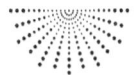

I HAVEN'T SLEPT AT ALL. I STRAIGHTEN IN MY CHAIR AND rub my aching eyes, see Peter falling asleep with his back to the storeroom that doubles as a jail. The rifle on his lap practically pins him to the floor.

If we survive this, I'd love to see a real jail built, not have to worry about having some unsavory character locked in a back room—especially as Carson keeps leaving. Mortimer's men probably set the fire to the courthouse for that very reason.

"Peter, go upstairs and get some sleep."

He starts awake. "I'm not tired," he says, finally.

"You are...you were falling asleep. Go on."

He continues to stare at me blankly. I've about given up hope when he stands up, leans the rifle against the wall, and disappears upstairs.

"Good morning." Mr. Trasker comes in, looking like he

hasn't slept either. He sits down wearily at one of the tables.

I stretch my shoulders, a little stiff. "Well, if they're coming it wasn't last night."

"I suppose so."

"Want some coffee?"

"More than anything." He scratches the side of his head slowly.

"How is the other side of town?"

"Quiet," he says. "Old Trevain spelled me out there."

My head hurts and all I want to do is sleep.

"We should call a meeting," I say, forcing myself out of the chair. I go to the bar and take the coffee tin down from the shelf.

"I should gather folks, then. What few of us there are."

"Wait until there's coffee. If they want to surprise us, they won't do it in the daylight when we can see them riding down from the hills. There's time."

"Right you are." He groans and leans back.

I open the tin. It's getting low. "Mr. Trasker?"

"Eh?"

"Never mind." If we survive this, I'll need to buy more coffee from him. But I reckon first things come first.


WE HOLD the meeting in the saloon. Garth Levine's gone and locked his office after him, and anyway, the saloon had room.

There's not many of us—around thirty, half women, the rest old men and boys, plus a few dandies from the cattle and mining syndicates who are all talk and hopes of getting rich.

Dying in Glory Mesa sure wasn't part of their plans.

One of the men from the mining company, heavy and loud-voiced, gets to his feet as if the meeting was his doing.

"Gentlemen, ladies, we have heard the startling news that one of us has turned against—"

"Not now," speaks up Trasker, emboldened by a sleepless night and dire circumstances. "To business, please."

"This is business," the man says, annoyed, and clears his throat. "One of our very own, a trusted member of this community...."

He trails off, staring at the doorway.

As a rule, Maria Pike never sullies her reputation by setting foot in the saloon. But wonders never cease. Here she is, framed in the doorway like the stern portrait of someone's great-aunt who disapproves of everything in life and continues to do so via her portrait, in death.

"I heard we were meeting. There is an attack coming?"

"Perhaps, ma'am," speaks up one of the old trappers. "We reckon it's coming."

"How much is fact and how much is supposition?" She eyes the filled tables as if I've been bribing folks in with rumors to drive up customers.

When no one replies, she pulls out a chair well away from the tables and seats herself gracefully. "Proceed, then. No need to wait on my account."

Old Trevain, normally quiet and unobtrusive, takes the opportunity to stand up and cut off our good friend from the mining syndicate.

EMILY HAYSE

"We all know Mortimer's going to attack this town again. We are having a meetin' so we can defend ourselves proper this time."

"If they're trying to catch us off guard, those south hills are where they'd do it," says another old fellow, taking his pipe out of his mouth to speak.

"But they came from the northeast last time," one of the women objects.

"Perhaps a lookout should be placed in the church tower." Maria's rich, soft voice cuts through the general murmur. "That way, whichever way they approach, the bells may be rung at first sight."

"Not a bad idea," concedes the old man with the pipe.

"I—I think," says Trasker, "we should have every able-bodied person armed, with ammunition on hand, and posts set up with more in case of need. If we have anyone here with skill in scouting—"

"I'm your man," says the fellow with the pipe. "I trapped and prospected in these durn hills for over thirty years."

"Good. Then—let's gather our firearms and ammunition. If anyone wants to learn how to shoot, I reckon there's people who can help with that."

The room agrees. The meeting disperses, people fetching firearms, finding ammunition, putting their children somewhere away from the edges of town.

Maria stops beside me. She smells of fine perfume.

"Poor brave fools," she says sadly, and sails from the room like a breeze.

. . .

THE WIND IS BRISK, blowing wisps of dust into the air. Glory Mesa is still and quiet. It's not an uneasy feeling yet, but it's strange—like those long dreams that go on forever, and you feel you've lived a lifetime by the time you wake up.

I'm heading up the street when the bells begin to ring.

I dash toward the south side of town, where Trevain is running toward me.

"Are they coming?" I shout.

"Look!" Trevain points back, toward the south hills. A small group of horses is riding toward us, fast. "I told them to hold their fire," he says. "It's kin."

"Kin?"

"Auki," he says, and grins.


MINUTES LATER, ten Auki men ride into Glory Mesa. We are all gathered, most of us, because of the bells, and their leader reins in beside us.

It's Tagweiah, an old friend of Archer's. It's been said they patched up each other's wounds after a fight with a *darani,* but the story has been retold so many times it's practically a legend now.

"Is Archer Scott here?" Tagweiah asks.

"No, he rode north," I say.

"That's bad." He gestures back the way they came. "We saw a force coming in from the south hills. Seven-score."

I wet my lips. That's a lot.

"We were to meet our cousins in the hills, and they did not come."

"We haven't seen them," I answer. The only cousins of the Auki up this direction are the Swift boys. "But Mortimer is up north. Our men, most of them, left after we received a wire from the railroad. He's attacked it."

Tagweiah nods slowly.

"They would have gone to help." He says it with confidence. "We have come to your defense." He gestures to the others. "We will strengthen your numbers."

"You didn't have to!" Maria's voice is all pleasure and humility. I think they make her nervous.

"No." Tagweiah dismounts with a smile that's mostly in his eyes. "But we have had nothing but friendship with Glory Mesa and its people. Archer Scott would do the same for us."

They are only ten, but that's ten more we didn't have, and all good fighting men.

"What about this land being cursed? Don't you believe in that?" Maria's hair is pale against the black of her dress, her manner strangely pathetic.

"It is not our land, therefore it is not our curse."

She says nothing to this.

"They will be here by morning." Tagweiah looks at me, then at Trevain, with a brief but pleasant glance. "We have time to be ready."

He gestures to his companions, and they dismount and disperse among us.

"We have plenty of ammunition," I tell him. "Let us know what you need."

# 48

## ROSAMUND

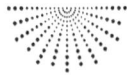

THE RAILHEAD APPEARS BELOW US AS WE RIDE DOWN THE ridge. A few buildings, around them blackened ruins, and tracks that lead away and disappear into the horizon.

To the south, smoke or dust.

I don't see Archer or the men.

Jack Selby disappeared not far from the spot where we were captured, casting one glance over his shoulder at me as he went. I wish I knew why he was there.

Holt leads us down into the camp and toward the railroad office. It still has the sign up. He gestures for the others to take Sam and Barnes away.

"Remember what I said," I say coldly. Holt gives them a nod, confirming my order.

It's strange to wield power like that.

"Mortimer, sir!" Holt bawls, banging on the door. "There's someone to see you."

The door opens, and Alexander Mortimer stands there as if he was expecting someone. The sun illuminates his red hair, making the edges gold, and slants down half of his sharp-angled cheeks. He looks as haughty as ever.

"Says she was coming to see you." Holt's voice is bitter, and I try not to smile.

"Rosamund?"

Holt steps aside. He's just dull enough, I think, not to recognize from Mortimer's tone that he wasn't expecting me.

I give Mortimer a cold nod.

He smiles. There's a new glint in his eye that I do not remember. "Well, this makes it better. Come in, you must be tired from your trip."

"Thank you, but it was not too tiring."

I follow him in with all the boldness I can muster.

"Archer Scott should not send his wife to do what he is afraid to do himself," he chides, pulling out a chair for me. "Coffee?"

"He doesn't know I'm here." I fold my hands, serenely ignoring him. "I came to talk to you myself."

He pours me coffee anyway, and then a cup for himself. He sits down across the desk from me.

I can smell his cologne now, strong and rich. He's thinner than he was when last I saw him—there's a gauntness that doesn't become him and a look under his eyes like he hasn't slept.

He takes a long drink, but his eyes remain on me.

I sip the coffee delicately.

"How long do you think you will hold out?" I ask, when

I can stand the silence no longer. I must not seem rushed, but I cannot wait.

"What do you mean?"

"I mean that you are not the only one who wants this territory."

"Talk to your husband, then. Why come talk to me?"

"I'm not talking about my husband. I mean the person who wanted me dead."

His face is a hard blank. "I don't know what you mean."

"You know exactly what I mean." I push the coffee gently aside and lean forward. "There is someone else who wants this territory, and I hear even you have taken orders from him."

"Whoever told you that was lying."

"Then who sent Terhune to kill me?"

"Not I, if that's what you're thinking."

"No, that's not what I'm thinking; otherwise I would not have come to you."

He shifts faintly, uncomfortably.

"You may think you are winning this fight, but it's a single battle in a much larger war. You cannot deny that to yourself, even if you do it to my face."

He laughs under his breath.

"If you were to make terms with Archer, there would be a chance for amnesty. He would listen to me, I know, no matter what has passed between you two—"

"There's no bargaining." He cuts me off with a swiftness that almost takes my breath away. "You have no leverage anymore."

"There is strength in numbers," I continue calmly.

"Together we'd be strong enough to stop any threats to this territory. You'd have what you wanted, and peace besides."

"I'd rather rot in hell than have peace with Archer."

"Is that really how you see it?"

"I have the upper hand. I don't need to join anyone for that."

"Then tell me who it is that wants this territory."

He smiles bitterly. "Just me, Miss Lacey."

That's a lie. I can see it in his face.

I stand up to leave.

"Wait." He halts me with a word. "Miss Lacey—or should I say Mrs. Scott? You married him, didn't you?"

"I did." Even face to face with Mortimer, my heart warms at the concession.

"*Salut.* A pity it'll be short lived."

That doesn't deserve an answer.

"Mrs. Scott," he continues, "I do not wish your death. You may refuse to believe me, but I want to see you live long in this land. Let Archer Scott be. His fate doesn't have to be yours."

Everything goes oddly hot and still. He's echoed Sikes, nearly word for word. For a moment, the fearful sense of destiny is overpowering.

But I made my choice; I'm not going back on it.

"Did you ever think about the proposition I once made you?"

I stiffen. "I believe I gave you my answer then."

"I beg you to reconsider. I'd rather you have a place in this future with me than no future at all."

"I'll see a future without you first."

"Is that a threat?" He laughs. His expression would be a pleasant one if the joke wasn't so grim.

A hasty knock.

"Come," orders Mortimer.

"It's Archer Scott. He's coming under a flag of truce."

Mortimer starts to his feet. "Quick, get her out of here." One of the men grabs my arm roughly. If Mortimer sees, he doesn't say anything. "If she makes a noise, he's dead."

He looks at me to make sure I heard the threat.

I heard. And I can hardly see for fury.

My newly appointed guard and I go into the adjoining room. It is dark and cramped and smells of paper and ink. From where we stand, we can both see into the front office.

Mortimer sits hastily—combing back his hair, the conceited fool.

I hear heavy footsteps and Archer comes into my line of sight.

It's only been a few days, and still I forgot how much I love his face. That honest expression, that hard jaw with a mouth that moves so quickly to smile.

He's sweaty and tired, and his shirt is stained with gunpowder. They've been fighting, then—but where? I heard no gunfire on our ride in.

"What can I do for you, Governor Scott?" Mortimer's voice makes the title a mockery.

"I'm here to talk peace. I have requested a ceasefire until terms are met."

"It's granted." Mortimer opens his palms. "What terms do you wish to discuss?"

"Terms that grant you pardon, for one."

"Oh, look how he changes his tune," Mortimer chuckles.

"It's more than you deserve." Archer isn't concerned by Mortimer's antics. "But this territory is going to endure. If you kill me, rest assured there are others who will not rest until they have eradicated you and your kind. Come to terms, and you are under my protection."

Mortimer stands. "We'll bargain, but not here."

"So be it."

"Take Governor Scott to the train." Mortimer gives his man a nod. "My car."

They walk out, and the moment the door shuts, I stride in to confront Mortimer.

"I thought you said there was no bargaining with you." Everything is still. I'm livid, nearly shaking.

"Well, now, he doesn't need to know that, does he?" Mortimer's smile is sweet. He offers his arm and I step back.

"Don't touch me."

"Have it your way." He makes a brief gesture to the man behind me. "Send word out to that canyon to let loose. Scott won't know the difference."

"Yessir." The outlaw gives him a nod and heads out. I hear his horse clatter away.

We step outside. It's hot and strangely bright. Close to the train is a swift hum of voices, a gathering crowd.

There's trouble.

"Stay." Mortimer picks a man to take my arm and walks on. Somewhere in the crowd, I see Archer—and Jack Selby.

Selby has a gun out.

The milling bodies shift and I lose sight of Archer in the crowd. We move on, toward the waiting train.

We reach the spot to find Mortimer facing Selby, who stands with his arms pinned behind him.

"You're clever, Selby. It almost worked. But fate is on my side today. Archer Scott is ready to listen to my demands."

Selby doesn't say anything.

"Clever, as I said. But after all is said and done, just a poor boy from a losing cause." Mortimer laughs too, and for an instant, I see in his eyes that Selby must have been very close to succeeding. There's a touch of fear in that madness. "You'll pay for this, Selby."

"Fine by me," he says gently, and he means just that.

"Take him out, string him up. Follow when he's dead, not before." Mortimer spits on the ground at his feet. "I never did care for Abernathy's dirty renegades."

I pass close by Selby, see his gentle blue eyes watching me quietly. Why is it my fate to see the faces of dying men?

"Your car, sir?" asks the outlaw holding my arm.

Mortimer glances at me. He's angry—no, it's something else.

A smile curls his lip. "No, throw her in one of the other cars. I want to deal with Archer first."

He leaves us, walking on through the cloud of steam that billows from under the car.

The outlaw drags me by my elbow to an empty train car that smells of musty hay. "Get in." He hands me up and I no sooner gain my feet than the door slams shut, leaving me alone in the dark.

# 49

## THATCHER

Thunder, so hard the ground shakes.

Raymond reins in sharply. Listens. "That's no storm," he says.

"Cannon fire?" asks Jem.

"Or explosives." Raymond urges his horse forward.

We've made it around the hills and we're heading into some lower, dusty country, full of hidden canyons and strange switchbacks to get up them.

I hear gunfire.

Raymond whips out his field glasses and gazes down at the land before us. He makes a long, slow noise in his throat like a growl.

"We got us some Abernathys, boys," he says, turning in the saddle. "Looks like they've got someone pinned down. What do you say we go show them some Western Territory hospitality?"

Someone lets out a whoop and cheers follow.

"Come on, boys!" shouts Raymond. He whistles to his horse and we take off in a rush, following his lead. I can see them now—probably a hundred men, flat on their bellies, firing down into a half-canyon.

In a canyon, the ricochets will kill you faster than an aimed bullet will.

The Swifts whip past, guns in hand, leaning hard over the necks of their ponies.

We're racing so hard the world blurs.

Over the rocks we scramble—my pony jumps and lands hard, almost slides on his hocks. We stream down, sweeping across their open, unsuspecting flank, and they crumble like the edge of the cliff.

I don't think they even knew what hit them.


IT'S OVER FAST. There's nothing left of the resistance. Only a few got to their horses before we shot them down.

Again that odd feeling takes me in the pit of my stomach. I wish I didn't have to be part of it at all.

Raymond hails the people below and a cheer greets him.

"About time!" one man shouts gaily.

"Where've you been gallivanting?" another calls.

Laughter.

"Well, come on up out of that death trap and we'll talk," calls down Raymond.

They're men from Glory Mesa. They spill over the rim,

covered in sweat and blood, faces flushed with heat and laughter.

I run over, clasp hands heartily with Garth Levine, then Jensen. "Didn't expect to find you boys up this way! Where's Archer?"

"He's not here."

"What? Did he stay behind?" That's not like my cousin at all.

"No." Levine shakes his gray head. "He went up to the railhead to parley, because we were getting slaughtered. He didn't come back."

From a distance comes the long, drawn-out whistle of a train. We all pause to listen.

Mortimer. He's getting away. And I'd bet the ranch he's double-crossed Archer.

I don't care anymore. I will show that man what happens when you mess with my kin. I've lived in this territory since the day I came into this world, and it's high time he learned he's trespassed once too often.

I grab the bridle of my pony, mount up.

"Where are you going?" Garth Levine wipes the sweat off his forehead. He's no fool.

"I'm going after Archer."

"Thatcher, don't do it. You'll be killed." Jem seizes my horse's bridle.

"Won't live with not trying. You catch up if you can."

"In that case, take my pony. He's the fastest." Max swings off his horse and brings him over. He's a trim little pony, built with hind legs like a hare's.

"Thanks, Max."

I throw my leg over, turn the pony's head east.

I catch Raymond's glance briefly. I tug my brim in farewell and see the glint in his eye.

They'll be following after me.

I clap spurs to the horse and it shoots away.

## 50

## CARNEGIE

IT COULD BE ANY HOUR. THE PLACE IS AS DARK AND STILL as a ghost town. The wind sighs down the street.

We will have one advantage. We know they're coming, and they are expecting a sleeping town.

There's a single light on in the saloon, flickering and dancing over the bar. By its thin light I look Peter in the eyes.

"Are you sure you can do this?"

"I'm sure."

"You take this rifle, you watch him carefully. If anyone tries to get in, you can shoot them, all right?"

"I have my knife too," he answers brightly.

"Good. You may need it."

I reach out and put my arm around his shoulder, giving him a squeeze. He doesn't wriggle away.

"Don't worry, Kate," he says. "I'll be careful."

I don't know if I've done the right thing, leaving Peter

in charge of guarding the prisoner. But the enemy will have no way of knowing where he is, and I'm hoping this will keep Peter away from the fighting.

I stop in the doorway and glance back at him once more.

He waves cheerfully and holds up the gun. He's promised me to barricade himself behind tables if he hears even one shot.

I step out into the street.

It's dark, that bluish dark that comes right before dawn. We've put the main force on the south end, but we have guns posted at every good entry point in town. My footsteps sound deafening on the hard, rutted ground.

Mr. Trasker comes out of his store, locking it after him. He grips a tin mug in his fist.

"Coffee?" He holds it out.

I take a swig and hand it back as if it were a flask of whiskey.

He laughs softly and I laugh too. It's good to go stout-hearted to a fight like this, since we don't know who's walking away from it and who isn't.

That old rifle of Carson's is waiting for me down at the old barn on the south end of town, but I'm wearing a gun belt, and it hangs heavy on my hips.

We don't talk, either of us, on the way down the street. I'm glad of it.

An odd pair we make. Shy Mr. Trasker, a little too old and too store-bred to ever pick a fight, but solid as a rock when it's a matter of our defense.

And me? Just a lonesome thing like a tumbleweed on a mesa.

It's dusty inside the old barn. Seven or eight shadowy shapes wait there already, and Tagweiah is one of them. He gets up from crouching at a hole in the wall and comes to meet us.

"They are coming. Your scout sighted their fires just over that hill. Those fires are out now."

"Let them come," I reply cheerfully.

"You have good spirit," he says, and there's a flash of a smile. It reminds me of the Swift boys—Alan in particular.

"I am grateful you have made this your fight." I want him to know that, beyond a doubt. If we have any chance at all, they're the ones who have made it so.

"There is no need for thanks." He pulls a bullet out of his belt and feeds it into the chamber of his gun.

"I want to give it anyway."

His eyes warm. "And so I will take it."

He goes to his place at the wall again, and I go to mine, kneeling down by a hole in the slats of the wall.

It's shelter, but it's not thick. A bullet could rip through these boards and still kill someone.

Better not to think on that.

A rifle shot breaks the morning stillness in half. I've heard rifles more times than I can count, but the strength of this one against the quiet of the sky feels like a cannon shot.

Then a whole volley breaks loose.

There's no going back now.

I watch my space, see the swift-moving figures ride across the open ground. They're on horses, many of them.

I take a breath, hold, squeeze the trigger. Carson's rifle has a good kick.

I lose track of time. I cover for the man beside me as he loads, and then he covers for me as I load. There's another woman in the barn, a tall blonde in a dusty blue dress.

She's a fast loader.

A sliver of sunlight slants through the barn behind us. Dawn has arrived.

Tagweiah raises his head and looks to the light.

Then, even as he puts his rifle to his shoulder and fires, he begins to sing. It's low, sweet music in the Auki tongue, of which I only know words, not sentences; and it rises in strength alongside the morning sun.

Across the barn, Old Trevain sings it too, and for a few glorious moments, the world is full of the sound of their song.

There's a brief space in the firing and I hear singing elsewhere, somewhere down the line.

If I'm to die today, this is a mighty fine way to go.

They don't seem to stop coming. There are no more breaks, and I'm glad. If there was time to rest, I might be able to think, and it might sink in that every time I squeeze the trigger it's a man on the other end of that bullet.

A bad man, but still a man.

Someone's down, hit. He's groaning as someone ties off the wound, I hear him send his friend back to fight.

The shooting is all around us. I've stopped straining my ears, trying to tell if there is fighting anywhere else in town.

I try not to think of Peter.

Then, like a pump running out, the onslaught of men trickles away and I realize they are no longer coming.

Gunshots still break the hot morning air at intervals, but there is no more fight.

Tagweiah grins. A strand of dark hair is plastered to his cheek with sweat. "They're gone."

I could almost faint with relief.

A cheer rises. I'm surprised that these men have the energy to cheer.

"Will they be back?" I ask, getting up slowly. I'm uninjured but awfully stiff.

"Not with those dead." He nods at the space of ground outside town, littered with bodies. I look away.

He holds out his hand—our custom. I shake it, then touch my forehead and press my fingers to my shoulder for his.

He returns the gesture.

"Are you leaving now?"

"If the wounded can travel." He ducks his head under the strap of his rifle and walks out into the sun.

I follow slowly, in a daze.

I turn around and look back at Glory Mesa, standing. Windows are boarded, but the glass behind them is just fine. Doors are locked with locks that weren't even tried.

We did it.

Mr. Trasker is dusty and his fingers are stained gray-black.

"I declare, I could dance a jig," he says with conviction.
"So could I!"

I seize his hands and we twirl—admittedly not a jig—until Glory Mesa and the hills beyond tilt and spin. We let go and I'm laughing so hard I can hardly breathe.

"That felt good," I say, panting. "Let's do it again."

We do, and I'm dizzy, laughing so hard my sides ache.

Tagweiah rides by slowly. Two of the Auki men have bloodied rags tied on various places. I raise a hand in farewell to them, a gesture Tagweiah returns.

There's amusement in his eyes. I rather wish I hadn't twirled so much—the world is swaying around me like a top before it collapses.

I slide to the ground, my hands pushing back the sweat-soaked strands of my hair, my back resting against the dusty, bullet-torn boards of the old barn.

I'm exhausted. All the weariness and fear that should have been here during the fight flood over me, making me weak.

I feel like I could sit here 'til kingdom come and never stir an inch.

Somewhere, across town, someone starts to play a fiddle.

# 51

## THATCHER

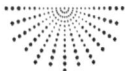

I hit Shiloh's Crossing and I see the smoke pumping down the tracks. I'm almost too late.

Maybe I am. Maybe there's no hope. Maybe they killed him already, threw him in the Shiloh River. Maybe he's strung up in the cluster of shacks.

But something tells me, powerful strong, that he's on that train.

Last time.

I slap the pony's flank with the end of my reins, let out a long-drawn whoop. The pony is tired—the brave little thing has carried me well. But its hooves tear up dirt, it starts so quick.

I'm coming, Archer. Flesh and blood don't let their own go without a fight.

· · ·

THE PONY IS HUFFING, almost sobbing, but it doesn't slow. I'm gaining on the train, coming up alongside, almost within reaching distance. I dig my spurs in, asking for more speed, speed I wouldn't feel right asking under any other circumstances.

The daring little thing gives. A tiny burst of speed I know it can't keep up for long. I knot the reins, loop them over the pommel, giving the pony enough head, but not so much that it'll trip once I let go.

I'm almost there, up alongside the second-to-last car. The railing is right there. I knife the pony in, inches closer, drop my stirrups.

"Run free. You earned it," I whisper, grab hold, and kick free of the pony. It sheers away immediately, still running, ears flattened—slows, fades in the distance.

Good pony.

I climb up onto the roof of the train, get my bearings. It's ten cars long. If they had him, where would they be keeping him?

I thrust my eye to a knot-hole in the wood, peer inside the dim car. Horses.

I move on to the next, and then the next. Supplies. Guns. More horses.

Near the front, the cars have men in them. I count a hundred, maybe—around thirty per car. Some of them have guns, some don't. I can't tell if they're all outlaws or if some are hostages.

Up front, there are two passenger coaches, and I cannot see into them without climbing off the roof.

I take my chances. Make my way to the nearest coach, clamber down carefully, checking for guards.

There are two, both inside the coach. Pressing my back against the painted wood of the swaying car, I peer in further.

Archer is seated at a table, a stack of papers in front of him. It would have looked normal if his nose wasn't bleeding.

There's a slim man, dressed in gingham and rawhide, looking at the paper. He turns slightly and I catch the gleam of an *isark* claw at his throat.

Tora-Teth.

He kicks the chair out from under Archer.

That's it. I've seen more than enough. I cock my gun, reach for the door handle. Take a breath. Feel my heart-beat. Right here. *Focus.*

I shove the door open and fire, dropping one guard.

"Drop it," I say to the other, and he lays his rifle down, then his pistol. I jerk my head to the far corner. "Over there, where I can keep an eye on you."

They obey, the wounded one dragging a little.

"Step back," I tell Tora-Teth. "Over there—with them."

He gives a mocking smile that I don't like, but he backs up slowly.

I hurry forward, keeping my gun on him. My cousin is on the ground, moving slowly. His head is bleeding.

My gaze goes back to the renegade. "I'd sure like to give you a taste of your own medicine."

He has a faint smile on his face, as if this just amuses him.

EMILY HAYSE

I don't have time to think how ridiculous it must seem, a rancher taking on outlaws alone. The thought flits through my mind and is gone.

"Jesse?" Archer sounds dazed.

"Stay down," I say, glancing at him and back to the men in front of me.

"Mortimer will be back in a few minutes." Tora-Teth shows his teeth in a mean sort of smile. "You had best leave, Jesse Thatcher, before we take offense."

"Well, I've taken a heap of offense to you, so I'm not worried."

He glances behind me, a swift, dangerous look.

I look back briefly, and Archer shouts. A hot tearing sensation rips through my arm and I see, as if in a slow dream, a knife buried deep in my sleeve.

There is a jolt, a deafening crash, and suddenly the world rocks and tilts sideways.

## 52

## ROSAMUND

I'm shaking. We must have derailed. There was a tremendous crash, an impact which shook the very boards of the car. I was thrown against one wall as the car tilted.

I am unsure whether I should move now, afraid the car will tilt further and slam against the ground—or—perhaps fall and fall, with nothing after that.

This thought stirs me to action. I move slowly, getting my feet under me, then standing, legs shaking.

The door is bolted shut, but I see grass through the crack. My fears of falling off a trestle are relieved.

I have to get out. I brace against the door and shove.

No good.

I'm running out of time. Surely there will be men coming soon, checking the cars, stopping any chance of escape.

Gunfire breaks out somewhere—in the echoing car, I cannot tell which direction it comes from.

EMILY HAYSE

I shove the door again.

The lock—or perhaps the chain—gives and the door scrapes open. It hits against the ground, digging into the dirt, only opening halfway.

I climb out, ducking low.

Men are tumbling out of the cars ahead of me, fire spreading across the grass, smoke pumping from the wreckage.

I look behind me and my heart jumps to my throat.

I scramble back a step or two. It's Mortimer.

His eyes are dull like stone. There's nothing in them, pleased or angry. He's leading his big black horse. It looks nervous, but not jumpy.

He stops in front of me, his eyes searching my face, and I draw myself up tall. He's no longer in control of this situation, whatever he says.

Fate, in his words, has not favored him entirely today, and I see the doubt in his eyes.

"Do you see now?" he asks softly. "It's the good that get crushed. And life chooses whether you're lucky or not."

I open my mouth to protest, but I don't know what to say. I hear his every word, but I cannot make any sense of them put together.

He takes one more step toward me. I back up and am stopped by the train car. I'm frozen in place.

"Everything's burning." He looks up the tracks. "Now that we're derailed, the afternoon train will run into this wreckage. I promised the governor I would set his world on fire, and I've kept my word. But I'll have you away from it, if it's the last thing I do."

"Why should you care?"

He shakes his head, laughs ironically, but his face is twisted.

"Rosamund, I lied. The day I met you, I was supposed to kill you." He rolls his next words around slowly, looks away toward the hills. "I took gold to do it."

The horse stamps impatiently. The ground shakes at the impact.

"There are powers at work stronger than any of us, evil that lives beyond a line even I dare not cross. I must fight this fight until I win it or die, but you—you must live. If I die, I shall lie in ground I have chosen to fight for. But if that be my fate, you will live on, and thus I shall have a hand in the destiny I sought."

Gunfire pops through the air, sporadic, deadly. My ears hurt.

The cars up front are on fire. Blazing fire. Billowing smoke reaches out as if to swallow us all.

He shoves the reins into my hand. I look quickly up into his face.

Tears stand in his eyes, and his flame-red hair blows in the hot wind until you can't quite tell the difference between it and the pulsing flames.

"You could have had the world with me. We would have been history—you would have had only good in your life. I would have done anything to secure it. But you saddled yourself with a cursed man and now that curse is on you."

He reaches out and touches me gently on the forehead with his ash-streak finger.

"I do not think that you will see me again, Rosamund.

But one day, you'll wish you had accepted my offer. Remember this moment."

He steps back. The smoke swallows him up, and he is gone.

I reach up and touch my forehead. My fingers come away black.

# 53

## THATCHER

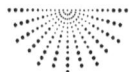

THE GRASS IS BURNING. MY EYES SNAP OPEN FROM A thick, momentary blackness. There's soot in the air. My ears are dull, muffled. There are shouts and screams, but I can't hear them clearly. I feel like someone's thrust my head underwater.

I can't be underwater, otherwise the grass wouldn't be burning.

My heartbeat is galloping, galloping, shaking the ground with each wild thump. I move my hand, a gesture that takes all my strength.

I push up on my arm, feel pain like shards of glass race up it, bury into my neck, and everything ends abruptly, like a candle being blown out.

SEARING PAIN BRINGS ME TO, and I look up into Raymond Lacey's keen-eyed face.

"You'll live."

"What happened?" A bullet whistles overhead.

Perhaps it's not so much what happened as what's happening.

"The train derailed and you were knifed pretty bad, son."

"How'd it derail?" I'm dazed, still trying to reconcile Raymond's presence with my memories.

"Bridge was out at the crossing. Train's down in a ten-foot gully."

"Did you do that?" I don't remember us doing it.

"Nope. Now, are you up to a fight or do you want me to get you out here?"

I feel my hands. They're still here. The pain is in my left shoulder, not my right.

"Give me a gun."

"Good man." He pulls his own pistol from his holster and presses it into my hand. "Enemy's that way." He points vaguely eastward, and he's up and gone.

I roll over in the grass, take a look around. A train car lies sideways in the ground, a huge furrow cut in the ground where it skidded and fell. It's sheltering me in part from a rainstorm of bullets coming across the tracks.

Jack Selby is sitting with his back against it, maybe ten yards down from me, loading. He turns, whips his rifle to his shoulder, and fires.

"Where'd you come from, you coyote?"

Selby barely tilts his head. "Over yonder."

There's blood on his collar. A fair sight of it. His face is bruised up, including an eye.

"How can you shoot with that eye?"

"The same way you shoot with that mouth."

I raise my gun and fire, just to show him.

Smoke and fire are everywhere. The front cars of the train are engulfed in flame, leaving trails of fire through the grass like blood.

"I mean it, Selby, where'd you come from?"

"A hanging party. Before that, I was blowing up bridges."

"Is there any—connection between the two?"

There's irony in his expression. He lifts his rifle and fires again. "Not as much as you'd expect."

Alan Swift throws himself down between us. "How many?"

"Fifteen or so, pinned down over there," says Selby, dropping down and pulling bullets from his belt.

"The boys have another twenty out there."

"You boys finally got here." I look over at him, pretending severity.

He only laughs and moves on, ducking low, disappearing into the smoke.

And then I see him. Archer, blood streaming down his face, running heedless of bullets, man to man, hiding place to hiding place.

Fearless. He's shouting something I cannot make out, but he's mesmerizing.

This was what he must have been like in the war—confident, fearless.

I've seen my cousin fight the elements, fight the land, even a bronc or steer on occasion, but this is different.

There's a blazing courage in his eyes I've never seen before. I've never had occasion to see it until now.

The fight is dying down, the firing thinning. Smoke drifts in and out. I feel as if I have lived this moment a hundred times today. My arms ache horribly.

Selby is panting—the fellow's a bit pale. I wish he would be more forthright about all this hanging and blowing up of bridges, but I know better than to press him.

Archer dashes up the hill, a couple of the braver men at his heels, bent low, going after whoever's left up behind the tracks.

And the smoke clears, suddenly thinning out like the gunfire, leaving Archer standing there below the track. Mortimer is standing above, crouched low.

They spot each other immediately, without surprise. It's as if this is where things were always meant to lead.

They straighten slowly, almost as one, their pistols trained on each other.

Luck of war, you come face to face with your enemy. I know nothing of it, but I feel the moment, the weight of what's at stake between them.

Mortimer squeezes the trigger and I hear—or perhaps my ears trick me into hearing—a click. Nothing happens.

For the space between a heartbeat, I can't breathe.

"Get out of my territory." Archer lowers his gun. "I'm giving you a chance. Get out, and if I see you again, it'll be a bullet or the rope."

Mortimer is swaying, staring hatred into my cousin's eyes, but there is no wavering in Archer's gaze. The kindness that I see in them so often is not there.

He's a rock you could dash yourself to pieces on.

Mortimer throws his gun onto the tracks and limps away, up into the smoke until he's lost from sight.

Archer stays. Watches until he's sure he's not coming back.

"Move, get back!" The shout runs up the track like wildfire.

Selby is already on his feet, running from our shelter.

"Get back, get back! It's going to blow!"

The shout has meaning now—clicks like the hammer of a pistol. I shove my gun into my belt and run. Bullets be hanged, I'd rather die running than blown to bits.

There's a sound like prairie thunder, but all around, as if it has swallowed me.

I throw myself to the thundering ground, covering my head as I'm pelted with something sharp, stinging.

I drag myself to my elbow, ears ringing. It's dirt. Sprayed over the top of me, around me. A glance back shows nothing but smoke everywhere, and dimly through it, new small fires.

My heart's pounding in my throat so hard I might be sick.

I rise up in the middle of the smoke, slowly, tentatively. Jack Selby is rising too, his rifle still gripped in his hand.

He gives me the barest smile, the first real one I've seen out of him.

"Close," he volunteers.

The outlaws that are left are throwing down their weapons, coming forward with hands raised. The wounded ones are dragging themselves, probably hoping for medical help.

The Swifts round them up like they would their stock, aided by men from all the homesteads and towns, men who left their own places and rallied to the common defense.

Archer walks toward them and they begin to cheer. Cheer until their lungs burst, filling the wide, open sky with the sound of it.

This must be it—the part of war men remember. The thing that makes a young man want to go. I don't know if I'm awed or repulsed.

Archer comes up to me and lets his breath out in a long, weary sigh. He's looking at me with tired, haunted eyes. He's seen and done things today he had hoped never to do again.

I throw my arm over his shoulder and slap his back, hard.

"Well," I say. I have no words beyond that.

Carson comes up, covered in soot. If there's any blood on him, it's not his.

"What do you say, Governor Scott? Did we do it? Are we going to go after those clans now?"

Archer raises his eyebrows and wipes sweat from his nose, shakes his hair back. He looks to Raymond. "Did we find Abernathy?"

"He's six feet under at the rim of a canyon," says Raymond, matter-of-factly. "A few miles back."

"I don't need to see. I'll take your word." Archer breaks suddenly into a smile.

Carson chuckles grimly.

"No sign of his sons, though," says Raymond.

"We won't worry about it yet. The fight's out of them today."

He turns to face us. We're all dirt-streaked, bloody, covered in soot and gunpowder. The wind blows through our hair, whisking smoke between us like clouds on a mountain.

He opens his mouth to speak, but can't seem to find the words.

"Gentlemen." He holds out his hand, clasps each of ours in turn. "Thanks, I reckon."

# 54

## MORTIMER

MY COAT IS SODDEN WITH BLOOD. I'M IN NO PAIN. THE world meets me sideways; I pull myself up on my arm and go on.

The day is drenched in golden light, the last good moments before the sun goes raging down. Before it fights the losing fight for its life.

I fall, the sweet grass against my face. I roll over with an effort, stiff. There's pain now, but it's muffled. I'm mostly warm, pleasantly so. But I can't move any more. There are flowers here. Green grass. Good, like home. When I was a child.

It's a good place to lie. Lie down and rest.

I wanted her to see me as a hero, just once. Just once.

One bloody horse, one bloody fight, one chance. One chance to be a hero.

I wonder if she'll even remember it.

It was my lot in life. I wasn't given a choice. What a

sore, bloody world this is. Forces a man into his life's course. How can one be sorry for his deeds if he had no choice?

But I am. I feel it rising like tears in my throat, this deep regret. Deep as a pebble dropped in a well, when it takes forever to hear it hit the water....

I could have been more. I should have been more. It should not have ended here. I—*I* was a king once. They called me king. Outlaw King of the Western Territory.

Not many men can say that.

I was used. All my life, men trod over me, built their empires on my back.

But I had an empire. For a fleeting moment, I had one too.

They're all fools. Everything is fleeting. They congratulate themselves on living—and what does it bring them?

Better to live, and die in the open air.

Better to lie down and sleep in the flowers....

It comes like my mother's caress, her whisper as I fall asleep: I could have been a hero.

## 55

## ROSAMUND

HE'S STANDING THERE, LOOKING AT THE WRECKAGE strewn across the beautiful land, his back to me. He doesn't even know I'm here.

He thinks I'm safe in Glory Mesa.

Part of me almost wants to turn the horse around, ride all the way home and never tell him about my part in the events today. But I don't know the way.

I dismount and drop to the ground softly.

The horse follows me obediently. In Mortimer's hands, he always seemed willful; with me he's quiet and curious.

"Archer?"

He turns and looks at me. There are tears in his eyes. "Rosamund."

His face clouds over with confusion.

I throw myself against him, wrap my arms around his chest, burying my face in his shoulder. He smells a little of the desert air and leather, but mostly smoke and sweat.

He's here, he isn't going anywhere. I tell myself this again and again.

He holds me tightly and says nothing.

## 56

## SELBY

THE SUNSET CASTS STRONG LIGHT TONIGHT. THE railroad crews are already starting to clear the hijacked train away, the wreckage. Men that can pick themselves up and gather what's theirs, make ready to leave.

Carson is in charge of the burying detail. The Swifts are rounding up the loose horses that got free in the fight, in the derailing. Garth Levine the surveyor is dead. Spilled his blood for the land he mapped so much of. If anyone understood its worth, perhaps it was him.

A dun horse wanders around, its reins dragging. I whistle to it and it comes, wandering and slow. Three white socks, a snip.

It's mine. Miraculously, it doesn't appear to be hurt at all. I gather up its reins, unwrap one end from around its foreleg where it's tangled, lead it along behind me.

The men are starting to leave. Perhaps there will be some organization under Raymond Lacey—Marshal Lacey, now—but I don't think all the men are going back to Glory Mesa. Many of them were gathered from their homes, and after the taste of killing, want to go straight back to their plows and corrals.

I would, if I were them.

I pass by men, men walking limping horses, here and there a cowboy riding off in a quick lick of dust that stands red-gold above the western flats, lingering long after horse and rider are out of sight. Those left are already talking about celebration. How quickly they forget the blood and smoke and death.

How quickly men are cursed to forget—yet it is a blessing too.

I look at my stained hands, rub my fingers together. Soot dusts off them, but the stains don't go away.

First river I hit, I'll scrub them with sand.

Raymond Lacey passes, a tall shadow against the fading light.

"Selby." He holds out his lean hand and I shake it firmly. He doesn't ask if I'm going or staying, just nods and moves on.

My horse presses its nose against the back of my arm and blows gently. Absently I reach back and scratch its neck.

I pass Archer Scott on my way out. He's saddling up a horse, a big rangy black. I wonder if he knows it's Mortimer's.

"I hope you understand—" I begin, but he cuts me off, shakes his head.

"Jack, you don't have to prove anything to me. Thank

you." He turns and holds out his hand, grasps mine in both of his.

I nod.

"I mean it. Without you—"

I shake my head. It doesn't need to be said.

"You moving on?"

"I reckon I should."

"There's going to be a celebration back in town. You don't have to come, but you sure are welcome. If any man deserves it, it's you."

He smiles that white smile, and I know now for certain that I like this man.

"I'm moving on," I say.

"Is there anything I can get you before you go?"

"Cartridges are a mite low."

He reaches into the saddlebags, pulls out a small white box, sets it firmly into my hand.

"Obliged."

"Pretty sure I still owe you," he says with a tired laugh.

He doesn't owe me anything.

"You need me, you know where to find me," I say.

"Godspeed, Selby."

I cluck to the horse briefly, and it quits pulling up the weedy grass and falls into step behind me. I hear the slow crunch as it eats, feel the calm, heavy steps in the dust near my feet.

The sunset is rose-gold, bathing the living and dead alike in its gentle glow.

# 57

## ROSAMUND

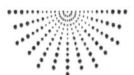

"ROSAMUND, ARE YOU HAPPY?"

The question takes me by surprise. I pull the knife from the pie and set it down. "Yes, my love. Why wouldn't I be?"

Archer sits at the kitchen table sipping his coffee, one knee over the other. "You've seemed a little down."

"I am happy, Archer." It's the truth. "Very happy, truly. But one doesn't get over everything right away. The fighting, the dying."

He sets down his coffee and I'm suddenly enveloped in his arms. He's holding me close. Softly, he kisses the top of my head.

I smile up at him, and he looks at my face like he never wants to forget it.

"I'm sorry," he says, after a long moment of studying.

"For what?"

"Asking you to this life. It's been months, and we haven't even had a week put together in the same house."

"We've talked about this. I want to help you, Archer. I want to make this land a good place. This is my work now —whatever it takes."

He smiles, one hand reaching down to find mine, entwining his fingers tightly with mine. "Is it too much to hope that it gets better from here?"

I lean my head against his shoulder and he rests his chin on my head. It feels good to be here, to be close and not apart. "I don't think so." I reach up and run my hand over the back of his shoulder.

"Archer?"

"What, love?"

"What about Mortimer's father?"

"What about him?"

"Is he going to be all right? I hope somebody told him about his son gently."

Archer looks at me as if I'm a puzzle he can't decipher. "He'll be fine. Your brother saw to everything. He'll get a pension and a cabin."

"And all the others?"

"Well, like I said, there'll be a trial."

"Will you do something for me?"

His hand is warm in mine, his eyes taking in my face as if to reassure himself that I am actually here.

"Ask if there's a man by the name of O'Meagher. It's important."

"Why?" His eyes darken with concern.

"He was their cook—and he was good to me. I

406

promised that if you won, I'd remember him and his kindness."

Archer is looking away, out the window.

"I promised him, Archer."

"Don't worry." He kisses me. "I'll see to it first thing in the morning."

A knock at the door—such a comforting, familiar sound that I don't even need to see it's Raymond.

"Afternoon," he greets, ducking into the window.

I let him in and he looks down at me, his eyes twinkling.

"All set, marshal?" asks Archer, his arms folded.

"Sure."

The celebration is tonight. Carson will have drinks on the house, Maria has made some kind of dessert with a name half the town cannot pronounce, and Mr. Trasker has hung banners outside the general store reading *Hurrah for Gov. Scott* because there wasn't room for the whole phrase.

Raymond will see to it that there are no disturbances or rough play, especially as there are free drinks involved.

"I just came to give you a report—and see my sister." His face gentles and he holds out a rose. He must have plucked it from someone's garden, but it's our secret language.

The last time he gave me one, it was from O'Meagher.

I shiver, even though the day is warm. I put the rose in water.

It's all over now.

.   .   .

IT'S DARK. Lanterns hang from the porches, the lights bright up and down the street. The air is full of laughter and shouting and fireworks.

But I feel like I'm in a dream. I can't shake it. I can't get the feeling to go away—this morose, lonely feeling.

All the people I care about are here. Mortimer is no longer here to threaten them. His outlaws, the troublemakers, they've all been scattered, to be dealt with another day. And whoever it was who had paid to have me killed seems to have disappeared or gone into hiding with the rest of the lot.

Why can't I be happy again? What is it?

I leave Archer talking to Sam. He and Barnes had been rescued at the railhead by Raymond's men—another happy ending.

I wish I could feel it.

I wander up the dark street toward home. Home feels right, though it is dark and quiet right now.

There's snorting from the corral. The horses are nervous from the fireworks. I walk up to the railing, lean my arms and chin on the poles.

There's Archer's bay, eating. He's not too concerned. There's the white horse Archer is breaking in right now, and the chestnut that's mine.

And the black horse. Every time I look at it, I'm flooded with revulsion and a strange regret.

The black throws up its head, its ears flickering at the sound of the fireworks.

"Easy." It jerks its head around.

The leads hang from the fence; I take one and slip

softly into the corral. The horses come to meet me, curious, and I slip the lead onto the black.

I lead him out, out to the hills southwest of town. The stars cluster thick over the hills. They are so strong tonight.

The black blows quietly through his nose. Out here, the fireworks are only vague lights, hardly different from the rest of the glow the town gives, and he isn't afraid.

He presses his nose against my arm, curious.

"Good boy." I reach up, scratch his neck. He had no choice in the matter, same as me. We were both tools, willing or unwilling.

He lowers his head, blows at the sand. There's no grass, so he turns back to me, questioning.

I reach up, unbuckle the halter, and slip it off his face.

At first, he's uncertain. He swings his head around, looking at me, looking at the hills.

"Go on," I urge quietly. "You're free."

He's a stallion—he'll be happy out there.

He takes a few steps, his head snaking along the ground, sniffing.

Then he raises his head, looking west, toward the far hills. The dust rises in a cloud as his hooves scramble over sand, and then he's away, headed toward some unknown scent. Some far place his instincts call him to.

I feel the burden fall off my shoulders as clearly as if I'd actually been carrying it.

Waste of a horse, some would say. Maybe. But the only thing I feel right now is—free.

# 58

## SIKES

I BEND DOWN, REACH MY HAND DEEP INTO THE DUST. *The ground is cursed.* The land stretches out before me, shimmering with the heat. I can feel it groaning in its sleep.

I feel it in my bones—the promise of the future. Fire, death, hope, glory. Liberation. This boy, this man. The one whom my hands held first in this world, the one who is chosen.

It's as if I've known, from the beginning, where this would lead.

It is a wild land. Deep rivers, mountains stretching for miles like bands of constellations, hot flats, tall pine forests, lakes like basins of water for dusty hands to dip in and be refreshed.

It senses the war brewing. It senses the possibility of liberation, just around the corner. It seems to shiver under my hand with anticipation.

Let him celebrate now. Let him enjoy this victory, this fleeting rest on this restless land.

Tomorrow will come. Soon enough, it will come.

I straighten, shade my eyes as I look across the land. There's a whisk of dust—raised by wind perhaps, or a wild horse.

*Soon,* I tell it.

An exclusive preview of
Knights of Tin and Lead: Book 2
*THE BEAUTIFUL ONES*

Coming October 2021

# I.

# ALAN

THE SETTING SUN IS RUDDY, RIMMED WITH GOLD, turning the green hills and the cloudless blue into the colors of a dream I once had.

At least—I thought it was a dream.

I stare over the backs of the roving cattle, drinking in the light and color. Every day in this country is like watching poetry unfold over the hills in front of you. I wish I could come up with words for it like the poets do, but I reckon that's why I'm out here pushing cattle.

When Jem went to war, he sent Max to live with the Auki and left the ranch to me and the foreman. I wish he'd left Max with me, but he did what he thought was right.

I worked sunup to sundown those three, four years he was gone.

He and I, we never talk about those years. I reckon he thinks I'm respecting him, not wanting to pry into the war, not wanting to make him feeling guilty for leaving. We're folk who tend to let bygones stay bygones.

But he doesn't know that I keep silence for my own reasons, too.

The warm, evening breeze blows a strand of hair into my face—it catches gold in the sunlight before I brush it aside.

The cattle are bunching, rubbing long, angled horns

against each other's hides, thrusting their heads up over the sea of milling backs as if swimming through it.

We'll have to make camp before long.

"Max!" I call, cupping one heavy-gloved hand to my mouth. He turns in the saddle—I'm amazed he can hear me—and I whistle, making a quick turning gesture with my hand.

He rides up to the front; he'll turn point riders in and we'll circle the herd for the night. Just ahead is a good spot.

The boys have the cattle well enough in hand. I peel my horse off the herd and canter up to the crest of the nearest hill.

The sun floods the valley between the hills like a mountain river after a storm. There's a wildness to this land. Even the peaceful moments mirror the deadly ones.

It was dusk then too, when the dream happened.

There'd been trouble between a couple Eastern clans that year—nothing we wanted a corner of—so we had decided to drive the herd over the Northwestern ridgelands to a settlement beyond the territory borders. It was a promising settlement, sure to pay top dollar.

For a week we traveled through strange territory—it was timberland, mountain, and low barren places with rocks and pools that steamed.

The pools were made of nearly every color a man could think—yellow, orange, blue and green—and we kept the cattle steered clear of them.

I was scouting ahead and a little to the south of the herd, and I found myself up on a high ridge, looking down at the land around me.

To one side lay timberland, spotted with deep meadows; on the other, a wide, flat stretch of land pocked with those hot holes, shooting boiling water, and pools of every color, steaming slowly.

And as I gazed down, I saw in the pools a simultaneous movement like the reflections of clouds moving across the sky above, but the sky was empty and blue.

It was a moment, a moment only, but I saw in the flatlands the likeness of an eye, half a mile wide, the pools like golden flecks in the iris.

And then it was gone.

I was up on that ridge alone. I don't know if any living man had been up there before or has been since.

I look long at the fading valley below me.

I'll never know or understand what happened that day.

CAMP IS SET up by the time I ride down. The world is just blurred shadows as men move along the edge of the firelight, trail-dusted.

"Where were you?" Jem pours out coffee into a tin mug and hands it over. Always the eagle eye, Jem, watching for trouble.

"Just looking over the lay of the land." The coffee is good, hot and thick and bracing.

"And?"

"We'll have good grazing."

"Good." Jem looks around the circle at the half dozen of us not on the herd. "Eat up. I want the riders out and the others in before it's too dark."

He turns to me. "You're on night hawk."

I only nod. I'm not tired anyway.

I finish my bacon and beans and pull a fresh horse from the string. The clear sky is darkening gently, the first of the stars coming out across the sky like markings on a map.

I've never been back there, to that ridge. But on nights like these, I think of it.

# ACKNOWLEDGMENTS

As a very young child, I was afraid of many things. Some of my earliest memories are pretending I was a knight or a cowboy riding alone, often saving or protecting someone. Both these figures gave me someone brave to emulate, and by practice and pretending, I learned to face my fears. It's fitting, I think, that this venture into a much-loved genre of mine is an homage to both of them.

To my beta readers, Lucy, Audrey, Elizabeth, Mollie, Haylie, Heidi, Joshua, Schuyler, Lydia, and Anna, thank you for your time, dedication, and quality feedback.

To Elisabeth, who has been here since the very beginning. Stories have been our thing. Thanks for sticking with me on the journey and for always being my editorial voice of reason.

To James Egan, who makes the most brilliant covers, thank you.

To my proofreaders Anna and Heidi, thank you for your sharp eyes and invaluable time.

To my street team, who are probably the coolest bunch of people I've had the honor of meeting online, thank you for all the help, shares, and encouragement. You are the best!

To the Inkwell, the Storyteller's Hall, and Heidi, who sustained me with many hours of support, check-ins, and sprints, thank you. The crazy deadlines I pulled were largely thanks to all of you.

To my family for the support, the snacks, and the extra time and understanding when I'm on deadline and have a brain full of holes, thank you so very much.

And to my drink squad, Ethan, Alice, and Merry. The endless coffees and La Croix you ply me with are the fuel of my books.

Special thanks to Mary Weber, Cindy Worrell, Lydia Hayse, Claire Banschbach, Morgan Busse, Gillian Adams, Lani Forbes, Shannon Dittemore, Nadine Brandes, and all of those friends and readers who shared encouragement, excitement, and good westerns with me.

To the Creator and Chief Storyteller: thank you for the grace and strength to tell this story.

# ABOUT THE AUTHOR

EMILY HAYSE is a lover of log cabins, strong coffee, and the smell of old books. Her writing is fueled by good characters and a lifelong passion for storytelling. When she is not busy turning words into worlds, she can often be found baking, singing, or caring for one of the many dogs and horses in her life. She lives with her family in Michigan.

ALSO BY EMILY HAYSE

Crowning Heaven

Seventh City

The Last Atlantean

The Rivers Lead Home

www.ingramcontent.com/pod-product-compliance
Lightning Source LLC
Chambersburg PA
CBHW021952120726
47898CB00001BA/89